"Ryan, he'll never make it on foot."

"But we daren't take him back. The hue and cry could begin any moment. Elmo, can you ride?" asked Ryan abruptly.

"Yes, Mas'r Ryan."

"Good. You'll have to take my horse if you're going to make it out of South Carolina. That will make it harder to set the dogs on your trail, as well." Ryan tossed the boy into the saddle.

Elmo needed no further urging. He dug his bare heels into the huge gelding's flanks and headed north through the trees. Kathryn regarded Ryan accusingly. "You never said you were giving him your horse! It could be recognized."

"That's a chance I'll have to take," he replied.

She opened her mouth to protest, but he stopped her with a deep, demanding kiss. His embrace tightened and he was just drawing her down onto the thick carpet of pine needles beneath them, when a shot rang out in the woods behind them.

"Elmo!"

Brenda Hiatt

BRIDGE OVER TIME

Harlequin Books

TORONTO • NEW YORK • LONDON
AMSTERDAM • PARIS • SYDNEY • HAMBURG
STOCKHOLM • ATHENS • TOKYO • MILAN
MADRID • WARSAW • BUDAPEST • AUCKLAND

ISBN 0-373-70592-1

BRIDGE OVER TIME

ABOUT THE AUTHOR

"I always thought it would be fun to have a friend from another time," says author Brenda Hiatt. "I'd show her my world and she'd show me hers. This book was based on that fantasy."

Brenda lives in Texas with her husband and two children. Currently a prolific author of Regency romances, Brenda has broken new ground with *Bridge Over Time* and she's anxious to hear your comments.

Write to Brenda, c/o Harlequin Superromance at:

Harlequin Enterprises
225 Duncan Mill Road
Don Mills, Ontario
Canada M3B 3K9

Books by Brenda Hiatt

HARLEQUIN REGENCY ROMANCE

70—GABRIELLA
81—THE UGLY DUCKLING
91—LORD DEARBORN'S DESTINY
102—DARING DECEPTION
112—A CHRISTMAS BRIDE

**For Brenda Chin,
who brings out
the best in me**

CHAPTER ONE

KATHRYN HATED DRIVING in the rain, especially at interstate speeds, but her mother would never forgive her if she didn't reach South Carolina in time for the costume ball. She'd surprised herself as much as her mother by agreeing to attend, but she needed a change of scenery, and a rest. The pace was bound to be slower in Columbia than in Washington, D.C. If only it hadn't started to rain! It had picked up as she left and was still going strong as she neared the southern border of North Carolina. Methodically, she practiced the relaxation exercises she always used when driving, beginning with her tense hands on the steering wheel.

Out of the corner of her eye, she suddenly saw something coming toward her—a minivan changing lanes at too high a speed was now spinning out of control in her direction. Kathryn hit the brakes hard, holding the wheel in a death grip and praying incoherently. The van continued to spin, skidding from the right lane completely across the highway and stopping with its front bumper only inches from that of Kathryn's Porsche. In a state of near shock, Kathryn stared at the other driver—a boy still in his teens. He looked as white and frightened as she felt. What a narrow escape!

She remained frozen in place while he backed around onto the shoulder and turned the minivan—probably the family car, she thought irrelevantly—to face the right direction. Once he was gone, Kathryn shakily resumed her journey south, cursing cars, interstates, rain and the entire rat race of the modern world.

At the next exit, she pulled off to stop at a garishly lit diner that obviously catered to the eighteen-wheeler crowd. As a high-profile political and social activist, Kathryn Sykes-Monroe would normally never consider entering such a place, but after that harrowing experience, she felt an overpowering need for a cup of coffee and a stationary place to sit.

She pushed open the glass door and chose an isolated stool at the far end of the counter. Several of the men eyed her speculatively as she ordered a cup of coffee but she coolly ignored them with an ease born of long practice.

Funny, she thought, how she could be a basket case behind the wheel but completely at ease when being ogled by strange men. Still, she took the precaution of putting her money on the counter in advance in case she needed to make a quick exit.

As she stirred extra sugar into her coffee, one of the truckers, a great hulking brute in a plaid flannel shirt and two days' growth of beard, leered at her from the far end of the counter. Briefly encountering his eye, Kathryn pierced him with the blank stare she used to discourage unwanted advances. As always, it worked—the trucker backed off, and Kathryn finished her coffee, rose and reluctantly returned to her car.

"KATHY! I WAS AFRAID you wouldn't make it." A slim, stylishly dressed woman walked rapidly down the wide circular driveway toward her.

"I said I'd be here, Mother. You know I'd have called if anything came up."

"Oh, no, I didn't mean that, but the weather reports showed rain all up the Eastern Seaboard and I know how you are about driving in bad weather. I hope it wasn't too traumatic for you."

Kathryn grimaced. "No, Mother, I managed just fine. I'm a big girl now, remember?" Turning back to the car, she removed her cosmetic bag and small suitcase.

"Is that all of your luggage?" her mother asked in dismay.

"It should be plenty for a few days. You said you had my costume for tomorrow night." Then, sensing her mother's disappointment, Kathryn gave her a quick hug. "Look, if I decide to stay longer, I can go shopping. I don't have any definite plans since I'm between projects right now."

She turned to gaze up at the house. "So this is the ancestral mansion." She remembered the three-story brick front and white pillars from the pictures her mother had sent. It wasn't really a mansion in the modern sense; in fact, it was not much bigger than the family's five-bedroom New Jersey home had been, but it had a sense of history that gave it a dignity deserving of the name. "I like it," she decided aloud.

Beaming at what she apparently considered a personal compliment, her mother took Kathryn's cosmetic case and steered her toward what was now the Sykes-Monroe home. "Come in and see what I've done with the interior," she invited eagerly.

Kathryn paused briefly at the foot of the front steps to look around her. Mid-March in South Carolina was definitely spring—there were daffodils and early tulips in the grassy central circle of the drive. Laurel Street was busy, but the expanse of the grounds made the house seem distant from the downtown traffic. Columbia was a softer, greener, homier city than Washington.

"I, ah, take it you didn't get that role you auditioned for on Broadway?" Her mother broke into her observations.

Kathryn's laugh held just a trace of bitterness. "Off-Broadway, actually, but no. It looks like my future will lie in organizing charity luncheons for senators' wives instead of on the stage. At least that pays well and gives me plenty of visibility."

"Yes, Mrs. Hardison told me she sees your name in the 'Life-Style' section nearly every month. I really am proud of the work you're doing in Washington, sweetheart."

Kathryn smiled but said nothing as they mounted the broad brick steps to the front door. The noble causes that had fired her with such enthusiasm when she'd been fresh out of college had begun to seem trite, more politics than substance. But there was no need to tell her mother that.

The door opened onto an impressive front hall with a wide, curving staircase at the far end. Leading her into a formal drawing room on the right, her mother said, "Oh, I forgot to mention that we will be having another houseguest."

Kathryn stiffened as the tall, dark-blond man rose to greet them. Though he was undeniably handsome, her expression was wary. "Hello, Logan," she said coolly, casting an accusing glance at her mother.

"Good to see you again, Kathy." His voice was also more cautious than welcoming.

They regarded each other in silence. Oblivious to their discomfort, Mrs. Sykes-Monroe went on chattering. "Well, I'll just let you two get caught up while I tell Alice where to put your things." She tripped busily from the room, leaving Kathryn and Logan little option but to talk.

"You're looking well," said Logan. "Washington doesn't seem to have eaten you alive just yet."

"As you were so sure it would." Kathryn forced a smile. "You're looking good, too, Logan. You'll have to forgive Mother—she had no way of knowing this meeting would be ... awkward."

Logan's smile took on a cynical edge. "I should have known you never told her."

Kathryn shrugged. "There was no particular reason to. Why upset her over nothing?"

"So I bet she's wondering why we're not falling into each other's arms. I take it you had nothing to do with my invitation, then?"

"Is that what you thought?" asked Kathryn, stung. "That I'd arranged this 'old home week' just so I could grovel and beg your forgiveness? You, of all people, should know that I go my own way and make my own decisions. I'd hardly ask my *mother* to stage a reconciliation, even if I wanted one."

"I can believe it," he replied, inspecting her at some length. Another woman might have blushed, but not Kathryn Monroe. "You've become quite the young socialite, haven't you?" he asked cynically.

"And you don't care for socialites?"

It was Logan's turn to shrug. "Let's just say I was hoping to find something a little different in the gentle South. See you at dinner, Kathy." He quirked a half smile at her and left the room.

Kathryn frowned at his retreating back for a moment, but then her brow cleared. She really didn't care in the least what Logan thought of her. Not anymore. She'd worked hard to cultivate this image and wasn't about to change it to please a man who persisted in behaving like a protective big brother.

MRS. SYKES-MONROE dominated the dinner conversation as she did any remotely social event. Her audience consisted only of Kathryn, Logan and her husband, but she spoke as if addressing a packed auditorium. It disturbed Kathryn a bit to realize that she'd begun copying her mother's style when she solicited contributions at Washington functions. Surely her own speeches weren't this pompous?

"Tomorrow night," began Mrs. Sykes-Monroe grandly, "we will celebrate the restoration of this historic home, back in the family after nearly sixty years. The costumes will reflect the period of its construction, around 1815 to 1820.

Most of the records were burned during the Civil War, so we can't be more precise than that."

"Surely fashions couldn't have changed much over five years," commented Kathryn dryly.

"That's not the point. I want to be as authentic as possible. In my case, it shouldn't be too hard. I came across a portrait of Catherine Sykes-Prescott, my great-great-great-great-great-grandmother, and I modeled my ball gown and hairstyle after her. She spelled her name with a *C* by the way. It was her daughter who broke with tradition and named *her* first daughter with the spelling you and I have, Kathy. Have you seen the portrait? She really looked amazingly like me, except for the hairstyle and dress. The picture is in the gallery at the back of the house."

"I'm afraid I haven't been in there yet. I'll be sure to look after dinner. I don't suppose there's a similar ancestor to pattern me after?" Kathryn tried to sound sincere, but she had never been able to share her mother's passion for family history. She preferred to direct her energy into more useful channels.

"No, unfortunately I haven't found a likeness of the next Catherine. From one or two surviving letters I got the impression she was a bit of a black sheep, but I'm not sure exactly why. Wouldn't it be wonderful if she had dark hair and blue eyes like yours? Let's just assume she did. I had the seamstress copy your dress from an 1820s fashion magazine I found at the State Library, so you'll look nearly as authentic as I will."

"You relieve me."

Mrs. Sykes-Monroe frowned slightly. "Oh, Kathy, *do* try to enter into the spirit of things. Some of the most prominent families in Columbia will be attending, and several from Charleston, as well. I've contacted the local DAR chapter and..."

Kathryn's attention started to wander at this point, and she picked up the low-voiced conversation between her father and Logan. The men were discussing business, as she should have expected. Her father was trying again to convince Logan to become a partner in his development firm.

Plump, balding Paul Monroe possessed a business acumen completely at odds with his pleasant, cherubic demeanor. He'd built what amounted to a construction empire in New Jersey and other parts of the northeast, extending his interests from single-family homes to office buildings and shopping complexes. Kathryn suspected he'd given in to her mother's desire to move to South Carolina mainly because it offered a chance to expand into fresh territory.

No doubt this was where Logan came in. At twenty-eight, he was considered something of a "whiz kid" in architectural circles. But to Kathryn he was still the same old Logan—her self-appointed big brother. When his father died twelve years ago, Mr. Monroe had taken Logan under his wing and encouraged him while he pursued his degree in architecture. Within two years of graduating, Logan had made quite a name for himself.

According to her father, Logan's designs were both fresh and practical, generating excitement in developers from all over the country. But though he'd worked with Monroe Building and Design several times, Logan had been careful not to tie himself to any one company. He was too much a free spirit, she suspected, to follow company rules or play office politics. She couldn't even remember the last time she'd seen him in a suit. All of which made his interference in her own life even more galling, smacking as it did of hypocrisy.

"The whole downstairs will be decorated with fresh flowers, and I expect to produce quite an effect with a miniature fountain in the center of the hall," Kathryn heard her mother saying.

"Won't that interfere with the dancing?" asked Kathryn, startled at this detail even though she was well acquainted with her mother's penchant for the flamboyant.

"Not at all. The front hall is simply huge, and it shouldn't be too crowded. Remember, I am inviting only the best families, as well as a few friends. Which reminds me, someone is coming over tonight whom I think you'll be happy to see."

"Oh, really? Who?"

"She wanted it to be a surprise, but— Oh, here she is already!" she exclaimed as a short, dark-haired girl in her early twenties peeked into the dining room.

"I just wanted to let you know I'm here. I'll wait in the living room until you're finished eating. Oh, Kathy, you look *great!*"

"Annette!" cried Kathryn joyfully, nearly overturning her chair in her haste to greet her friend. The two girls hugged, then Kathryn turned to her mother. "I think I'll skip dessert. Annette and I will be in the living room if you need us." Her mother nodded understandingly and Kathryn hurried out, pulling Annette with her.

"What are you doing in South Carolina?" Kathryn demanded at once. She and Annette had been roommates their last two years of college, and even though Annette had married two weeks after graduation, they'd kept in touch by letter and phone.

"I live here!" She laughed. "David is stationed at Fort Jackson, right here in Columbia."

"He didn't come tonight? Why didn't you write to tell me?"

"We only got orders a month ago and had to move two weeks later. Everything was so crazy, I decided to wait until we had an address to write to you—and then your mother convinced me to make it a surprise. And no, David's not here. He's TDY in Kansas for two months, as of last Thursday. A great way for me to get settled in, huh?"

"TDY?" asked Kathryn.

"Oh, I'm sorry. I'm so used to the army jargon I forget everyone else doesn't know it. It means temporary duty. It also means extra money, though, which will come in handy right now."

"What do you—Annette! Is that a *maternity* dress?" Her friend nodded happily. "Now don't tell me you've only known about *that* for a month."

"Well, no," Annette admitted. "My mother didn't want me to tell anyone until after the first trimester, so I went along with her. But I'm five months along now and ready to tell the world!"

"It doesn't look like you can keep it a secret much longer, anyway." Annette was tiny, which made her pregnancy that much more obvious.

"Can you imagine how big I'll be in a couple of months?" She laughed. "Will you be here long, Kathy? I hardly know anyone on post yet."

"I haven't decided," Kathryn replied honestly, "but now that I know you're here, I won't be in such a hurry to get back to D.C. Not that I really was, anyway."

"Things aren't going so hot?" asked Annette with ready sympathy.

There had never been secrets between Annette and Kathryn, even during their wild college days. "It's not things, so much. It's me," she confessed. "I was going to make such a difference there you know, set the world on fire. All the social training Mother subjected me to in my teens—the modeling and charm schooling—was going to help me to influence people, to get funding for the causes I care about. And it has. But so much of it is politics, knowing the right people, which charity is fashionable this month . . . the actual issues seem to get lost in the shuffle. To tell you the truth, it's all starting to seem pretty shallow—and making *me* feel shallow by association."

"What about the theater?"

"No luck there, either—and I've gone up to New York to audition six times in the past year. But I'm not sure that's really the life for me, either. What I need is a rest, a chance to sort things out."

Annette blinked. "A rest? You? You were always dragging me around to everything, trying to get me involved. Women's rights one week, saving the whales the next..." She sighed enviously. "And you're still so thin!"

"Aerobics." Kathryn grimaced. "It's boring and time-consuming, but pleasantly plump actresses don't get cast as leading ladies—or make for good photo ops. I took some dance and voice lessons, too, so I wouldn't get rusty. You never know when a musical might be auditioning. But enough about me. Like I said, I came here to get away from it all."

"Well, here comes some diversion," whispered Annette, gesturing toward the door, where they could hear voices approaching. "Isn't that the same guy that came to visit you once or twice at school? What was his name?"

By way of answer, Kathryn stood to make introductions. "Annette, you remember Logan Thorne, a business associate of my father's and an old family friend. Logan, my very dear friend, Annette Kent."

Annette promptly seated herself next to Logan, obviously determined to find out all she could about him. Forthright and bubbly, she had a way of getting people to spill their secrets that Kathryn could only envy. Though articulate and persuasive with a roomful of potential donors, on a more personal level Kathryn had always had a difficult time making friends.

Mrs. Sykes-Monroe was quick to corner Kathryn with her plans for the following evening, giving her no chance to learn what kind of headway Annette might be making with Logan. She heard Annette's frequent laughter, though, and was surprised. She hadn't thought Logan had much of a sense of humor, at least not in recent years.

"Come on, Kathy, let me show you what I mean." Kathryn reluctantly followed her mother to a long, narrow room where more than a dozen family portraits were hanging on the walls.

"They used this room as a dining hall when this house was a girls' dormitory sixty years ago," remarked her mother, "but now I've restored it to its intended purpose. Ah! Here's the portrait I wanted you to see." She stopped in front of a painting two-thirds of the way down the room, and Kathryn saw that it did indeed bear a striking resemblance to her mother.

"This was Catherine Sykes-Prescott," said Mrs. Sykes-Monroe. "It was her mother who began the tradition of hyphenating 'Sykes' before her married name, so we wouldn't forget our fine English heritage, no matter what nationalities later generations married into. The tradition of naming the first daughter Catherine dates from nearly a century earlier."

Kathryn nodded. She'd heard it all many times before, and it had been impressed on her since childhood what her duty was in this regard, when—if—she married. She'd gone by plain Kathryn Monroe when she was younger, only recently copying her mother's hyphenation to give her name more distinction for the stage and social scene.

"I plan to have my hair styled just like this," her mother was saying, "and my dress will look almost the same as the one in the painting. I took a photo of it to show the seamstress."

Kathryn duly admired the portrait and several other paintings of note in the gallery, and then returned with her mother to the living room. Only Annette and her father were there.

"Logan's gone upstairs to get some drawings he wants me to see," said Mr. Monroe. "Some upscale town homes he's designed." He then launched into the business plans he and Logan had been discussing, while Annette accosted her friend.

"Logan's looking pretty good, don't you think?" she asked as soon as they were seated on the white linen couch in the far corner. "But he seems too settled into his carefree bachelor life-style, if you ask me."

"Annette!" Kathryn had to laugh. "I'm sure he didn't tell you that."

"He didn't need to," replied Annette, tossing her short dark curls. "He's got that lazy way of talking some men have when there's not enough going on in their lives. He needs an interest." She waggled her eyebrows at Kathryn suggestively, making her laugh again.

"You're probably right. If anyone needs shaking up, it's Logan ... but I'm not going to be the one to do it. Mother tried some matchmaking along those lines once, too, but I've known him too long to even think of him that way. And it's mutual. He's practically a brother to me. A tyrannical, overbearing big brother, who tried to run my life once too often."

Annette wrinkled her nose. "Yeah, I seem to remember something about that, now that you mention it. Still—I've got a funny feeling about you and Logan."

Kathryn's chuckle held a hint of alarm—she knew from experience that Annette's predictions often had an uncanny way of coming true. "You and your feelings. Don't start. By the way, I'm not sure things here *will* be so different from Washington. Mother's got the next two weeks scheduled right down to the minute with luncheons, fund-raisers, the works." She sighed. "I was looking forward to a change of pace, but it doesn't look like I'm going to get it."

KATHRYN TWIRLED, delighted, before the antique pier glass in her room. It reflected a young lady from a bygone age, in a blue-and-silver gown that looked exactly like the one in the 1822 ladies' fashion magazine downstairs. Of course, they hadn't used a polyester blend back then, but it made the dress both comfortable and washable, if not absolutely authentic. Her rich brown-black hair was piled high on her head, adorned with royal blue ribbons that matched both the dress and her eyes.

Turning from the mirror, Kathryn wandered around the room, trying to get into the part as she would for an audition. This party was important to her mother, and she was determined to do her best. She'd never studied the particular time period being reenacted, but maybe this room could help her—much of this was the original furniture, her mother had told her, bought back when the house was restored. Gently, Kathryn touched the needlepoint on the chair cushions, the damask of the draperies and the intricately carved woodwork of the antique desk.

Peering into the various recesses of the desk, she opened tiny drawers and fingered the carvings. One of the wooden rose petals along the edge of the desktop seemed to move beneath her fingers and she looked more closely, worried that the valuable piece of furniture might have been damaged. No, the carved piece wasn't broken—it seemed to turn on a sort of pivot. As she played with it, she heard a tiny click and another piece of carving on the front of the desk sprang forward.

Kathryn gasped and snatched her hand away, sure now that she'd broken something, but then saw that instead of falling off, the section of carving had opened downward on a hinge. Intrigued, she felt inside the secret recess and carefully drew out a small leather-bound book. Could it be as old as the desk? Curious, she opened it. On the flyleaf she read "Personal Diary of Catherine Prescott—Private."

Smiling, she wondered if her long-dead ancestor would curse her from the grave for reading her girlish secrets nearly two hundred years after the fact. Never superstitious, she turned to the first page, dated June 22, 1823. That young Catherine had written of her excitement at an impending trip to London to stay for a Season or two with her Aunt

Sykes. The next several pages Kathryn was forced to skim as the writing was faded and difficult to decipher, the *S*s looking like *F*s. Catherine described travel preparations and farewells to local friends, with little mention of the dresses she was packing, which Kathryn would rather have read about.

"I shall write absolutely everything that I see and hear," she had penned on the seventh of July, the eve of her departure. "I must close now, to be well rested for the drive to the coast."

Kathryn turned the page, interested to read her ancestor's impressions of London as a young girl, but apparently Catherine had neglected to take her diary along on the trip. The next entry was dated March 13, 1825—today's date, except for the year. Kathryn shivered involuntarily at the coincidence.

I have just remembered this old diary. Perhaps if I set down my thoughts in writing, I will be less prone to voice them aloud tonight and ruin my mother's plans. Truly, I would as lief ruin them, however, for I have no wish in the world to wed Ryan James. It is apparent that the man cares nothing for me, only for Papa's lands, which I stand to inherit someday. This ball tonight is most important to my mother, however, so I shall create no scandal for the present. Also, I should like to see, and perhaps to dance with, the Marquis de Lafayette. A true hero in our home! Mother hopes to outshine the ball given at the State House yesterday night—and well she may. The slaves, poor things, have been working inside and out for days to produce her idea of perfection. The result is lovely, but I fear my stay in England has made me intolerant of slavery, though I dare not mention it again to my father. Of course, he is nowhere near so harsh a master as Mr. James, but he thinks a lady should have no opinion on such matters, which is most vexing. In England, the gentlemen are vastly more polite, nor do they pressure a lady to do what she knows to be wrong, as R.J. has done in his efforts to force my hand. If I doubted the gossip about him before, I do so no longer! Had I known what fate awaited me this side of the Atlantic I would have accepted Sir Mark Fenton after all, I think. It grows late, so I must stop. Perhaps Mr. James will not attend. I hope not, for I vow the man frightens me and I would not wish him to discover it.

Mention of the time made Kathryn glance at the clock by the bed. Nearly eight o'clock. Bending over to slip into the authentic but comfortable silk-ribboned dancing slippers that matched her dress, she thought over what she'd read so far. Imagine living in a time when a girl could be forced by her parents to marry a man of *their* choice! She wished she could have a few moments to advise that young Catherine of what *she* would do in her position. Then she chuckled. This was her great-great-great-great-great-grandmother she was talking about—a woman who had lived out her life more than a century and a half ago.

There were several more pages of writing, and she was tempted to continue reading to find out what had happened. She glanced back at the diary, vaguely bothered by something about the handwriting on the next page. As soon as the party was over, she would read the rest, she promised herself. There was no time now. Rising hurriedly, she took one last look at herself in the mirror and left the room.

Descending the graceful, curving staircase, Kathryn found it easy to pretend that it was two centuries earlier. Her mother had chosen every furnishing, drapery and knick-knack to reflect the early 1800s. She was so caught up in the history around her that, on reaching the second-floor landing, she suddenly felt a strange sense of disorientation, even dizziness. As she put a hand on the banister to steady herself, the antique grandfather clock that stood on the landing began to strike the hour.

Kathryn remembered the clock from her childhood and knew it had been in her mother's family for generations. But she could never remember the clock working. Had it been repaired for this evening? It struck four times and hummed to silence, though the hands pointed to eight o'clock. Her head clearing, she made a mental note to tell her mother that the clock was still not working perfectly and continued down the stairs.

Several guests had already arrived, all historically garbed. She supposed that period costume balls must be commonplace among this crowd. If the majority of these ladies were like her mother, they probably liked nothing better than emulating their notable ancestors. To her surprise, though, even the gentlemen had gotten into the spirit of things, wearing realistic Early American outfits. Kathryn rather doubted her own father—or Logan—would be in costume, but she didn't see them anywhere around.

In fact, she didn't recognize anyone—but then, she admitted, she hadn't expected to. She smiled politely at a few people, scanning the large hall for her mother. Annette would be here, too, but probably not this early. Annette had never been on time for anything.

"Good evening, Miss Catherine. You are looking exceptionally lovely this evening," came a masculine voice at her elbow. Turning, she saw a tall, ruggedly handsome man with shoulder-length dark hair—probably a wig—and compelling, deep brown eyes.

She was certain she'd never seen him before, but his gaze implied otherwise. In fact, he was regarding her with an intimate intensity that would have made most women either tremble or melt. Kathryn did neither. She'd met his type before, though they were usually less magnetically handsome than this obvious pick-up artist.

She couldn't help noticing his build was as provocative as his face, his powerful shoulders and thighs nicely displayed by the tight-fitting jacket and knee-breeches he wore. The snowy lace at his throat, rather than looking girlish, only emphasized the tanned strength of his face and jawline. No doubt he was used to impressionable young women falling hook, line and sinker for his flattery and hypnotic leer.

"Excuse me, sir, but I don't believe we've been properly introduced," she said coolly, deciding to play the part of a prim 1820s miss rather than shoot down one of her mother's guests.

His broad smile made Kathryn steel herself against his palpable charm, but he followed her lead. "I can well understand such a sought-after young lady as yourself forgetting the least of your numerous admirers," he drawled with an elegant, sweeping bow. "Allow me to refresh your memory. I am Ryan James."

Kathryn frowned. She'd heard that name before, and recently—but where? *The diary*, she suddenly realized. But how could this man possibly have known? Remembering again that the guests tonight were from Columbia's oldest families, she wondered if he might be a descendent of the very Ryan James that Catherine Prescott had been all but engaged to. Had they married? If so, this man must be some sort of relation, which would account for his boldness.

"You obviously know me already," she said, thawing slightly. "My mother didn't tell me exactly who was going to be here tonight, so you must forgive me if I seemed rude."

"Perhaps she feared you would remain in hiding in your room had you known I was to attend," Ryan returned mockingly, his eyes caressing her face and figure in a way that revived her original suspicions about him.

Kathryn narrowed her eyes, ready to cut him down to size. But before she could speak, she saw her mother bearing down on them, regal in her antique gown and upswept hairstyle.

"Catherine! Mr. James! I see you two have mended your quarrel. I am so pleased."

"Quarrel? We only just met." Even as Kathryn spoke, she noticed something jarringly wrong with her mother's voice—and face, now that she looked closely. Were those pockmarks on her cheeks? Surely even she wouldn't go *that* far in her zeal for authenticity. The slight British accent she could more readily believe, though she wouldn't have thought her mother could so easily disguise her New Jersey twang.

Her mother—*was* it her mother?—looked at her just as strangely. "Just met? What game are you playing at, Catherine?"

"You've found us out, Mrs. Sykes-Prescott. Miss Prescott and I were simply playing a little game," interposed Ryan smoothly. "It was my idea. All is well between us now."

Her mother smiled uncertainly and left them to greet some newly arriving guests. Kathryn, meanwhile, was beginning to sense that something was *very* wrong. Her mother had never mentioned using the name Prescott this evening, though apparently this Mr. James knew about it.

"I'll expect payment in full for that favor, Miss Prescott," he said with a wolfish grin, interrupting her musings. "I'm sure you are grateful to me for deflecting your mother's wrath—for wrathful she would certainly be to find you, ah, toying with my affections." He allowed his hand to brush hers, and then to slide caressingly up her arm in a manner that was far from cousinly.

Kathryn stepped away from him hastily, trying to marshal her confused thoughts. "I'm afraid your affections will have to wait, Mr. James," she said with formal politeness. "Right now, I need to speak to my father." Without waiting for a reply, she turned and made her way to the front of the house.

The hall seemed to be getting full. Hadn't her mother said that she'd invited only the "best" families? As she made her way between the richly dressed strangers, Kathryn noticed some unlikely odors. Many of the women—and men!—were wearing heavy perfume, and those that weren't seemed long overdue for a good shower. Surely that was taking authenticity a bit too far!

Her mother was still by the front door, and Kathryn hoped to find her father nearby. *He'd* always been solidly rooted in reality, and might be able to shed some light on whatever was going on. A portly, middle-aged man she'd never seen before stood at her mother's side, apparently greeting people as they came in. Her father was nowhere in sight.

"Here you are, Catherine." Her mother beckoned to her as she approached. "I was hoping you would join me in greeting our guests. Many of them are anxious to see you now that you are back in South Carolina."

Kathryn smiled and nodded graciously to an elderly couple just entering before turning back to her mother. "I really need to speak to Father, if you don't mind, Mother. I'll be back in a minute."

"Certainly," she replied with a surprised look. "In private, I presume you mean? Joseph," she said, nudging the man at her side, "Catherine has something to tell you. Don't keep her long, I beg you."

The man nodded and held out his arm. "Shall we go into the music room, my dear? I believe it is as yet unoccupied."

They went into the formal parlor where she'd met Logan yesterday, only now it was furnished primarily with an old-fashioned piano and a large harp. How odd, thought Kathryn. Those instruments hadn't been here before. And who was this Joseph? She'd wanted to speak to her father. She was feeling increasingly disoriented by now, but the man's next words caused a real surge of alarm.

"You're not going to berate me again about the slaves, are you, Catherine?" he asked with gruff affection. "I told you before that I won't have a daughter of mine concerning herself in such matters, regardless of what radical ideas she may have picked up in England. The cotton could never be gathered without them, even with those newfangled machines you keep pressing on me."

Kathryn's head swam. This had to be a dream. There was absolutely no other explanation for what was going on. Trying desperately to remain calm, she decided to play along with this man who seemed to think he was her father.

"No, I suppose you're right. I...I just wanted to say I was sorry for upsetting you about it earlier." She barely knew what she was saying. She *had* to get away by herself to think. "Um, tell Mother I'll be with her in a couple of minutes. I think I forgot something in my room."

Before her father, who looked nothing like her father, could reply, she bolted from the room, making for the staircase at the rear of the house. Several guests, all complete strangers, spoke to her as she hurried by, but she was now too distraught to answer. There was no sign of the man who'd introduced himself as Ryan James, and Kathryn breathed a sigh of relief. She didn't feel up to another encounter with him right then.

It wasn't until she was partway up the staircase, holding her gown up in front so that she wouldn't trip on it, that Kathryn noticed the material between her hands. It was heavier, much heavier, than the silky polyester blend she'd donned earlier. And, more surprising, it was a pale apricot color instead of blue.

Kathryn only just managed to reach the landing, where she was out of sight of the guests below. Trembling, she sank into a small straight-backed chair next to the grandfather clock, unable to go any farther.

What is going on? she asked herself wildly. *What the hell could possibly be going on?*

CHAPTER TWO

CATHERINE GRIMACED as Nancy tightened the laces of her corset. Why did clothing have to be so uncomfortable? Fleetingly, she longed for her childhood, when she had worn simple, loose-fitting frocks, or even, when away from her mother, breeches. Then, she could be comfortable without scandalizing anyone. Even in England, these torture devices had not been necessary for girls of her build, as flowing, high-waisted dresses had been all the rage there.

"That's enough, Nancy. Don't pinch!" she admonished when the maid gave a final tug to the lacings. "I have no desire to compete with Leslie Allerby's nineteen-inch waist. Twenty-two is dainty enough, if you ask me." After Nancy helped her into an apricot satin gown and put the finishing touches to her hair, Catherine dismissed her. "I should like to relax for a few minutes before I go down," she said.

"Yes, Miss Catherine. Mind you don't fall asleep, though, or the Missus'll give you a tongue-lashing for sure and certain."

"I won't. Thank you, Nancy."

The maid left, and Catherine slowly crossed to the window to stare down at the gardens below. Her mother, proud of her heritage as granddaughter of an earl, had had them laid out in traditional English style with massed plantings of yew, ivy and spring flowers. Catherine scarcely noticed. She was dreading the evening ahead, playing the role her mother demanded while Ryan James leered and embarrassed her at every turn. If she weren't so eager to meet General Lafa-yette, she'd pretend a headache and refuse to go down at all.

Why were her parents so set on her marrying? Her father had trained her extensively to manage the plantation that would one day be hers. She could handle it quite well, she thought, without any help from Ryan James. As his wife, she would no doubt be relegated to a purely social role, her opinions on the management of their combined lands counting for naught. Such a life would bore her into an early grave, she was certain.

Oh, he was handsome enough, she had to admit. In fact, several young ladies of her acquaintance had pronounced him the handsomest—and most eligible—bachelor in Co-lumbia. But she, herself, could never remain above five minutes in his company without feeling uneasy. Rumor held that he was an incorrigible ladies' man who would make his wife's life a misery and, even worse, that he was dreadfully cruel to his slaves. She saw no reason to disbelieve either rumor.

For a moment Catherine tried to imagine another sort of man, the one she *would* marry. Somehow she knew, with a certainty that went beyond wishful thinking, that such a man existed somewhere, and that he waited for her as she did for him. He would encourage her to read, to explore, to enjoy what life had to offer—not expect her to conform to some silly stereotype of what a woman should be. And he would be a real gentleman. What he looked like, she didn't know. Sometimes she imagined him one way, sometimes another. No matter, though—when she met him, she would know him at once.

On sudden impulse, she left the window and walked over to her writing desk, unerringly twisting a carved wooden rose petal at one corner. Sitting down, she pulled her diary from the recess revealed and opened it to reread what she had written of her expectations about London. About half had come true. It *had* been exciting, especially at first, and she'd learned much—too much!—about how to go on in civilized society. The etiquette her mother prized so highly was elevated to an art in London. In a way, it was a relief to return to her plain-speaking American neighbors. But some, notably Ryan James, were too plain-spoken for even her liking.

Catherine picked up the pen and dipped it into the almost-empty inkwell. There was something to be said for recording one's feelings for future perusal. She had only put down a few paragraphs, though, when she heard voices below. Her mother had specifically said she was to be downstairs before eight o'clock, and here she was dawdling! Scribbling one last sentence, she replaced the pen in its stand and the diary in its cubbyhole before leaving the room in a flurry. She and her mother were at odds about enough things without adding one more.

Yes, she was definitely late—the grandfather clock on the landing began striking the hour as she passed it. It stopped abruptly after four chimes, however, and Catherine glanced at it, suddenly feeling strangely light-headed. The hands had stopped at twelve-twenty and the pendulum was still. Shaking her head to clear it, she hoped her mother wouldn't add the broken clock to her already long list of sins.

Resuming her descent of the curving staircase, Catherine suddenly realized she was breathing more easily than she had a moment before. "Perhaps I am finally growing used to these damnable corsets," she muttered, then guiltily glanced around. If her mother had overheard that expletive, she'd be set to a week of prayers.

On reaching the ground floor, she noticed that the lights seemed abnormally bright. Had her mother added more sconces for the occasion? She looked up at the nearest chandelier and blinked. Those flames looked like nothing she'd ever seen before—they were white, rather than yellow, and did not flicker in the least.

"Kathy, there you are!" came her mother's voice. Relieved, Catherine realized that she must not be upset at her tardiness, or she would not have used the affectionate nickname.

"I'm sorry if I am a bit late, Mama," she said, turning quickly. "I did hurry. Did you know that something is wrong with the clock on the landing?"

"Yes, of course, it hasn't worked for years. I did mean to have it repaired before this evening, but the time seemed to slip away." She paused to chuckle at her own wit. "I must say, Kathy, you look splendid. You must plan to really play the part!"

"Yes, of...of course, Mama," Catherine answered reluctantly. Was it so obvious that she detested these social games? Why else would her mother have phrased it so? Still, she *would* try tonight, though she knew if Ryan James began his outrageous flirting, her resolution would vanish like a puff of smoke.

"Good, good!" Her mother beamed at her, then bustled off to the parlor to make certain that everything was ready for the first guests.

Catherine glanced after her thoughtfully. Mama looked unusually well tonight, she thought, with an almost youthful glow. There had been something different about her voice, as well, though she could not quite place what it was.

On her way to the front door, where she knew she would be required to play hostess alongside her parents, Catherine paused in amazement at the sight of a small fountain spraying miniature cascades of water down its ornamental sides. How on earth had her mother managed that? The unusual brightness was even more noticeable by the door, where a chandelier hung lower, and she took the moment to examine the new candles more closely. Why, they were not candles at all! Where the flame should be, there appeared to be little globes of glass, lit from within. She had seen gas lights in London, but they had looked nothing like this—

nor, in all her extensive reading, had she come across any new inventions fitting this description.

An approaching figure drew her rapt attention reluctantly away from the chandelier. From his height she at first feared it was Ryan James, but then saw that this man had dark blond hair, not brown, and that it was cropped short, according to the new fashion in England. Just as she noticed that there was something decidedly odd about his attire, he spoke.

"Something wrong with the light?" he asked, glancing at the chandelier. His voice was deep and rich, and affected her profoundly. "All the bulbs seem to be working. I'm glad I found you here early. I wanted to apologize for my—attitude—yesterday. I was in a foul mood, but it wasn't your fault and I had no right to take it out on you."

Catherine stared at the man, torn between admiration and perplexity. He was the handsomest man she had ever seen. A tingle, first icy and then warm, curled through her as she gazed at him. Though his features were unfamiliar, she felt as if she knew him. In fact, she felt inexplicably drawn to him—to the strength in the chiseled lines of his face, the kindness in his eyes. But she had absolutely no idea what he was talking about.

"I . . . I beg your pardon?" she finally asked. "Have we met, sir?"

"That's carrying a grudge a bit far, Kathy," he said, the softness leaving his hazel eyes. "I wouldn't have thought it of you—or maybe I would. I'd nearly forgotten that sharp tongue of yours. If you decide to accept my apology, fine. But don't expect me to repeat it." He turned on his heel and strode away, leaving her to stare in confusion at his retreating back.

Now she had offended him, and she didn't even know why. Even in that outlandish outfit—what had that thing around his neck been, some new sort of cravat?—he looked splendid. She wondered again who he could be. Some foreign visitor, perhaps? His accent had been unusual, but not precisely foreign. More as though he came from some part of the English-speaking world that spoke in a strange dialect. And there was that tantalizing familiarity that made her wonder if they had, indeed, met before, as he had implied. Could it be . . . ?

She felt a surge of sudden, wild hope. Determined to discover all she could about this fascinating man during the course of the evening, she looked for her mother. She saw her coming out of the front parlor, which had apparently been set up for refreshments.

"Sorry to leave you alone by the door, Kathy, but no harm done, I see. No one has arrived yet," she said breathlessly as she hurried over.

"Someone has, however, Mama," replied Catherine, glancing over to where the man she had unwittingly insulted stood with his back to them.

"Logan doesn't count. He's almost family," replied her mother, dismissing that intriguing gentleman with a wave of her hand. Catherine noticed again a change in her mother's manner of speech and regarded her more closely, although most of her attention was still claimed by this enigmatic stranger. Could her parents have an alternative to Ryan James in mind?

"You look wonderful tonight, Mama," said Catherine as the results of her inspection finally sank in. However had she achieved that clearness of complexion? No heavy, covering cosmetic was evident that might account for it.

"Why, thank you, sweetheart!" Her mother gave her a quick hug, her eyes suddenly moist. "You don't know how I've missed you calling me 'Mama'—"

Just then the bell rang, and the attention of both ladies was claimed by a steady stream of visitors for the next half hour. Strangely, Catherine didn't recognize anybody, though she had thought she knew nearly everyone in Columbia. Ryan James must not be coming after all, she thought with relief. But where were Priscilla, Jane, or even the preten-tious Leslie Allerby? They had all been invited, and none were prone to tardiness.

As greetings were exchanged, she had ample opportunity to listen more closely to her mother's voice. Something had definitely changed. She spoke more quickly, and with a trace of the same accent she had first noticed in Logan's voice. Was it some new fashion that no one had told her about? She found herself mimicking it, almost unconsciously.

"So this is our actress!" a woman of about her mother's age exclaimed, breaking into her thoughts. "When will we see 'Kathryn Sykes-Monroe' up in lights?"

Catherine blinked at the woman in utter confusion, but her mother answered smoothly, "Kathy's other work has taken precedence over the theater lately, Mary. Did you not read about the Animal Rights Foundation demonstration that she spearheaded? It was in all the papers. We're so proud of the good she's doing."

The woman moved on, leaving Catherine shaken by the incomprehensible exchange. She began to pay closer atten-tion to the comments between her mother and the arriving guests, noticing several oddities. For one thing, although those who appeared to know her mother well addressed her as "Catherine," as might have been expected (although Catherine herself knew none of these "close friends"), more than one guest greeted her as Mrs. Sykes-Monroe—and her mother made no effort to correct them. No mention was made of General Lafayette's incipient arrival, which she expected to be on everyone's lips, and a few of the gentle-men were attired in the same odd style as Logan had been, although most wore the proper knee-breeches and cutaway coats.

She had not yet seen her father, whom she had expected to share their post by the door, but could not but be re-lieved at his absence. They had argued violently that very morning about his treatment of the slaves, and she doubted he had yet forgiven her. Certainly she had not forgiven him. And by now, he might have discovered that she had taken the forbidden Xerxes from his stable for one last gallop this afternoon (and not sidesaddle, either) before he was delivered to Colonel Hampton, his new owner. For that, he would likely be furious.

"Oh, Kathy, I'm sorry I'm late!" A pretty, dark-haired girl that Catherine was certain she had never seen before, ran forward to embrace her with the familiarity of an old, dear friend. "I've gotten a little bigger since I started making this dress, and I had a hard time getting into it." Glancing down at the girl's pink satin gown, Catherine realized that the young lady was "increasing."

"I'm sure Kathy doesn't mind in the least, Annette," commented her mother, smiling fondly on the two girls. "I'll let you go join the guests, Kathy, since nearly everyone is here. I'm sure some of the people who said they wouldn't miss it were politely lying, anyway."

Catherine blinked at her mother's outspokenness, but Annette was already pulling her away from the door. "You look like you need a few minutes to yourself, Kathy. Doesn't your mother know you came to Columbia to unwind?"

Even though she didn't recognize her, Catherine instinctively liked this lively girl and followed her obediently into the music room. Only it *wasn't* the music room! The pianoforte was missing, and so was the harp. Had her mother had them moved for tonight? It seemed a lot of trouble, even if she did have the slaves do it.

Surveying the room critically, she realized that even more had changed. The claw-footed divan was upholstered in deep rose, when only this morning it had sported a green-and-yellow floral print. The rest of the room's decor had been altered to coordinate, from the pink-striped draperies in place of the green velvet that had hung on the long windows, to the rose-and-gray patterned carpet covering what had before been highly polished bare boards.

Catherine sat down heavily on the new divan, her mind reeling. Her dress billowed up around her and she stared at its blue folds in something like shock. The room began to spin and she feared for a moment that she would swoon, much as she had always detested that particular bit of artifice in other young ladies.

"Kathy, what is it?" asked Annette in alarm. "Don't tell me it's nothing—I know you too well. What's wrong?"

Catherine looked up at her helplessly, trying to force her numb brain to function. "I don't know. I honestly have no idea!"

Annette sat down next to Catherine on the divan and began rubbing her hands briskly. "You look like you've seen a ghost! As a matter of fact, you look as white as one. Come on, tell me about it. You've always been able to tell me anything."

"But I haven't! Told you anything, I mean. I do not even know you, although you seem to know me perfectly well. My gown, this room, everything is wrong! Am I mad, or is everyone else? What is happening?" Her voice rose in panic and Annette tried to calm her, glancing at the open archway.

"Sshh, Kathy! Everything will be all right, I promise. Just calmly tell me what you think is wrong. Have you lost your memory? Did you bump your head or something?"

"No. At least . . . I don't believe so. I remember perfectly well who I am and everything that has happened today, and even yesterday, but things seem to have changed. This room, for example. Only this afternoon there was a pianoforte right here, and my grandmother's harp there, in the corner." She pointed with a shaking finger. "They're gone! And the colors are different. Even my gown. When I put it on, no more than an hour ago, it was a peach or apricot color. Now it's blue. The fabric is different, as well. It is certainly not satin!"

Annette regarded her strangely. "Are you playing a part, Kathy? It's not like you to mess with my mind this way. You're not just 'getting into character,' or whatever actors call it, are you?"

"Actors again!" exclaimed Catherine. "That is what another woman said, and Mama did not even seem surprised by it. Am I supposed to have been an actress?"

Annette now appeared almost as bewildered as Catherine felt, but before she could answer, Kathryn's mother appeared in the archway. "There you are, girls. Come, Kathy, you two will have time for gossip later. I need you to help me hostess. There are a few people you still need to meet, and the band will be starting soon. I can't get over how well you look the part tonight—I'm surprised that you didn't get the part in that play."

"Acting yet again!" exclaimed Catherine in dismay. "Mama, how can you? You know you would have my head if I, a Prescott, ever set foot on a stage."

"Prescott! Oh, marvelous, Kathy! Keep it up—everyone will love it." Her mother seemed genuinely delighted at her words, which confused Catherine even more. She tried a different approach.

"Mama, what are these new candles you have in the chandeliers? They burn so steadily, and so much more brightly than the ordinary ones. Are they a new invention?" She really wanted to know, thinking they might be implemented at the plantation, as well.

But though she still smiled, her mother only said, "That's good, Kathy, but don't overdo it. I'd rather you didn't draw attention to my less-than-authentic details. I could hardly replace the bulbs with candles for this one evening. For one thing, they'd probably drip and ruin the fixtures, though it would have been a nice touch. Do come along and meet some people."

Catherine rose and followed, afraid for the moment to ask any more questions, since none of the answers made any sense. She forced herself to smile, hoping her fit, or dream, or whatever it was, would pass quickly.

"Kathy, this is Mr. and Mrs. Brentwood, of Charleston. She was a member of my New Jersey DAR before she moved down here two years ago, but I don't believe you've ever met her."

Catherine was certain she had not, but managed to murmur an appropriate greeting and curtsied deeply, which seemed to charm the Brentwoods. Her mother then took control of the conversation and Catherine was able to observe her companions more closely.

Both of the Brentwoods were dressed in suitable evening attire, though there was something decidedly strange about Mr. Brentwood's shoes, she thought. They spoke with an accent similar to the one her mother was affecting. When the Brentwoods wandered off to greet other acquaintances, Catherine became aware of the intriguing man she had met earlier watching the guests from the other side of the room.

"Can you tell me about that man, Mama? That one there, in the strange clothing," she asked impulsively.

"Strange... Oh, of course! He refused to wear a costume, and I was afraid if I insisted he wouldn't come down at all. Very well, sweetheart, I'll play along. This was all my idea, after all." Mrs. Sykes-Monroe primmed up her mouth and continued in an affected tone. "That, Miss Prescott, is Mr. Logan Thorne, a promising young architect and very eligible bachelor. Would you care for an introduction?"

Though not understanding the first half of what her mother had said, Catherine very much wanted a chance to speak to Mr. Thorne again. Perhaps she could undo whatever offense he felt she had committed against him. "Yes, thank you, I would," she replied just as primly, which seemed to please her mother. She was therefore led across the room as the small orchestra began to tune their instruments.

"Logan, ah, Mr. Thorne?" said her mother as they reached the gentleman in question. "Might I present to you my daughter, Miss Catherine Prescott? She has expressed a desire to make your acquaintance."

Logan bowed civilly, though he raised one eyebrow questioningly as he did so. Catherine flushed to the roots of her dark hair. How could Mama have been so gauche? One did not say that a lady wished to make a gentleman's acquaintance. How forward he must think her!

"Do I take it this means you're finally willing to accept my apology?" asked Logan in an undertone, examining her furiously blushing face with something like surprise. Though she still had no idea what he meant, Catherine nodded, mindful of her mother beside them. "Eligible bachelor" she had termed him. Her earlier suspicion about her parents' motives must have been well founded.

The orchestra began playing in earnest at that moment, a tune that Catherine recognized. She wondered whether Logan might ask her to dance. She had been much admired in the ballrooms of London and found she was not at all averse to displaying one of her few social graces for this man. But when she glanced at him, she saw that he was scowling.

"I hope you're not having them play this antique stuff all night," he remarked. Catherine nearly gasped at such rudeness, but her mother was already answering.

"You can hear rock or rap or whatever it is you listen to every other day of the year, Logan. Consider this a cultural education."

"At a party?" he exclaimed in mock horror. "Do you really think anyone will know how to dance to this?"

"I do," said Catherine, feeling that he needed some sort of set-down for such behavior. Both Logan and her mother turned to look at her in astonishment.

"Marvelous!" cried her mother, recovering first. "Then you can show Logan how it's done. Maybe the other guests will follow suit."

Logan looked as though he wanted to refuse, but his hostess fixed him with a challenging stare that dared him to back down. He nodded and held out his hand to Catherine. "Very well, Miss... Prescott, was it? Show me the steps."

She had the feeling he thought he was calling her bluff. Well, she would call his, instead. She led him out near the center of the floor—the actual center was occupied by that astonishing fountain—and proceeded to instruct him in the quadrille.

"Hold my hand so, Mr. Thorne, and begin with your right foot. Yes. Watch what I do and try to perform as a sort of mirror image. I believe we will omit the more complicated portions of the dance for now."

"Oh, no you don't. Show me the whole thing, please."

He thought she was trying to get out of it! Catherine bowed her head to him slightly, and began her part of the dance. The quadrille was a lively dance, requiring very little contact between them, and she was able to perform it as a solo, her anger at his attitude giving her added energy.

She finished one set of the intricate steps and paused, waiting for him to partner her. Instead, he began to applaud, and to her intense embarrassment, the majority of the guests joined in. Suddenly realizing how she must have looked to everyone, dancing alone in the middle of the big room, she fervently wished that the floor might open up and swallow her.

Thankfully, the orchestra paused at that moment and Logan led her from the floor as she desperately tried to recover some shred of dignity. "*That* is how it is done, Mr. Thorne." She tried to speak haughtily, but her voice came out in a high quaver instead. Would this madness never end?

"So I see," he replied and, to her surprise, she thought she detected respect in his eyes. "You really did know what you were doing. I apologize—again—for doubting you."

She looked up at him uncertainly. Surely he must despise her for such a display? But no, his expression, while puzzled, showed nothing like distaste. Her mother would be another matter, though, she thought suddenly. She would likely banish her to her room for the rest of the evening—or even the rest of the year.

"Kathy, that was *wonderful!*" Mrs. Sykes-Monroe exclaimed as the couple reached the edge of the floor, astonishing her daughter once again on this most astonishing evening. "You never said a word about having learned the dances of the period. Did you do it to surprise me?"

Catherine stared before managing a slight nod. She had nearly forgotten how her mother had changed along with everything else. She would just try to brazen her way through until the world—or her own mind—returned to normal.

"Now, this I know how to do. Shall we?" Logan was holding out his hand to her again and she realized that a waltz had begun. Two or three other couples drifted onto the floor, and no one seemed to be staring at her now. Would they let her live down that ridiculous demonstration? Breathing a bit easier, she allowed Logan to lead her back onto the floor.

He waltzed somewhat differently than the English gentlemen had, but she found his steps easy enough to follow. Nor did he try to hold her too tightly, as an occasional London beau had done, for which she was grateful. Being this close to him did crazy things to her heart. By the time the waltz ended at least ten couples had joined them, and as the last strains of music sounded she decided that perhaps madness wasn't such a bad thing. She allowed a small, contented sigh to escape her lips as Logan held her for a moment after the dance ended. She looked up at him shyly, hoping he had enjoyed the experience as much as she.

He was smiling, too, but when their eyes met, he suddenly frowned and stepped away. "Well, I, ah, have work to do. Good night, Kathy, er, Miss Prescott." He sketched a stiff half bow and left her, bowing again to his hostess as he passed. And then he was gone.

Surely I did nothing to offend him this time, thought Catherine indignantly. What could have caused such a change in his manner? Was she the one who was mad, or was he? Walking slowly from the floor, she decided the answer was beyond her, at least for the moment. But now she renewed her determination to discover just what *was* going on.

"Well, he didn't stay long, but at least he came," said her mother as Catherine reached her side. "And I didn't have to prod him into that second dance, I hope you noticed."

"Mama, are you matchmaking again?" asked Catherine bluntly. This new, changed mother of hers didn't seem to mind plain speaking.

"No, of... of course not," she said almost guiltily, to Catherine's surprise. "I've about given up on Logan for you. It was pretty obvious last night the two of you don't..." Her voice trailed off wistfully. "Oh, run along and enjoy yourself, Kathy. I'm sure there are other young men to dance with, maybe more to your taste. Though most of the men here are closer to your father's age, I have to admit."

The orchestra was now playing a polonaise, but no one was dancing to it and Catherine certainly had no intention of giving another demonstration. She saw that friendly young matron, Annette, standing nearby and made her way over to her side.

"I thought you and Logan didn't get along," said Annette teasingly as Catherine approached her. "That was quite a dance lesson you gave us! Where did you learn to do that?"

"In London," replied Catherine without thinking, feeling her cheeks grow hot again at the memory of what she had done.

"London? When was that?" asked Annette with great interest. "You never sent me a postcard."

"I . . . I was there these two years past," said Catherine faintly. "Do you suppose we could slip away somewhere to speak privately? I simply *must* discover what is going on." She had little interest in the ball, now that Logan had left. In his arms, she had nearly forgotten that her world had turned topsy-turvy. But now she had to know.

"Sure," said Annette. "Do you want to go up to your room? Nobody would bother us there, unless your mother comes looking for you again."

"I don't believe she will." Catherine led the way up the stairs but paused at the top. "I hope I am in the same room. So much else seems to have changed." She cautiously opened the door on the right, then breathed a sigh of relief. This room, at least, looked as it should, or nearly so. She motioned Annette to enter and the women sat half facing each other on the bed.

"Oh!" exclaimed Catherine as she sat down. "The bed looks right, but it certainly doesn't *feel* right. It is so hard!"

Annette frowned slightly. "It feels fine to me. What did you expect it to feel like?"

"Goose down. I have—or had—a down mattress. This feels almost like wood."

"It's better for your back, trust me. Lordy, nowadays I'd never even be able to get out of a feather bed." She patted her round stomach. "But never mind the mattress. Tell me what's wrong."

"I was rather hoping you could tell me," said Catherine plaintively. "So much seems different, and I don't see how it could have happened. Will you tell me what you know about me?"

"Sounds like amnesia to me," murmured Annette.

"What?"

"Never mind. You're Kathryn Monroe, though sometimes you call yourself Kathryn Sykes-Monroe, like your mother. You said it made a more distinctive stage name. Yes, stage," she repeated, when Catherine started to speak. "For the past two years you've been trying to break into theater, as well as pursuing your fund-raising work in Washington, D.C. I've known you since we were college roommates at William and Mary, more than six years. I don't *think* you've ever been to England. How much of this do you remember?"

"None of it," said Catherine simply. "Are you mad, or am I? My name is Catherine Prescott, though my mother uses the name Sykes-Prescott and will wish me to add the Sykes to my name when I marry. I have never even visited Washington. I spent the past two Seasons in London with my Aunt Sykes and returned to America only a few weeks ago. This ball was to have been in honor of General Lafayette, but I don't believe he is here at all, nor does anyone seem to expect him. I suppose it must be I who is mad, for *everyone* else cannot be!"

Annette regarded her intently for a moment, then asked a single, irrelevant question. "What year is it?"

Catherine blinked. "It is 1825, of course. But what has that to do with anything?"

"Whoa! This is getting too weird." Annette pushed herself up from the bed and paced the room, muttering to herself, then stopped and took a deep breath. "Listen, I'm no psychiatrist, so I can't say for sure if you're crazy or not, but it sounds like *you* believe everything you're saying. I don't know what's going on with you, but I do know for a fact that this is 1994."

For a moment Catherine merely stared at her, not quite comprehending. Finally, she said faintly, "I must have misunderstood you. What did you say?"

"This is 1994. If you're from 1825, you've somehow come nearly two hundred years into the future."

"That...that doesn't seem very likely, does it?" Catherine was now staring at Annette as intently as the other girl was regarding her. What sort of game could she be playing at?

"No, it doesn't," admitted Annette. "I'm afraid it's a lot more likely that you're crazy. For one thing, if you're really Catherine Prescott from 1825, what happened to Kathy Monroe, my best friend?" She raked a hand through her upswept hair, sending pins flying. "But... I'm almost starting to believe you're really not her—you don't talk or act much like her. But that's definitely her body you're in!"

Catherine whirled to the mirror over the dressing table. "What do you mean?" she demanded, when one glance reassured her. "This is my face, my body." Even as she said it, though, she realized it was not quite true. Her complexion was darker, her hairstyle different than she had ever worn it, and... were those *freckles* on the bridge of her nose?

Annette shrugged, her hands spread wide. "Maybe Kathy looks as much like you as her mother looks like your mother. I know that's Kathy's costume—she showed it to me last night."

Catherine started to tremble. Why was this girl saying these things? Who was she, anyway? "I... I think perhaps you had better leave," she finally said shakily.

"You don't believe me, do you?" asked Annette. "Well, I'm not at all sure I believe you, either." She chewed her lip for a moment. "Look. We're not going to solve anything until we're both convinced the other is telling the truth. It should be pretty easy for me to prove this is 1994. Can you *prove* you're really Catherine Prescott? I mean, is there anything you can tell me that Kathy couldn't have known about?"

"What kind of things? And how could you verify them?"

"Hmm. I guess if I could look something up, Kathy could have, too. And if you are Kathy, you'd only tell me the things you know are in a book somewhere."

"A book—my diary! Only I would know what I wrote in my diary. I wonder.... That certainly looks like my writing

desk. Perhaps my diary is still in its place." She jumped up
and went over to the desk. "How odd! Here it is, on top of
the desk. I know I put it away earlier this evening." She
reached for it, but Annette stopped her.

"Just a minute! Shouldn't I look at it first?"

"Oh, yes, I suppose so. Here you are." She handed the
small, leather-bound book to the other girl. "The last entry
should be dated March 13, 1825."

Annette looked up from the diary. "In case you're interested, this *is* March 13." She turned the pages until she
reached the date specified. "I've found it. But it's not the
last entry. Oh!" She read silently for a few minutes, while
Catherine watched with growing perplexity.

Finally, Annette slowly set the book down on her lap, her
face pale. "I...I believe you now," she said in an odd voice.
"And I know what happened to Kathy."

"What are you talking about? I've not yet told you what
I'd written. It was about the ball tonight, and how I didn't
wish to marry Ryan James.... How can it not be the last
entry?"

"See for yourself," replied Annette, handing the diary
back to her.

Catherine's words were written there, just as she had
penned them not two hours earlier, but the ink looked
strangely faded and the pages, yellowed with age, crackled
as she handled them. But that was not what held her attention. On the next page, in the same faded ink, was another
entry in an entirely different hand. It was dated March 14,
1825.

I don't dare tell anyone in this time what seems to have
happened, but I decided it might be a good idea to write
it down here, for posterity or whatever. Maybe, if
Catherine and I have switched places like I think we
have, she'll be able to read this in my time. If we switch

back before that happens, at least I can use this diary as proof I'm not crazy.

Sometime last night, just before Mother's party, something very strange happened and I gradually realized I was no longer in 1994. Thinking back carefully, I believe the time shift occurred after I left my room but before I got downstairs, maybe while I was on the landing. I figured I was dreaming for most of the evening, especially since I'd just been reading Catherine's diary—this diary—before I left the room. But my experiences today have finally convinced me this is real. I don't know if I'll still be here tomorrow, but in case I'm not, I wanted to write this now. If I stay here for long, I'll try to keep a record here. I'm not very good at journals, though, so forgive me, Catherine (if you read this), if I forget. I'm sure this strange situation won't be permanent—we both have our own lives to get back to. Somehow we'll figure out how to switch back. In the meantime, I plan to enjoy myself, and I suggest you do the same. Maybe when we switch back you can get rich trading on your knowledge of the future.

Catherine looked up, her face as white as Annette's. "I certainly didn't write this—it's not even my handwriting."

"I know," said Annette. "It's Kathy's."

"How . . . how did you manage this? Why are you doing this to me?" Suddenly, Catherine was furious that her fate had somehow been taken out of her hands, and she found herself directing that fury at the only person available. "Get out of here! And take this with you!" She threw the diary at Annette, who caught it and tucked it into her reticule.

"Look, I know this is a shock to you. It is to me, too. I've suddenly lost my best friend." Annette stood there studying Catherine. "Look, you've convinced me of your side, or rather Kathy has. Now it's my turn. It's pretty late now, but what do you say first thing tomorrow I come pick you up and show you what the 1990s are like?''

Catherine's anger evaporated as quickly as it had appeared. "I...I apologize. You are right, of course. This *has* been a shock, but it is hardly your fault and I had no right to shout at you. You may have your chance to convince me tomorrow, though I find I almost believe you already. No other explanation seems to fit. Suddenly I am very tired. Will you ask Mama to send up my maid?''

"I'm not surprised you're tired. But...I don't think you have a maid now. Do you need me to help you get ready for bed?''

"Oh! And...and I suppose that is not really my mother, either, though the resemblance is almost perfect.''

"Yes, she's shown everyone that portrait of her great-great-however-many-greats grandmother. That must be your mother. Mrs. Sykes-Monroe had herself done up for tonight to look just like her. Try not to be too shocked when you see everyone in regular clothes tomorrow.'' While she spoke, Annette was opening drawers and pulling out what appeared to be wisps of sheer fabric. "You might not consider any of Kathy's stuff decent to sleep in, but it will have to do for tonight. I'll take you shopping tomorrow.'' She handed Catherine an almost transparent garment.

Catherine regarded the tiny thing dubiously, but nodded. "All right. I'll undoubtedly have dozens of questions to ask you by then.''

"I hope I can answer them.'' Annette smiled, apparently regaining her composure more quickly than Catherine could. "Anything else I can do for you?''

"No, I'll manage,'' said Catherine firmly, fingering the skimpy nightgown.

"G'night, then. See you tomorrow!'' Annette smiled encouragingly and left.

Alone, Catherine sat heavily on the bed and tried to organize her thoughts. Could it really be true? Could she have been suddenly, magically, whisked into the future? As she thought about it, Catherine realized that she was becoming more excited and less frightened by the idea. What was the world like now? New inventions, such as the cotton gin and the steam engine, had been sweeping the country in 1825. What other inventions might there be now?

She looked up at the light fixture on the ceiling. Annette had somehow turned it on from the doorway when they entered the room. Examining the walls around the door, she saw the switch in its ornate brass plate and experimentally moved it. The light went out. She moved it back to its original position and the light flared on again. What a wonderful device! No more searching for candles in the dark or fumbling with matches. These new lights probably did not start fires so easily, either.

Inspecting the little bedside lamp, which, at first glance had looked like an oil lamp such as she remembered, she noticed that it had the same thin glass bulb under its shade that the chandeliers downstairs had sported. She twisted the little heart-shaped brass handle and the bulb glowed with light. Marvelous!

In spite of her fascination with the lights, Catherine was feeling more tired by the minute. Yawning, she looked around for her basin and chamber pot. The ornate china pitcher on the dressing table was filled with flowers and plainly not intended for washing. Catherine remembered that Nancy sometimes set the chamber pot just inside the dressing room if she planned to entertain a girlfriend in her room, thinking it more genteel that it be out of sight. She opened the dressing room door to look and gasped in amazement.

This was not at all the dressing room she remembered. Feeling along the wall by the door, she found another switch and flooded the small room with light. "Aahh!" she breathed.

The room was carpeted in pale green, and the walls glistened with ceramic tiles of white peppered with tiny green specks. A gleaming white bathing tub, apparently built right into the wall, peeped at her from behind a peach-and-green curtain, and a long white marble counter with a built-in basin ran along one side. The entire wall above the counter appeared to be one huge mirror. Catherine advanced reverently into the room and hesitantly touched the golden knobs and faucet over the basin.

First she tried to move the faucet, as it rather resembled a pump handle, but found it firmly fixed in place. She then gingerly twisted the knob on the right and a trickle of clear, cold water splashed into the basin, draining out through the hole at its base. Experimentally, she twisted the other knob and the stream of water became stronger and warmer. She turned off the cold water and increased the flow from the left-hand knob and produced a stream of steaming hot water. Oh, heaven! No more fires to light or pails of water to carry. Catherine luxuriously washed her face in the hot water and dried it on one of the soft peach towels hanging on a rod by the basin. She then began exploring the rest of this room of magical bathing delights.

Between the tub and the counter was a large ceramic bowl with a carpeted green lid. When she raised the lid, Catherine found that the basin was half full of water and had what could only be a seat along the top. A chamber pot of the future! It had to be. There was a gold handle on the tank above the basin. When she twisted it the water in the basin swirled away and disappeared with an alarming "whoosh," to be replaced in moments by more water from an unknown source. Catherine was dubious about this device, but her need was great by then, so she gingerly seated herself on the automatic chamber pot and made use of it. She considered the roll of soft, peach-colored paper a great improvement over cloths that had to be washed and reused.

Next, she experimented with the bathing tub. The right- and left-hand knobs worked just as those on the counter-top basin had, she found. But what did the one in the middle do? She twisted it, then jumped back with a squeal when a stream of water hit the back of her head.

"I should have asked Annette to demonstrate this room before she left," murmured Catherine as she toweled off her hair. She was sorely tempted to take a bath, but decided she was just too tired.

Changing into Kathryn's negligee, Catherine had to admit it was comfortable, if not entirely decent. Telling herself that she would work out the answers to her incredible plight tomorrow, she slipped between the satiny-smooth sheets on the hard bed and fell instantly asleep.

CHAPTER THREE

AS THE TREMORS in her body gradually subsided, Kathryn sat very still in the chair by the clock and tried to think. The most logical explanation, of course, was that she was dreaming. She'd been getting into her role, reading that old diary, and had fallen asleep in her room. Now she was dreaming that she was back in 1825, with her subconscious using information from the diary to fill in the details. She just hoped she would wake up in time for her mother's party.

Experimentally, Kathryn tried pinching herself. It hurt, and her dress was still apricot silk. Maybe that pinching thing was a myth. Taking a deep breath, she suddenly noticed an uncomfortably tight girdle of some sort under her dress that made deep breathing difficult.

Pushing away panic, she stood to look into a small gilt-framed mirror that hung on the wall above the chair. The same deep blue eyes and heart-shaped face she'd always had looked back at her, though her dark hair was styled differently. She smiled at herself in relief. She'd half-expected to see a stranger or, worse, no reflection at all. Dreams were strange things.

Since none of this could possibly matter, anyway, she decided to look for that annoying but interesting Ryan James. If she couldn't wake up, she might as well have some fun. Going back downstairs, she found Ryan at the door to the gallery. "You must excuse me for running off earlier, Mr.

James. I thought something was wrong, but it turns out I was mistaken.''

He regarded her with apparent surprise. "I am pleased that you returned, Miss Prescott. Dare I hope that your opinion of me has improved on further acquaintance?"

Kathryn treated him to a bewitching smile, reminding herself that this was all fantasy—*her* fantasy—no matter how real it seemed right now. "Let's become better acquainted, and I'll let you know," she said teasingly.

"Of course, if that is what you wish," he replied without hesitation, though she thought he looked startled.

The Catherine he knew would never have answered him like that, of course. Or rather, she amended quickly, the Catherine she was dreaming he would know.

"Shall we dance?" he inquired as the musicians began to play. She nodded. Dancing might be safer than trying to carry on a conversation until she could get herself firmly in hand.

The first dance was a waltz which, fortunately, Kathryn knew how to do, since she'd studied both modern and classical dancing as part of her theater arts degree. She tried to remember when her dance instructor had said that the waltz became popular, hoping to find an anachronism that would prove she was dreaming once and for all. Unable to dredge that detail from her memory, she decided to ask her partner.

Kathryn suspected Ryan was holding her more closely than was required by the dance, but since she was used to modern slow dancing, it didn't occur to her to object. "How long has the waltz been popular in America?" she asked, keenly aware of his strong arm around her waist.

"Not for very long," Ryan replied. "In fact, I've no doubt many of the matrons present are thoroughly shocked at its being played. Your mother has obviously heard that the General is fond of the waltz and began with it in his honor. I must say that I share his preference."

"The General?" asked Kathryn in complete confusion. Some mention had been made in Catherine's diary about a guest of honor, but she was positive it had not been a general.

"Lafayette, you know." He looked at her strangely. "I suppose in England they would refer to him as the Marquis, if they refer to him at all. But in America the honor of an earned title is higher than that of an hereditary one, I assure you. You weren't there long enough to exchange American values for British ones, I hope."

"No, of course not," she said weakly. "I was just daydreaming." A daydream inside a dream?

The dance ended and Kathryn suddenly remembered her promise to her mother—or was it Catherine's mother? Either way, it gave her an excuse to leave this disturbingly real man for a few moments. She was finding herself more flustered than amused by their conversation. But when she reached the front door, she found that her mother had deserted her post to take a place on the dance floor—her mother had always had a passion for dancing.

Making her way back through the ballroom, she saw Mrs. Sykes-Prescott dancing with an elderly gentleman whose air of elegance set him apart from the other men present. Kathryn realized at once that this must be General Lafayette. His manners seemed somehow too polished for an American—at least, for an early-nineteenth-century American.

When the music stopped, she approached her mother and found her guess was correct. The French nobleman declared he was charmed to make her acquaintance and requested the next dance. In spite of her wavering conviction that this was all a dream, Kathryn couldn't help but be honored by his notice. During the dance, General Lafayette conversed in almost flawless English, relating an incident that had occurred the day before.

"Would you believe, mademoiselle, that old Pompey Fortune, my body servant from the days of your country's fight for independence, rode all the way from Winnsboro to see me? Thirty rough miles on a donkey, and he as gray as I. He is a free man now, in reward for his faithful service—I wish such were true for all his unfortunate brethren in America. But no—with such a charming young lady I will speak only of pleasantries."

The conversation turned to other topics, but Kathryn couldn't help remembering the reference to slavery in Catherine's diary and the comments made by Mr. Prescott on the subject. How long would it be? She vaguely recalled from high school history that the Civil War would still be some forty years in coming—a very long time for someone living as another's property. Even though it had all been so long in the past, Kathryn felt a stirring of indignation against a society that would allow such a thing. Thank heaven things were more civilized in the modern world. She'd protested plenty of injustices over the years, but none came close to human bondage.

The evening was long but fascinating to Kathryn. Several times, though, she wondered where she could ever, even subconsciously, have absorbed enough history to provide the wealth of detail in this dream. Her mother's long-winded lectures on this time period hadn't included the vials of smelling salts she saw more than one lady resort to during the evening, nor the tiny flasks of what had to be some sort of liquor that many people carried.

The first time she saw a man take something from a little box and sniff it with a flourish, she was shocked. Was he snorting cocaine in her mother's house? True, she'd seen it at theater parties in college, but here . . . ? After seeing several others do it, however, she figured out that it must be snuff. She'd heard of it, but never seen it actually used.

Then there were the details of the house itself. As the evening wore on, she found several things that were definitely different than they'd been earlier. The most obvious things were the chandeliers, lit by candles rather than electric bulbs, and the gallery, which contained completely different paintings than it had last night.

And, of course, there was Ryan James. Try as she might, Kathryn could think of no one she'd ever met that he might be based on. She mentally reviewed every man she knew, slightly or intimately, but came up with no parallel. And she was positive she would have remembered anyone remotely resembling that unsettling gentleman. She was not sure the term "gentleman" even applied. In many ways, he seemed as out of place in this genteel, antique setting as she was. His speech was authentic to the period, in form if not always in content, and his dress appeared to be appropriate, but his manner was mercurial, varying from a polished drawing room beau to a back-alley rogue.

By the time she finally made her way up the stairs to her room, Kathryn's faith in her dream theory had been badly shaken. And she knew for certain that even if this *was* a dream, she'd never forget an impossible man, named Ryan James.

KATHRYN AWOKE the next morning to sunlight streaming through the many-paned window and sat up in alarm. She'd slept through the night and missed her mother's party! And she'd had the strangest dream! Maybe she should write about it before she forgot. What a story she'd have to tell her mother!

Glancing around for paper and pencil, her eye lighted on the desk and she remembered the diary that had started the trouble. Suddenly she was curious. *Had* Catherine gone on to marry Ryan James? Kathryn wasn't sure what answer she hoped for, but she somehow needed to know.

Stretching, she rose and went to the desk, but the diary was not where she'd left it last night. Could she have put it back in its recess without thinking? Fumbling a little, she managed to release the secret panel, and there, sure enough, was the diary. She opened it to the place she'd left off reading the night before, only to find the next page blank. Riffling through the rest of the small volume, she discovered that all the pages were empty. Nothing had been written after March 13, 1825.

Sinking dazedly down onto the softness of the bed, Kathryn tried to remember. She *had* glanced ahead in the book before going downstairs, and had seen several more pages of writing, though there'd been something different—familiar, almost—about it. Could that have been part of her dream? Obviously the diary itself wasn't, since she held it firmly in her hand.

Casting back in her mind, she struggled to recall the start and finish of that strange and so-vivid dream. Try as she might, she could not remember where waking left off and the dream began. Mentally retracing every step and action, she found no point where she had lain down or even closed her eyes. Finally she gave up and concentrated on the ending.

After the party, she'd come upstairs to prepare for bed. She'd discovered, to her dismay, that the apricot gown was fastened down the back with intricate little hooks instead of buttons, and that she couldn't seem to undo them herself. Just as she'd been about to resign herself to sleeping in the dress, a black maid she'd never seen before had appeared to help her, acting as though it were a nightly occurrence.

Kathryn had said little, not wanting to look a fool, while the maid helped her out of the dress and into a cotton nightgown that was equally unfamiliar to her. After the maid left, she opened the door to the adjoining bathroom only to find the fixtures gone and a mirror and hooks in their place. It was apparently a dressing room now, which left her with a problem.

Glancing back into the bedroom, she noticed a china pitcher and a large bowl on the dresser. The pitcher turned out to be filled with cold water, and on the floor next to the dresser she found a copper kettle of hot water and an empty pot with a lid. Wishing her dream included modern conveniences, she managed to wash and relieve herself, and finally crawled under the quilts on the down-filled bed to sleep.

Kathryn pressed her hands into the mattress beneath her. It was still down-filled! Wildly, she looked around . . . yes, there were the pitcher and bowl on the dresser, with the chamber pot beside it. Who ever heard of going to sleep and waking up *inside* a dream? But it couldn't be real . . . could it?

Now Kathryn noticed details she'd been too tired to observe last night. The room was the same one she had occupied her first night in Columbia, but some things had changed—the bed for instance, with its down-filled mattress. The spread was still white, as she remembered, but the blanket seemed to be made of wool. The desk was the same, though it looked much newer, without the darkening around the carvings she remembered from last night.

Some things were missing, like the pull-down shades on the windows and the overhead light fixture. Nor was her travel alarm clock in its place on the nightstand, though she knew it was the last thing she'd looked at before going downstairs last night. She couldn't see her purse or her overnight bag and she got up quickly to check the bathroom. It was still a dressing room, and none of the clothes hanging on the hooks were familiar to her. Fear rose up in her throat, almost choking her. What was she going to do?

At that moment there was a light tap on the door and the maid from last night entered. She looked plump and motherly, her smiling chocolate-colored face framed by a ruffled white cap that completely concealed her hair. "I heard you movin' 'round, Miss Catherine, and thought you might be ready to dress. Or d'you rather have a tray in your room after such a late night?"

"Yes, that...would be nice," replied Kathryn faintly, wanting to postpone leaving the relative security of this room for as long as possible. She wished she knew the maid's name, but couldn't think of a discreet way to ask before the woman was gone.

Alone again, she quickly availed herself of the chamber pot, wrinkling her nose and thinking that if this aberration, whatever it was, lasted very long she was really going to miss flush toilets, not to mention good old everyday toilet paper. Splashing her face with the cold water in the basin, she went back to the dressing room to choose an outfit. The clothes were gorgeous, she had to admit. She'd always loved sumptuous dresses. She chose a rich plum velvet gown, laying it on the bed for the maid to help her into when she returned, since there was no way she'd be able to manage the row of tiny buttons down the back.

A moment later the maid reappeared, bearing a steaming tray of something that smelled like a bit of heaven. Kathryn hadn't realized how hungry she was—last night she'd been too disoriented even to think about eating. The maid set the tray on a low table near the bed and removed the covering cloth.

"Goin' riding again this morning, are you, Missie?" she asked then, lifting the purple folds of the dress Kathryn had laid out on the bed. "I'll come help you dress when you're done eating." She bobbed a quick curtsy and left the room.

Oops. That was a riding habit, and Kathryn hadn't realized it. She'd chosen it simply because she loved the color and fabric. She certainly hadn't intended to ride a horse in it. In fact, it seemed pretty impractical for any sort of exercise—she'd be burning up after ten minutes.

At least she knew *how* to ride, though she'd given it up along with meat and animal products, when she'd become spokesperson for the Animal Rights Foundation last year. The Foundation held horseback riding to be a form of animal enslavement—but here they would be the only form of transportation available. Surely it would be okay to bend such high-flown principles for the duration of her stay.

Turning her attention to the breakfast tray, she found it contained two soft-boiled eggs, a thick slab of fried ham, and toast that was obviously cut from a home-baked loaf. A lump of what had to be fresh butter sat on the edge of the plate. The toast was the only politically correct item on the plate, she realized in dismay. Conscience fought a quick, hopeless battle with hunger before she dived into the meal with a vengeance, guiltily thinking it was the best she'd ever had.

True to her word, the maid reappeared seconds after Kathryn rose from the little table, making her wonder if the woman had been listening at the door. Another maid, a scrawny black girl of perhaps fourteen, entered behind her but stayed only long enough to collect the tray and the chamber pot. The older servant began pulling things from a chest of drawers.

Kathryn had no problem with most of the underthings, though she'd never been used to wearing so much, particularly under such a heavy dress. She supposed brassieres hadn't been invented yet, and was glad she was still young enough not to need too much support. When the maid held up the corset, though, Kathryn frowned, remembering how uncomfortable it had been last night. To her surprise, the woman spoke before she could open her mouth.

"Now, Miss Catherine, I know what you be thinkin', but it's no use. Your mama would have your head and mine too if you went down without it. I promise not to lace it too tight. Last night was special—I didn't want you shown up by any of them other girls."

Could the woman read her mind? Kathryn wondered incredulously. As she allowed the maid—she *must* find out her name—to lace her into the dreadful thing, she realized that a bra would have been superfluous. The corset did the job more than adequately, pushing up her ample bosom almost flagrantly. Maybe there was something to be said for these things, after all, she thought, admiring her profile. But why did they have to be so damned uncomfortable?

Next, the maid seated her at the dressing table and went to work on her hair. While she brushed and pinned, Kathryn had an opportunity to examine her reflection. It was her face, and yet it wasn't. Her hair was the same brown-black, falling in waves past her shoulders, and her eyes were still blue, fringed with long, dark lashes. But her complexion was extremely pale, and where were her freckles?

The face staring back at her also looked somehow younger than her own, with an openness, an innocence, that seemed to imply that this face had seen less of the world than she had. She raised a skeptical eyebrow at the thought and suddenly it was her own face, after all—or at least she was in control of it. Mindful of the maid behind her, she resisted the urge to experiment in the mirror. She was going to look crazy enough trying to adjust to this new—or rather, old—culture without being caught making faces at herself.

"There you go, miss," said the maid finally. Kathryn was sure she was wearing at least a pound of hairpins, but she thanked the woman graciously. Time to face the world, she thought grimly, following the maid out of the room and down the wide staircase.

Voices emanated from the large front room that had been a living room yesterday and now seemed to be a formal salon or parlor. Squaring her shoulders and lifting her chin, she entered. If ever she needed acting talent, it was now. She had no idea what would happen if anyone here suspected that she wasn't Catherine.

"Good morning, darling," her mother, or rather, Catherine's mother, greeted her as she stepped through the archway into the sunny parlor. The blue-striped curtains were pulled back from the tall windows to display the front lawn and drive beyond. The claw-footed divan and slope-back chairs were similar to what her mother had decorated with, but in different colors.

Today Mrs. Sykes-Prescott was wearing a less formal dress of deep rose, though her hair was still upswept as it had been last night. The morning sunlight was less kind than the candles had been, however, picking out the gray. "I hope you slept well," she continued.

"Oh, yes, very well," replied Kathryn, trying to appear calm and collected while feeling anything but. "I was so tired after the dancing last night that I dropped right off." Did they use that expression in the 1820s? she suddenly wondered—she was really going to have to watch the slang. But Catherine's mother didn't seem to find anything odd in her phrasing.

"I'm so glad, since that nice Mr. James asked if he might take you riding today. I accepted on your behalf, but I see from your attire that he must have spoken to you as well."

Something in her voice told Kathryn that Mrs. Sykes-Prescott had been prepared to cajole or even bully her into riding with Ryan James.

"No, he didn't," Kathryn heard herself saying. "Is it so strange that I might want to go riding by myself?" She waited, actually needing to know the answer to that question.

"Hardly that!" Mrs. Sykes-Prescott said with a laugh. "But I would have thought after yesterday you might wish to refrain for a while. By the way, I fear your father was quite displeased this morning when the groom told him of that escapade."

Oh, no! What kind of trouble had Catherine got into now? It dawned on her that she had a lot more than social customs to contend with. She was missing a whole lifetime of memories. "I . . . I suppose I did overdo it," she said tentatively, fishing for more information.

"That, my girl, is quite an understatement!" exclaimed Mrs. Sykes-Prescott, in a tone Kathryn's own mother hadn't used since she was twelve. "You knew perfectly well you were not to ride that horse again. It is much too high-spirited for a lady, and simply enormous. I vow, I would not go near it myself! And now that it has been sold, 'twas doubly wrong. Suppose the horse had been injured during that gallop?"

"The *horse*—?" Kathryn began indignantly, but was interrupted by an authoritative knock on the front door.

A black man, tall, thin and balding, who Kathryn remembered from the night before, hurried to open it before she could embarrass herself by rising. She realized, belatedly, that this must be the butler.

"Mr. James," he intoned.

Kathryn looked up eagerly. She liked Ryan James better than anyone else she'd met here so far, even if he did seem to be mocking her half the time. If anything, that only added to her fascination, since the men in her life had generally either flung themselves at her feet or avoided her, finding her self-confidence threatening. Ryan, so far, had done neither.

"Good day, ladies," he drawled as he sauntered into the room. He looked every bit as handsome as he had last night, though now he was clad in trousers, boots and a tailed riding coat of deep green. "I see you are ready for our ride, Miss Prescott."

"Yes, let's go," said Kathryn quickly, not particularly caring if this woman who was not really her mother thought her rude. Ryan appeared equally unconcerned, merely smiling at Mrs. Sykes-Prescott before bowing Kathryn out of the room ahead of him.

The butler silently held the door for them and they walked down the broad front steps where a black groom was waiting with two horses. After the breakfast she'd eaten, she saw no point in balking at riding. The Foundation would never know. Then— *Oh, Lord,* she thought in sudden panic, *is that a sidesaddle?* How on earth was she supposed to get into it?

"You are quiet today, Miss Prescott," said Ryan. "I hope you are not repenting of your unwonted friendliness to me last night."

"Not yet," replied Kathryn, as lightly as she could. "Would you be so kind as to help me onto my horse?" She moved toward the silvery-gray mare wearing the sidesaddle, wishing that she could ride the other horse instead. She stifled a laugh at the thought of Ryan in a sidesaddle, but her amusement abruptly evaporated when he suddenly grasped her around the waist and tossed her onto the mare's back.

Kathryn gasped, wondering desperately if this was the normal method of getting a lady into this ridiculous contraption. The groom's face was impassive, and nothing in Ryan's expression indicated that he had taken a liberty, so she rather shakily turned her attention to arranging her legs.

"Oh, dear," she said innocently. "My skirts seem to be tangling up my feet." As she'd hoped he would, Ryan stepped quickly back to her side, deftly pulling the velvet folds out of her way so that he could fit her foot into the stirrup. One hand brushed her ankle and she regarded him suspiciously, resolutely ignoring the tingle she felt at his touch.

"My presence isn't flustering you, is it Miss Prescott?" he asked with a grin.

"Of course not," she snapped before remembering that the real Catherine would have had no such trouble arranging her feet otherwise. Kathryn's knee was already hooked over the pommel and there was no other stirrup, so she tucked her other foot behind the knee of the leg in the stirrup. It felt like a secure-enough position, if rather awkward, and she hoped she'd gotten it right. She was going to be sore later, though.

"Your parents tell me they've no objection to announcing our engagement immediately," remarked Ryan offhandedly as they trotted up the drive and turned left onto Laurel Street.

Kathryn glanced at him sharply. She knew from the diary that Catherine's parents were pushing this match. She also knew that Catherine herself wanted no part of it. Her safest course, she decided, was to hedge—and to get back to her own time as quickly as possible.

"I had no idea you were in such a hurry."

Ryan's deep chuckle vibrated through her. "I'll take that response as a good sign. At least you didn't rip up at me. I am willing to wait, but not forever, Catherine."

His use of her first name was almost insolent, and she knew instinctively that her counterpart would not have liked it. "Miss Prescott to you, sir," she correctly primly. "We're not engaged yet."

With that, she flicked the reins to urge her mount into a canter and was pleasantly surprised to find her seat as secure as she'd hoped, though she had to tense her stomach muscles to avoid falling backward. The groom, she noticed, accompanied them, though he stayed a discreet distance behind. Kathryn decided that this was no bad thing; she probably needed a chaperon in Mr. James's company. She stole a sideways look at him, admiring the strength of his handsome profile. It was just possible that later she *would* want to dispense with the groom for a while.

Turning onto busier Richardson Street, they were forced to rein to a walk, as the horse-and-carriage traffic was fairly heavy. Kathryn looked around her with interest, taking in the planked sidewalks, the quaint brick-and-wooden-frame storefronts, the pedestrians in their period clothing. History in books had always bored her, but living it was entirely different.

Even in the 1990s Columbia was hardly a large city, but now, in 1825, it seemed barely more than a village. Water pumps on occasional street corners were being plied by maidservants, making Kathryn wonder whether these were the only sources of water in the town.

"Here is a dry goods store," said Ryan abruptly, breaking into her silent observations. "Why don't you do some shopping? I have some business to attend to at the warehouses."

Kathryn glanced at him in surprise, but his gaze was directed across the street, where a voluptuous blonde leaned seductively against the doorway of a three-story brick building labeled Nagel's Hotel. Her red-and-black dress was cut low even by modern standards, with one side of the hem hiked up to show a shapely expanse of calf and ankle. She smiled invitingly at Ryan, and he turned his horse in her direction, apparently anticipating no interference from Kathryn.

"I see you have some shopping of your own to do," she commented caustically, forgetting to stay in character. "That one should be discounted as used merchandise."

Ryan swung around to stare at her incredulously. "What did you say?"

Kathryn slanted a knowing glance at him through her lashes. "You heard me. Run along and play. I can find my way home without your help." Gesturing to the groom, she turned the mare and headed back the way they'd come. She had gone less than half a block before Ryan caught up with her.

"Of course I cannot let you ride back alone. Your parents' good opinion is very important to me." His cajoling tone reminded her of a small boy caught with his hand in the cookie jar.

"But mine isn't?" asked Kathryn, far from conciliated. Why on earth should she be upset about his philandering? she asked herself impatiently. It wasn't as though this man actually *meant* anything to her.

"Of course it is. You were completely out in what you suspected back there. How could a strumpet like that turn my head when you were within sight?"

"I was wondering the same thing myself," murmured Kathryn as demurely as she could manage. Demureness had never been her strong suit.

Ryan shot her a frowning glance but said nothing, and they rode on in silence for some way. Kathryn couldn't help wondering whether Catherine would have pulled Ryan away from the tramp downtown, or if she would even have cared. Probably not, she thought, recalling the diary. She was beginning to see why a sheltered girl like Catherine Prescott might not care for Mr. James. For herself, though, she found him . . . intriguing.

They passed from the business district onto Walnut Street, a quieter avenue that bore no resemblance to anything Kathryn could remember. Wisteria climbed over some of the houses and the sandy street was lined with trees. Inhaling deeply of the clean, sweet spring air, she realized that this, after all, was the kind of unwinding she needed to do. With Ryan James to keep things amusing, she thought she just might enjoy a stay in 1825—as long as it was a short one.

Lunch was being laid on the table when they returned. Mrs. Sykes-Prescott greeted them warmly, but when she pressed Ryan to stay to dinner, as she called the meal, he pleaded business in town and left, avoiding Kathryn's knowing glance. *I hope she proves a disappointment, Mr. James,* she thought as the door closed behind him. She wondered how much the Prescotts really knew about this oh-so-eligible suitor of Catherine's.

"Run on upstairs and change out of your habit, dear," Mrs. Sykes-Prescott said briskly. "I told Nancy to lay out your ivory cotton gown, for I believe it will be getting warm today."

Nancy—that must be the maid's name. Upstairs, Kathryn made a point of using it at every opportunity. "Thank you, Nancy," she said as she left her room to join the Prescotts downstairs. "We'll let the loose corset be our little secret, all right?"

The woman nodded and put her finger to smiling lips, apparently at ease with Kathryn's new friendliness toward her. They had worked together on a compromise that allowed the corset to do its job without pinching, though Kathryn still would have given a lot for some elastic. At least the food was good, she thought, hurrying down the stairs. The aromas were causing her stomach to grumble already.

"Your father sent word that he would eat dinner at the plantation, and quite probably supper as well," her mother informed her as she entered the dining room.

Kathryn was hardly disappointed. She wanted to know more about this man whom she must now treat as a father, but she was willing to postpone a meeting since she was apparently on his black list right now. Sitting down to a veritable banquet, she gave her full attention to the meal. Afterward, Kathryn spent the long afternoon ostensibly embroidering pillow covers with Mrs. S-P (as she began calling Catherine's mother to herself). Though she could sew rather well from her time spent on costume crews in college, Kathryn had never embroidered, so she faked it, trying to look convincingly busy. They hardly talked at all, and Kathryn suspected that Mrs. S-P preferred it that way. She and her daughter did not see eye to eye on more subjects than Mr. James's suitability as a husband, it would seem.

The light supper of deep-fried chicken and steamed peas, which was served at dusk, was every bit as good as breakfast and dinner had been. Kathryn had to force herself to eat sparingly, afraid Nancy wouldn't tolerate another inch to her waist. Finally, reluctantly, she'd become convinced that all of this was absolutely real. No dream, or even any madness she'd ever heard of, could account for her experiences.

As she mounted the stairs at the close of the evening, the throbbing of her knee and backside from this morning's ride added to her conviction that she'd pay full price for any indiscretions she committed here. And that reminded her that she still hadn't seen Mr. Prescott since he'd heard about Catherine's wild ride. With any luck, though, she'd be gone before he could do anything about it, and Catherine could pay for her own crimes.

Alone in her room for the night, she sat down to consider her situation. She wondered if she could possibly be reliving a past life, as some of her theater friends had claimed to have done. But wouldn't she *feel* like Catherine in that case? Instead, she felt very much herself. She had none of the early Catherine's memories to draw on, that was for sure.

It was more as though her mind was somehow trapped in her great-great-great-great-great-grandmother's body. Could some sort of switch have occurred? Had they somehow overlapped in time and . . . traded places?

Kathryn's eyes fell on the diary, still lying on the desk. Sitting down, she picked up the quill and, after a bit of effort, managed to ink it—but then paused. If she and Catherine *had* exchanged places, surely there must be a way for them to trade back. But how? And what on earth was going on in her own time?

CHAPTER FOUR

CATHERINE AWOKE EARLY, feeling surprisingly refreshed, considering the hard mattress. Perhaps Annette had been right about it being good for her back, she thought. She got up and went to listen at the door, but heard no sounds without. There no longer seemed to be a plethora of servants in and about the house, she had noticed. Perhaps they were no longer necessary, considering the advances made in such everyday conveniences as bathing. Bathing!

Cautiously, she opened the bathroom door, wondering whether she had dreamed its marvels, but no, all was as she remembered from last night. With a guilty sense of satisfaction, she ran hot water into the beautiful white bathtub, plugging the hole under the faucet with the gold stopper. It was better, much better, she thought, not to require help in order to attend to one's personal hygiene. She used the automatic chamber pot again, wondering in sudden embarrassment how audible its noise might be in other portions of the house. Surely, though, people from this time must be quite used to it.

Easing herself into the steaming bath, Catherine sighed in pure delight. This was lovely! She leisurely soaped and rinsed herself, then washed her hair with soap. It was only as she was letting the water drain from the tub that she noticed the elegant green bottle labeled "shampoo" and realized its purpose. She would use it tomorrow, she promised herself, and also try standing under the stream of water from the faucet near the ceiling.

Tomorrow? She caught herself up short. Surely she would not be here that long. During her blissful bath she had pushed the dilemma facing her to the back of her mind, but now it nearly overwhelmed her. What if she could not get back? Her parents must be nigh frantic by now! But no— Kathryn was there in her place, she remembered. Was she finding 1825 as strange as Catherine was finding 1994? In the diary, she had written that Catherine should enjoy herself while the switch lasted. No doubt that was excellent advice.

Poking through Kathryn's drawers and what appeared to be a built-in wardrobe in the bathroom, she remembered what Annette had said last night about "regular clothes." Fashions certainly had changed since her time! From her survey of the few things hanging in the closet, she was forced to the welcome conclusion that women must now be wearing breeches. The first order of business, however, must be undergarments. Recalling what she'd had on under her dress last night, Catherine nearly blushed—thin silken drawers and a contraption about her upper body that apparently served a corset's support function. And that was all.

After a brief process of trial and error, Catherine managed to fasten the lacy brassiere. These new underthings were vastly more comfortable than what she had been used to, however indecent they appeared. Returning to the closet, she tried on a pair of beige linen trousers and found them equally comfortable. There was a patterned beige-and-rust blouse that went well with the pants, as well as a matching jacket, so Catherine donned these, as well. In sudden excitement, she wondered if these new styles meant that ladies were no longer required to ride sidesaddle. That would be marvelous!

She was not sure what to do with her hair, always having had Nancy or Aunt Sykes's maid, Pyms, to dress it for her. Finally she simply brushed it out and pulled it back with a golden hair clip she found on the dressing table. Annette would let her know if she was not dressed appropriately for their shopping trip.

Emerging into the hallway, she heard voices below and a surge of alarm swept through her. How could she possibly conceal her true identity? For a moment she was tempted to stay in her room, but then realized that her only hope of breakfast was downstairs. Straightening her shoulders, she went down.

"Good morning, dear, I hope you slept well," the woman who looked so like her mother greeted her as she entered the room. "Annette said you weren't feeling too well last night and went to bed early. Are you all right now?"

"Perfectly," replied Catherine, very much aware of Logan Thorne's presence. He was watching her from his place at the table and it was all she could do to refrain from staring back. "A good night's sleep has set me up wonderfully." She tried to mimic her mother's accent, cautioning herself to say as little as possible until she had it right.

"Good, good," said her mother—it was so much easier to think of her that way—rising to push open the kitchen door. "Alice, would you fix a plate for Kathy, please?"

A moment later a big woman with frizzy red hair bustled out of the kitchen bearing a plate of fruit, fried potatoes and pastry, as well as a large glass of orange juice. "There you go, sweetie," she said with a wink, thumping them down on the table.

Catherine obediently sat down in front of her breakfast, glad to have found out so easily which was her place at the table, and began to eat. Unfortunately for her concentration, she was seated directly across from Logan, who now seemed to be giving his full attention to his own plate. After a moment, however, she saw that he was regarding her curiously.

"Were you in a hurry this morning or are you trying for a natural look? If so, I have to say I like it."

Did he mean her hair? she wondered. "I was hungry," she replied briefly, afraid to reveal her ignorance by saying more.

"I always thought your face looked better without the war paint, myself."

Before she could reply to this astonishing statement, her mother broke in. "Nonsense, Logan. You know a girl in Kathy's position wouldn't be taken seriously without makeup. I certainly wouldn't be caught dead without mine. Of course, at my age... I have to admit, though, Kathy, you look pretty good. Different, but good."

"Different?" asked Annette, walking in at that moment. Catherine swung around to smile at her in relief.

"Without her makeup, I meant," said Mrs. Sykes-Monroe. "I was just envying her for still being young enough to get away without it."

"Oh." Annette sounded relieved, herself. Then in a different tone, she said, "You wouldn't believe what happened when I got home last night." After a dramatic pause to be sure she had everyone's attention, she continued. "I was *mugged!* Right on post! I thought I'd left that kind of thing back in New Jersey. So much for Southern hospitality."

Catherine looked bewildered, not knowing what the word "mugged" meant, though it was obviously something unpleasant. Her mother, however, let out a small shriek. "How could anyone mug an expectant mother?" she cried. "Were you hurt?"

"No, I just kept my mouth shut, gave him my purse and called the MPs as soon as I got inside. Luckily, I had my keys in my hand, so he didn't get those. And I doubt he noticed I was pregnant, not that that would have made much difference."

"You canceled your credit cards, didn't you?"

"First thing this morning. I was robbed once before, so I knew what to do. At least he didn't get much cash. I only had twenty or so in my wallet. But what a hassle getting everything replaced! Anyway, I have to go to the MP station this morning to file a report, and if I know army bureaucracy, it could take hours. So I'm afraid our trip to the mall will have to wait, Cathy.''

Catherine nodded quickly, trying not to stare. Robbed! Annette had been robbed last night, and yet here she was talking calmly about it instead of having the vapors.

''I'll be going by the mall myself this morning,'' said Logan from across the table, immediately diverting her attention from Annette. ''I can drop you there if you'd like, Kathy.''

Was he inviting her to go driving with him—alone? She knew it was improper, but it seemed a perfect opportunity to learn more about him. ''Why, thank you,'' she said quickly, before she could change her mind. ''How nice of you to offer.''

Annette stared at her, wide-eyed. She opened her mouth, closed it, then said to Logan, ''Well, uh, thanks, then. Cathy really doesn't know her way around Columbia yet.''

''I didn't think she'd want to drive even if she did.'' Logan's tone was almost mocking, and to Catherine's surprise, Annette agreed. Did he know? she wondered confusedly.

''Could I maybe scrounge a Danish or something?'' Annette asked, changing the subject. ''I only had a cup of coffee before I left.''

''Of course.'' Passing her a plate of sweet rolls, Mrs. Sykes-Monroe continued, ''I've been thinking, Annette, since Dave is away for a while, why don't you just move in here until he gets back? I'm sure Kathy would love having you.''

''Oh, yes, I would!'' That would be a perfect way to have Annette here to help her out as she went along, Catherine realized. Besides, she genuinely liked her.

Annette caught the look in Catherine's eye and hesitated for only a second. "If you're sure it wouldn't be too much trouble?"

"Of course not! There are still two empty bedrooms, though you'll have to use the hall bath. I really don't like to think of you living alone, especially after what happened last night."

"Well, okay, then," Annette capitulated readily. "I really don't much like staying alone, either, especially at night. Our quarters are old and they creak. Though I guess they're not nearly as old as this house! I don't mind creaking when I'm not by myself, though."

"This house has been fully renovated," Mrs. Sykes-Monroe informed her archly. "It wouldn't *dare* creak!"

As soon as she finished eating, Annette turned to Catherine. "Would you mind lending me some lipstick? Mine was in my purse." With her eyes, she communicated that she wanted a chance to speak to Catherine privately. Catherine agreed at once, though she wasn't quite sure what "lipstick" was, and led her upstairs.

As soon as they were in her room, Annette asked, "*Are* you still Catherine Prescott, or did I dream that?"

"No, I'm afraid it is true."

"And how do you plan to keep that a secret from Logan? I couldn't believe it when you agreed to go to the mall with him!"

"I thought perhaps if...if we were to show him the diary... That reminds me, do you still have it? I am sorry I threw it at you last night."

"Yeah, I guess I do. I stuck it in my purse and...oh, no!" Annette's eyes widened in horror. "It was in my purse! Boy, now I *really* hope the MPs get it back for me. We never finished reading what Kathy wrote."

"You...were robbed last night." Catherine's horror returned abruptly.

"Yes, but don't get all upset. Crime is probably worse than it was in your time, but that sort of thing is still pretty rare, at least in smaller cities like Columbia. As long as you don't go out by yourself at night, you'll be fine. Anyway, I'll give the MPs this number, in case they find my purse—that is, if you really want me to stay."

"Please do! I fear I shall need all of the help you can give me. For example, about this morning—should I not have agreed to go out with Mr. Thorne alone?"

"The 'alone' part isn't the problem—I mean, there's nothing improper about it or anything like that. The question is, do you think you can pretend to be Kathy—our Kathy—during the ride there and back?"

"Would it not be much simpler to tell him the truth?" Catherine asked hopefully.

To her disappointment, Annette shook her head. "I don't think so. I mean, he'd think we were both nuts or, more likely, that we were playing some kind of joke on him. I got the impression that Logan and Kathy didn't get along all that well, even though they've known each other for ages. And with the diary gone, we have no proof." She hesitated. "Maybe you should just wait and go shopping with me tomorrow."

"No, no," said Catherine quickly. "If you can advise me about what will be expected, I believe I shall do well enough."

Annette still looked skeptical, but she shrugged. "Okay, if you insist. I doubt he'll actually hang around to shop with you, anyway, if he's like most men. But don't say I didn't warn you!" Catherine smiled gratefully. "Do you want me to help you put a little bit of makeup on, or would you rather do without?" asked Annette, apparently resigned.

"Whichever is right, I guess. In my time, nice girls didn't paint at all."

"Now I'd just say nice girls don't overdo it. Let's see," Annette went on, looking around her, "where would Kathy keep her makeup? Ah! Here it is. I'll bet she's lost in 1825 without it.'' She bit her lip and Catherine suspected she was missing her friend.

"It is probably just as well," Catherine said as briskly as she could. "She would be much more out of place wearing face paint there than I am without it here. My mother would likely throw her out of the house. I certainly hope she doesn't let on that she has been an actress!"

"Well, it was only in college, actually, but . . . I get your point. Here, smooth this lightly over your face—" she handed Catherine a small bottle "—while I tell you as much as I can about the nineties. The most important thing you need to know about is money. Let's see what Kathy has in her purse." She picked up the small bag from its place by the bed.

At first, Catherine objected to spending Kathryn's money—it seemed almost like stealing—but Annette managed to persuade her that she had no choice.

"Besides, when you switch back, Kathy will still have anything you buy," she pointed out. "Now, I'll bet you've never seen one of these before." She handed her a small card that was as shiny as metal but felt more like polished wood. "It's a credit card," she explained as Catherine rubbed her fingers over the raised numbers on its surface. "It can be used just like money. Here, why don't you practice forging Kathy's signature?"

Catherine did so, since it was easier than arguing, and Annette quickly told her how a credit card worked. "You'll have to use it, too, since Kathy doesn't have much cash."

"And the mall? What is that?"

Annette rolled her eyes. "We really are starting from scratch, aren't we? And I don't have time right now to tell you even a fraction of what you need to know. Are you sure you want to do this? There's still time to back out, you know."

But Catherine shook her head firmly. If she spent the day holed up indoors, she would never learn anything about this new world she'd landed in—or about Logan Thorne. And she might switch back at any time. "Please, just tell me all you can before you must leave."

FIFTEEN MINUTES LATER, armed with a bewildering jumble of information ranging from which stores to patronize to what subjects to avoid talking about with Logan, Catherine followed Annette from her room. Catherine wore a neutral shade of foundation, a tiny bit of blush and some mascara. She had balked at the idea of color on her eyelids.

"I'll see you this afternoon," Annette promised, still looking more than a little worried. "If I can, I'll run by the post library and pick up some books to help fill in the gaps. And believe me, I've left plenty of them!"

Unfortunately, Catherine did not doubt her word for a moment. Still, nervousness could not quite dampen her excitement at the thought of spending time alone in Logan's company. He was waiting for Catherine as she and Annette came down the stairs, and he looked even handsomer than he had last night. His shirt was open at the throat and his trousers, in the same faded blue as the shirt, were as tight as the buckskins worn by some men of her own time. But for some reason, no other man in snug-fitting nether garments had ever affected her so.

Logan cleared his throat and Catherine suddenly realized that she had been staring. She looked away quickly, willing herself not to blush.

"Ready to go?" he asked.

The trace of amusement in his voice told her he had noticed the improper direction of her eyes. Drawing on all of her Aunt Sykes's social training, she lifted her chin and looked him squarely in the eye. *A lady never admitted to doing, or thinking, anything improper.* Not one of her favorite lessons, but it stood her in good stead now.

"Certainly, sir," she replied with a slight, condescending tilt of her head.

He raised one eyebrow at her phrasing but turned away to open the front door for her. "I assume you want me to drive."

Again, she had the feeling that he was mocking her. Perhaps Kathryn was a terrible driver, but Catherine was not, and she resented the implication. She could drive anything from a farmer's gig to a high-perch phaeton, as she had once proved in London, to her aunt's horror. She smiled at the memory.

"Indeed, if you would prefer, I—" she began loftily, but broke off in amazement at the sight of a silver metallic contraption on fat black wheels in the driveway before them. Not a horse was in sight. Wildly, she glanced at Annette, who shrugged and smiled sheepishly. *Gaps,* indeed!

"Yes?" Logan prodded.

She gulped hastily. "I . . . it was nothing."

He nodded with a maddeningly knowing air and she knew he thought she had lost her nerve. It rankled, but what could she do? Certainly if she attempted to drive one of these futuristic carriages she would expose herself instantly.

Preceding her to the silver coach, Logan opened one door. "Don't worry. I promise not to drive too fast," he said kindly.

Catherine stared. *Had* he figured out her secret? But he was smiling as though nothing were amiss. "You may drive as fast as you wish," she told him. She had never been one to creep along, whether driving or riding, and it seemed hypocritical to expect Logan to do so for her sake.

"Oh, have you overcome that little phobia of yours?" he asked in surprise.

"Phobia?" Catherine had never heard the word before and glanced over at Annette, who was already out of earshot, climbing into a brown coach a short distance away. She caught Catherine's eye and waved cheerily before closing the door. A lot of help she was proving to be!

"Your fear of driving—and being driven," explained Logan. "I'd rather drive at a snail's pace than have you clutching the door handle every time I turn a corner." He gestured for her to get inside. "It was hard not to notice."

"Oh. I . . . I'll be fine." So it was Kathryn he meant, after all, she thought. Catherine climbed in. It was certainly easier to get into than a carriage, she had to admit. Indeed, one had required a small ladder to reach the seat of the high-perch phaetons in London.

Logan climbed in beside her, sitting behind a small wheel that she guessed must steer the coach, though she couldn't imagine how. He pulled a ring of odd-looking keys from his pocket and fitted one into a hole near the wheel. Catherine almost jumped out of her skin at the roar the vehicle produced when he turned the key.

"So cars do still bother you," said Logan, glancing at her. "Actually, it's sort of nice to see that *some* things haven't changed."

Catherine pondered that cryptic remark as he backed the "car"—short for "carriage," she supposed—and headed down the drive toward the street. Suddenly, she choked back a laugh. To think that she had been wondering whether women still rode sidesaddle!

In a moment, they were traveling as quickly as Xerxes's fastest gallop, though they were in the middle of the city. Catherine watched everything around her, the other cars, which were moving just as quickly, the tall buildings, and the red-and-green lights at the intersections. She managed to figure out for herself that the red lights meant that the cars were to stop and the green ones meant they could proceed. She was unsure about the yellow one in the middle, as once it caused Logan to slow and twice to increase his speed.

Once past Harden Street, going east on Taylor, they were beyond the Columbia that had existed in Catherine's time.

Yet Annette had still referred to it as a small city. A few minutes later, Logan turned off the road and slowed down. Catherine's mouth nearly dropped open in astonishment. "Whatever is this place? It is enormous!" she cried without thinking.

"Richland Fashion Mall. But surely it's no bigger than the ones around Washington, D.C.?"

Quickly, she tried to cover her mistake. "No, of... of course not. But I did not expect Columbia to have such a large... mall." She remembered the word at the last moment.

Logan jockeyed the car into what Catherine considered an impossibly small space and turned off the engine. She couldn't help staring at her surroundings as she climbed out of the car, and though Logan regarded her curiously, he did not look suspicious. "I guess you *have* been busy in D.C., if you haven't had time to shop," he said. "It used to be your life, as I recall. Well, enjoy!"

She certainly would, thought Catherine, as they passed through one of the many glass doors. What an incredible place! It seemed to be a pink-and-gray tiled street with shops on either side, but it was all under one vast roof. There were indoor gardens of flowers and shrubbery and spectacular fountains—the most intriguing of these had a dozen or more of what appeared to be permanent bubbles composed of flowing water that glistened and quivered, casting back rainbows from the bright lights overhead.

"I need some stuff at an auto parts place just down the street. Was there a particular store you had in mind?" Logan asked her. "I'll help you find it if you'd like before I go."

She named one of the stores Annette had recommended and he nodded. "There's a directory." He led her to a multicolored panel that she realized was a map of the mall and located the store for her. "It's down here on our left."

Pulling her attention away from the map with its stagger-ing array of shops, Catherine followed him, nearly as fas-cinated by her surroundings as by the man at her side.

Logan noticed her rapt expression and frowned. It hadn't been his imagination. Something about her was definitely different. And whatever it was, it did something to him that he wasn't sure he wanted to examine too closely.

"Oh!" she exclaimed, half pointing but then quickly dropping her arm to her side. He followed her gaze but saw nothing out of the ordinary. Just a group of shoppers, most of them black, probably local high school or college stu-dents. The girls were whispering and giggling, trailing be-hind the boys. Two of them wore the traditional African garb that was now popular. Nothing she wouldn't have seen in D.C. Nor did he notice anything remarkable in the store windows behind them.

"Did you forget something?" he asked. To his amaze-ment, the color in her cheeks deepened slightly. He remem-bered now that she had blushed once last night, too. Even when she was in her teens he couldn't ever remember Kathy blushing. Could she be feeling that same strange pull of at-traction that he was?

"No, I . . . oh, there's the store." She seemed almost anx-ious to get away from him now, which was more in line with her usual attitude toward him. He knew she had always lumped him in with her parents—an authority figure. When he was younger, it had amused him. It didn't anymore.

"I'll leave you to it, then," he said, oddly reluctant to go. It was foolish to think Kathy, of all women, might need any help from him. Even as a child, she'd been stubbornly in-dependent. "How many hours do you think you'll need?"

Her blue eyes widened with something like alarm. "I, ah . . . perhaps two hours?"

"Fine. I'll meet you in the food court for lunch."

"All right. Thank you, Mr. Thorne." She went into the store, leaving him to stare after her.

Finally, he turned away, feeling immeasurably older than twenty-eight. As he walked away slowly, Logan tried to put his finger on just what it was about her that had changed. She looked the same, with the heart-shaped face she'd had since childhood, now matured into startling beauty. Why hadn't he noticed that before? Two days ago, he'd still seen her as a little sister who'd grown up to be a bit of a disappointment. It was also apparent that she hadn't forgiven him yet for his criticism of her friends and life-style two years earlier.

Mr. Thorne. Did she really see him that way—on the other side of the generation gap? Or had she just said it to needle him, to show him that she hadn't forgotten his judgmental attitude? She'd been right, of course. He'd had no right to lecture her, then or ever. But it had been such a shock to find her at that party, with drugs in the back room and drinking in the front, kissing and fondling everywhere. And that jerk with the earring, with his hands all over her—!

Logan snorted now at his own hypocrisy. He'd done pretty much the same stuff in college. In fact, no one but Kathy would dare call him conservative—the architects and developers he'd worked with sure didn't see him that way. But he'd always been protective of Kathy, feeling that he owed it to Mr. Monroe to keep an eye on her. He'd offered to bring her to the mall in an attempt to mend his fences with the one member of his adopted family he was on the outs with. But now, suddenly, she didn't feel so much like family anymore. *Had* she changed? Or had he?

CATHERINE, MEANWHILE, was finding the boutique far different from any store of her experience. The elegant little shop turned out to be bigger than it looked, built narrow but deep, and it held racks upon racks of ready-made dresses, hundreds of them, sure to fit any figure or taste imaginable. But then—"Eighty-three dollars?" she gasped aloud at the first price tag she examined. It wasn't even a ball gown!

"Actually, that's quite a bargain for a Liz Claiborne," commented a hovering saleswoman, startling her. "And that classic styling will last you for years."

Catherine remembered that in London, where style was everything, some ball gowns there had cost upward of 300 pounds, once trimming was taken into account, though she herself had never spent nearly that much. But these dresses seemed so...so tiny!

"Can I help you to find something?" the woman asked.

Catherine thought for a minute. "A nightgown, I suppose, and some underthings." It hadn't looked as though Kathryn had brought much. "And perhaps a dress or two."

The next hour and a half passed quickly for Catherine. She tried to keep her actual purchases to a minimum, unable to shake the feeling that she was stealing from the real Kathryn, but the totals still mounted alarmingly. Leaving the shop with a large bag, she looked around, eager to explore the mall until it was time to meet Logan.

Rounding one corner, Catherine was assailed by a burst of loud music resembling some of the rhythmic chants she had heard in the slave quarters. It had a strong, almost primal beat that both attracted and repelled her.

"Whatever do you sell in here?" she asked the long-haired young man at the counter, raising her voice to be heard over the din.

"Records, tapes, CDs. It's a music store," he said slowly, treating her as though she didn't understand English very well. Catherine nodded and smiled to hide her confusion at his answer. How could anyone sell music?

Leaving the raucous shop, Catherine's attention was diverted by the sight of a moving metal staircase. People were riding up and down, being carried, as if by magic, from one floor to another without moving their feet. That was something she *had* to try! She watched a few other shoppers step onto the bottom stairs as they appeared out of the floor before imitating them gingerly. She held the rail, which moved with her, and delightedly watched the ground floor recede. At the top, though, she tripped as the step she was on disappeared.

"Careful there!" Logan materialized out of nowhere to steady her before she could fall. "I was just coming to look for you. Ready for some lunch?"

His hand on her arm sent a tingling sensation through Catherine that was unlike anything she'd ever felt. She had to concentrate to reply lightly to his question. "Certainly. I have completed my shopping."

He released her, and she felt a sense of disappointment. "Food court's this way," he said. He did not offer her his arm, as a gentleman of her own time would have done, but she had already noticed that such was apparently no longer the custom. A pity.

"I hope you won't read me the riot act if I have a burger," he said as they came to a wide area filled with tables. "That stir-fry place has a vegetable plate, I think. I assume that's what you want."

"Just vegetables?" Catherine asked in surprise.

"That's part of ARF's line, isn't it? Don't tell me their spokeswoman doesn't abide by it?" He sounded cynical now. "Or didn't you know I'd been following your career?"

Catherine blinked in confusion, very aware of the charade she was playing. He glanced curiously at her and she tried to smile, torn between the necessity of acting like the girl she appeared to be and the desire to let him know who she really was. And what on earth was *arf,* or its vegetable line? "I'll eat whatever you're having," she said finally.

His brows went up. "Even if it's a cheeseburger?" She nodded. "Okay. I guess I can restrain myself from taking it to the papers. Or are you moving on to a worthier cause?"

She just smiled noncommittally and followed him to a counter. Despite the delicious aromas assailing her from all sides, Catherine suddenly longed for her own time. It became more apparent with every word Logan spoke that she didn't belong here. She hated to lie to him, but she didn't seem to have any other option.

"Diet Coke okay?" he asked. At her nod, he relayed the order to the strangely uniformed girl behind the counter.

To her amazement, by the time Logan received his change, their entire meal had been assembled by another server. They sat at a nearby table and she watched him carefully to be certain that she did everything correctly, from removing the paper from the clear flexible tubes they drank through to dipping the thin strips of potato into a tangy red sauce before eating them. Logan didn't appear to notice that she was copying his every move. He chatted easily during the meal and she nodded and murmured in response, using a full mouth as an excuse to avoid speaking too much.

"Had enough, or do you want some frozen yogurt for dessert?" asked Logan at last, gathering the disposable debris and piling it onto the tray.

"No, thank you. This was wonderful. I had never, I mean, I have always loved cheeseburgers. And...and Coke, and fries..." Logan's slight frown warned her that she was overdoing it. The meal *had* been wonderful though—and not only because of the food. Already her sudden desire to return home was ebbing.

"So, Kathy, are you shopped out yet?" asked Logan.

"Heavens, yes." She almost mentioned the prices, but realized in time that Kathryn would not have found them remarkable.

"Let's go, then. I parked on the roof this time, so we'll take the elevator."

Catherine's eyes widened at the sight of the glass-sided box that descended to open its silvery doors in front of them. The escalator had been fun, but this flying glass box ...!

Behave as Kathryn would!

Chin up, she stepped into the elevator ahead of Logan, trying to look as though she had done so a hundred times before. He followed her in and the doors closed behind them, apparently of their own volition. Logan pressed a little round light on a panel beside the doors and they began to rise into the air, the mall spread out below them. Just as she began to enjoy the ride, though, the elevator stopped and reopened its doors to bright sunlight. Catherine blinked.

"It's over here," said Logan, leading the way back to the car.

This time Catherine was ready for the roar of the engine and did not flinch when he turned the key in the ignition. As he had before, Logan drove very carefully, and more slowly than Catherine would have liked. She knew he was watching her out of the corner of his eye and wondered if she should pretend to be nervous in order to appear more like Kathryn. But if she did that he would never drive any faster. Better to make him believe she had overcome "her" fear. She looked out of the window, taking in the incredible changes 170 years had wrought on the city.

"You weren't kidding," commented Logan after a few minutes. "You really are a lot calmer in a car than I remember. Still, I don't think I'll ask you to watch me race."

"Oh, do you ... I mean, I would like to see that."

He looked at her curiously. "Are you serious? You always hated the fact that I raced—even more than your father did."

Catherine had no idea what he meant, but she didn't want to miss a chance to see these wonderful cars race each other like horses. "I am perfectly serious."

"I'm tempted to call your bluff. Okay, if you mean it, I'm planning to race at the Columbia Speedway on Friday. Are you game?"

"Certainly!" Her smile seemed to convince him that she was sincere. He gave her another sidelong glance and lapsed into silence. The trip home seemed shorter, and Catherine was disappointed when he dropped her off at the front door.

"You're not coming in?"

"No, your father wants me to see a project he's considering out near Lake Murray. I'm picking him up at his office. We'll probably be back in time for dinner."

Catherine thanked him for the ride and watched him drive away. Dinner? Wasn't that what they had just eaten? No, Logan had called that "lunch." Dinner must now mean the later meal she'd known as supper. So many little things to learn about this time—and big things, as well! She began to climb the front steps, but just then Annette's brown car pulled into the driveway and Catherine went back down to greet her. Along with clothes and toilet articles, she had brought an armload of books.

"Are you doing some kind of research project, Annette?" asked Mrs. Sykes-Monroe, when she saw the stack of volumes.

"Not exactly," she answered. "I've been thinking about taking some courses at USC while we're stationed here, so I want to bone up on the subjects I'm weak in before I take the GRE."

"You certainly had a quick answer for my mother," commented Catherine a few minutes later. "What are USC and GRE?"

"USC is the University of South Carolina—I think it was South Carolina College in your time. And GRE stands for Graduate Record Exam. It's a test colleges require before they'll admit you to graduate school. And it's true, I *am* thinking of enrolling, so I didn't exactly lie."

"Do you have a college degree?" asked Catherine, impressed. When Annette nodded, she breathed, "I've never known a woman with a college degree before. That is wonderful!"

"You make me feel like a genius," laughed Annette, "which I'm definitely not! Nowadays just as many women go to college as men. There are female executives, doctors, lawyers, you name it. That's one way the world really has improved since your time."

Catherine shook her head. "I don't know if I will ever take it all in, or get used to it—but I like it. Perhaps *I* will go to college . . . if . . . if I stay here long enough."

Annette frowned. "Yeah, *if*. I wonder how Kathy's managing. The MPs still haven't found my purse and I'd sure like to get that diary back! She went to college, too, you know—we were roommates at William and Mary. Neither of us were exactly Phi Beta Kappa material, but she did pretty well in theater and political science."

"The College of William and Mary? In Williamsburg? I knew a young man who went to study there."

"Well, I don't expect I knew him," said Annette with a chuckle. The humor of it struck Catherine as well and the two of them burst out laughing.

"We can't enroll you in school right away, but you can get a start on your studies with these," Annette said once they sobered. "I got you a recent history of the United States, from the Civil War on, and a history of South Carolina."

"The . . . Civil War?"

Annette groaned. "You'll have to read these books. I'm afraid I'm no expert—I used to sleep in history class in high school and never took any in college. About all I remember about the Civil War is that it freed the slaves."

"Freed the slaves? At the mall I saw quite a few free Negroes. There were almost none in Columbia in my time. Are they all free now?" She was delighted.

"Of course. And they prefer to be called blacks, these days, or African-Americans."

"Why, that is wonderful! To think I was arguing with my father over his treatment of the slaves only yesterday. When was this Civil War?"

"In the early 1860s, I think. I told you I'm not real big on history. Anyway, I also brought you a couple of novels, to give you an idea of the culture now—but don't take the stuff in there too literally. I figured you could pick up some slang that way, at least. It's an awful lot to read, I know, but you can do a little at a time. And tonight we're going to watch at least an hour of prime time TV. How's that for a beginner's course on the nineties?"

"I read rather quickly, for I love it—the local bookstores never ordered enough to satisfy me. And of course, Mother never considered it as proper a pastime as embroidery." She made a face. "I can scarcely wait to start on these. But what is . . . prime time *teevee?*"

That started Annette giggling again. "You'll see. I just hope we can manage to be alone when I turn it on, because I can't wait to see your face!"

CHAPTER FIVE

KATHRYN WAS absolutely furious.

This morning she'd had her first encounter with Mr. Prescott since the party. She had been halfway down the stairs on her way to breakfast, feeling perfectly glamorous in a lacy dress of green and white, when he'd spotted her from the hall.

"A word with you, Missy, if you please!" he almost thundered, startling her to a standstill.

Mr. Prescott's florid complexion was even redder than usual at the moment. Kathryn merely regarded him questioningly, wanting to be absolutely certain what he was angry about before attempting to defend herself.

"Yes, Father?" she said in what she hoped was a suitably submissive tone of voice. Her own father never shouted at her, and she doubted she'd be able to control her temper if this man started bullying her.

"Don't you 'yes, Father' me, young lady! You know perfectly well what I have on my mind, and if you were hoping that one day would make me forget, you are far off the mark. It merely gave me more time to consider a just punishment."

Kathryn sucked in her breath. "Punishment?"

"Punishment," he repeated. "You knew damned well you were to stay away from that horse. That brute Xerxes is dangerous—you could have been killed! Do you know why I sold him to Colonel Hampton? I'll tell you why," he went on, before she could answer. "Because I knew you wouldn't be able to resist trying your hand at him. I know I used to encourage you in such escapades, but your mother is right. You're a young lady now and it is no longer proper—or safe!''

"I wasn't hurt, was I?" She kept her voice low, trying to suppress her resentment. At least he seemed more concerned with her safety than the wretched horse's, unlike Mrs. S-P.

"No, thank God. It seems your time in high society didn't quite drive all of my lessons out of your head." A ghost of a smile flitted across his face, but then his expression hardened. "Still, I plan to make damned sure you never take such a risk again."

"I'll do what I damned well please," Kathryn snapped before considering her words.

His beefy jaw dropped. "How dare you use such language to me, young lady! I was going to forbid you to ride for a week, but now I'm minded to make it a month. Until I say otherwise, you are not to mount a horse at all...except in the company of young James. Now what have you to say?" He clearly expected that condition to upset her as much as the restriction—and if she'd really been Catherine, it probably would have.

"Very well, Father," she said, narrowing her eyes wickedly. "May I send a note to Mr. James asking him if he'd like to go riding?"

Mr. Prescott's jowls quivered and his face darkened even further. "You . . . you young hussy!" he spluttered at last. "You may spend the remainder of the day in your room for your impudence, that's what you may do. Upstairs, Catherine! At once!"

Kathryn's eyes widened in disbelief. Was this man actually sending her *to her room?* "You can't be serious?"

"If you are not up there in ten seconds you'll discover just how serious I am!" Mr. Prescott advanced menacingly on her, and though she could see pain mixed with the anger on

his face, she took a step backward. Her own father had
never lost control like this.

"Catherine, please," pleaded Mrs. S-P from the dining
room, appearing almost frightened by the scene she had
come out to witness. Kathryn considered bolting for the
front door, but doubted she'd make it past the enraged man
facing her. And where would she go then?

"You needn't shout, Father," she said softly, to empha-
size his lack of control. "I just remembered something I
need to do upstairs." She turned as casually as she could
manage, drawing on every ounce of her stage training, and
made a graceful exit up the stairs. She could tell from the
blustering below that she had effectively taken the wind out
of "Father's" sails and smiled in bitter satisfaction.

That smile disappeared abruptly a few minutes later when
she heard the incredible sound of a key turning in the lock
of her bedroom door. He wouldn't dare! But when the knob
would not turn under her hand, she was forced to admit that
she was indeed locked in her room. And for a sin she hadn't
even committed!

She threw a silver-plated hairbrush across the room in a
fury, narrowly missing the mirror. "I want to go home
now!" she shouted to the empty room. "Whoever's idea of
a sick joke this is, listen to me. I've had enough. Send me
back." She waited expectantly for a moment, but nothing
happened.

Kathryn flung herself into the chair at her dressing table
and fumed at her reflection. "I can't handle this," she informed the girl scowling back at her from the mirror. "I just
don't have the temperament to be a second-class citizen."
She paused, observing her image critically. "You're awfully pale, you know. That's probably the in thing now, but
I don't like it. First chance we get, you and I are going to
spend some time in the sun."

Feeling a little calmer, she tried to think rationally. So what if she couldn't ride? She didn't believe in it, anyway. It was no hardship to have it forbidden.

But it was no use. She wasn't about to let a man—any man—dictate to her. Her feminist beliefs went far deeper than any ARF rhetoric. Kathryn went to the wardrobe and pulled out the habit she'd worn yesterday. The three middle hooks were beyond her reach, but she didn't really care. If the slightest opportunity occurred, she damned well intended to ride.

On that thought, she got up and went to look out the window. The ornamental shrubs and flowers in the gardens were lovely, but she was more interested in finding a tree close enough to her window so she could escape. There wasn't. However, as she opened the sash, she saw a rider in the lane that ran along the side of the property. Ryan James!

Kathryn leaned as far out of the window as she dared and whistled piercingly. As she'd hoped, Ryan looked her way and spotted her as she waved her arms wildly. Undoubtedly curious as to the cause of this unusual display, he tethered his horse to the fence and opened the gate leading into the gardens.

"May I be of some assistance to you, Miss Prescott?" he asked when he stood directly below her, a grin tugging at the corners of his mouth.

"You most definitely may," she replied, acting as coquettishly as she could. "Would you inform my parents that you wish to take me riding again? I'll explain once I'm out of here." She hoped the vagueness of her reply would pique his curiosity enough for him to do what she asked.

"In trouble, eh? Very well, but you will owe me yet again, Miss Prescott."

Kathryn ran back to the dressing table and patted a few stray hairs into place. Oh, for some makeup! She felt naked without it. Except for a couple of times when she'd been sick in bed, she couldn't remember a day since junior high that she hadn't worn it. She'd have to check some of the stores in town. Maybe if she was discreet she could use just enough to bolster her confidence without causing comment from Catherine's parents.

A knock at the door, followed by the key turning in the lock, interrupted her thoughts. "Kathryn, Mr. James is here and would like you to ride with him," said Mrs. S-P, peering anxiously around the door. She stopped and stared, obviously amazed to see Kathryn already dressed for riding. "Your father has gone out, but he *did* say earlier that you could ride with Mr. James. So if you wish to go..."

Her mother was obviously hoping she would refuse, as Catherine apparently had been doing whenever Ryan invited her out, but Kathryn was more concerned now with escaping than she was with staying in character.

"Certainly, Mother, I'd love to," she said breezily, watching the woman's expression change. "Would you mind doing up these last hooks for me?" Reluctantly, her mother complied. Kathryn smiled her thanks, then swept past her to go downstairs.

Ryan was waiting in the hallway, looking particularly handsome in his cutaway coat and high collar. There was something to be said for these old-fashioned styles, thought Kathryn, gazing at him appreciatively. They might not be as comfortable as the modern ones, but the men looked like men and the women like women. She'd never cared for androgynous clothing and hairstyles, and had always been careful to cultivate a feminine image for herself.

"Why, good morning, Mr. James," she called out, and was gratified to see his eyes light up as he caught sight of her. "Whatever brings you here this morning?"

"You do, of course, Miss Prescott," he replied with a twinkle in his eye. "I found myself somehow drawn here."

Kathryn was glad her back was to her mother, or her expression might have aroused suspicion. "Shall we go?" she managed to say without a quiver in her voice.

As he did yesterday, Ryan bowed her out of the house and they waited on the front steps for the groom to bring her horse around. "Now, what is all of this about?" asked Ryan in an undertone as soon as the door had shut behind them. "Believe it or not, I do have some business to attend to this morning."

"You can attend to any business you please once we're away from the house," replied Kathryn. "I just needed a means of escape."

Ryan raised an eyebrow and waited for her to continue, but at that moment the groom rounded the corner, leading the mare Kathryn had ridden yesterday. As before, Ryan tossed her into the sidesaddle, but instead of gasping, she reveled in his brief touch. She arranged her legs herself, and couldn't help a small smile of triumph at the accomplishment.

"We won't be needing you today, Jeller," said Ryan abruptly to the groom. "Isn't that right, Miss Prescott?" His gaze challenged her.

"That's right, Jeller. We won't be gone long." The groom bowed his head, though his eyes were alight with curiosity, and he went back to the stables.

"I hope he doesn't mention this to my mother," said Kathryn as they turned the horses. "I wasn't sure I could talk freely in front of him."

"Oh, Jeller's all right," Ryan assured her as if he knew. "But I wanted a bit of privacy. What exactly is going on?"

Kathryn related the scene with her father that morning, concluding, "So you see, you were the only one who could rescue me. Don't you feel like a knight in shining armor?"

"Is that how you see me?" They stopped a few blocks from the Prescott house. An open cotton field stretched before them; overgrown azaleas in full bloom crowded along the edge of the field and pines whispered overhead in the spring breeze. No one was in sight.

"Right now, I do," answered Kathryn softly, with a warm smile. She was very conscious of his overpowering masculinity. He returned her look, and she had the disconcerting feeling that he was reading her thoughts. Swinging down from his horse, he held a hand up to her. Kathryn hesitated only the barest moment before allowing him to hand her down from the saddle, her eyes never leaving his. Instead of releasing her hand after she dismounted, he pulled her closer to him. Boring into her very soul with dark, hypnotic eyes, he lowered his lips to hers.

Kathryn had kissed many men in her twenty-three years, but never one who compelled such a response from her. Ryan's kiss was both tender and demanding, making her burn to give in to anything he might ask, and more. It was an unfamiliar and exciting sensation, and she gave herself up to it, twining her arms around his neck as his hands slid down to her waist. For a few incredible moments, no one existed but the two of them, pressed so closely that they almost became one.

Finally it was Ryan who pulled away, resting his hands on her shoulders. His eyes were aflame with desire, but she could see a question in them, as well.

"Who are you, Catherine Prescott?" he asked.

Kathryn felt her insides contract. What did he mean? How did he know? Panic warred with the desire he had aroused in her, but she forced herself to appear outwardly calm. "Who do you want me to be?" she finally responded, her heart hammering wildly.

Ryan smiled, a slow smile that made the warmth creep back through her body. "Whoever you are right now. Not the prim, innocent miss I met a few weeks ago, but the woman you've just shown me. This was hardly your first kiss."

So that was it! "Surely you don't expect me to admit to that, sir?" she asked, lowering her lashes flirtatiously. Relief washed through her so strongly that she hardly knew what she said. He didn't suspect her, after all.

Ryan regarded her for a long moment, his expression unreadable. "No, I will have to draw my own conclusions, I suppose. Dare I hope this means our engagement can be announced now?"

Kathryn blinked. Catherine had been convinced he only wanted the Prescott lands, she recalled. Nor was this a romantic proposal, in spite of that incredible kiss they had just shared. "Whatever is your hurry, Mr. James?" she asked, covering her conflicting feelings with a playful air. "Only yesterday you were willing to wait."

"I find myself somehow more impatient today." Again, he gave her that warm smile that turned her insides to jelly.

"I'll consider it." She still forced herself to speak lightly, refusing to commit herself. After all, Catherine might well be back here tomorrow. She experienced an unexpected twinge of jealousy at the thought. "Didn't you say you had some business you had to attend to this morning?"

His gaze narrowed and the warm smile cooled slightly. "Yes, I did. And much as I would prefer to let it go hang, it really can't wait much longer. Would you care to ride into town with me, or shall I escort you home?"

"I have *no* desire to go home just yet. Would you help me up, please?"

He threw her into the saddle and they turned toward town.

"You asked who I am, but I could ask the same question of you, Mr. James," ventured Kathryn after a moment. "I seem to know very little about you." She hoped that this was true of Catherine. It did seem unlikely she'd have tried to find out much about a man she disliked.

"You never seemed particularly interested before," he said pointedly, confirming her guess.

"Well, now I am."

"Hmm." He sent her a long, lingering look. "I'm from up north—Maryland—and have gradually wandered south over the years. When I found Columbia, I liked it and decided to stay, at least for a while. The land is fertile, there's plenty of space and the people are friendly." His smile on the last phrase made Kathryn look quickly away. How could this man affect her so strongly? "I've done well for myself here and have every intention of doing even better. I'm really quite a catch, you know." He grinned, waiting for her response.

Kathryn met his look squarely this time. "I can see that you're very highly regarded, Mr. James—especially by yourself."

He choked on a laugh. "Touché, Miss Prescott. But why not? Everything I have I've worked hard for. No one has ever gone out of their way to make things easy for me, and I've learned to get what I want, whatever obstacles might present themselves."

"The work ethic personified," she said lightly, feeling a twinge of what might possibly be guilt for the easy life she had led. At his questioning look, she changed the subject. "So, what do you grow on that fertile land of yours?"

His expression told her she should have known. "Cotton, of course. Fair Fields is the third largest plantation in the area, in terms of acreage, though it may well be first in production. I think I've proved . . . Well, never mind that. I have also planted an apple orchard, but of course it will be some time before it produces."

"So, it's true about the apples," she said brightly, trying to cover her slip. "I think Father mentioned them."

It seemed to work, for he talked of various types of apples and their characteristics, which he had obviously studied in depth, until they reached the downtown area of Columbia. "I fear we must part company here, Miss Prescott," he said with a reluctance she couldn't help savoring. "I see two of your friends outside Beecher Porter's shop there. Perhaps I can escort you home after my business is concluded.''

Kathryn nodded, then crossed the street to join the young ladies mentioned, since they had seen her and were beckoning eagerly. She recognized both girls from the ball two nights ago, but could not at the moment remember their names. Her heart beat uncomfortably fast. This was going to be a hard act to pull off.

"Cathy, I am so glad to see you out today," one of the girls, a tall blonde, exclaimed. "Leslie was saying that your father was angry and might not let you ride. It would have been such a shame, for Mr. Porter has some new lace that you simply *must* see."

Leslie, a dainty brown-haired girl with an impossibly small waist, reddened slightly but gave Kathryn a dimpled smile as she spoke. "Yes, you see, my brother overheard your father telling mine how you had ridden that stallion he sold to Colonel Hampton, and how he was going to forbid you from riding. I *am* so glad he changed his mind!"

Kathryn, whose keen assessment of character had helped her countless times in the backstabbing social arena of Washington, decided that this girl would bear watching. There was something catlike about her.

"Or did Mr. James talk him round?" Leslie continued, her green eyes glittering. "I can't believe it was *your* idea to ride out with him!" Both girls tittered and looked across to the saddlery warehouse, where Ryan's horse was tethered.

"You had better be nicer to him, Cathy, or you're going to lose him to someone else," confided the other girl in an undertone as the three of them entered the shop. "I know several ladies, some younger than you, who would accept him in a second, despite his reputation." She said this with a significant glance at Leslie, who'd gone ahead to the counter.

"I'll keep that in mind," Kathryn replied with a smile. But then her attention was claimed by the charming little shop. It was like a small fabric store, but with far more character, packed almost to overflowing with miscellaneous trinkets, many of which she had never seen before. On the counter were displayed gloves in every pale shade from white through beige to gray, and a basket on the floor at one side was filled with frilled parasols. And here she was without any money!

Kathryn had always adored shopping and had no intention of changing her ways because of a mere time displacement. She examined the goods intently, wondering if credit existed yet. The laces the blond girl—her name turned out to be Priscilla—had mentioned were exquisite, and Kathryn was already imagining what they'd look like with two or three of Catherine's dresses.

She was a decent seamstress, thanks to her stints on theater costume crews, though she was sure sewing without a machine could get tedious after a while. Still, it was something she could do instead of the bewildering embroidery Mrs. S-P expected of her.

Watching carefully as her two companions made their choices known to the shopkeeper, Kathryn was relieved to see no money changing hands. Credit was alive and well, thank God!

"I'll take two cards of this lace and the pink parasol," she informed the plump little man when he had wrapped Leslie's and Priscilla's purchases. It wouldn't do to go overboard while she was still in disgrace.

"Certainly, Miss Prescott," responded the shopkeeper eagerly. "Will there be anything else?"

"Not today, thank you, Mr. Porter." Her smile assured the man that she'd soon be back for more.

Once outside, Leslie left them, explaining that her mother expected guests for dinner. Kathryn was just as glad to have an opportunity to talk with the friendlier Priscilla.

"This is a lovely time of year, isn't it?" she began. The weather seemed like a safe topic to begin with.

"Yes. Before long it will be too hot, but right now I love being out of doors," replied Priscilla. "The next month or two are the best time for flowers, too," she added with a sidelong look at Kathryn. "If I were getting married, that's when I would want my wedding to be held."

Kathryn chuckled—she wasn't the only one hoping to pick up information during this conversation. "I'll admit Ryan can be pleasant when he tries, but I haven't agreed to a wedding yet."

"Oooh, Cathy! Is it 'Ryan' now? Your feelings toward him *have* changed."

Oops.

"I daresay he *can* be pleasant," Priscilla continued. "He certainly is handsome enough! And he may change his ways after marriage. Many men do, I hear. You just need to keep him busy at home." She held a handkerchief to her lips and giggled at her own naughtiness, which Kathryn found amusing. Priscilla would be awfully easy to shock—she'd have to watch her mouth.

"Many men *don't* change their ways after marriage," she pointed out.

"He might, though," insisted Priscilla. "And it's not as though you have any particular woman to worry about— just all of them! I've not heard that he's lost his heart to anyone, at any rate. If you can capture that, I have a feeling he is the sort that would be yours forever. There is something—well—*intense* about him."

Kathryn had noticed that, too, almost the moment she met him. No wonder he drew women like flies. But she herself could *not* afford to get involved with him, since she had no idea how long she'd be here. Nor did she dare do anything that would force Catherine's hand when she returned. The idea of her ancestor being forced into marriage, even with someone like Ryan—especially with Ryan—disturbed her greatly.

Perhaps there was something she could do. At the very least, she could teach Mr. James a lesson about his wandering ways. And maybe she could find a way to give Catherine more options. A woman should be free to choose her own future.

Priscilla's elbow prodded her ribs, interrupting Kathryn's noble plans. "Speak of the devil," she whispered, gesturing down the street.

There was Ryan, in conversation with three fashionably dressed ladies whose ages appeared to range from about eighteen to forty. All three were giggling and flicking their fans at him. He seemed to be enjoying himself enormously.

Kathryn watched the group for a moment, then turned to Priscilla. "Please come to visit me soon, maybe even this evening if you can. It seems ages since we've had a good talk."

Priscilla blinked, then smiled. "Certainly. I'll come after tea if my father has no plans. It has been a long time."

"Mr. James offered to escort me home, so I'd better reclaim him. Care to come along?"

"No, no, you go on. I still have some shopping to do, and our groom is to meet me at Mr. Arthur's bookstore." She paused for a moment, following Kathryn's gaze before adding, "Good luck," under her breath. It was almost as though she knew what Kathryn was planning. Their glances met in understanding before they exchanged farewells.

Kathryn's mouth curved in a small, secret smile as she began walking slowly in his direction. Her smile broadened as Ryan tweaked the cheek of the youngest of the three ladies and whispered something in her ear that made her blush and rap his knuckles with an ivory fan.

You may be too much for poor innocent little Catherine to handle, but I'm just the one to tame you. En garde, Mr. James!

CHAPTER SIX

As KATHRYN APPROACHED the charming little group, Ryan took the hand of the prettiest lady, whom Kathryn judged to be a year or two older than herself. If she'd expected him to be disconcerted when he noticed her, she was disappointed. He smoothly brushed the lady's fingertips with a brief kiss and turned toward Kathryn with an apparently genuine smile of welcome. The echoing smiles of the ladies were both less genuine and less welcoming.

"Miss Prescott! Do I take it that you are ready to return, or have you more shopping to do?" Neither his voice nor his manner held the slightest trace of embarrassment.

"I'm quite finished, thank you," she replied, with a similarly carefree smile.

The ladies murmured insincere greetings to her while looking daggers at her. Kathryn, never good with names, used the technique she'd cultivated in recent years of smiling to acknowledge the greetings, without revealing that she had never met these women before. They hadn't been at the Prescotts' ball, which told her their social standing was probably a notch or two below hers, so she allowed the merest touch of condescension to creep into her manner.

After five minutes of polite nothings, Ryan made his bows and led her to where their horses were tethered. "Mrs. Hankins was just mentioning how you had matured during your stay in London," he remarked as he mounted. "I told her that I prefer a woman with some polish."

Kathryn chuckled. "I doubt she intended it as a compliment, but I thank you, sir." She was careful to keep her smile cool. She knew from experience that a man like Ryan would be far more attracted to a challenge than to an easy conquest. She intended to be the greatest challenge he had ever encountered.

"As she has at least ten years on you, she construed my response as a personal homage. Perhaps I should have been more specific in my praise," replied Ryan with a searching look.

Kathryn slanted him a glance from beneath her lashes. "Perhaps you still can be."

Ryan shot her a wide grin. "Fishing for flowery phrases, Miss Prescott? That's hardly my style, but I'll do my best to oblige you."

"I would never want you to do anything that makes you feel uncomfortable," replied Kathryn archly, softening her words with the curve of her lips.

They continued in a bantering vein during the short ride, and Kathryn reveled in the lingering looks he sent her way though she sternly refused to return them. The more firmly hooked he was before Catherine's return, the better, she decided, feeling almost protective of the girl whose place she'd taken.

"Thank you, Mr. James," she said with a polite smile when they reached the sandy drive of her house.

"Let me know if you need rescuing again, Miss Prescott. It will be my extreme pleasure." His gaze held hers.

"Hopefully, it won't be necessary," she replied coolly, turning to glance at the house before her eyes could betray her. "My mother is at the window. I'd better go in. Goodbye, sir!"

"Until next time, Catherine," he replied softly.

She didn't dare look directly at him, but nodded in his general direction before trotting up the drive to the waiting Jeller. Mrs. S-P was not actually in evidence when Kathryn quietly opened the front door, nor were any of the servants, so she was able to whisk up the stairs to change for dinner without being seen. It seemed that Catherine was adept enough at getting into trouble without any help from her. Nancy was puttering around her room, making a show of straightening the trinkets on the dresser when she came in.

"How long before we eat, Nancy?" asked Kathryn breathlessly, closing the door behind her.

The maid gave her a long, knowing look before answering. "Jes' five minutes or thereabouts, Missie. We'd best get you out of that habit and into something fit for the table right away." Kathryn was sure Nancy was well aware not only that she was in disgrace—the entire household had to know that—but also that she'd ridden without Jeller.

"Thank you, Nancy," she said sincerely as the woman helped her to change. "I don't know how I'd manage without you." She wondered whether the maid's first loyalty was to her or her parents. Deftly, Nancy brushed and repinned her hair, sending her out the door only four minutes after her arrival. Her reassuring wink told Kathryn her secret was safe.

Catherine's parents were entering the dining room as she descended, and she quickened her steps to follow. Once they were seated, Mr. Prescott turned to her with an accusing glare that made her tremble, more at the thought of missing another meal than in fear of another tirade. She was ravenous, and the mouth-watering aromas assailing her from the kitchen made her want to postpone any further confrontation until after the meal.

"Your mother tells me you managed to cozen young James into riding out with you, after all." At least he was not shouting.

"Now, Joseph, that is not what I said at all," interposed Mrs. S-P, obviously wanting to avert another scene. "There is no possible way she could have got any sort of message to

Mr. James before he called. She had been in her room only half an hour, and had not even spoken to any of the servants." Kathryn wondered if Catherine's mother remembered that she'd already been dressed for riding.

"You said I might ride out with him, Father," murmured Kathryn, keeping her eyes downcast. *You're playing a sweet little Southern belle! Remember that!*

"I also said that you were to spend the day in your room, or had you forgotten that?"

Kathryn felt her temper rising, but forced herself to keep her eyes on her plate. "Am I not even allowed to eat? You sent me upstairs before I had any breakfast, and I'm hungry." She had been blinking rapidly during this plaintive speech and was able to lift tear-filled eyes to convince Mr. Prescott. Her last statement, at least, was absolutely true.

She could see that he hadn't thought of this, and that he felt some remorse, though he'd never admit it. His wife was more vocal.

"Oh, Cathy! I should have sent you up a tray. I was so distracted this morning that I never even thought."

"Well, girl, perhaps you've learned your lesson," said Mr. Prescott gruffly. "You may eat with us, of course, but you are still to remain within doors for the rest of the day."

"Thank you, Father. I have learned my lesson." She managed to sound contrite, though it cost her an effort. "May Priscilla call on me later today? I saw her downtown and invited her, but of course she must ask her father first."

Honestly! Grown women are treated like grade school children here! "Can I go over to Kathy's to play?"

Mr. Prescott was now in a mood to be generous. "Certainly, she may. Miss Blake is an unexceptionable companion for you and a very well-behaved girl. You might take a leaf from her book, missie." But now his eyes were twinkling.

"I'll try," she said honestly. She had hopes of learning a great deal from Miss Blake. For starters, she now knew her last name. Steaming platters were carried in at that moment, and Kathryn's whole attention was claimed by her empty stomach.

MRS. SYKES-PRESCOTT was charmed by the new lace Kathryn had purchased earlier that day. She agreed that the cream lace would look lovely on her daughter's deep-gold day dress, so Kathryn was able to substitute sewing for embroidery during the long afternoon in the parlor. Her fingers ached by the time the tea tray was brought in at four, however, and she was glad to lay the nearly completed project aside. They were just sitting down to enjoy the cakes and tarts when Miss Blake was announced.

"Priscilla!" Kathryn exclaimed with a genuine smile. "I'm so glad you could come!" She wasn't sure what the previous degree of intimacy between Catherine and this girl had been, but she meant to increase it. She'd had ample time to think while sewing, and had hatched the beginnings of a plan to help Catherine.

Priscilla curtsied to her host and hostess before taking the chair next to Kathryn. "You have been so busy since your return from London, it seems we have hardly seen each other," she said, implying again that they'd been good friends before Catherine's trip to England, and hadn't yet had a chance to catch up. This suited Kathryn's purposes perfectly.

"Maybe we can sit in the gardens for a while after tea and talk, since it's such a beautiful day," Kathryn suggested. "If that's all right, Father?" she remembered to ask.

"Certainly, certainly, my girl," he said jovially. "The gardens count as part of the house, in my thinking." He excused himself a few moments later, saying that he needed to speak to his overseer about something.

"I have a few letters to write, myself," added Mrs. S-P when he left. "You girls have a nice visit." She rustled from the room.

"Would you like to go outside?" asked Priscilla almost timidly, and Kathryn realized she'd been frowning.

"Of course! It's awfully stuffy in here, anyway," said Kathryn, turning back to her new friend with a smile. "Let's go."

Kathryn had to suppress the urge to exclaim at the spring beauty of the gardens, since Priscilla would expect them to be old hat to her, but she looked around in appreciation at the rows of tulips and irises. "Spring is such a pretty time of year" was her only comment, and Priscilla agreed wholeheartedly. Who wouldn't in such a setting?

"So, Priscilla, tell me what's gone on in Columbia while I was away. I need to catch up on all the local gossip."

Priscilla blinked at her in surprise. "Your sojourn in London *has* changed you, Cathy," she said. "You used to hate gossip. But I've heard it is a positive passion in London society, so I shouldn't be surprised if you've caught the fever."

"Yes, it's almost the only thing anyone talks about there," Kathryn adlibbed. "I couldn't help getting hooked. So, tell!"

"Well, let's see, you left . . . my word! It will be two years ago this summer! I suppose a lot *has* happened since then. The most recent news is that Mary Mellick was to marry Jim Allston at Christmastime and jilted him at the last minute to run off with John Young. Can you imagine? Both of their fathers were furious. . . ." She continued at some length, trying to recall every tidbit of interest over the past two years, while Kathryn listened attentively, absorbing not only names but customs, which were made very clear by this recital of their violations.

Occasionally Priscilla strayed into political news, always important to the men of this capital city, especially with the installment of South Carolina's own John C. Calhoun as Vice President only three weeks ago. Kathryn tried to absorb some of that as well, not wanting to appear ignorant about things she'd be expected to know, but she couldn't help linking the names and issues with the history she'd been forced to study—and hated—in high school. Luckily, Priscilla's knowledge of political matters wasn't broad and she quickly returned to social gossip. Kathryn couldn't help thinking it was all pretty tame stuff—none of it would even have rated as news in her time, much less scandal.

Gradually, Kathryn managed to steer her friend to the topic she really wanted to hear about: Ryan James. She was able to discover, without appearing *too* interested, that Ryan had appeared in Columbia soon after her own supposed departure for England and that his origins were a bit of a mystery. She also, more unwillingly, learned that this mystery had fascinated the local ladies almost from the moment of his arrival and that he was rarely without feminine pursuit—or company—of some sort.

"There's just something about him. He has a way of making a lady feel special, whether she's a farm girl or a senator's wife. I've noticed it myself. I vow he knows the name of every female in Columbia, and never forgets."

Kathryn managed to stop herself from commenting that in a town that consisted of only a few hundred houses this was not a particularly remarkable feat. "But what about the rumors?" she prompted. "There seems to be a conspiracy to keep them from me." This seemed likely, if she were expected to marry the man.

"Oh, mostly what you'd expect about a handsome single man, only more so in Mr. James's case. You can't condemn him for being human, Cathy! But I don't believe he's actually ruined anyone respectable. He seems to limit his—well, *you* know—to ladies who aren't really ladies, if you know what I mean.

"Until you returned, it seemed he was being careful not to get into a situation that might lead to marriage. Oh, he loves to flirt, but he knows exactly how far he can safely go with each lady without her papa intervening. Of course, he's won three duels since he's been here, and I imagine the papas keep that in mind." She giggled. "Mary Mellick told me that he's been an expert shot since he was in his teens, though how Mary could have known that is beyond me. In any event, he's considered a prime catch by almost any standards!"

"I suppose that depends on your definition of 'prime,'" retorted Kathryn. She could see why Catherine, apparent innocent that she was, might fear such a marriage. If she herself could be sure of staying here... No, she *couldn't* get involved with him. "What about the way he treats his slaves?" She had reread Catherine's diary and picked that bit out.

Priscilla sighed. "I knew that would bother you. Nor can I claim it's exaggerated, for I had it from my own maid, Polly. But the way a man treats his slaves generally has no bearing on the way he treats his wife."

Kathryn swallowed hard. She hadn't wanted to believe that particular rumor and realized now that she had been hoping Priscilla would deny it. All the more reason to go ahead with her plan. "Priscilla," she said urgently, "will you help me do something?"

"Of course! What is it?"

"Well, it's starting to look like I might *have* to marry Mr. James. My father's extremely insistent. Do you think, between us, we might sort of, well, scare the other ladies away from him? I could face it better if they weren't always after him."

"We can't very well chase them off with sticks, can we? Besides, I rather doubt Mr. James himself would appreciate our interference. He might withdraw his suit altogether!" Priscilla plainly considered that the ultimate catastrophe.

"No, no, we'd have to be subtle. Since rumors of his mysterious past seem to attract women like flies, maybe we can add a little vinegar to the honey pot."

"What do you mean?"

"I mean we could spread some rumors of our own—a hint here, an innuendo there. Something to make him a little less appealing."

"Do you have any ideas?" Priscilla was looking every bit as interested as Kathryn had hoped she would.

"As a matter of fact, I do." Kathryn had been thinking about this all afternoon and was sure she'd hit on just the thing. "Suppose we circulate a story that he's been married before. And that his first wife died under, ah, mysterious circumstances. That way we don't actually accuse him of anything, but it leaves room for doubt."

Priscilla thought for a moment. "I suppose so. But mightn't it get Mr. James into trouble?"

"Of course not, unless it turns out to be true—in which case he deserves it! If anyone were to check it out, they'd find out he never even had a wife. But until then, it might just do the trick." And, with any luck, it would also make the Prescotts less set on having Ryan as a son-in-law. She was determined to give Catherine a choice in the matter.

"I suppose that might work," Priscilla admitted. "In fact, when he first arrived here there *was* a rumor following him—that he was a fugitive or some such thing."

"Great! If you can think of anything like that, anything at all, weave it in. I'm afraid you're going to have to do most of this rumor spreading, Priscilla. It might look a little obvious if I say things to warn other women off."

"Oh, I don't mind. It's for a good cause. And I can think of at least two ladies who will spread any rumor like wildfire if I so much as whisper it to them. It won't be difficult, I assure you. The Columbia ladies love to gossip as much as the London ones do!"

THE NEXT DAY at breakfast, Mr. Prescott suggested that Kathryn accompany him on his rounds of the family's plantation, The Glen. Apparently he was already willing to forget the restriction on her riding. Kathryn thought it wise to agree.

Seeing a cotton plantation was a new experience for Kathryn, and not a particularly pleasant one. It shocked her to realize that the black men sweating under the lukewarm March morning sun were slaves—actual slaves. With a vague sense of embarrassment, she thought of the "injustices" she'd protested over the years. As part of the Animal Rights Foundation, for example, she had been strident in her opposition to animal "enslavement." Now she was seeing the real thing. Slavery. Human beings owning other human beings. Treating them like animals. Kathryn knew she'd never be able to take ARF's rhetoric seriously again. She struggled to appear as if she'd been used to such barbarism all her life. But then—

"Father, what's that woman wearing?" she cried, completely unable to conceal her dismay at the sight of a contraption on one slave woman's back that extended up behind her for all the world like a rooftop television antenna covered with bells.

"A darky that tried to escape," he answered, after a glance in the indicated direction. "Standard practice, so don't start on me again. I'm a kinder master than many, but I can't be letting escape attempts go unpunished. The bells merely let the overseer keep a closer eye—and ear—on her." He chuckled at his own wit.

Riding closer, Kathryn saw that the horrid thing was made of iron and had to weigh twenty or thirty pounds. And the poor woman was expected to hoe cotton all day wearing that horrible device! Kathryn also noticed the brownish stains across the back of the slave woman's rough cotton dress and realized, with a sickening wrench, that she must have been brutally whipped for her "crime." A surge of anger against injustice, familiar but far stronger than she'd ever felt it before, welled up inside her.

"Rather a clever idea of old man Johnson's, even you must admit, eh, Cathy?" asked Mr. Prescott jovially, noticing her interest. "Just as useful as some of those new-fangled gadgets you're always pressing me to try."

She remained silent, sure that she'd betray herself if she tried to answer him.

As he continued discussing changes and improvements, Mr. Prescott explained little, plainly expecting her to understand, and she realized that Catherine must have been well on her way to learning about the plantation. Surely that was unusual for a woman in this age? But while Mr. Prescott obviously took enormous pride in his cotton crop and expected her to do likewise, all Kathryn could see was the human misery it was built on.

As they rode back to town around noon, Kathryn realized that her visit to The Glen had been educational in ways she never would have expected. It had given her insight not only to the time, but to herself, and the relative triviality of the causes she'd espoused. With an effort, she thrust aside her disturbing thoughts, forcing herself to look forward to Priscilla's expected visit that afternoon.

"CATHY, I CAN ALMOST swear it is working already!" The girls were alone in the garden again, although the freshening breeze and gathering clouds warned that their time outdoors was limited. "I haven't spoken to Mr. James myself, but I saw him at the Little Theater last night and the Harkness sisters gave him the cold shoulder. They've been among his most persistent flirts!"

"Would they have heard the rumor already?"

"Oh, undoubtedly! If there is anything Mary and Eliza love more than flirting it is gossiping, and Mrs. Greene, who was the first person I dropped hints to, is a bosom bow of theirs. Between the three of them, I daresay half of Columbia has heard the story by now!"

Kathryn smiled. Step one was complete, it would seem. "Are you going to the party at Leslie Allerby's tonight?" she asked. It was time to do some more work on step two.

"Of course. It will be the biggest event of the month—not counting General Lafayette's visit, of course. Everyone who matters will be there." Priscilla was a bit of a snob, Kathryn had noticed, but no more so than anyone else of her class and time. Probably less so than many. Besides, who was she to pass judgment? As an only daughter of a wealthy family, she'd been guilty of her share of snobbery over the years. She was only now beginning to realize that.

Her thoughts turned again to Ryan James. Had he been born rich? Almost certainly not. He'd mentioned working hard for everything he had, something Kathryn now regarded with respect—and admiration. In spite of her idealistic determination to make a difference through her charity work, she'd always had the family money to fall back on if things got rough. Working, even for good causes, had been almost a game to her.

"What do you plan to wear?" Priscilla's question was a welcome distraction, and the girls fell into an animated discussion of fashions until a rumble of thunder and a few large drops of rain interrupted them. This conversation had been almost as valuable as the one on gossip, Kathryn thought as they ran for the back door. She now knew all about the current styles, for one thing. Priscilla had also told her that Ryan James would likely be at the Allerby do. She'd have to be at her most fascinating tonight if the second step of her plan was to be successful.

KATHRYN SURVEYED her reflection with satisfaction. The dress she had chosen was blue, remarkably similar to the polyester creation she had worn before the "switch" had occurred last week—the dress Catherine had found herself in, if Kathryn's theory was correct. This dress, however, was of real silk, and its creamy blue folds shimmered beautifully as she moved. It had a tight bodice with a fairly low neckline, puffed sleeves that narrowed below the elbows and a full skirt with three layers of petticoats beneath it. Not quite *Gone With the Wind*, but, of course, this was about three decades earlier.

She had Nancy lace her corset as tight as she could stand it, remembering that scene from the movie. For the first time, it began to sink in that Nancy was a slave, as much as those workers in the fields had been. Somehow, she hadn't thought of her that way before, though in the back of her mind she must have known it.

"Thank you, Nancy, that's fine," she said with a warm smile, wishing she could communicate her feelings to the woman. Instead, she turned to the mirror. The tiny waist produced by the tight corset was attractive, she had to admit. Breathing was difficult, though—no wonder ladies fainted so easily now. She turned back to Nancy. "Please tell Mother I'll be down in a few moments." Kathryn wanted no witnesses for what she planned to do next.

When Nancy was gone, Kathryn pulled out the piece of folded paper she'd hidden in the secret recess with Catherine's diary. While watching Moses, the houseboy, shine Mr. Prescott's boots that afternoon, she'd been inspired. When his attention was called away by the cook for a few minutes, she'd quickly scooped out a tiny bit of the blacking and hurried upstairs, where she'd saved it in a scrap of paper for tonight.

Carefully, using the edge of her fingernail, she traced the merest bit of the blacking along her lash line, then tipped the lashes themselves with the color. There! She wiped her fingers clean with a cloth and touched up the corners of her eyes. The effect was just what she had hoped for, emphasizing her eyes and lashes without looking made up. With any luck, not even Catherine's mother would notice.

More important, it gave her the added confidence she would need tonight. Her brows were naturally dark and needed no attention. Pinching her cheeks would have to substitute for blush—she would wait until they arrived to tend to that detail so it wouldn't fade before Ryan saw her. Flicking a dark curl into place with a smile, she went to join her parents downstairs.

The Allerbys' house on Gervais Street, located within sight of the State House, was built on a similar plan to the Prescotts'. Leslie's parents were just what Kathryn had expected, fashionable and pompous. Mrs. Allerby, a large, plain woman, ordered her diminutive, shifty-eyed husband around unmercifully.

Ryan arrived only moments after the Prescotts and greeted Kathryn warmly with an outrageous compliment on her appearance. She gave him what she hoped was a bewitching smile, but a group of politically minded gentlemen immediately herded him away from her.

For an hour or so before supper, the guests congregated in the formal front parlor, the ladies on one side and the gentlemen on the other. *Some things never change,* thought Kathryn. Straining to hear the men's conversation, she picked up the words *tariff* and *nullification,* but they meant nothing to her. She tried to remember anything of significance that had happened between the War of 1812 and the Civil War, but she drew a complete blank.

"...exactly the color of your eyes," Mrs. Allerby was saying to her, and with a start Kathryn brought her attention back to the ladies in her group. She realized that she'd just been complimented again on the gown and thanked her hostess graciously, returning the compliment by remarking on the loveliness of the decorations. Mrs. Allerby beamed. "I've always said there is nothing like a London Season to polish a girl's manners. Perhaps we shall send Leslie next spring, if she is not yet engaged."

This caused an excited outburst of questions from the other ladies in the circle wanting to know exactly what was meant by that hint. It reminded Kathryn of the way she and her friends had squealed and gossiped about boys in junior high school.

"No, no, nothing definite." Mrs. Allerby calmed them with a fond look at Leslie, whose waist was tinier than ever tonight in a rose silk gown. "But there are so many eligible young men courting her that I must admit it is a distinct possibility. She could have been married three times over by now if her father would have allowed it before she was seventeen." Leslie preened and said nothing, confirming Kathryn's first impression of her.

At supper, Kathryn found herself seated across and down the table from Ryan, which suited her plans quite well. He was not close enough to speak to, but in a perfect position to observe and admire her. As the soup was served, she devoted her attention to Mr. Hammond, a young gentleman of no more than eighteen or nineteen, who was seated on her right. She didn't dare try to flirt with her fan as she saw some of the other ladies doing, but she smiled, demurely or roguishly, as the conversation demanded. She amused Mr. Hammond with some success if the frequency of his laughter was any indicator, and she was aware that Ryan was not the only one sending admiring glances her way.

During the second course, she directed her wit and charm at Mr. Mills, on her left. He was an architect, she discovered, and she was able to converse with some intelligence on the topic, having absorbed various details from her father and Logan over the years. She was careful to stick to the basics without mentioning anything that might be anachronistic, but he clearly found her fascinating. He was married, but that hardly mattered to Kathryn.

Her purpose tonight was to show Mr. James that other gentlemen found her worthy of attention and, perhaps, of pursuit. Then he'd be less likely to take her—no, Catherine—for granted. Sneaking a glance at him, she accidentally caught his eye. Ignoring the sudden flutter of her pulse, she smiled brilliantly at him and turned back to Mr. Mills. She hoped she hadn't imagined Ryan's slight frown.

After dessert the ladies left the men to their wine and cigars and retired to the parlor as was the English custom. Priscilla came over to Kathryn, looking very pleased with herself.

"I was right," she whispered. "Our little rumor has spread like wildfire. Why, just before supper, Miss Caroline, Colonel Blanding's wife, actually repeated it to *me!* In fact, she was saying—" She broke off as Leslie Allerby approached, along with a few others. Kathryn joined in their gossip, learning far more than she revealed and adding it to the store of knowledge she'd gleaned from Priscilla. A few minutes later, a hum of deeper voices warned them that the gentlemen had left the dining room.

"They must have been unusually eager to rejoin us," giggled Leslie, apparently construing it as a compliment to herself alone.

"Perhaps they found their conversation growing dull," some devil prompted Kathryn to reply. Leslie's eyes narrowed suspiciously and Kathryn knew that the other girl had noticed the way she'd amused her own supper partners earlier.

The gentlemen entered at that moment and Leslie went forward eagerly to greet them—too eagerly, Kathryn thought. Ryan responded easily to her flagrant flirtation and she shot Kathryn a triumphant glance. Apparently Leslie hadn't heard the rumors yet—or didn't care if she had.

"Miss Prescott, is it true?" Mrs. Allerby broke into her thoughts. Her expression, when Kathryn turned, was avid. She was obviously hoping for confirmation of some bit of gossip.

"Is what true, ma'am?"

"What Miss Blake was just hinting about Mr. James. I thought you might know, he is such a friend of...your father's."

"I fear it may be, ma'am. Mr. James has even implied as much to me." She allowed her voice to tremble slightly, as though she were frightened.

"You poor dear! And your father still wishes to go ahead with the match?"

"I don't think he gives the rumor much credit," Kathryn explained, looking fixedly at the floor so that Mrs. Allerby could not see her expression.

"But surely there is evidence?"

"None of a concrete nature. But taking everything together, I can't quite dismiss it."

"I should think not. I shall have my husband look into this if your father won't, Miss Prescott, fear not!" Rigid with an indignation Kathryn couldn't help feeling was rather out of proportion to the cause, Mrs. Allerby hurried to extricate her daughter from her flirtation with the gentleman in question.

Kathryn used the rest of the evening to show Mr. James just how fascinating the other gentlemen present found her. While she didn't exactly snub Ryan, she didn't show him any favoritism, either. She discussed the growth of Columbia with Governor Manning and the growth of South Carolina College with Professor Henry Nott, as well as politics, local and national, with Jacob I'on, president of the South Carolina Senate.

By allowing the men to do most of the talking, Kathryn skillfully managed to hide her ignorance while flattering their egos. The only ones present that failed to find her utterly charming were certain ladies who were generally used to being the center of masculine attention at such gatherings. For this evening, at least, they found themselves totally eclipsed by a newly polished Miss Prescott who neither chattered about horses nor upset the teacups as she used to do before she went off to London. Mrs. Allerby was not the only mother to consider giving her own daughter the same advantage in the near future.

Priscilla made several attempts to speak privately with Kathryn before the party broke up, but there was such a crowd of gentlemen around her that it was impossible. Young James Hammond, for one, scarcely left Kathryn's side for the remainder of the evening. Priscilla would have to wait until tomorrow to tell her friend about her own addition to their scheme.

CHAPTER SEVEN

"YOU TOLD THEM WHAT?" Kathryn regarded Priscilla with dismay. The girls were in the small parlor, where the heavy draperies were open to admit the sparkling morning sunshine. Priscilla had called shortly after breakfast, eager to discuss last night's supper party and to share her cleverness. Kathryn was anything but delighted, however.

"That Mr. James has a wife still living, in addition to the one that, er, died. And I didn't *tell* anyone that, precisely, I only hinted at it. I thought it an admirable way to ward off the ladies who had not been frightened by the first rumor."

"You actually implied he was a bigamist?"

Priscilla looked uncomfortable. "I meant to imply that he had married again, *after* his first wife's death. But Mrs. Allerby seemed to leap at once to a conclusion similar to your own. I could hardly set her straight, particularly since I had been deliberately vague."

"And I practically confirmed it. I thought she was over-reacting to a mere rumor!" Kathryn thought hard for a few moments. "Did you tell anyone else?"

"No, but I'm sure Mrs. Allerby did. She is as avid a gossip as Mrs. Greene. And she *did* warn Leslie away from him afterward...." She broke off and sighed dejectedly. "I'm so sorry, Cathy, but it seemed such a good idea at the time. I really thought you would be pleased." Priscilla looked almost on the point of tears.

"It's okay, Priscilla, really it is. It's not as if there's any evidence to back it up. The worst that's likely to happen is that the truth will come out sooner than I'd hoped." Hopefully not before she and Catherine traded back, though.

The other girl smiled with relief and they moved on to other topics. It turned out that Priscilla's opinion of Leslie Allerby and her tactics was even lower than Kathryn's, and they had just finished dissecting that young lady's character most satisfactorily when Mr. James was announced. Priscilla rose quickly, almost crimson with embarrassment over the two rumors she had spread, and excused herself after a brief, incoherent greeting to the gentleman she had maligned. Kathryn looked after her with pity before turning her attention to her caller.

"Good morning, Mr. James. You'll have to excuse Miss Blake—she's not herself this morning. Too much excitement last night, I expect."

"She was hardly the center of the excitement, if I recall correctly, Miss Prescott," he drawled, one eyebrow raised.

"Why, sir! Whatever can you mean?" asked Kathryn with mock coyness.

"Never mind." Ryan didn't rise to the bait, but a smile tugged at the corners of his handsome mouth. "I came to invite you to ride out to my plantation, as you expressed curiosity about it the other day. There are some aspects of my operation I think you may find interesting."

She remembered her revulsion at viewing her father's cotton plantation only yesterday—and Ryan was reported to be a far crueler master than Mr. Prescott. "I'll have to ask my mother," she said reluctantly. "She may need me at home." As she rose, he stopped her with his voice.

"I can see you would rather not. Might I ask why?"

Had she been that transparent? "Well, no offense, but my father took me riding across his cotton fields only yesterday. How different can yours be?"

"Why not see them and find out?" His eyes challenged her. And intrigued her.

"All right, then," she capitulated. "Though I'd still better check first."

She returned only a brief moment later. "My mother doesn't mind," said Kathryn, barely suppressing a smile at such an understatement. Mrs. S-P was so delighted to have her ride out with Ryan that Kathryn was sure she was hearing imaginary wedding bells. But she, or rather, Catherine, would not be railroaded into such a wedding—that is, if her plan worked. And if Catherine did choose to marry Ryan—Kathryn swallowed at the thought—she was taking steps to ensure that he'd be a more devoted husband than he'd have been otherwise.

"I'll have Jeller bring my horse around," she said.

"That won't be necessary. I took the liberty of driving my curricle, in anticipation of your acquiescence. I also had my cook pack one of her excellent picnic dinners, so you can see that we shall be quite prepared for any eventuality." His expression was limpidly innocent and Kathryn had to suppress a smile.

"How very resourceful of you. Let's go."

Without further ado, they set off. Kathryn found it a welcome relief to sit back and be driven rather than constantly having to control a horse. Conversation was easier this way, too.

"Can't you give me a hint of what it is that makes your plantation so different, Mr. James?" she asked before a noticeable silence could set in. Sitting next to Ryan in the open curricle, she found herself stimulated by his nearness—*too* stimulated. Concentrating on the evils of slavery would help her to ignore the effect he had on her, she hoped.

"Tell me, Catherine, when you have observed the slaves working your father's plantation, and others like it, have they appeared to be particularly happy?"

Her jaw nearly dropped. "Why, no, they...they haven't." How could he have known what she was thinking?

"That is where I fancy you will see a difference on my plantation. I have found the carrot to be enormously more effective than the stick—not to mention more humane. But it is the economics of my methods I am hoping to use to convince others to follow my lead, as most of my fellow planters seem little concerned with the happiness or dignity of a black man."

Kathryn blinked. This went completely against what she had heard about him. She managed to answer, "I think it's high time someone took that view, Mr. James. I'm more eager than ever to see your plantation now."

Ryan regarded her for a few seconds with that disturbing intensity of his. "Somehow, I thought you would see it that way, Catherine. Do you know, I am beginning to believe we might be kindred spirits, you and I."

He looked away just as Kathryn was beginning to think she might drown in that gaze. The effect lingered and she had to draw on all of her training to change the subject, mentioning the unlikely blackness of Mrs. Hankins's hair. The conversation lightened and they chatted amiably about the personalities present at the Allerby dinner for the rest of the journey.

"Now—" Ryan's tone changed abruptly "—when we cross this stream we will be on Fair Fields. The house is just over that rise, but it is the fields themselves I wanted you to see."

They were passing through a lightly wooded area, thick with blooming azaleas, and came to a wooden planked bridge crossing a clear, chattering stream. On the other side, the trees continued for a few hundred yards before ending abruptly before a seemingly endless expanse of tilled earth. The field closest to them had already been plowed, but, following Ryan's pointing arm, Kathryn saw a group of slaves moving slowly across the acreage to their left.

"Jeb and Ezekiel are father and son. They can plow that field in half the time a pair of your father's slaves would take," said Ryan. "Ginny, Ezekiel's sister, is only fourteen, but she can keep up with them and put the seed exactly where it belongs. Her mother taught her the trick of it." He gestured toward a young black girl following the men, her apron full of the cotton seeds that she cast behind the plow in wide, sweeping arcs. "Her little sister Beulah is almost as good at it."

There was genuine pride in his voice and Kathryn turned to watch his face. As her father's had been the day before, it was alight, but with a difference. With Ryan, it was the *people* he was proud of, not the amount of cotton "his land" could produce. Glancing back at the field, she noticed another difference.

"Don't you have an overseer?" she asked. She remembered the heavily armed white overseers presiding over each one of Mr. Prescott's fields. Their presence had emphasized the fact that the slaves were just that, possessions to be trained like animals and kept strictly under control.

"I haven't really needed one for more than six months now," he replied. "You see, my hands have a motive to work, a far better one than a whip. Half the profit from this plantation goes to them, which means the better they do their work, the more quickly they can redeem themselves. Why should they try to escape, risking death, or at best the life of a fugitive, when in a year or less they can buy their freedom and answer to no man?"

Kathryn stared, open-mouthed. "You actually pay them? And allow them to buy themselves back? Is that . . . legal?"

"Yes, it is legal, but not very popular. The planters have a real fear of free Negroes. They are afraid they'll stir up unrest among their own slaves, as happened near Charleston not long ago. I hope my people will learn that peaceful means to freedom are better in the long run than armed revolt. I learned that lesson myself the hard way."

"What do you mean?"

Ryan looked at her for a long moment, a question in his eyes. "No, not yet. You are probably one of the few people I could trust with the story, and I am certain I will tell you sometime—sometime soon—but not yet."

Kathryn had never been one to pry secrets out of people, but her curiosity was thoroughly aroused. She made herself turn back toward the cotton fields and change the subject.

"Are your fields putting up shoots yet? Yesterday, I noticed a few of my father's were."

"Yes, the east side was planted nearly two weeks ago and should be showing green by now. Would you like to ride over?" If he were surprised at her willingness to drop the previous subject, he gave no sign.

"Aren't I here for the grand tour?" she replied.

He nodded, chuckling. "Not so reluctant now, I see. Let's drive on to the house to eat something first, then we can tour the rest of the plantation on horseback. It will be the best way to see everything."

Kathryn agreed and they followed the road up to the imposing plantation house, white and columned in classic style. The trees surrounding it were mature, and she realized, as they approached the wide front steps, that this was no new house. She commented on it.

"No, I bought the house along with the plantation from a Mr. Fry, who was forced to sell." Kathryn regarded him questioningly. "He stuck his neck out too far," Ryan explained. "Borrowed more money then he could repay. He also had no notion of how to run a plantation. Like so many others, he heard there was money in cotton and moved to South Carolina to get in on the gold. He bought land and slaves, built a house and waited for the money to roll in, trusting his hired overseers to take care of the plantation for him. Of course, they robbed him blind. I bought him out—house, land, furniture, everything—and he moved back to Boston where he belonged. I might add that I more than tripled his production on our first harvest."

"So these were all his slaves?"

"Yes. There were 140 when I bought the place, second only to the Taylors. Now, two years later, I'm down to less than eighty, though most of those who bought their freedom have stayed on to work for wages. A few of the most industrious families have even bought some land from me to work for themselves."

Kathryn regarded Ryan with increasing respect, almost awe. This man was decades ahead of his time! If only she could tell him how things were going to turn out.

"I think this is a wonderful thing you're doing" was all she found to say. The words were inadequate, but she meant them.

At the foot of the stairs, Ryan helped her from the curricle. "I don't stay in this house often enough to justify a full-time cook, so we'll just lay out our picnic on the dining room table."

"I'd like to see the house, but couldn't we eat outside? It's such a beautiful day," said Kathryn impulsively. It was true. The blooming dogwoods and azaleas gave the lawn an almost fairyland look, and the air was both warm and fresh. But beyond that, she was not sure she was ready for the intimacy a cozy meal indoors might precipitate. The great outdoors was safer.

Ryan's look told her he guessed her thoughts. "Very well, if you insist. I'll take you on a formal tour of the *downstairs,* and then we'll spread a cloth on the grass."

Kathryn acknowledged his teasing with a wry smile but did not object to his plan. She knew it was cowardly, but something about this man made her doubt her ability to remain in control of the situation—a doubt she'd never had before.

"The entryway, mademoiselle," announced Ryan, flinging open the front door with a flourish and sweeping her a mocking bow. Kathryn entered into the playful spirit, "oohing" and "aahing" at everything she was shown. It was a handsome house, though nothing marked it as Ryan's own; not surprising, as he'd done none of the decorating.

"Now, admit, Miss Prescott, that I could hardly carry on a seduction in such a setting," he remarked as he opened the double doors to the dining room. The table and sideboard were solid and practical oak, as was the paneling that extended halfway up the walls. Three large paintings graphically depicting hunting scenes graced the papered upper portion, and a huge buck's head gazed benignly at them from above the fireplace.

Kathryn tried unsuccessfully to turn a chuckle into a cough. "Perhaps not, sir, but it *is* a lovely day. Anyway, I don't think this room is any more conducive to eating than to romance."

He laughed. "You have a definite point, though I can't say I ever thought about it before. Would you care to see the second floor?" He asked it casually, watching for her reaction.

Kathryn suddenly realized she very much wanted to see the second floor, the floor his bedroom would be on. She was shaken by a temptation so strong that it took all of her willpower not to agree to his suggestion. *Catherine! Think of Catherine!*

"No, all of a sudden I'm really hungry," she answered firmly. Ryan arched one eyebrow and she wondered if he were aware of her mental struggle.

Outside, they found that a lacy tablecloth had already been spread for them under a graceful willow tree, and the contents of the picnic basket were being set out by an elderly black woman.

"Thank you, Mama Ruth. You didn't have to do this," said Ryan warmly as they approached the inviting repast. "I see you have added some of your wonderful corn muffins to our feast."

"Yassuh, Mistah James. And it weren't no trouble settin' things up pretty like. I knows you like things special when there's a young lady to show off fer.'' Her creased face split into a knowing grin and she winked roguishly at Ryan. ''My boys, they done plowin' the first task now, so I best go get their dinner ready. You have yourselves a nice picnic, now.'' Winking again and still chuckling, she strode away with a speed that was startling in so old a woman.

Ryan looked after her fondly. ''Mama Ruth is the hardest-working person, male or female, black or white, that I've ever known. I'm not sure she ever sleeps. I don't think she knows any other way to be.''

''She seems to really care about you,'' offered Kathryn tentatively, touched by the obvious affection between Ryan and the old woman.

''Oh, she does. Treats me like one of her own sons. She was more respectful than usual just now because of you. Normally she'd have scolded me for not bringing enough to eat.''

''Not enough?'' Kathryn looked at the meal laid before them in disbelief. People in this time seemed to eat roughly twice what they did in the 1990s. No wonder nearly everyone who didn't do hard labor was on the hefty side.

Not Ryan, though. Either he worked harder than she'd been able to observe, or he ate less than most men. His lean, well-muscled body showed no signs of overindulgence.

''Didn't you say you were hungry?''

With a start, Kathryn realized that she had been staring at his physique, and her thoughts gave his question another meaning entirely. ''Yes. Yes, let's eat,'' she said lamely, avoiding his eyes. Suddenly, she realized the tables had turned. Somehow he was doing to her just what she'd planned to do to him.

''Here, let me fill a plate for you.''

There was cold ham, crisp-fried chicken, apple fritters and, of course, Mama Ruth's fresh corn muffins. As Ryan loaded a fragile china dish—no paper plates yet, Kathryn reminded herself—with the fragrant selections, her eyes kept

straying to his strong hands, his tanned throat, the curve of
his mouth.

The bright spring sunshine threw dappled shadows that
moved and shimmered across them as the light breeze stirred
the drooping willow branches, giving the scene a dreamlike
quality. Kathryn began to think that the dining room might
have been safer, after all. Ryan seemed in tune with her
mood, and they ate slowly and in silence, occasionally exchanging a long, intimate look.

Everything was delicious, but Kathryn was more aware of
Ryan than of her own food. When he bit into a drumstick
with his strong, white teeth, she swallowed hard and responded by slowly licking imaginary crumbs from the corners of her mouth. Their gazes held lingeringly, knowingly,
before they continued their meal.

Kathryn stopped eating before she really wanted to, her
hunger and another need vaguely unsatisfied. The meal had
been an intensely sensual experience, and she felt that,
somehow, without a word, she and Ryan had reached an
understanding. She wondered if she would ever be able to
eat again without thinking of him.

Ryan stood and smiled languidly down at her, extending
a hand to help her to her feet. A current, almost electrical
in nature, passed between them as their fingers touched, and
Kathryn had to fight a desire to prolong the contact.

"Well, what about that tour?" she asked brightly, deliberately breaking the spell. It would be fatally easy to fall in
love with this man. And that was something she couldn't
risk.

HER TOUR OF FAIR FIELDS taught Kathryn a lot, not only
about the cotton plantation but also about the man who
owned it. Against her will, her respect for Ryan James continued to increase.

They began at the small apple orchard planted a short
distance behind the plantation house, which he explained

should bear its first fruit the autumn after next. The trees were in full flower now, shedding fragrance and white petals on the pair as they rode between them. Then they proceeded to the cotton fields themselves, in various stages of planting.

"I'm letting these fields lie fallow this year, something few of my fellow planters ever do, I might mention," Ryan said as they rode past the acres farthest from the house. "It was discovered long ago that such a course improves the yield of other crops, so I decided to try it with cotton. I never claimed to be an orthodox planter, after all."

"No, that you certainly aren't," replied Kathryn warmly, making it a compliment. He flashed her a grin that made her heart beat faster.

"And you like that, I think," he said with an air of pleased discovery. "Have I actually found a woman who does not value conformity above all else?"

"Conformity was never my strong suit," replied Kathryn, remembering her rebellious college years. "Of course, women aren't all cut from the same pattern, either."

"Oh, no, there are at least two or three patterns out there," he said with a grin, "but you don't seem to fit any of them. I ask you again—just who are you, Catherine Prescott?"

The question reminded her abruptly of the kiss they had shared—was it really less than a week ago?—and overwhelmed her with a desire to repeat the experience. "I'm just me," she finally replied, but her voice sounded weak and breathless, even to her own ears. "No one else. And I don't want to be!" she finished more strongly.

"I wouldn't want you to be anyone else, either," he said with unexpected softness. "I am just coming to realize that, I think."

The moment was intimate, but the mood was suddenly broken by a shout from one of the field workers.

"Masah James! Masah James!" A young black man was trotting toward them on foot, waving his arms in excitement.

"What is it, Japheth?" called Ryan as soon as the man was within hailing distance. "Is anything wrong with Magda?"

"No, suh, but I seed you out here and wanted to let you know the news. I's a new father, suh, with a new baby boy!" The man slowed as he neared them, and now fairly strutted with pride.

Ryan burst into a delighted grin. "That's wonderful, Japheth! Tell Magda I will come to see the child whenever she feels recovered enough. Congratulations!"

"Thank you, Masah James!"

"Mr. James, Japheth. You're a free man now, don't forget, and no longer have to call any man master."

"Yes, suh, *Mistah* James, suh. But Magda, she feel fine! You c'n come see little Nathan soon as ever you want."

Ryan glanced questioningly at Kathryn. "It wasn't a planned part of my tour, but would you like to see Japheth's new babe?"

Kathryn cringed inwardly for a moment, recalling the squalor of the slave quarters on the Prescott plantation. But nothing she'd yet seen at Fair Fields had compared to The Glen. "If you want to," she managed to reply with a smile.

"You go on ahead, Japheth, and tell Magda we're coming," said Ryan to the beaming field hand. "She'll want a few minutes to prepare, if I know women at all."

"Thank you, suh! I'll tell her, suh!" He smiled broadly at both of them before loping off with a wave of his hand. Ryan was chuckling.

"You should have seen him last week, Catherine. This is his first child, and I'll swear he was having labor pains himself, he was so nervous. Magda was taking the whole thing much more calmly, but then I've noticed that women generally do. It's we men who get rattled at the simple facts of life and death.''

"You really care, don't you?" she asked wonderingly.

"What?" Ryan pulled his attention back to her.

"About your workers. You really care about them. I mean personally, not just in some abstract, philosophical way.''

"Of course. They are people just as we are, with intelligence, feelings and souls. I find it hard to understand the prevailing attitude that equates slaves with beasts, to be owned, fed only enough for effective work, and punished, even beaten or killed, when they don't perform to standard.'' His face clearly expressed his disgust at his fellow planters' tactics.

Kathryn remembered Mr. Prescott yesterday. He had not spoken to a slave once in her presence, only to his white overseer. And even then, he'd been interested solely in the land, the potential harvest, not in the welfare of his slaves. No doubt Mr. Prescott was the epitome of the "orthodox planter.''

"I have to agree with you," said Kathryn finally. On inspiration, she added, "I suppose my stay in England has made me more intolerant of slavery than ever." Catherine had said something like that in her diary. "I must say I'm glad to find the rumors I've heard about you were wrong."

"I'm no saint, Catherine, believe me." He hesitated as they rode slowly along the dirt road between the fields, then said, "There's something I want you to know, for two separate reasons. Firstly, I feel I can trust you with the information. You seem sympathetic to what I'm trying to do here in a way few, if any, others of your class have shown themselves to be. Secondly, it seems only fair that you know the truth about me before you consent to become my wife."

Kathryn chose to ignore those last words, unwilling to provoke an argument—at least until she found out what this "truth" about him was. "Go on" was all she said.

He watched her closely for a moment with that look that gave her the uncomfortable feeling he could read her mind, but instead of elaborating he said, "I think we've given Japheth a good enough head start. And the carriage would be a better place for serious discussion than horseback, don't you agree?"

Kathryn was now intensely curious about what he might have to tell her, but Ryan was already dismounting in front of a tiny cottage and she had no choice but to follow. Japheth opened the door wide in welcome and she was struck at once by the cheerfulness as well as the cleanliness of his home, a marked contrast to what she had seen at The Glen yesterday. The few furnishings were in good repair and fresh straw had been strewn over the dirt floor. There were even flowers on the table.

Magda was sitting up in the narrow bed on the far side of the cabin's one room, her face wreathed in smiles. "Mistah James, do come in," she said, inclining her head with a dignity that startled Kathryn.

"Thank you, Magda," replied Ryan as if addressing any high-born lady. "I hear congratulations are in order. Miss Prescott and I have come to pay our respects to your new addition."

Magda carefully lifted the bundle in her lap, smiling tenderly down at the infant while Japheth gestured for Kathryn and Ryan to approach. Now eager, Kathryn stepped forward for a sight of little Nathan and was rewarded by a glimpse of wide gray eyes that stared knowingly at her out of a cherubic face crowned by thick, curly black hair. She sighed unconsciously, bemused by the amazing smallness of a new baby.

A miniature fist escaped the tight swaddling and waved in her direction, and without thinking she reached out to touch it. The tiny fingers uncurled to clasp her forefinger tightly and she grinned, first at the baby and then at the proud parents and Ryan, who stood watching her. "He's just perfect," she said sincerely to Magda. "Congratulations."

"I guess I can't add anything to that," said Ryan heartily. "You have a fine son there, Magda, Japheth. I'm certain he'll grow into a man you can be proud of."

"Yes," agreed Magda while Japheth beamed. "Our Nathan'll have opportunities that neither of us ever dreamed of. Why, he can be anythin' he wants to be when he's grown."

They took their leave, not wanting to tire Magda, and both were silent during the ride back to the plantation house, contemplating the miracle of new life they had just seen. Kathryn had never been around young children and had never really given babies much thought, but now she understood the fascination they held for so many people. Remembering Ryan's tender expression as he gazed at the infant, her thoughts meandered off in another direction.

The remnants of their picnic had disappeared, Kathryn noticed on their return, and she had no doubt that the vigilant Mama Ruth was responsible. Not only did Ryan care for his people, they obviously cared for him as well—not such a hard thing to do, she thought, as he took their horses to be stabled and brought the carriage around. He handed her into the curricle and flicked the reins, putting the horses into a sedate trot.

"I believe there was something you wanted to tell me," Kathryn prompted him after they'd driven several minutes in silence. The baby had temporarily distracted her, but now her curiosity returned in full force. "Some 'truth' about you?"

"Trust a woman to be as curious as a cat," he commented, but without malice. "Yes, I believe it's time you knew." He paused for a moment, as though arranging the words in his mind.

"I know the inhabitants of this town consider me a bit of a mystery," he finally began. "I've revealed little of my background to anyone here, trusting money to pave my way in society—which it has!'' His smile was cynical. ''It is generally known that I lived in Charleston before coming here two years ago, but I've purposely tried to keep my life there very much a mystery.''

Kathryn expected now to hear that he came from a lower-class family, something that wouldn't matter to her but might to Catherine—and certainly would to Catherine's parents.

''After our second war with Britain, I gradually worked my way south, ending up in Charleston some years ago. I was born, if you will believe it, into a most respectable and prosperous Maryland family, though I have nothing to show for it. My father and I were of diverse personalities, and as a result, he turned me out of the house shortly before my fifteenth birthday. When I crawled into Charleston I had little besides the clothes on my back and my wits, though I had received some small compensation for my part in the war.''

''You fought in the War of 1812?'' interrupted Kathryn, doing some quick mental subtraction. ''You must have been awfully young!''

''I was forced to grow up rather quickly,'' he replied with more than a trace of bitterness.

''Yes. Yes, I imagine you were.'' Kathryn could not comprehend how a father could turn a fourteen-year-old boy adrift. Her own upbringing had been so privileged, so...pampered.

''At any rate, it turned out that my wits were enough. I worked my way up in various ways, becoming quite a rich man in Charleston before I left, though never one of the more respected ones. Charleston's sense of class is much stronger than Columbia's. My friends tended to be among the working classes and even included some of the free Negroes. That is how I met Denmark Vesey.'' He looked at her significantly, and she wondered if she were expected to recognize the name. She did not, and her expression obviously told him that.

"You haven't heard of the Vesey Insurrection? Granted, it happened while you were in England, but I would have thought— Well, no matter. I'll tell you the bare bones of it. Vesey was a free mulatto, originally from St. Thomas, or so he told me. I know now how naive I was to believe everything he said. He bought his own freedom in Charleston, more than twenty years ago. Won six hundred dollars in the lottery, the story went, though he never discussed it with me. He must have been near forty when I met him, but he looked twenty-five—a strong, handsome fellow, and brilliant as well. He told me himself that when he was in his teens he pretended insanity to avoid being sold." He snorted with something that was not quite laughter.

"And this Vesey plotted some sort of slave revolt?"

"Exactly. He drew me in. I became one of the secret leaders of the conspiracy, along with several others, white and colored, slave and free. He never told some of us the full extent of his plan, however. To me, and to all of the other whites and several of the coloreds, he put it forth as simply a mass escape—the slaves were to work their way north and west through the wild country. What he really planned was a bloody massacre. It was set for July 14, but in May the word leaked out. I suspect some of the slaves involved found out about the proposed killings and were loyal enough to warn their masters. Vesey had time to burn most of his papers, which was the only thing that saved me, but he and thirty-four others hanged for it. I found it—expedient—to liquidate my assets and leave Charleston before the incident could be investigated further."

"You mean you could have been executed for your involvement?" Kathryn was aghast.

"Of course." He looked at her strangely. "After all, a massacre was planned and I was involved, however the technicalities may absolve my conscience. Legally, I assure you, I am guilty of a capital crime.''

Kathryn sat back, stunned. To think that a man could be hanged for simple plotting that hadn't even harmed anyone—that thirty-five men already had been! In spite of what had been intended, such so-called justice seemed incredibly harsh to her.

"I shock you, do I not? I will give you ample time to think about it before pressing my suit again, but I must ask you to say nothing of this to anyone. If it were suspected, inquiries in Charleston could be dangerous to me—and to others—even now."

"Others?"

"Yes. I did not flee here alone. One man and his wife came with me, posing as my personal slaves. I have reason to believe that he may have been implicated in the little evidence that remained to the magistrates. It is for his sake, more than my own, that I must ask you to remain silent on this.''

"Of course!" Kathryn assured him quickly. As if she would betray such a secret, especially when it carried such a penalty! "You can trust me, I promise."

He searched her face for a moment and was apparently satisfied. "My motives have not changed since that time, as you have seen today, but I have, ah, moderated my methods.''

"I'm glad of that," she exclaimed fervently. When his look questioned her, she forced a smile and a wink to mask her true feelings. "You're much too ornamental to be hanged, Mr. James. I doubt if a noose would be very becoming."

"If I didn't know better, I might almost suspect you cared," he responded. She smiled mysteriously, but said nothing, in keeping with her plan to leave him guessing.

Ryan came in for tea when they reached the Prescott house and was all that was charming to his host and hostess. Kathryn was more drawn to him every minute and had to force herself to dwell on the more unsavory aspects of his reputation—the womanizing, the dueling, his apparently legendary temper. It was hard to do, since beyond some innocent flirting, she'd seen no evidence of any of these things. The rumor of his cruelty to slaves had proved false—maybe the others were, too. Guiltily, she thought of the rumors she herself had begun.

He left after half an hour and Kathryn resigned herself to the inevitable sewing session with Mrs. S-P. She finished adding the last of the lace she'd bought to Catherine's dresses and was forced to finish out the time with another wretched attempt at embroidery. "What the hell good is embroidery to anyone, anyway?" she muttered to herself, tearing out everything she'd done for the third time.

"What was that dear?" asked Mrs. S-P, her needle never stopping its rapid motions.

"Oh, nothing. I'm just tired, I suppose. I believe I'll go upstairs and rest until supper."

"You do that, dear."

Though she didn't sleep, Kathryn felt more refreshed when she joined the Prescotts at the supper table. She ate slowly, ignoring her parents' talk of politics and remembering instead her picnic with Ryan that afternoon. Suddenly, Mr. Prescott's words jolted her out of her reverie.

"If Ryan James murdered a wife in Charleston, it couldn't have gone undiscovered for this long. And if he had another, she'd have come after him. Mind you, I don't give the slightest credence to this rumor, but Jonathan Allerby has always been a slave to his wife's whims."

"What...does Mr. Allerby plan to do?" asked Kathryn, striving to keep her voice level.

"First, he was simply going to write to an acquaintance there, asking a few questions about young James, but that did not satisfy Joanna. No, she insists that he go himself to ferret out anything he can."

"Sour grapes, if you ask me, my dear," interposed Mrs. Sykes-Prescott.

"Precisely," agreed Mr. Prescott. "I've no doubt you have hit the nail on the head, my love. She recognizes that her own daughter is unlikely to shackle him, and so wishes to tarnish *your* victory, Catherine."

Kathryn tried to smile, but she knew it was a feeble effort. Her thoughts darted this way and that like a trapped animal, remembering what Ryan had told her that afternoon. A capital crime! If his part in that abortive uprising in Charleston came out, he could be hanged—all because of some stupid jealousy and scheming on her part.

What have I done? Oh, dear God, what have I done?

Kathryn found it impossible to fall asleep that night, worrying about the consequences of Mr. Allerby's inquiries. She began to suspect, as well, that she might possibly be falling in love with Ryan James. The irony of timing did not escape her—that she should discover her feelings just when she had done something for which Ryan might reasonably despise her. The only thing more ironic, she thought, would be for the switch back with Catherine to occur now. On that thought, she began, almost involuntarily to pray.

Not yet! Don't send me back yet!

CHAPTER EIGHT

BY SUPPERTIME, CATHERINE had read nearly all of the U.S. history book and scanned the other books Annette had brought her, and felt confident of her ability to conceal what had happened from Kathryn's parents—and Logan. Much of what she had read shocked her: the incredible wars, the bombs that had been used to kill thousands of people at once, the assassinations of two presidents. Still, she found herself beginning to hope that somehow she might be able to remain in this new time. There was more to be afraid of here, but there was also so much more to experience, and to aspire to, especially as a woman. And, of course, there was Logan.

Catherine consulted with Annette about the proper attire for supper and was surprised to hear that she could wear the slacks she had worn all day. "At least, that's what I'm going to do," Annette told her. "It's just family tonight, not like going to a fancy restaurant or anything."

It seemed inappropriate, almost disrespectful, to Catherine not to dress more formally for the evening meal, but she had to admit it was nice not to worry about clothes the way she'd had to since being declared a young lady at sixteen. Remembering that Logan might be at the table, she compromised by changing into a pretty, but hardly formal, flowered dress. Touching up her makeup with only minor supervision from Annette, she knew she looked her best.

"Daddy called to say he and Logan won't be back until late," said Mrs. Sykes-Monroe when they came downstairs. "They couldn't schedule a meeting with the property owners until eight, so it's just us girls for dinner." She beamed at them. "This will be our first chance for a cozy chat since you got home, Kathy."

Catherine cringed inwardly, hoping she would not give herself away during this "cozy chat." She knew enough history now not to sound like a complete idiot, but what about personal details? Her mother wasn't likely to ask who the last president was, she suddenly realized. Annette helped her, to her relief.

"I'd love any advice you could give me about babies, Mrs. Sykes-Monroe. I haven't even picked out names yet."

This was a masterful move, diverting Mrs. Sykes-Monroe throughout the salad and chicken Kiev. It wasn't until they all decided to forgo dessert for the sake of their figures that she turned to Catherine, saying, "Well, darling, have you decided on your plans for the future yet? I hope you can stay in Columbia for a while. I read in *The State* today that Town Theater is auditioning for *A Midsummer Night's Dream*. It's not Broadway, I know, but any acting credits are worthwhile, aren't they?"

Catherine glanced at Annette, remembering what she had told her about Kathryn's plans, before saying tentatively, "I... I really came to Columbia to rest, Mama, and to... think things over. To be perfectly honest, I'm not certain that acting is what I want to do with my life." That much was true, at least.

Mrs. Sykes-Monroe's face lit up. "Why, that's an excellent idea, darling, to take some time out to 'find yourself,' as they used to say. Your father always thought you had a wonderful head for business, and you did well in the economics courses you took in college."

"Well, that is something to consider," Catherine agreed. She would doubtless make a better businesswoman than an actress, at any rate. But first she would need to do an enormous amount of studying. Business had probably changed as much as everything else since 1825, and her father's tutoring on plantation management would likely count for little here. "I haven't decided on anything yet."

"Well, since you want to rest, Kathy, I won't drag you around the entire Columbia social circuit. I do want to show you off to a few of my friends who weren't here last night at the party, though, so I hope you won't mind a brunch or two."

"Not in the least, ma'am," replied Catherine graciously. "Indeed, I'd be flattered." Mrs. Sykes-Monroe blinked as though in surprise and Annette was suddenly seized by a fit of coughing. Had she said something wrong?

But her mother was smiling again now. "Very nicely put, sweetheart. One thing I'll say for the political scene in Washington, it's given you class. No wonder you're making such a name for yourself there." As they left the table, she added, "I have to make a few phone calls. I'll be down in a while."

"Great!" exclaimed Annette as soon as she had gone upstairs, and before Catherine could ask what "phone calls" were. "We can just catch the start of a new comedy I wanted to see—but I'll bet your face will be funnier!" Motioning Catherine to follow her, she led her to the front parlor—the "living room," as it was now called—and made her sit on the sofa. Catherine watched, mystified, as Annette picked up a small black box and sat down next to her.

"No, don't watch me, watch the television set," said Annette, pointing to a large, square, wooden box with a black glassy front that was set into a recess in the wall.

"Is that some sort of display case?" asked Catherine.

"Something like that," said Annette with a mysterious smile. She pointed the little black box at the television and pushed a button. At once, a man's voice emanated from the case. "—For a limited time only, so order today!" Catherine jumped and stared, first at the television, then at Annette.

"How...?"

"Just watch!"

Catherine did. After a brief silence, another voice began speaking and the glass screen began to light up. A display case indeed! A man's face materialized, his mouth moving along with the words. "...And the school board will meet to discuss the plan. In the weather, we'll hear whether this sunny spell will last. Join us at eleven." Another brief silence, and a new picture came on, along with sprightly music. Bright, confusing images flashed across the screen in rapid succession, then the scene stabilized into one room— a "living room" of a house. People began talking to one another and she realized that the "show" had begun.

"I see!" she said excitedly. "It is like a play, is it not?"

"That's right," said Annette. "I didn't think to explain it like that. Let's watch the show and see if we like it."

Catherine found the dialogue and action, especially the instantaneous scene changes, hard to follow at first, but after a few minutes, she was following the plot almost as well as Annette. Much of it seemed improbable to her, but she had seen plays where that was so also. Some of the lines Annette chuckled at eluded her, but she found others funny and remembered Annette had said it was a comedy. She was just deciding that this was a fun, and incredibly convenient, form of entertainment, when the action stopped and a woman who had not been in the cast began to speak matter-of-factly about something called "denture adhesive." Annette pushed another button on her small black box which caused the sound, but not the picture, to cease, and turned to her.

"Well, what do you think?"

"It is amazing—wonderful! Is this not part of the show?"

"No, this is just a commercial. That's where the companies who pay for the show break into it to advertise their products."

"Oh. I suppose that makes sense. You mean that they make these shows so that people will watch them and see demonstrations of new products at the same time."

"Pretty much," said Annette. "There are movies, in theaters, which are even more like plays. They don't have commercials but you have to pay to see them. I'll take you to one soon—or maybe Logan will." She winked.

Catherine blushed and changed the subject. "How do you control the . . . the television set with that little box?" She indicated the one Annette held.

"This is a remote control. A pretty new invention, really, just fifteen or twenty years old. It sends some sort of beam to the TV that tells it what to do. See? This button turns it on and off, this one controls the volume—that's how loud it is—and these numbered ones change the channel." She demonstrated.

"All of those shows are being performed at once?" asked Catherine in amazement. "No wonder there is such a demand for actors!"

"Most of these shows are actually taped. That means they were filmed earlier to be shown later." Catherine's confusion must have shown. "I'll try to explain it better later on. The show's starting again." She restored the sound with the remarkable little box and they fell silent to watch.

The show was just ending when Mrs. Sykes-Monroe joined them. "I expect the men will be here soon," she said, "but if they're not, we won't wait up. You need your rest now, you know, Annette!"

"Thanks, but even I don't need to go to bed at nine-thirty! You missed a halfway decent show, by the way."

"Decent? I didn't think anything on television was that, nowadays!" Her hostess laughed.

"Well, maybe not in the moral sense, but it was pretty funny. Was there anything special you wanted to watch?"

Catherine was surprised and disappointed that the show was over already. Who ever heard of a play that lasted half an hour? It hardly seemed worth the trouble of costuming the actors.

"Not until ten," answered Mrs. Sykes-Monroe. "I'm addicted to 'L.A. Law,' and tonight they're showing an episode I missed last fall."

Catherine opened her mouth to ask what "L.A. Law" was, but caught herself in time. She'd find out soon enough.

Annette pushed two of the buttons on the remote control box. "Let's see if anything important happened in the world today. I usually trust Dave to tell me the news, but when he's gone I like to check on it myself." She and Mrs. Sykes-Monroe made comments, both about the program and other topics during the show that followed, but Catherine was too intent upon the events pictured on the screen to pay much attention to them.

Both from Annette's comments and from the seriousness of the faces on the television she understood immediately that this was no fictional drama being portrayed. The things being shown and discussed were real happenings in the real world, and apparently all were things that had happened just today. Even a bombing—she remembered bombs from her history book—in Northern Ireland, across the Atlantic, was known here, in America, almost as soon as it had occurred. How could that be? She longed to ask.

The content of the stories was just as startling, not to mention alarming. Murders were mentioned casually; even a man who had been arrested for killing twelve people seemed to evoke no emotion in the woman—the woman!—who told about the incident. How could these people be so calm about such terrible crimes? Could she get used to such a world? She remembered how offhand Annette had been that morning about having her reticule—no, her "purse"—stolen. Was crime so commonplace?

Of course, there were areas in London, even in 1825, where it was by no means safe to venture. Cutthroats and cutpurses abounded in the unsavory quarters of the city.

Only in and around elegant Mayfair could a well-dressed person safely walk the streets. Perhaps things had not changed so very much, after all. The only difference now was that one heard instantly about terrible things that had always happened. The thought gave her an odd sense of comfort.

After shifting to less serious matters, such as the outcomes of various sporting events and the making of a new movie, the news program ended. Annette changed the channel again, presumably to the one Mrs. Sykes-Monroe wished to watch. Catherine wondered whether present-day Americans spent all of their evenings in front of this marvelous new invention. If so, it might account for the ladies' obsession with watching their diets.

"Previously on 'L.A. Law,'" a voice announced importantly, and a few scenes followed that involved various people kissing, crying and shouting at one another. After some music, the show began in earnest, and Catherine realized that the plot must be picking up where it had ended the week before. So that was why the programs were so short! They continued from week to week. No wonder people were so eager to see the next show in such a series—it would be like picking up a book to read the next chapter.

"We're home!" called Mr. Monroe as the front door slammed. A moment later, he and Logan came into the living room and Catherine felt the now-familiar tingle at Logan's entrance. She glanced at him and he caught her eye with a smile.

Breathless, she turned her attention to Mr. Monroe. It was the first time she had seen him since understanding what had happened, and she was startled to see how little he resembled her own father. He was a much smaller man, for one thing, and his face, while pleasant, was not so jovial. Suddenly, she missed her father. They had always been close, despite their disagreements. How would he manage The

Glen without her if she could not get back? A lump rose in her throat.

"Did you save us any dinner?" asked Mr. Monroe, breaking her reverie.

"You said you would eat there! But yes, I'm sure Alice has some leftovers, since she cooked for all of us," replied Mrs. Sykes-Monroe, rising to kiss her husband on the cheek.

"We saw only a burger joint along the way and Logan said he had a burger for lunch, so we decided to come back here and see what we could scrounge. Let's go see what Alice has for us, Logan. I'm starved!" Logan gave the ladies a collective wink and followed the older man.

"And that means I can watch 'L.A. Law,'" said Mrs. Sykes-Monroe contentedly, settling back on the divan.

"Not me," said Annette decisively. "I never did get hooked on it, but this is one of the few episodes I *have* seen. I'll leave you to it, since I won't be able to keep my mouth shut."

"I'll come with you," said Catherine, rising. She had seen enough television for one evening—it had somehow lost its charm on Logan's return. She couldn't help hoping for another glimpse of him as she followed Annette into the foyer. His voice mingled with Mr. Monroe's from the direction of the dining room, but Catherine couldn't think of any particular reason for her to go there.

"How about that dessert now?" asked Annette with a wicked twinkle in her eye. "I'm always hungry these days, and I hear the best way to avoid morning sickness is not to let your stomach get too empty." She tried to put on a pitiful expression and failed utterly.

Catherine giggled at her foolishness, though her heart leapt at the chance to join Logan. "And what is my excuse?"

"You're keeping me company," Annette informed her, loftily. "I hate to eat alone." Catherine refrained from pointing out that with Logan and Mr. Monroe there, she would not be alone. She wondered nervously, almost giddily, whether Annette was matchmaking.

The two men were demolishing fully loaded plates when they entered. "I see Alice found you a scrap or two," teased Annette. "We skipped dessert earlier, but I've had second thoughts. Mind if we join you?"

"Not at all," answered Logan. Mr. Monroe, his mouth full, merely shook his head. "As a matter of fact, Kathy, I wanted to talk to you," Logan continued. "About the race on Friday. The Columbia Speedway is a dirt track, not the asphalt I normally race on. It'll be pretty muddy, and the people there aren't going to be exactly—uh—your type, I'm afraid. You still want to go?"

"Of course." Catherine was aware of Annette's surprised regard, but refused to look at her. She thought she heard something like a snort from Mr. Monroe's direction.

"All right, then, if you're sure. The gates open at six, and it's a good half-hour drive. We'll leave just after five, if you can be ready that early." He was grinning now, and her heart turned over. She swallowed hard before answering.

"Certainly, if Mother has no plans for me. I...I'll go ask her." She rose.

"You're going to ask your mother?" For some reason, Logan looked almost astonished.

Catherine regarded him uncertainly. "She did say something about a luncheon, I believe," she offered. He shrugged and she went out, returning in a moment, still confused. Her mother had seemed almost as surprised as Logan that she had asked. "There *is* a luncheon she would like me to attend," she informed him now, "but we should be back before three."

Annette had finished her dessert by this time, and was making it clear by little motions with her head and eyes that she wanted to talk to Catherine alone. With a smile that she hoped would reassure her friend, Catherine stood up. "Good night, Logan. Good night...Father."

"Are you out of your mind?" asked Annette as soon as they reached the landing. "You agreed to go to a stock car race?"

Catherine nodded. "He asked me on the way home this afternoon. I know it is probably something Kathryn would not have done, but—"

"Probably, nothing! Kathy wouldn't be caught dead at a stock car race—or any kind of race. She gets nervous riding with me!"

"I know. Logan mentioned something about that. I managed to convince him that I've overcome my fear of cars, and I think he invited me to the race to test me. But I truly do wish to go. I loved the few horse races I was able to attend, and this sounds ever so much more exciting."

Annette smiled reluctantly. "Oh, you'll probably love it. I have to keep reminding myself that you're really nothing at all like Kathy. I'm just afraid Logan is going to start realizing it, too."

"Would that be so bad?" She'd love to be able to tell him the truth, especially since he seemed critical of Kathryn.

Instead of answering, Annette looked at her thoughtfully. "You know," she said slowly, "before the switch, I told Kathy I had a feeling about her and Logan. My feelings are never wrong. But maybe, just maybe, it was *you* and Logan who are supposed to get together. Hmm . . . I wonder. . . ." She stared into space, obviously thinking hard.

Catherine started to question her, but Annette only smiled vaguely. "You go on up to bed. I just remembered something I left downstairs."

"FORGET SOMETHING, Annette?" Mr. Monroe asked teasingly as Annette reentered the dining room. "Maybe another slice of pie?"

Annette made a face at him. "I know I'm getting fat— you don't have to remind me! No, I just wanted to ask Logan something."

"I'll leave you then. 'L.A. Law' should be over by now."
He went in search of his wife.

Logan pushed his plate away and looked up at Annette
expectantly. "What can I do for you?" he asked, smiling.
He wondered again how the cool, sophisticated Kathryn
could have such a bubbly, outgoing, *fun* best friend. It was
impossible for anybody not to like Annette.

"I have a favor to ask of you," she said with an impish
grin. "Are you busy tomorrow night?"

He nodded. "We have another meeting with that Lake
Murray client."

"Okay, how about Thursday?"

"No, not that I know of," he replied, wondering what she
was up to. "Why?"

"There's a new movie, a documentary on the Civil War,
that I wanted to see. I hate to go alone and was wondering
if you'd come with me. I'll pay your way." She batted her
eyes in a mock flirtation that made him laugh.

"That won't be necessary, but I'll be glad to be of service, ma'am." He gave her a half bow from his seat. "I take
it Kathy doesn't want to go?"

Annette gave him a sideways, sly look that almost made
him laugh again. "Actually, I haven't asked her. But since
you mentioned it, I'll see if she'd like to come along."

So that's what she was up to, thought Logan. Hadn't
Kathy told her that any romance was out of the question?
They were almost like family. Still, he had to admit to a
slightly more than brotherly interest in going out with her
again. "All right," he said. "But if she doesn't want to
come, we won't let her interfere with *our* plans, okay?"

"Of course not," exclaimed Annette. "It's a date, then.
Good night." She rose, still looking pleased with herself,
and scurried out of the room.

Logan sat shaking his head and chuckling for a moment,
but then he grew thoughtful. Even if he hadn't known Kathy
for so long that the idea of dating her seemed almost inces-

tuous, she really wasn't his type. She'd become a slick socialite, always in the Washington gossip pages. When he went out with a woman, he wanted to relax and be himself, not play any silly social games. So why did Kathryn's face keep returning to haunt him? Guiltily thrusting away the thought, he went up to his room to immerse himself in plans for the new business complex.

ANNETTE CAME BOUNCING into Catherine's room before she had turned out the light. "Remember I mentioned movies? Well Thursday night you'll get to see one—with Logan!" She waited expectantly for Catherine's reaction and grinned when she blushed deeply.

"How...when...what do you mean?" was all that Catherine managed to say. How could the mere mention of the man's name affect her so profoundly?

"I got him to agree to take me. I was planning to ask you along at the last minute—as far as he knew, anyway—but he asked if you'd like to go. It's practically like he asked you himself!" She looked as smug as the cat that got the cream.

"I thought you were up to something." Catherine smiled in spite of herself. "You are as much a matchmaker as my mother. My *real* mother, that is."

"Oh, Kathy's mom does that, too. I guess they have more than looks in common—more in common than you and Kathy do, as a matter of fact."

"Perhaps all mothers are like that," said Catherine. Then, curiously, she asked, "Are Kathryn and I really that different?"

Annette considered for a moment. "I guess you could say Kathy's the cool, sophisticated type. She always knows just what to say and is never at a loss for words. And I've *never* seen her blush." She looked pointedly at Catherine.

"I suppose we *are* different," she said, pinkening again. "I tend to say the first thing that comes into my head, and it's usually the wrong thing. I only hope I can continue to act her part successfully."

Annette sat on the bed, thoughtfully flipping the pillow over and over. "Maybe when you're with Logan, you shouldn't try so hard," she finally suggested.

"What do you mean?"

"I can't say I really know him well, but from the few conversations I've had with him, I'd say you were more his type than Kathy was. She always loved life in the fast lane, but I think he's more laid-back—the kind of guy who'd go for an old-fashioned girl. And there aren't that many left these days."

Catherine had to giggle. "He's not likely to find one more old-fashioned than I am!"

"That's for sure!" Annette choked on a laugh. "Well, I'd better get to bed." She paused in the open doorway to look back. "I've been wondering.... Do you think that could be why you and Kathy switched? Because you and Logan were *meant* to be together?" Catherine gasped, but before she could answer, Annette shrugged and closed the door.

Could it be true? she wondered, turning off the light and slowly climbing into bed. She *had* always felt there was one right man out there waiting for her, that somehow they would find each other. If that man were Logan Thorne, could the bond between them be so strong that it actually brought her forward in time? But how could Annette have known? And why, she thought wryly, did Logan seem completely unaware that any bond existed?

THREE EVENINGS LATER, when Logan found both Annette and Catherine dressed and waiting for him, he felt a sudden, inexplicable lift of his spirits. Annette had said she would ask Kathy to go along, but he hadn't expected a documentary to be her kind of movie. But then, he hadn't expected her to ask to go to a race, either.

Annette chattered cheerfully as they all walked out to Logan's car, but as he opened the passenger door, her mood changed. "Suddenly I don't feel so well," she said, assuming a tired expression. "I don't think I'm up to sitting through a movie tonight. Tell you what—you and Kathy go on and I'll get to bed early. You can tell me about it tomorrow." She smiled wanly at the suspicious looks she received, managing a weary little sigh with a perfectly straight face.

Logan glanced from her to Catherine and shrugged. "Well, I don't suppose we can insist."

Catherine shook her head, though she looked knowingly at Annette. "I'm certain the moment you lie down you'll feel much better," she said with a significance that Logan didn't miss.

"You're probably right," Annette replied, quickly turning her face toward the house. "Have a good time!" she called over her shoulder, moving briskly for one so tired.

"I guess it's just us," said Logan, amusement warring with doubt. Had Kathy planned this with Annette? Why? "Do you still want to go?"

Catherine looked up at him, her eyes wide and innocent, and he felt an unsettling tug at his heart. "If you do." She sounded uncertain, as though she thought he might refuse.

"Get in, then," he said, struggling to keep his smile brotherly.

Once they were both sitting in the car, Logan turned to her. "Listen, are you really set on this Civil War thing?" he asked. "I didn't say so to Annette, but I've already seen it."

"Oh. Is there something else you'd rather see?" Catherine had been somewhat prepared for the historical movie, hoping to learn more about the past she'd missed, but she knew she would enjoy any movie if she saw it with Logan.

"I heard on the radio that there's a *Star Wars* marathon at USC tonight. It's been years since I've seen it on the big screen, and it's one of my favorites. Would that be okay?"

"Certainly," replied Catherine readily. "I've never seen it," she added, since that seemed to be some sort of criterion for enjoyment.

Logan looked at her strangely. "You've never seen *Star Wars?* You're kidding!"

Catherine could only shake her head. Had she somehow blundered again?

"I knew you weren't a sci-fi fan, but I thought *everyone* had seen *Star Wars,* at least on TV. Well, you're in for a treat. If this movie doesn't make a sci-fi fan out of you, nothing will."

Catherine didn't dare ask what "sci-fi" was, but she was beginning to look forward to what was apparently a classic movie in this time. But *Star Wars*—what a strange title.

They drove the short distance to the university, and Catherine managed with difficulty to keep her astonishment to herself. For the first time since her arrival in 1994 she was traveling over an area she had been very familiar with in 1825, and the changes nearly overwhelmed her.

South Carolina College itself—oops, USC, now—was enormous. In 1825 there had been only 120 students enrolled here. Even Logan had to stop once to ask a passerby where the movie was being shown before turning into a parking lot near Pickens Street. Medium Street had been renamed College, she noticed, which seemed appropriate. She wished she dared ask Logan how many students attended now. Perhaps many of them were women! She smiled secretly.

As they walked from the car to Russell House, where the movie would be shown, she caught Logan watching her curiously. Was he noticing a change in her? She longed to tell him the truth, but could think of no way to open the subject that would not sound incredible. Annette was right. He would think she was either mad or playing a prank on him.

When the movie began, Catherine nearly forgot Logan as she entered the world—or rather, worlds—on the screen.

The beginning words that scrolled across the stars, "Long ago, in a galaxy far, far away..." told her that this was not a true story—though she was not quite certain what a galaxy was. She quickly realized that the story was about a civilization that had gone beyond the flights to the moon she had read about, one that traveled between planets the way people now traveled between cities. She longed to ask Logan if such things might really happen.

Inexorably, she got caught up in the lives of the characters in the movie, finding herself able to relate to their problems even without understanding the setting they were in. When Luke Skywalker destroyed the Death Star near the end of the film, it was all she could do to refrain from clapping and cheering out loud. No play had ever affected her like this.

"That was amazing!" was all she dared say to Logan as the lights came up after the credits. She didn't realize that her sparkling eyes and glowing cheeks said far more, and wondered why Logan was regarding her with something like startled recognition.

He blinked, shaking his head slightly. "Do you want to stay?"

"Stay?"

"They're showing all three tonight. I'd only planned to watch *Star Wars,* since I have to work tomorrow, but we can stay at least for *Empire,* if you want to. It's not very late yet."

"*Empire?*" Catherine knew she must sound like a fool.

"You know, *The Empire Strikes Back*—the second *Star Wars* movie. The third is *Return of the Jedi,* but that won't be over until well past midnight, and I do have to race tomorrow, too." He was regarding her strangely again, and Catherine realized that she should have known of those other films. Well, she hadn't had time to study *everything*.

"I'd love to see the others—" oh, how much she wanted to "—but you really should get to bed early tonight."

Logan chuckled. "Sounds like I've made a *Star Wars* fanatic of you already. Tell you what, we'll rent them sometime to make up for missing them tonight. Okay?"

Catherine nodded happily, though she had no idea how one could "rent" a movie.

During the drive back Logan was strangely silent, but Catherine hardly noticed as she relived the marvelous movie she had just seen. How had they made those spaceships look so real? she wondered. She wished she could ask Logan. Annette might not know, but she thought that Logan would.

"I need to stop for gas." Logan turned the car into what looked like a small covered parking lot with odd rectangular boxes mounted on raised platforms. He stopped the car alongside one of the tall boxes. Catherine noticed it had a black hose protruding from each side, ending in some sort of metal contraption that rested against the upper part of the box. "I'll have to put it on my card," he said, opening the door. "Could you pump the gas while I go inside to pay?"

Catherine looked at him in alarm. How on earth did one "pump gas"? "Ah, I don't—"

He misinterpreted her hesitation. "Oh, I forgot. Kathy Monroe doesn't pump gas." He was out of the car before she could respond and Catherine sat there, feeling rather foolish, but not knowing what she could have done differently. There was just so much she didn't know!

Logan pumped the gas and paid for it, struggling with his conflicting emotions as he restarted the engine and pulled out of the service station. It was obvious that Kathy and Annette had set up this "date" in advance, but why? Kathy had never given him the slightest hint before that she was romantically interested in him. But she seemed different tonight, just as she had at the mall. That eager innocence could all be an act, he supposed, but again—why? Could she be feeling the same strange tug of attraction that he did?

"Well, we're back," he said unnecessarily as he pulled the car to a stop before the broad front steps of the Monroe house. "Um, thanks for coming tonight." He felt a sudden urge to prolong the moment. She'd get out of the car any second now and the evening would be over—and he wasn't ready for it to end just yet.

"Thank you for taking me, Logan," she replied. "I don't know when I've enjoyed anything so much."

She made no move to leave, Logan noticed. Was she waiting for him to come around and open the door for her? Kathy had snapped at him more than once in the past for doing that, saying she wanted to be treated as an equal. But now he recalled that at the mall, and again tonight, she'd allowed him to hold doors for her. The change he noticed in her was more than imaginary, then.

"I enjoyed it too, Kathy—more than I expected to." Tentatively, he reached out and touched her arm and felt something—a current, a bond—leap between them. She half turned, her eyes questioning, and suddenly he no longer saw her as a little sister, but as a woman. "Kathy, I—"

The rest of whatever he would have said was lost as she swayed slightly toward him and his arms went around her without conscious thought. He lowered his lips to hers and the bond he'd already felt crackled into life, twining them together. She responded at once, but timidly, inexpertly, though he knew Kathy was no novice—she'd made that brutally clear to him during their flare-up at college. If he didn't know better, he'd have sworn he held a different woman in his arms. Abruptly, more for his own sake than hers, he released her.

Catherine sat back quickly, a sigh that was almost a gasp escaping her trembling lips. What must he think of her? She had . . . had *encouraged* him to kiss her! She was glad the darkness hid the deep blush she could feel staining her cheeks.

"I'm sorry," said Logan after a moment. "I shouldn't have done that. I . . . I don't know what got into me. Let's forget it, okay?"

"If . . . if that is what you wish," replied Catherine shakily. She had felt the current that crackled between them, but wasn't sure if Logan had. She was ready to die of embarrassment.

"Look, Kathy, I really am sorry. It's just we hadn't seen each other in so long and . . . Will you accept my apology?" His look was almost pleading.

Catherine thought she was the one who had behaved wantonly, but he apparently didn't see it that way. A surge of relief swept through her. "Of course, Logan," she said softly, afraid that her voice might give away her feelings. "We won't mention it again."

"Are we still on for tomorrow?" Logan asked as they climbed the front steps, his smile so appealing that Catherine was tempted to throw herself back into his arms.

"Why shouldn't we be?" she managed to reply lightly.

His smile broadened and he opened the door. "All right, then. Good night, Kathy."

She watched his broad back wistfully as he climbed the stairs to the second floor. If only she dared tell him who she really was! They had agreed to forget what had happened in the car, and Catherine resolved to do her best, but there was a problem. She didn't *want* to forget. The memory of Logan's kiss warmed her as she finally drifted off to sleep.

CHAPTER NINE

WHEN LOGAN CAME downstairs for breakfast the next morning, he found Catherine in the living room switching through the channels on the TV. "Have you eaten yet?" he asked from the doorway.

She dropped the remote onto the coffee table as if it were hot. "No! No, I haven't," she replied, avoiding his gaze.

Surely a polished sophisticate like Kathryn Monroe couldn't still be flustered by—or even remember—that kiss last night? Logan himself had been unable to forget it, but he doubted an experienced woman like Kathy would have similar trouble.

"No one was in the dining room when I came down," she continued when Logan didn't speak, "so I thought I would wait until someone else was ready for breakfast. I...I didn't like to bother Alice for just me."

Logan blinked, but only said, "Now I'm here. We don't have to feel guilty asking your high-paid housekeeper to cook for two of us, do we?"

Catherine looked at him uncertainly, not sure if he was teasing. She had been unprepared for the feelings, stronger than ever, that surged through her at the sight of him, and struggled to maintain her composure. Her mother breezed in at that moment, sparing her the need to answer.

"Why is everyone in the living room instead of the dining room? I've just asked Alice to fix us pancakes for a change, and they should be ready any minute. Is Annette up yet?"

"I haven't seen her, ma'am," replied Catherine, earning a puzzled look from both of her companions. "I'll go upstairs to find out, if you'd like." She stepped into the foyer in time to see Annette descending the stairs.

"Do I smell pancakes?" she asked eagerly. "I'm starved!"

The conversation was light and general during the meal, with Annette and Mrs. Sykes-Monroe carrying the bulk of it. Logan left while the others were still eating, saying that he had to meet Mr. Monroe if they were to finish their business by four.

"I'll be back in time to change before the race," he told Catherine on his way out the door. "You should probably wear grubbies tonight, since we'll be in the pit. Jeans and a T-shirt'll do—if you have any."

"Grubbies?" echoed Mrs. Sykes-Monroe distastefully when he had gone. "What race? You told me that you were going out with Logan tonight, but you didn't say where." Annette raised her eyes heavenward, Catherine noticed, but luckily her hostess didn't.

"We are going to the Columbia Speedway, Mother," she said as calmly as she could, expecting a tirade like the one she had received from Annette last night.

Instead, Mrs. Sykes-Monroe merely said, "I've never heard of it. I didn't realize Logan was still racing—but I suppose it will be all right. I'm sure he wouldn't take you among undesirable people."

Remembering what Logan had said on that point before, Catherine did not comment. "What should I wear for the luncheon today?" she asked, changing the subject.

"Oh, daytime-dressy, I think. There will be mostly older ladies there, and they like to see a young person looking nice."

Some things never change. "What time will we be leaving?"

"Oh, not until eleven-thirty or so. And I promise to have you back in plenty of time to change into your 'grubbies.'" Mrs. Sykes-Monroe shuddered delicately.

Annette followed Catherine upstairs to explain the mysteries of "daytime-dressy" and "grubbies" and to pick them out of Kathryn's wardrobe. There were several tailored afternoon dresses to choose from, any of which would be appropriate for the luncheon, but Annette despaired of Kathryn's jeans.

"Not only are they one hundred dollar designer labels, but they look like she never even wore them," she exclaimed. "Come to think of it, I can't remember ever seeing her in jeans at all, even in college, when everyone else practically lived in them. Well, try them on and let's hope they're not too tight!"

They were a bit snug, but after Catherine did a few deep knee bends, at Annette's direction, she could almost sit down in them. "I thought I had left corsets behind in 1825," she said, laughing.

"Don't worry, it's not permanent. Once you've broken them in, there's nothing more comfortable," Annette assured her. "Now, what about a T-shirt?" Some more rummaging brought to light an appropriately well-worn black shirt with *Cats* emblazoned across the front. With jeans, shirt and Kathryn's jogging shoes laid aside for later, Annette helped Catherine dress for the luncheon, though by this time she needed very little help.

"You catch on fast," commented Annette as Catherine donned the blue-and-lavender dress without assistance and knotted a matching scarf around her throat. "You look as fashionable as Kathy ever did, in fact."

"She has such a beautiful wardrobe, I can't imagine *not* being fashionable in it," replied Catherine honestly. "And the clothes are so *comfortable* here. Except for new jeans, that is," she admitted. "I hope Kathryn is managing with corsets and long skirts. And sidesaddles."

"Well, I don't know about the sidesaddles, but she's probably in heaven with the clothes. She always loved costumes, and comfort *never* took precedence over fashion with her. She even jogs and exercises, to make sure she looks her best."

"She enjoys exercise?" asked Catherine, suddenly intrigued by how little she knew about this person whose body she now inhabited. They looked so much alike that it was easy to forget that only her spirit had been transported through time. What was Kathryn doing in 1825 with *her* body? Somehow she hadn't thought to worry about it before.

"Kathy is a real go-getter," Annette was saying. "Always into causes— Save the Snail Darter one week, Handicapped Albino Skydivers the next. She'd jump on one bandwagon, then get lured away by another one, usually before she had a chance to do any good. She used to try to drag me along, but I was too lazy. We sort of anchored each other."

Catherine gave Annette a sympathetic smile, knowing that she was missing her friend again. But she couldn't say she was anxious to get back to 1825—not anymore. She toyed with the idea of telling Annette about that unexpected kiss last night and asking her advice, but decided against it. Logan had wanted to forget it, though she hadn't been able to.

"Perhaps Kathryn has found an outlet for her energies in my time," she finally suggested. "She has likely found many things there she would like to change." Annette agreed with a laugh and they went down.

"IT'S NOT FIVE YET, but what do you say we get an early start?" asked Logan with a glance at his wristwatch—a clever improvement over the pocket watch, Catherine thought—after they had finished an early dinner. Catherine had eaten little, for the luncheon had started late and she had consumed more there than was probably wise, especially considering the jeans she was now wearing.

"That would be fine," she replied. "I'll run upstairs for a sweater. I won't be a moment." True to her word, she was back in less than two minutes with Kathryn's lightweight white cardigan over her arm. "Ready when you are," she said airily, mimicking an expression she had heard Annette use.

"You know, I've been wanting to try out a Porsche," said Logan as they stepped outside. "What do you say we take your car?"

"My car?" Catherine almost squeaked.

"It hasn't been driven since you got here, has it? Oh." He started to chuckle. "Don't worry, I'll drive—that's the whole point."

"You mean you want to race in it?"

Now Logan looked incredulous. "Race it? Of course not. My racing buddy, Billy Clark, has got the car I'll be racing in. I just wanted to drive it to the track—if that's okay."

"Ah, certainly," replied Catherine with relief. Just for a moment there...

"Um—can I have the keys, then?" She froze. The keys? What keys? "Aren't they in your purse somewhere?" he prodded.

"Of... of course!" Catherine dug into the bag she carried, hoping he was right. He was. At the bottom was a ring of jingling keys. She pulled it out and offered it to him, hoping he would know which one was for the car.

He did, for he unlocked the passenger door and motioned her inside, went around to his own seat and fitted one of them into the keyhole by the wheel. "What a waste," he remarked, glancing down. "There ought to be a law against building a Porsche with an automatic transmission—but I can't say I'm surprised you'd have one."

Since she had no idea what he was talking about, Catherine examined the array of dials and indicators on the dashboard instead of answering while Logan started the engine. This time she didn't even have to brace herself for the roar.

"Will the car you will be racing travel more quickly than this one?" she asked once they were under way.

"Of course," said Logan, taking his eyes off the traffic to glance at her in surprise. "I did some street legal racing when I was younger, but stock cars are specially made to go much faster than even sports models like this. And dragsters can go as fast as 250 miles per hour."

"Two...my goodness!" Catherine gasped. Surely, that *must* be impossible!

"I know I've told you this stuff before—it sounds like you've blocked everything about racing out. Part of your therapy?"

"Therapy?"

"To shake your phobia. You mean you did it on your own? I'm impressed." She didn't know what to say, but after a moment he continued, "We'll be stopping in a few minutes to check on my sportsman car. I left it with Billy so his mechanic could go over it before tonight. It should be fueled up and ready to go by now."

When Catherine saw the car Logan would be racing, she realized no one could mistake it for the type normally driven on the streets. It was long, low and solid white, with huge tires and space for only the driver. In fact, the tires and steering wheel looked like the only things it had in common with the other automobiles Catherine had seen. The driver would sit in a sort of metal cage, which he would apparently have to climb into, since the car had no doors. The back end of the car was higher than the front and had transparent "fins" (as Logan called them) extending even higher, making it wedge-shaped.

Billy Clark was a friendly, stocky man with sandy hair and mustache, perhaps a year or two older than Logan. He greeted them effusively on their arrival. "Good to see you again, Logan," he exclaimed in obvious delight. "I told Carol, the track owner, you were coming, so don't be surprised if she makes a big deal over you. It's not often we get a big name at our little dirt track!"

"Big name? Me?" Logan was amusedly disbelieving.

"Shoot, yeah. Here, anyone who's ever NASCAR raced is a big name. For a while there, it looked like you had a shot at the Winston Cup."

"Yeah, well, I was taking myself too seriously then. Now it's just a hobby. Kathy, meet Billy. This is Kathy Monroe. She's a mover and shaker in Washington, and also an actress—or should I say, aspiring actress?" He glanced at Catherine.

"Aspiring," she said firmly.

"Aspiring, then. One day *she* may be a big name, who knows?" Billy seemed suitably impressed. "Well, we'd better get going. I'll follow you to the track. How are you getting your car there?"

"Joey took it down already. You ready?"

Catherine climbed back into the passenger seat, more eager than ever to see the race.

"He seems like a nice man," she commented as they turned onto Garners Ferry Road.

"He is. Always willing to help people. That's probably why he decided to become a police officer. That's what he does when he's not tinkering with cars."

They were leaving the downtown area now, and Logan began to drive faster. Delighted, Catherine watched trees and fence posts flash by, and then the car accelerated onto the freeway. Soon they were moving faster than the fastest racehorse and she exulted in the feel of it. She longed to ask Logan how fast they were going, but thought she had probably asked enough stupid questions for the time being. The scenery whipped past so quickly that she was at first unable to focus on anything, but after a few minutes she found that if she picked an object far enough away or far enough ahead, she could watch it long enough to make out what it was.

Speed Limit 55 MPH, she was able to read on a black-and-white sign before it was behind them. That must be their rate of speed! Now she knew, and without having to ask, she thought smugly. She vowed to become more observant in general, to speed her adaptation to 1994. In keeping with this resolve, she began to watch Logan carefully from the corner of her eye. He seemed to be driving effortlessly, with only one hand on the steering wheel while he tuned in music from the panel in front of him with the other. Could she ever learn to drive like that? So easily, so... casually? She would ask Annette to teach her, she decided.

Logan seemed unable to find the music he wanted, flipping through different songs much the way she had been able to change the channels on the television with the remote. She presumed this music mechanism worked much the same way. When he paused at a soft instrumental tune, she broke their lengthening silence.

"This is pretty. Can we listen to this?"

He glanced at her with that small frown that told her she had surprised him again—she fleetingly wondered what sort of music Kathryn liked—and took his hand away from the panel, placing it back on the steering wheel. "Sure."

"How far away is the racecourse?" she asked.

"It's in Gaston. We should be there in fifteen or twenty minutes. You're not regretting your decision already, are you?"

"Of course not. I was merely curious." She fell silent for a few moments, working out how far away Gaston must be from Columbia given their rate of speed. The answer amazed her. That would have been half a day's carriage ride in her day, given the usual state of the roads!

Logan broke the silence next. "Kathy, maybe it's just me, and you can tell me to go to hell if you want, but you seem, ah, different somehow. Is it anything you'd like to talk about?''

Alarm flared through her. So she wasn't fooling him, after all! But what could she say? Glancing at him, she saw that his face was set, as though he expected a rebuff. Hadn't Annette said that Kathryn regarded him as an interfering big brother? Doubtless she would have snapped at him for prying into her affairs. Catherine, however, longed to tell him everything—if only she could find the words that would ensure his belief.

"I see you don't," said Logan when she hesitated too long. "No problem. Just wanted you to know I was here if you needed an ear."

Oh, I do! she longed to cry. *If only I thought there was a chance you would believe me.* With a sigh, she turned back to the window. Soon she would tell him, she vowed. But it would have to be when they had more time, for a simple explanation would never do.

A few minutes later, Logan turned off the freeway onto a smaller highway, though their speed seemed about the same. There were more trees here, blocking her view of the more distant scenery. Finally Logan slowed and Catherine saw a sign that read "Columbia Speedway." Following the arrow to the left, they turned onto a much smaller paved road that, after a mile or so, turned to reddish dirt, the first dirt road Catherine had seen since the switch. In spite of the dust their passage raised, she felt a nostalgic pleasure in it.

The rutted, dusty road seemed to go on for some time, or perhaps it was simply that their speed was necessarily much less than it had been. Catherine realized that she was already used to going places more quickly than had been possible in 1825. She was getting spoiled.

Logan noticed her cynical expression and misinterpreted it. "Don't say I didn't warn you. It's too late to turn back now."

"I haven't the slightest desire to turn back," she assured him, earning another penetrating look from those handsome hazel eyes. He made no other comment, however, turning his attention back to the road, which certainly merited it.

Another turn, this time to the right, brought them to the speedway itself, where Billy was maneuvering his truck and the trailer into the waiting line of vehicles. Logan pulled in behind. When the line diverged to follow signs marked Grandstand or Pit, they stayed in the Pit line. Catherine presumed that those who went on to the Grandstand were spectators, as none of them towed cars. A blue-uniformed man came up to Logan's window, holding out a pen and pad.

"Here's where you sign your life away," he said jovially. Logan smiled and explained to Catherine that it was a liability waiver, which meant nothing to her, so she merely nodded.

After glancing at the signature, the police officer looked up. "Oh, so *you're* Logan Thorne! We heard you'd be here tonight. Give the folks a good show!" He waved them on.

"You *are* famous," remarked Catherine, only half teasing.

"And now I have to live up to it," said Logan wryly. "I shouldn't have let Billy talk me into this. Trust him to broadcast it!"

Logan paid their admission into the pit and they were motioned inside the red clay track, where two other men pointed out the area where the late-model cars were parked. They pulled to a halt next to the white race car on its trailer and Logan climbed out. He spoke to Billy for a minute, then the other man walked off with a cheery wave. As Catherine watched Logan unhitch the trailer and climb into his racer to back it onto the mud of the pit, she felt she should offer to help but had no idea what she might be able to do.

Instead, she looked around at the other cars and quickly decided that Logan's was the most attractive one there. The others had writing all over them: Ron's Plumbing, Katz Auto Parts and Earl's Garage were among the names she noticed. Logan's car, by contrast, was pure white with only a discreet number thirty-three written in silver-gray on each side.

Now Catherine was struck by the growing volume of engine noise in the pit. As more and more cars arrived, she wondered if she would be permanently deafened by the noise of the roaring engines. With difficulty, she resisted the urge to cover her ears.

"Let's go catch up with Billy," Logan shouted over the roar when he finished inspecting his own engine. She nodded and followed him through the sticky red mud, eagerly taking in the sights with only an occasional wince when a nearby car let out an especially ferocious sound. Billy was waving at them from another part of the pit, where more conventional-looking race cars were parked. "These are the hobby, super stock and pure stock cars," Logan informed her loudly, pointing out the different types as they walked over to Billy. Catherine examined the racers he indicated with interest.

Billy introduced Logan and Catherine to some friends, presumably other racers or perhaps even family members—she couldn't be sure, since she only heard about one word in every three. Logan and Billy talked for a few minutes, but from several feet away Catherine had no idea what they were saying.

"This your first time?" a woman Billy had introduced as Linda asked her.

"Yes," shouted Catherine in reply, not wanting these people to think her a mute.

The woman nodded knowingly. "Thought so. So, are you and Logan an item?"

Catherine blinked at the question and glanced quickly over her shoulder to be certain he hadn't somehow heard. Rather than shout an answer, not that she had one, she shrugged.

"Mind if I introduce him to my sister?" asked Linda when Catherine failed to lay claim to him.

Catherine was startled at the spurt of jealousy that shot through her. There was no civil way to object, though, so she shrugged again, which Linda took as permission. She walked over to another, younger woman whom Catherine had not met, but just then the engine roars subsided somewhat and a voice began booming announcements over the remaining noise.

"We'll start warm-up laps in a moment, folks, but first I want to welcome a driver you may have heard of from the NASCAR Grand Nationals...Logan Thorne!" There was applause and cheering, and Catherine noticed Billy beaming as if Logan were his own creation. After a moment the voice resumed, announcing that the late-model cars would have ten minutes to warm up before the super stocks took the track. Logan touched Catherine's arm to get her attention and she jumped.

"That's my cue," he said, able to speak without shouting for the moment. "Let's get back to my car, unless you'd rather stay here with Billy and his gang."

Catherine pondered the skepticism in his voice. He obviously liked Billy. Was he assuming she would not? From what she had learned about Kathryn, it seemed unlikely that this would be her sort of place, or these her sort of people.

"I'll watch from here, if you don't mind," she replied. His eyebrows shot up, but he only shrugged and strode quickly back to his racer. Drivers of all classes began revving up their motors in preparation for the warm-up laps, and the din was worse than before, the sound echoing and reechoing off the sides of the bowllike depression that housed the track. It sounded to Catherine like a continuous clap of thunder, directly overhead. Were these people used to it, or had they all lost their hearing long ago? It seemed not to bother them in the least.

"See that blue number twelve?" Billy shouted to her from a few inches away. She turned to see the car he indicated, circling the track at what seemed a perilous speed.

"That's Crazy Charlie," Billy yelled. "I should have told Logan to watch out for that guy. He's liable to do anything just to get attention for his sponsor. They don't seem to mind how many times he smashes up the car." As they watched, the blue car spun sideways on the turn before straightening out and continuing on at the same pace.

"Aren't those cars expensive?" Catherine asked.

"You bet! Thirty or forty thou, not to mention the tires, which are only good for one race. That's the rich man's class."

"What about everyone else?" She was genuinely curious.

"It still ain't cheap. I like to call dirt track racing a rich man's sport that poor people do." She smiled appreciatively, but he was pointing again. "There goes Logan," he shouted.

Catherine turned quickly and saw number thirty-three flash past. He seemed to be traveling just as quickly as Crazy Charlie, but he was negotiating the curves much more skillfully, with a minimum of skid.

"How fast are they going?" she asked Billy, who was donning a helmet for his own warm-up laps in a few minutes.

"Prob'ly no more than a hundred or so. They save the real speed for the heats. My God! Look at that!"

She whipped around to look. Crazy Charlie's number twelve had gone into a full spin on the curve. The other cars swerved violently to avoid hitting him, and a man standing on one of the huge tires that ringed the track waved a red flag frantically. Instead of slowing, the blue car spun faster, as if the driver were trying to keep it spinning.

Logan's white car came around the far curve then, moving faster than she had believed possible. Catherine saw Logan's car swerve first one way, then another, trying to stay clear of cars until he could stop. Another racer, a black one, skidded out of control on Logan's left. It careered into Logan's car rear-end first, knocking it into the path of Crazy Charlie's car, which still had not slowed its spin. The whirling blue car hit Logan's hard from the opposite direction. Slowly, each second seeming to take minutes, Catherine saw Logan's car flip entirely upside down on the track.

She barely heard the scream that broke from her throat—her only thought was to get to Logan. The announcer's voice was shouting something, but all of her attention was on the white car lying on its crumpled roof. She could see no movement inside it. Panicked, she began to run, only to slip and fall in the slick red mud. Pushing herself up with her arms, she saw that two men on three-wheeled vehicles had reached the scene of the accident and were carefully pulling Logan out.

A sizable crowd had gathered by the time she was able to reach the cluttered end of the track, but she shoved her way through, frantic to see Logan for herself. He was sitting on the ground, obviously conscious. She released her breath, only then aware that she had been holding it—and that she was shaking.

"Will he be all right?" she asked of the man examining Logan. The noise level was the lowest it had been since they had arrived at the speedway, and though her voice was weak and breathless, Logan looked up at her question.

"I'm fine, Kathy, just a bump on the head. But thanks for asking." He appeared shaken and pale—though no more so than Catherine had been. The man attending him must have noticed, too, for he hastened to reassure her.

"He'll be fine, ma'am, but he won't be racing tonight. He needs to go home to bed. He may experience some dizziness or a bad headache, so he shouldn't drive. If it still aches tomorrow, Mr. Thorne, you should go see your doctor and get a real examination."

"What, this doesn't count?" asked Logan.

"I'm just a medic," explained the man. "I don't think you've got a concussion, but a doctor ought to verify it. Let's get you out of this crowd now." The medic helped Logan to his feet, and Catherine was relieved to see he could stand without assistance.

He looked at Catherine again, appearing to really focus on her this time. "You're a mess," he said with a feeble smile.

"Yes, I . . . I fell." The other man handed her a cloth and she rubbed the worst of the mud from her hands and arms, then her knees. "Thank you." She handed it back and he left to check on some of the other drivers who had been involved in the pileup. "Are you certain you are all right?" she asked, turning back to Logan. "I've never been so frightened in my life!"

His smile became warmer, stirring an echoing warmth deep inside her. Though his voice was light, she could tell he was working to keep it that way. "Why, Kathy! I didn't know you cared. Does this mean—"

Billy came up to them then, his face still white. "Logan, man, don't scare me like that! I sure am glad you're okay. And don't worry about your racer—I'll take it back to my garage. It looks like it'll need some work, anyway. Where are the keys to your street car?"

Logan fished in his pocket and handed them to Billy. He still looked more than a little bit disoriented, though he tried to hide it.

"Here, ma'am," said Billy, handing the keys to Catherine. "You'll have to drive him home."

CHAPTER TEN

CATHERINE STARED at Billy Clark's retreating back, her mouth open. Drive Logan home? She was to drive Logan home? How on earth was she supposed to manage that? She had hoped to coax driving lessons out of Annette, but this was entirely different! Logan would know at once that something was wrong—and he was in no condition right now for complicated explanations.

She directed a searching look at the man by her side. Logan was standing, but he leaned heavily against the metal fence and still seemed rather dazed. Perhaps she could carry it off after all—and what an adventure it would be! She was a quick study, she told herself. In London she'd had to learn numerous dance steps, how to flirt with a fan, how to curtsy to persons of varying rank—all useless knowledge now. But she had watched Logan closely as he drove here earlier and was almost certain she had memorized his every move. Key in the ignition, turn it to the right, move the lever until the little arrow points to D. Then just steer with the wheel.

"Come, Logan, you can lean on me until we reach the car," she said. He nodded numbly. Their progress was slow, but by the time the warm-up laps were resumed, they had reached the Porsche. Catherine remembered with relief that Logan had backed the car in earlier, so at least she would not have to drive it in any direction but forward. Logan automatically headed for the driver's seat, but Catherine led him around to the passenger's side and helped him into the car. Once seated, he leaned back gratefully against the headrest and closed his eyes.

Catherine slid behind the steering wheel and closed the door, elation and nervousness warring within her. Which key was it? She glanced surreptitiously at Logan, but he seemed to be dozing. The third key she tried went in. That's the first step, she thought. Placing one foot firmly on the brake pedal, she turned the key to the right and the car roared to life. She eased her foot off of the brake and waited. Nothing happened. Now, what? She remembered the lever attached to the steering wheel. It resisted her attempt to move it at first, but finally, as she was getting desperate, it moved—and so did the car. Backward!

Catherine stepped hard on the brake, but not before the car bumped against the fence behind it. Logan stirred, but did not speak or open his eyes. The lever moved more easily now, and she was able to shift the indicator to the *D*, as Logan had done. She took a few deep breaths before easing her foot off the brake.

This time the car moved forward, very slowly. Catherine grinned. She'd be fine now. She was able to maneuver the Porsche out of the space it was in and turn it in the direction of the gate, still crawling along at no more than a mile an hour. Any time another car within sight moved, which was often, she hit the brake. Eventually, she made it to the Speedway exit. Once on the dirt road, she accelerated to five miles per hour, simply by keeping her foot off the brake. After a minute or two, she gained enough confidence to try the other pedal—lightly—and the car increased its speed.

The unpaved road seemed to go on forever—so long, in fact, that she began to wonder if she had missed a turn. Surely she wasn't going *that* much more slowly than Logan had? She was just considering the advisability of awakening Logan to ask directions when she saw the smooth, black pavement ahead. The ride became noticeably smoother. Pressing harder on the acceleration pedal, she held the car firmly to the middle of the road until she saw another vehicle coming in their direction—it was a truck! She gasped and swerved violently to the right, running up on the grassy shoulder to avoid a collision.

At that, Logan opened his eyes. "What ... what's going on?" he asked thickly.

"N-nothing," replied Catherine breathlessly. "I am simply driving you home, as Billy told me to."

Logan shook his head to clear it, then clutched it with a moan. Still, he sat up to look around. "Where are we?"

"On our way back to Columbia," said Catherine, thinking it unwise to go into detail.

"But why are we stopped on the side of the road?"

Catherine was already feeling foolish about her near-collision with the truck. Of course she should have been driving on the right-hand side, as Logan had. "I, ah, wasn't quite certain of my direction, but I didn't wish to wake you."

"Was I asleep? Maybe I have a concussion, after all. But I'm starting to feel better now."

"The doctor at the racetrack said you should see your own doctor tomorrow," she reminded him, not wanting the conversation to return to her driving.

"He wasn't a doctor. But he was probably right. I'll do that. Now, let's see, you need to follow this road out to 321, then take a right and follow it for several miles. I'll try to stay awake—the ramp onto the new highway is still poorly marked. Oh, and if you see any place that looks like it sells coffee, stop—I could sure use a cup."

Catherine nodded nervously and eased the car back onto the road. If he stayed awake, he would undoubtedly notice that she didn't know how to drive. On the other hand, if he went back to sleep she would just as undoubtedly get lost. What a predicament!

Keeping the car carefully to the right, Catherine dared to touch the accelerator pedal, bringing the car's speed to ten miles per hour. *Courage! I've driven carriages faster than this in London.* She eased the speedometer display up to fifteen, twenty, then twenty-five, as her confidence began to reassert itself.

"It's starting to get dark," commented Logan. "Why don't you turn on the headlights?"

"Headlights?" squeaked Catherine, trying not to panic.

"The little dial on the end of the turn-signal lever," said Logan, as if that would help. Catherine looked at the two levers extending from the steering column, then back at Logan, who was frowning curiously at her.

"Here." He reached across her and twisted the end of the left-hand lever, causing the display panel in front of her to glow softly. At the same time, she noticed a light on the dim road ahead and remembered seeing bright lamps shining on the fronts of cars they had passed last night. "I can't believe you've never driven this car at night before. How long have you had it?"

So she *hadn't* given herself away quite yet. "Not...not very long, I'm afraid. Thank you." She waited patiently until there was no car in sight in either direction and carefully turned onto the four-lane street. Centering the car between the dotted line and the shoulder, she pressed the accelerator until the indicator read forty miles per hour and glanced triumphantly at Logan. He had closed his eyes again.

'Twas just as well, she thought. The smooth stretch of highway beckoned to her, and with an exhilarating sense of freedom, Catherine increased their speed again until they were going fifty-five, as Logan had. She wondered how much faster this car could go, then decided there was only one way to find out. But as she began to accelerate further, a huge truck came up from behind them and roared past in the left lane. With a startled gasp, Catherine clutched at the steering wheel and swerved slightly to the right.

Logan opened his eyes. "Are you all right?" he asked. "You didn't have anything to drink at the track, did you?"

"Do you mean alcohol?" Did he think she was bosky? Surely her driving wasn't that bad! Her foot left the accelerator while she talked, and their speed slowed noticeably. *Oops!* She brought the speedometer back to fifty-five.

"That's it. Pull over," said Logan firmly. Reluctantly, Catherine obeyed, pulling onto the shoulder and stopping the car. "Put it in Park—that's *P*," he prompted when she hesitated. She moved the lever. "Now, tell me what's going on."

Catherine blinked at him. What could she say? "I...I suppose I'm not a very good driver," she offered.

"Not very good? I remember you were nervous behind the wheel before, but nothing like this. This is terrible. Are you sure you're not drunk?" His eyes narrowed.

"I think I've done very well for my first time!" she flared at him without thinking. He was accusing her of drinking liquor, something she had never done even in London.

"Your first time? What are you talking about?"

Suddenly she realized what she had said and desperately tried to retrieve the situation. "I mean...my first time driving on this road." She hoped it had grown dark enough by now that Logan couldn't see her face clearly. The blood was rushing to her cheeks and she feared her blush would betray her. She hated having to lie, especially to Logan.

"No, Kathy, I don't think that is what you meant. There's nothing especially remarkable about this stretch of highway." His voice was calm, almost analytical, and Catherine held her breath, afraid of what was coming next. "I knew something was wrong, that you'd changed. What kind of drugs are you taking?"

That was certainly not what she had expected. "Drugs?" Her surprise showed in her voice. "What do you mean?"

Logan stared heavenward, exasperated. "Okay, if you're not on drugs, you must be drunk—and I know for a fact it's not your first time drinking. So what the hell *did* you mean?"

Catherine felt a strange calm settle over her. It was time. "This is my first time driving a car. Any car."

Logan was silent for a long time. Finally, quietly, he said, "Kathy, are you crazy, or am I? I've seen you drive before. You know that. Have you developed a split personality or something? Now that I think of it, that might explain a lot."

"What exactly is a split personality?" asked Catherine curiously. Had something been discovered here in the future that might explain what had happened to her? Why hadn't Annette mentioned it?

"I'm no psychologist, but from what I've read it's where a person shifts from one personality to another, and may have no memories of what one personality did while acting as the other. They can be very different, even opposites, I think. There was a book out years ago about a woman who had sixteen different personalities, all distinct from one another."

Catherine was really interested now. "But how does it happen? I mean, how do one person's thoughts and memories come to be in another person's body?"

"Didn't you take any psychology at all? I'd have thought the theater arts department would have required it. There's not really another person's thoughts in there. The person just somehow divides the different facets of his or her personality."

Catherine was already shaking her head. "I don't think that's it, then. I don't have *any* of Kathryn's memories, but I have all of mine. And mine are of things she could never have experienced."

"Wait, wait!" Logan held up a hand. "What do you mean, 'Kathryn's memories'? Who, exactly, do you think you are?"

"Catherine Prescott. In a sense, I suppose I'm Kathryn Monroe's great-great-great-great-great-grandmother, though as I wasn't yet married when I left, I don't see how that can be. Perhaps she's my grandmother, instead.''

Logan leaned forward, supporting his forehead on his hands. ''I'm definitely not up to this conversation right now. I need a cup of coffee. Since you obviously can't drive, for whatever reason, I guess I'll have to.''

''But the doctor said—''

''He was just a medic. But don't worry, I definitely plan to go see a doctor first thing in the morning. I'm starting to think that bump on the noggin did more than give me a headache.''

Catherine slid over to the other seat as Logan went around the front of the car. She was relieved to see that he could walk without assistance now, but when he got in he sat down heavily.

''I'm still a little dizzy. We'll have to stop soon. Then I'll see if I can make it the rest of the way back to Columbia.''

Catherine felt guilty enough at not being able to drive, but now it was as if she had hit him on the head herself. She hated feeling so useless. *If I have to live in this time, I'm going to learn how to do it properly. I'll take driving lessons, I'll go to college, I'll...*

''There,'' said Logan suddenly. ''The Palmetto Lodge has a coffee shop. We'll stop here.'' He swung the car into the entrance, and Catherine marveled anew at his effortless handling of the vehicle. Now that she had tried it herself, she had an increased respect for his ability. No one would ever guess that he felt so poorly.

Catherine got out quickly so that Logan would not feel obliged to walk around the car for her, and together they approached the brightly lit dining room with its garish advertisements of breakfast specials painted on the windows. No one greeted them, and Logan led her to a corner booth away from the brightest lights. A heavyset blond waitress in an extremely short black skirt appeared from behind a swinging door and advanced on them.

"What c'n I getcha?" she asked loudly and saucily. Catherine saw Logan wince.

"Coffee for me, please," he replied in a soft voice that he probably hoped she would take as a cue. He looked at Catherine. "Kathy?"

"The same, please," she told the waitress, then turned her attention back to Logan. The bright lights revealed that he was paler than she had thought. "You look terrible," she commented as the waitress walked away.

"Thank you," he replied with a ghastly attempt at a smile. "I feel terrible."

"I'm sorry, I didn't mean—" Catherine began, then stopped. He didn't seem to be listening. "I really don't think you should drive any farther tonight," she finished. "Shall I send a message to my parents? Perhaps my father can fetch us."

"Send a message? You mean call them?" asked Logan, focusing on her face for the first time since sitting down. Catherine nodded, belatedly remembering the wonderful telephones she had seen Mrs. Sykes-Monroe use.

"What will you tell your father? That you don't remember how to drive a car? Just days after you drove here from Washington, D.C.?"

"Oh." She hadn't thought of that. Of course her parents would want to know why she couldn't drive Logan home herself.

"Besides," continued Logan, "I'd really rather your father didn't find out about my smashup. He always said I was nuts to race, and I'd hate to give him such a great opening for an 'I told you so.'"

"He doesn't like your racing? I didn't know that." Catherine realized that she really knew very little about Logan.

"I guess he never mentioned it to you—it was sort of a friendly feud between him and my father from when they were both fresh out of college and working for the same company. My dad was crazy for racing and used to try to get your dad interested, but he'd have nothing to do with it. He had just married your mother, and I imagine she had something to say about it. Anyway, whenever they saw each other, your dad would give mine a hard time about racing. Dad quit eventually, but not before I was bitten by the bug."

"Did he teach you to race?"

"No, he died before I was old enough to drive." Logan was looking at her strangely again—obviously, Kathryn knew that. "When I came to live at your house, your dad did all he could to discourage me, but I was so determined he finally gave in. I guess I saw it as a tribute to my father or something, following in his footsteps."

"Was he an architect, too?"

Logan nodded. "But he always preferred to work for a development firm—before he died he and your father became partners. I broke with tradition by staying independent. I'm too much of a rebel to fit in with the suit-and-tie crowd on a regular basis. It's not my style."

"Being tied down, you mean." Catherine wasn't sure that she hadn't learned more than she wanted to. Logan was obviously a man who valued his freedom.

"Right." He attempted a laugh, but winced and took a sip from the steaming cup the waitress had just deposited in front of him. "Ah, that's better."

"You two want a room or is the lady going to drive?" asked the waitress, eyeing Logan critically.

"We'll let you know," said Logan coolly, pointedly dismissing her. Logan grimaced after her as she sauntered off. "She thinks *I'm* drunk." He turned back to Catherine. "Speaking of which, I think we'd better continue the discussion we started in the car." He set down his cup and watched her expectantly.

There was no concealing darkness here, and Catherine knew that Logan could see her rising color perfectly well. "I, ah, it's rather hard to explain," she floundered.

Logan arched an eyebrow, but spoke gently. "Just try to tell me what you think is going on, in the order you remember it."

Catherine nodded and took a sip of her own coffee. It was almost as good as Alice's, and much better than they'd had in 1825. That thought steadied her, giving her the necessary link with her past to proceed. "I know this will sound unbelievable, but please don't think I'm mad," she began. "Despite appearances, I am not Kathryn Monroe. I am Catherine Prescott—that's Catherine with a *C*—from 1825. Somehow Kathryn and I...switched places, or rather times. It happened the night of the costume ball."

Folding her napkin over and over, she tried to choose her words carefully. "There was a similar ball being held in my home—the same house, by the way—that same night in 1825 in honor of General Lafayette's visit to Columbia. Only it wasn't a costume ball, of course. I'm certain that I was still in my own time as I was dressing for the reception, as Nancy was there to help me and she did not come forward. But when I went downstairs, things had...changed." She stopped toying with her napkin to look Logan squarely in the eye. "You came up and spoke to me just as I was noticing that the candles had somehow become light bulbs!"

Logan had to struggle against the instinct to believe her. It would explain everything so easily—the differences in her mannerisms, her speech, the new softness to her personality. In fact, it would explain everything that had confused—and attracted—him. She *did* seem like a completely different person. But time travel? He shook his head.

"I'm sorry. It's just...too incredible. This all must be in your head." He felt a twinge of regret. Whatever *had* happened to her, he was inclined to think the change was for the better.

"I told you it would be hard to believe." Surprisingly, Catherine didn't seem at all upset at his response. "Annette said the same thing, until she saw the diary. It is too

bad it was stolen, for it might prove my story to you, as well.
Perhaps if she were to tell you what it said—''

Logan's brows shot up. "Are you saying Annette is in on
this, too? Does she believe your story, or is this some prank
you two cooked up to make me look stupid? Are you still
carrying a grudge from two years ago?"

"I have only known Annette three days," said Catherine, "but I don't believe she is a woman who would inten-
tionally hurt anyone, do you?" She paused. "What
happened between you and Kathryn that she would still be
angry?"

Logan debated briefly with himself before speaking. "All
right. If your story is true, you really don't remember. And
if it's a hoax, at least it gives me a chance to tell you my side
of the story." He leaned back. "Like I said, after my father
died, your dad—or rather, Kathy's," he corrected with exaggerated politeness, "pretty much took over my upbringing. My parents had divorced years before and my mom had
remarried, so she didn't object. I never got along well with
Randy, her second husband, anyway. So I moved in, except
for holidays and one weekend a month."

"How old were you then?" asked Catherine.

"Sixteen. You, or rather Kathy, was eleven. I became a
sort of honorary big brother, and I'll admit I was probably
a lot more protective than most real brothers would be. I
think I felt like I owed it to your dad. Mr. Monroe pulled
some strings to get me into a top architectural school, since
my grades hadn't been all that great. I paid him back by
graduating at the head of my class."

He paused to take another sip of coffee. "Anyway, the
blowup that made Kathy so mad was due mainly to that
protective attitude of mine. I'd visited her two or three times
at William and Mary when I happened to be in southern
Virginia, and I dropped in one evening during her senior
year to watch her in a show. She invited me to the cast party
afterward and I went. Bad idea."

"What happened?" Catherine asked. She was hanging on to his words as though she'd really never heard any of this before, Logan noticed.

"Oh, nothing that doesn't go on at most college parties, I guess—especially theater parties. But I couldn't handle seeing Kathy in that setting—the booze, the pot, the guys coming on to her. I realize now I overreacted, but at the time I saw it as my sacred duty to save her from herself. She didn't appreciate my effort, to put it mildly. I made her leave, and on the way back to her dorm we had a shouting match. Some pretty harsh things were said on both sides— things I, at least, regretted pretty soon afterward." He stared down into his empty cup.

"Were you and Kathryn very close before that?" Catherine's voice was sympathetic.

"Oh, probably not as close as I tried to pretend, to justify my hero role. We really never had that much in common. Outside of architectural school, I was never particularly ambitious. I like to take time to smell the flowers, enjoy life. Kathy was more driven, an idealist—especially for her endless causes. I used to call her and her fellow activists TWERPS. She hated that." He chuckled at the memory.

"Twerps?" echoed Catherine.

"Those Who Enjoy Routinely Protesting Something," explained Logan. "And of course she hated the very idea of racing and used to razz me about that to get even. And she was always obsessed with clothes, which I'm not, obviously—but I guess that's true of most women."

"It's not true of me," said Catherine. "Though you are probably right. Even in 1825, every woman I knew was passionately interested in fashion. I was quite a disappointment to my mother in that area—among others."

Logan gave her a long, considering look that brought color to her cheeks again. Then he smiled. "Do you know how tempting it is to believe you? These past few days have been great. If you're crazy, I almost hope the cure doesn't take."

Catherine returned his smile. "I'm not crazy. I'm certain I can convince you of that somehow."

"So, you two want a room or not?" broke in the brassy voice of the waitress, effectively shattering the mood.

Reluctantly, Logan drew his wondering gaze away from Catherine. "No, just the check. I think we can make it home now. Unless you'd rather stay?" he asked softly as the waitress took his money to the cash register. The idea of sharing a motel room with this new Kathy, this Catherine, aroused feelings in Logan that made him feel more than a little bit guilty. Of course, if she really *were* telling the truth—

"Stay? Here, you mean?" Catherine looked around.

"It's a motel, too. Or maybe I should say an inn."

Her blush returned vividly and he savored it. "Oh! I...can you still not drive?"

"I was teasing," he said. "Let's go." Logan saw the uncertainty on her face as she rose and felt shaken by a sudden conviction that she had told him the truth. It stayed with him as they got into the car and headed back to town.

"You said you could convince me your story is true," he said after they'd driven in silence for several minutes. "How were you going to do that?"

Catherine had been berating herself for feeling more disappointed than relieved that they were not to spend the night together, but at his question she turned quickly, eager to abandon that line of thought. "Perhaps if Annette could verify it. She read my diary, you see, before it was stolen along with her purse."

"Your diary? What are you talking about?"

She told him about her conversation with Annette that first night, culminating with the discovery of Kathryn's faded handwriting in her old diary and Annette's subsequent belief. "So I thought perhaps if Annette were to tell you about it from her point of view..." She trailed off. It sounded incredible even to her. How could she expect him to believe it without physical evidence?

But Logan only said, "Then Annette has known about it from the start?"

Catherine nodded eagerly. "And she's been ever so much help to me. She showed me how to apply makeup, told me about credit cards and the mall, even procured history books for me from the library so that I would not give myself away. She seemed to think anyone else I told would think I was mad—even you."

He was silent for a long time, until they were pulling into the drive of the Monroe house. "Suppose you are telling the truth..." he said finally. Catherine's spirits soared. Then he continued, his words measured as though he found them painful. "That would mean Kathy, the Kathy I've known practically as a sister, is trapped back in the early nineteenth century. If that's the case, shouldn't we try to find a way to get her back?"

Catherine's heart fell. Of course Logan would think first of Kathryn, the girl he'd known since childhood. Why hadn't she considered that? Because she'd been too blind, too wrapped up in her attraction to Logan, she admitted to herself as she accompanied him into the house.

Though it was no later than ten, everyone had apparently retired already. Together they climbed the stairway to the second floor, Catherine as deep in thought as Logan seemed to be. As they reached the landing she suddenly thought she heard the grandfather clock beside her strike, as though from a distance. At the same time she felt a strange pull, and the sensation that she held a candle in her hand.

Alarmed, Catherine moved away from the clock, clutching at Logan's arm. Immediately, the pulling stopped and to her relief Logan still stood beside her on the landing.

"Is something wrong?" he asked as she released his arm.

If she told him the truth, or what she thought might be the truth—that she and Kathryn had nearly exchanged places again—would he demand that she go through with it? She wasn't ready, not yet!

"No, I . . . I just missed my footing," she said quickly, surprised at how easily the lie came to her. "Good night, Logan." She turned away and hurried up the remaining stairs, putting as much distance as possible between her and the clock.

CHAPTER ELEVEN

KATHRYN JUMPED BACK from the clock, nearly dropping the candle she held. Unable to sleep for worrying about Ryan, she'd decided to go down to the kitchen for a snack. But just as she passed the clock, striking the hour of ten, she'd felt the oddest sensation . . . that there were bright lights around her, and that someone—Logan?—stood beside her on the landing.

She and Catherine had nearly exchanged places again, she was almost sure of it. But instead of the satisfaction she'd have felt only yesterday at the prospect of returning to her own time, the idea now disturbed her deeply. She couldn't leave now, after putting Ryan in such danger—at least not before she could make amends. In sudden panic that it might happen again, she hurried on down the stairs, away from the clock.

RYAN DID NOT APPEAR at the Prescott house at all the next day, and Kathryn spent the time in an agony of self-recrimination and uncertainty. Should she make some attempt to warn him? Or might that in itself put him in danger?

When Jonas, the butler, finally announced him just after tea the following day, Kathryn felt like hugging the butler in relief. Even discovering the worst would be better than the anxiety she'd lived with for the past twenty-four hours. If he were here, surely things couldn't be quite as bad as she'd been imagining.

"Would you care to take a brief ride, Miss Prescott?"
Ryan asked after exchanging pleasantries with her parents.
She nodded quickly, unable to trust her voice, and flew upstairs to change into her habit. Had she imagined something strange in his manner? No matter. She would confess
her whole plot as soon as they were away from the house
and he could assure her, as she had assured Priscilla, that no
real damage had been done. At least she'd be able to sleep
again. She glanced at herself in the mirror, wishing vainly
for something to cover the dark circles under her eyes, before hurrying down the stairs.

Once outside, Ryan tossed her up into the saddle without
a word and then mounted his horse, spurring it into a brisk
trot that she was obliged to match. Studying his profile,
Kathryn thought Ryan looked rather grim. She briefly debated postponing her confession, but that would be cowardly. Of course she'd look foolish, confessing to spreading
rumors about him, but putting it off wouldn't change that—
it would only make it harder.

They were nearing the spot at the edge of town where he
had kissed her almost a week ago, and her heart began to
beat faster, remembering. Would he be completely dis-
gusted by what she told him? As he pulled his horse to a stop
and dismounted, helping her down from the saddle as well,
she tried to look contrite as she turned to face him.

"Ryan, I—" she began, but he cut her off angrily.

"You promised that I could trust you. What a fool I was
to believe the word of a woman!"

Kathryn could only stare, dumbfounded.

"No doubt you are wondering how I discovered your
treachery so quickly," he said mockingly. "It is lucky for me
that I am on such good terms with my workers—a trait that
you pretended to admire. They discovered what was afoot
from one of the Allerby slaves and told me at once."

Kathryn began to shake her head helplessly, but before
she could speak, he went on.

"Did you waste even an hour after I left you? Jonathan Allerby departed for Charleston today to find whether your tale was true. I don't know what he will discover, but I venture to fear that Columbia, nay, South Carolina, may no longer be safe for me. Certainly it will not be safe for Isaiah."

"You ... are you leaving?" Kathryn managed to gasp.

"I may well have to, thanks to you."

Suddenly she comprehended the enormity of his accusation. "You actually think I told Mr. Allerby about your part in that uprising?" she demanded, outraged.

"Do you deny you've given the Allerbys reason to suspect me?"

"I ... well ..." Her anger abruptly evaporated as she realized that what he accused her of was true, in a sense.

"Just as I thought," he said when she hesitated. "To think I believed you to be a kindred spirit, sympathetic to what I am trying to do."

"But I am!" she cried. "It's not what you think, Ryan—you've got to believe me!"

"I have done enough of that, I think," he replied tersely. "It is as I suspected all along—women of your class are good for only one thing."

With that, he grabbed her by the shoulders and forced his lips down upon hers. It was nothing like the gentle, sensual kiss they had shared before. This was a punishing, brutal kiss that conveyed his anger more clearly than words. He ground his teeth against her lips, bruising them, and suddenly Kathryn's fighting spirit awoke. She struggled, but he only gripped her tighter, pressing his fingers cruelly into the flesh of her upper arms. In desperation, she bit his lip and he released her abruptly, causing her to stumble. He made no move to help her, but she caught herself before she fell. She was panting with fury.

"How dare you, you bastard!" Her voice trembled with shock and anger. "First you insult me, and then you attack me! I can't *believe* I lost a night of sleep over you, you son of a bitch! And to think I passed up a chance to go back—"

Amazingly, Ryan grinned. "Just where did you pick up such language, Miss Prescott? Not from your mother, I'm certain. Go back where? And you say you lost sleep over me?"

"That's none of your damned business!" snapped Kathryn, still too angry to worry over her near slip.

Ryan clicked his tongue and shook his head in mock sternness at her swearing. "Strange what temper can reveal about a person. I wouldn't have thought it of you, Catherine." Her anger seemed to defuse his. "But you *will* tell me what you meant, you know."

"You mean you're willing to listen to me now?" she asked caustically. He inclined his head, motioning for her to proceed. She glared at him before speaking. "I did *not* tell Mr. Allerby, or *anyone* else what you told me the other day. And I think it's despicable that you would accuse me of it without even asking me first!"

"Granted," he said mildly. "Go on. Exactly what *did* you tell them that aroused their suspicions?"

Kathryn's confidence wavered as she remembered that she was far from innocent, but she forged on, still buoyed by anger. "It was the night before we went to Fair Fields, at the Allerbys' dinner party. I got a friend to help me to spread some rumors about your having been married before, and about her, um, dying mysteriously."

Ryan gave a shout of laughter. "So *that's* where that story came from. Now, why might you have spread such a rumor, Miss Prescott?" He looked smug now, which irritated Kathryn even further.

"Because I had no intention of being railroaded into marriage with you," she informed him. "I thought a rumor like that might make my parents think twice about it."

He blinked. "I see. You are quite a strong-minded young lady, my dear. I salute you. But why should Mr. Allerby have gone to Charleston to investigate such balderdash?"

"Well, I'm afraid that's not exactly what he's going to investigate. My friend got a little carried away with the plan and decided to, ah, elaborate. She meant to imply that you still had a wife living in Charleston but was so vague about it that Mrs. Allerby thought she meant you were a bigamist as well as a murderer. And when Mrs. Allerby asked me if it was true, I thought she meant the mysterious death story and confirmed it. I'm sorry, Ryan. I had no idea at the time that you *really* had something to hide."

"So you saddled me with two fictitious wives instead of just one. As I also dislike being forced to do anything, I really cannot condemn you for your motives." His mouth twisted in a half smile. "But I'm afraid that doesn't undo the very real damage. The fact remains that Isaiah and his wife may well be in danger, whether I am or not. Something will have to be done."

"I'll help," exclaimed Kathryn impulsively. "Anything I can do. Just tell me."

He gave her another long, searching look. "I suppose that *would* be appropriate. Very well. I have an idea, but the details must be worked out. When that is done, I shall let you know and hold you to that offer."

"I said anything and I meant it. You can count on me—I promise." Her look challenged him to disbelieve her.

KATHRYN HEARD NOTHING from Ryan for three more days, when he came to dine at Mrs. Sykes-Prescott's insistence. "I regret that circumstances have kept me so long from your side, Miss Prescott," he said gallantly when he arrived, bending over Kathryn's hand.

Mrs. S-P beamed at them both, her delight obvious. She had been vocal in her concern during Ryan's absence that he might have transferred his attentions elsewhere.

Catching the twinkle in Ryan's eyes Kathryn concluded that his efforts on Isaiah's behalf had been successful thus far. "I forgive you, Mr. James," she replied in the same spirit, "but I will want to hear your excuses later."

The Prescotts settled down in the parlor for some before-dinner conversation with their guest, which consisted largely of a discussion of the weather and its effects on the probable cotton yield. Kathryn tried to hold up her end of the conversation, but was burning with curiosity about Ryan's plans. She devoutly hoped they'd have a chance for a private word before he left.

That wish was not granted, mainly because both Prescotts were so eagerly solicitous. Mrs. S-P, in particular, continued to be scrupulously attentive to any need Mr. James might have, real or imagined. Was his turkey spiced as he liked it? Was it quite hot enough? If not, Cook could easily rewarm it for him. Kathryn would have been writhing with embarrassment if she hadn't found the whole situation so amusing.

Finally, after what seemed an endless meal, Ryan prepared to leave. "Might I call in the morning to take Miss Prescott riding?" he inquired of his host, almost on the doorstep. "We were in a fair way to making a custom of it before plantation business forced my absence this last week."

"Certainly, my boy, certainly," agreed Mr. Prescott with a heartiness that echoed his wife's smiling nod. "I'm not one to stand in the way of young love, you know!" He followed this with a guffaw that brought Kathryn close to a blush. She kept reminding herself that these were not her real parents, so their behavior did not reflect on her. It helped a little, even though Ryan didn't know the difference. She was also able to console herself that tomorrow morning she would finally find out everything she had been dying to know.

Kathryn was up much earlier than usual the next day, and had already washed and put on fresh underthings before Nancy even thought to look in on her.

"My habit please, Nancy," she replied briskly to the maid's surprised query.

Mrs. Sykes-Prescott was equally surprised to come downstairs a short time later to find her daughter already finishing a breakfast of eggs and toast. "You seem unusually eager to ride today, Cathy," she commented with a knowing smile.

Kathryn smiled back, in charity with the world. "Cook was kind enough to get me some breakfast when she made the servants', Mother. I'll tell her you've come down."

She walked quickly through the pantry and into the kitchen with its open brick oven and black iron stove sharing the same chimney. The smells were heavenly, though the heat was rather oppressive. A pump on the opposite wall was being plied by Alma, the girl who emptied the chamber pots; she apparently did double duty as some sort of under kitchen maid. As Kathryn watched, she filled a large pot with water and proceeded to scour pans and utensils in it.

Again, it struck her forcibly that Alma and the others were slaves—property—and had no choice but to perform such unpleasant chores. A wave of frustrated indignation swept over her, making it difficult for her to control her voice as she delivered her message to Cook. That done, Kathryn escaped through the side door into the cool morning air before she could betray herself.

Breathing deeply of the fresh, floral-scented air, she composed herself somewhat and headed for the stables to have her horse saddled, so she'd be ready whenever Ryan showed up. She walked down the center aisle of the building between the rows of stalls, stopping occasionally to stroke a curious, velvety nose, wondering why she'd let ARF convince her to give up riding.

Jeller was pouring out feed into various buckets at the opposite end of the stables, and Kathryn waited until he paused in his task to ask for her mare to be saddled and brought around. He didn't seem surprised to see her there, which told her that Catherine had been no stranger in the stables. She should have guessed that before, if she'd thought about it.

She was mounted and waiting, walking her mare slowly around the circular drive, when Ryan arrived. He smiled and waved as he trotted up, obviously still in high spirits, and called out, "Nearly as eager as I am this morning, I see!"

Kathryn didn't deny it. She had to admit she'd missed him more than she had expected to these past few days. There were times she actually found herself wondering whether it was her past life that was all a dream.

"Where are we headed?" she asked, appreciatively eyeing his deep blue cutaway coat and loose white shirt, open at the throat. She thought the style emphasized his masculinity in a way 1990s fashions were incapable of. And there was something about a man on horseback....

"In the general direction of Fair Fields, though we're not going so far," he replied. "I want you to meet someone."

He smilingly refused to answer any questions she put to him, replying to her increasingly frustrated queries about his plans with calm statements about the weather or the scenery.

"Ryan James, I'm warning you...."

"Do you hear that squirrel chattering, Miss Prescott? Little fellow sounds frightfully upset about something, doesn't he?"

She gave it up in disgust. Mercifully, they rode no more than fifteen or twenty minutes before he turned his horse onto an inconspicuous path and reined in at a small clearing well hidden from chance passersby. Pulling up behind him, Kathryn saw that two people were there before them, a man and a woman.

"This is Isaiah, Miss Prescott, and his wife, Coffee," said Ryan formally, swinging down from his horse.

Isaiah was a huge bear of a man with bushy, curling hair over his head and lower face; the little skin that showed was a rich mahogany. By contrast, Kathryn thought Coffee inappropriately named. Dwarfed by her husband, she was petite, pretty...and white. True, her hair was tightly curled, but her complexion was no darker than Kathryn's own, or at least what her own had been in 1994. Her features were delicate, refined, almost aristocratic, and her eyes a dark blue-gray instead of brown.

Kathryn dismounted and came forward to greet these two people she'd inadvertently endangered. "I am truly pleased to meet you," she said, covering her embarrassment and curiosity with a social smile, "though I apologize for the circumstances that make it necessary. Perhaps now Mr. James will tell me how I can help to make amends." She shot him a speaking glance.

He returned it with a grin. "Certainly. When you hear the plan, I think you will understand why I wanted you to meet Isaiah and Coffee first." He led her by the hand to a stump, seating her as graciously as if it were a drawing-room chair before continuing.

"I have managed to book passage from Savannah to New York for a Mrs. Murray and her servant. She will tell anyone who asks that she is going there to meet her husband—not so very far from the truth. I chose Savannah over Charleston for two reasons: first, Isaiah is known in Charleston, and even with the changes we shall make in his appearance he might easily be recognized there. Second, any pursuit is more likely to be directed toward the north than the south."

Isaiah and his wife nodded in agreement.

"Coffee will pose as this Mrs. Murray?" prompted Kathryn.

"Yes, and that is where you come in," said Ryan. "She will need a wig and clothing suitable to a lady of quality, and I cannot procure such items without provoking unwelcome questions. You can. Will you?"

"Of course," said Kathryn, lifting her chin at the challenge in his voice. "I'm willing to do much more, if necessary. I don't go back on my word." She turned her back on him and spoke to Coffee. "I can't believe anyone would take you for a slave, anyway."

"It is my hair that gives me away, miss. Otherwise, I could pass," said Coffee, surprising Kathryn with her cultured accent. "I am at least three-quarters white, and possibly more." At Kathryn's questioning glance she continued, "My father was a Charleston rice planter who took my mother against her will. Her mother had been similarly used. I never heard about my great-grandmother. I shouldn't say so to a young lady like yourself, but a great many slaves have white blood through such means."

"But it makes them no less slaves," said Ryan.

Kathryn felt an impotent rage boil up within her at the tale. She had considered herself a feminist for as long as she could remember. Slavery was evil enough, but that women could be routinely raped, while society turned a blind eye—!

Ryan continued, "Isaiah here was already a free man when I met him in Charleston, and he still is, of course, but no one in Columbia knows it, as he has posed as my slave since we arrived. He will carry his free papers concealed for use in New York, or for any unforeseen emergency that might arise before they reach port."

"But won't they be looking for him by name?" asked Kathryn, fighting down her anger.

"Yes, but we must hope that the news will not travel as fast as Isaiah and Coffee will, especially to the south."

Kathryn nodded, realizing that she'd been imagining the type of manhunt that was possible in the 1990s, where information could be broadcast any distance in an instant. Of course it would be easier to evade capture here in the past. But Ryan's next words showed her the error of that assumption.

"It is a good thing the slave catchers were here only a month ago and are unlikely to be back before high summer. I don't like to think of what might happen if they were to set their bloodhounds on your trail. They'd have to start from my land, though, which I would never allow."

"Bloodhounds?" asked Kathryn faintly.

"You didn't see them?" asked Ryan, his disgust clearly visible. "I thought the whole town turned out for the spectacle. They claim their dogs can track a runaway slave through swamp or stream, even on horseback. They are none too worried about keeping up with the hounds, either, which means a fugitive is as likely to be torn to shreds as returned to his master. Most reward notices read Dead or Alive. Do you mean to say your father had no runaways for them to hunt down this time?"

"He...he didn't mention it to me." Kathryn felt ill from the pictures conjured up by his words. Abolitionist though he was, Ryan was a product of his age, hardened to the horrors of slavery as she knew she'd never be. "Will you live in New York?" she asked Coffee, anxious to change the subject.

Isaiah answered, his accent broader than his wife's. "For a whiles, we might. Safer there than here, anyways, 'specially since we won't have a interested master paying for a search. Might be we'll go on to Canada, though. Can't no one touch us in Canada. It's a free country."

It's a free country. Kathryn had heard that phrase all her life, applied to the United States. But right now, nearly fifty years after the signing of the Declaration of Independence, it still wasn't free for everyone, she realized.

"We'll just do as the Lord directs," said Coffee serenely. "He's taken us this far safely, and He'll not fail us." She showed no trace of fear for what lay ahead, and Kathryn found herself envying the woman's steadfast courage born of faith.

"The ship sails in just over three weeks, so we haven't much time," Ryan broke into her thoughts. "Can you arrange to get the wig and gown by the day after tomorrow?"

"Yes." Kathryn felt a thrill at being able to do her small part against slavery—a thrill that went beyond any she'd felt at her various protest rallies in college or even in Washington. This was a cause far more worth fighting for than any of the others. "How will I get them to you?"

"I'll come to take you riding again the morning after next. If you can have the things in a bundle in the stables before I arrive, I'll take care of the rest." Kathryn nodded, and Ryan turned to the others. "You'll be out of Columbia that afternoon and out of South Carolina in two more days. You already know the best routes to Savannah, Isaiah. Coffee will do any talking, but she should say as little as possible to anyone. Her accent is good, but not perfect. You can read or write something if you have to, can't you, Coffee?"

Isaiah answered proudly, "Yes, I taught her 'most as soon as we were married. She can read anything now, and write as well as any white woman—better than most."

Coffee nodded in agreement, her eyes modestly lowered. "And you mustn't worry, Ryan. If we are caught, we'll not admit to any schooling on your lands. We were educated in Charleston."

"I'm hardly worried about that," said Ryan with a laugh. "I've always allowed my workers, slave or free, to learn anything they please, and to hell with the law. You two go on and make whatever preparations you can in the next two days. We'd best not meet again before then."

Coffee thanked Kathryn graciously for her help, which made her twitch with guilt since her own foolishness had made it necessary, and the couple left the clearing, heading back to Fair Fields on foot.

"I don't dare lend them a horse yet," commented Ryan as they disappeared among the trees. "It might prompt someone to question them, and I'd rather they were not noticed at all before they leave town two days hence." He turned to Kathryn, his eyes glinting dangerously. "Isaiah and Coffee have been happy here. I suppose we must be thankful at least that they haven't any children." His tone was accusing and Kathryn bristled defensively, knowing that the rebuke was largely deserved.

"I'll remind you that I didn't know about any of this when I spoke to the Allerbys, Mr. James. I've promised to do all I can to make up for it, so you don't have to keep treating me like some kind of low-life traitor."

"I'll reserve judgment until after your part is played," responded Ryan with a cynical twist to his mouth. "Don't forget that once you've helped this pair to escape you'll be as guilty as I in the eyes of the law. I can't help but wonder whether a gently nurtured young lady like yourself won't grow squeamish at putting her hand to such a task."

Kathryn lifted her chin defiantly. "Wonder away, Mr. James. You'll find you never had so able or willing an accomplice in your life."

They were standing face-to-face in the clearing, and Kathryn suddenly became aware of their isolation. Coffee and Isaiah's footsteps had faded away, leaving a deep silence broken only by her own hurried breathing. The fire in her eyes kindled an answering spark in Ryan's and suddenly she was in his arms.

"God, I hope you mean that, Catherine," he murmured against her lips. "You move me as no woman ever has, whatever your motives. To find that you truly share my ideals would be heaven indeed."

Kathryn did not answer, but pressed her body, her lips, to his in response. His hands explored her back, her waist, the

curve of her breast, as hers slid under his coat to caress the
hard lines of his body. Desire shot through her in an agonizing flame as he dropped his head to play along her throat
with his lips. Gasping, she brought his mouth back to her
own and kissed him deeply, her tongue intertwining with his.
He pulled her even closer and she heard a low moan shud-
der through his body. Her fingers, still trapped against his
chest, fumbled with his shirt.

Ryan loosened his hold to stare at her incredulously, a
question hovering on his lips. Instead of asking it, however, he blinked and looked around. "What are we doing?" he asked as if to himself. Thoroughly aroused,
Kathryn slid her hands up to his shoulders to draw him in
for another kiss, but he released her as though unaware of
her intent. He was flushed and breathing hard, but had
himself under control now.

"Time for this later," he said almost roughly, but Kathryn thought his harshness was directed more at himself than
at her. Still, it brought her to her senses and she realized how
close she had come to committing herself irrevocably to this
man, by the standards of the time. He was right.

"Come," he said more gently. "We both have work to
do."

CHAPTER TWELVE

"I AM SO GLAD you are finally beginning to show a healthy interest in your appearance," remarked Mrs. Sykes-Prescott the next morning when Kathryn told her she planned to shop for some new gowns and accessories. "I vow, before you left for London I had quite despaired of your ever becoming a young lady of fashion. You just didn't seem to *care*. And even the first week or two you were back, I thought nothing had changed. But now, I see I was mistaken. And you have done wonders with that French lace you bought. Would you like me to come along and advise you? I had planned to call on poor Mrs. Witchet today, but I daresay she will be just as happy to see me tomorrow."

"No, Mother, that won't be necessary," broke in Kathryn quickly. "I've already arranged to meet Priscilla downtown." It wouldn't suit her purpose at all to have a curious mother along. Or Priscilla, either, for that matter. She hoped she wouldn't actually run into her friend while shopping.

"I'll not change my plans, then. You young girls won't want an old woman along listening to all your gossip."

Relieved to have dissuaded her so easily, Kathryn protested that Mrs. S-P wasn't at all old, as was obviously expected, and prepared to leave.

With Jeller in tow, Kathryn went first to the same shop where she'd bought the French laces and was greeted as enthusiastically as before by the proprietor. She was pleased, and a bit surprised, to discover that he had a fair selection of ready-made dresses in stock, in four different sizes.

"The very latest from Europe, so they say!" the hovering Mr. Porter assured her. "All they require is a nip here or a tuck there to fit any figure!"

Kathryn rather doubted this last claim, but chose a patterned cotton and a luscious lavender silk for herself before selecting Coffee's disguise. "And that black-and-gray one, please, Mr. Porter," she decided. It was both discreet and elegant, and would make Coffee look even fairer.

"An excellent choice, Miss Prescott, excellent. The finest summer satin. It should suit you admirably!" he exclaimed, making Kathryn decide never to trust this man's taste. Black and gray were *not* her colors. She chose some gloves and a bonnet to match the dresses and waited while they were wrapped up in brown paper.

"Thank you so much, Mr. Porter," she said sincerely. "It seems I can always trust you to have whatever I need." The shopkeeper bowed and smiled as she went out the door.

Her next stop was the wig-maker's, and she hoped to arouse as little suspicion there as she had in the dry goods store. The woman behind the counter, who was obviously wearing her own wares in a glaring shade of titian, did not seem to know Kathryn—or Catherine, rather—which she took as a good sign.

"May I help you, miss?" she asked politely, but without Mr. Porter's obsequiousness.

"I'd like to look over what you have in brown, straight and a few shades lighter than my own hair," she said with the faint, cool smile that had stood her in good stead at many a celebrity gala.

The woman was immediately impressed by the obvious importance of this young lady, as Kathryn had intended. No explanations would be needed. "By all means, miss! Shall I line them up on the counter for you?" Kathryn nodded her assent and in a few minutes had made her choice.

"And where shall I have it sent?" The woman's manner was resembling Mr. Porter's more every moment.

"Wrap it up, please, and I'll take it with me. It's to be a surprise." She paid from the spending cash her mother had given her to avoid any awkward questions at home when the bills came. Upon leaving the shop, she was startled to see Priscilla just ahead of her on the wooden walkway. Her back was turned, so she could not have seen Kathryn yet, and after a moment's thought, Kathryn decided that this chance encounter might be for the best.

"Priscilla! I didn't know you planned to shop today."

The other girl turned quickly in surprise. "Oh, Catherine! I am merely ordering tobacco for my father, for he dislikes coming to town himself, you know. All the bustle makes him nervous."

Kathryn almost snorted. "You call this bustle? You should see—ah, London." Her guard was slipping as she grew more comfortable in the past. She'd almost said New York City.

"Oh, I suppose you are right, and Columbia is only a little hamlet by comparison, but it doesn't take much to make Papa nervous these days."

"Do you have to go right home or can you stay to shop for a while, and maybe come back with me for dinner?"

"That would be marvelous," exclaimed Priscilla. "No, I needn't go straight back, as the tobacco is to be delivered. Papa doesn't mind my ordering it, but he feels it would be unladylike for me to carry it. Though why it should matter when it is all wrapped up, I can't imagine."

Both girls laughed over the absurd conventions governing their behavior, though Kathryn's laugh held a note of alarm. She tended to forget how limited her freedom here was. Women couldn't even vote! Something else she'd work to change, if she stayed. They could shop, though, she consoled herself, and the two young women spent a pleasant

hour buying such absolute necessities of life as artificial
flowers and eau de cologne.

"MISS BLAKE IS A charming girl," remarked Mrs. Sykes-
Prescott that evening as the family rose from the supper table. "It was kind of you to invite her to dinner today, Catherine, for she must often be lonely shut up in that enormous
house with her hermit of a father. At least he is not so selfish as to prevent her from socializing." Her expression implied that being a recluse was sin enough.

"That reminds me, Mother," said Kathryn. "Might I
spend the day with Priscilla tomorrow? I offered to, if you
don't object."

"Why, I suppose so, if you like. I shall be busy for several hours, anyway, having my portrait taken by that young
James De Veaux, who painted Colonel Taylor two or three
years ago. He goes to Charleston again in a month and I
wish to take advantage of him while he is in town. Will the
mauve gown I wore at General Lafayette's ball look well for
it, do you think?"

Kathryn nodded, her attention suddenly caught. This
would be the same portrait that hung in the gallery in 1994!

"You and Miss Blake are very close these days, I notice," Mrs. S-P continued.

"I like her," said Kathryn simply. And it was true, unlike the story she had just told. Priscilla had a straightfor-
ward frankness that reminded her of Annette. For a
moment she missed her friend, but then more pressing matters pushed homesickness from her mind.

That night, Kathryn went over her plan. She had left the
dress and wig in the stables, as Ryan had directed, but she
was determined to have a more active hand in Coffee and
Isaiah's escape. As there was no gossiping Mrs. Blake, it was
unlikely Mrs. S-P would ever discover she hadn't gone to
Priscilla's. No, the greatest obstacle to her plan was going to
be Ryan himself.

She was right. Ryan called for her shortly after breakfast, and once greetings were exchanged, Kathryn said, "How lucky that you called today, sir! Would you mind escorting me to Miss Blake's house? I have promised to spend the day with her."

Ryan agreed, as his plans would run smoothly without her for at least the next hour. They had to ride somewhere, and the Blake mansion was as good a destination as any. So, after Kathryn's mare was brought around from the stables, he led off in the direction indicated.

"We can turn as soon as we are out of sight of the house," said Kathryn almost immediately. Jeller had not accompanied them, since Ryan had brought his own groom.

"What do you mean?" asked Ryan, lowering one eyebrow suspiciously. "This is the shortest route to the Blakes' house."

"I have no intention of going there, and Priscilla's not expecting me. I only said that to throw my mother off the scent. I'm coming with you."

"Absolutely not!" Ryan's tone brooked no argument, but Kathryn was undeterred.

"How do you intend to stop me?" she asked reasonably. "I'll follow you if you don't take me along, and I wouldn't think you'd want a scene today, of all days."

Ryan glared at her. "What start is this? Do you think it might be amusing to watch a couple of slaves escape, or are you gathering evidence against me?"

"You still don't trust me? I've done everything you asked so far and haven't raised anyone's suspicions. I don't want to be left out now."

"All the plans are made. You'll only be in the way, and possibly in some danger, as well." There! That would dissuade her.

"That's only fair, considering my part in this," she replied, surprising him. "Suppose the dress doesn't fit? Who's going to alter it at the last minute?"

"One of the other women . . ." began Ryan vaguely. The truth was, he hadn't thought of that, and his plan didn't call for any other woman learning of the escape. "Oh, very well. I don't suppose I could stop you, anyway," he said ungraciously. He was not used to being out-argued by a woman—but he was quickly discovering that Catherine was no ordinary woman.

"We'll be going out to Fair Fields now," he continued more civilly after a moment. "That's the only safe place for the 'transformation' I plan for Coffee and Isaiah. Then we have to get them on the road to Savannah without being seen."

"Lead on, then," said Kathryn brightly. Ryan sent her one more penetrating look and turned his horse. He'd thought he understood women, but this one had him out of his reckoning.

The ride to Fair Fields was pleasant, the day bright but not yet hot, and they passed no one except two farmers bringing their produce into town to sell. Once on Ryan's land, they proceeded to the slave quarters, almost a small village. Not all of his inhabitants were slaves now, but most wished to remain where they had grown up, among family and friends.

As they dismounted and entered the circle of cabins, Kathryn was surprised to hear crying from several windows, including those of the house she recognized as Japheth's. She turned to Ryan, but before she could ask any questions, he said, "In here, quickly, while no one is about," and ushered her through a low doorway. She found herself face-to-face with Coffee, who had tears running down her cheeks.

"What has happened?" demanded Ryan, looking from her to Isaiah, who stood next to her, his arm around his wife's shoulders.

"It be little Nathan, Japheth and Magda's new babe, suh," said Isaiah, his own voice shaky. "He done gone to his reward, and him not two weeks old. It be a blow to us all, and 'specially the women. You know how they dotes on a new babe.''

Kathryn caught her breath. She could see Nathan's perfect little face, feel the tiny fingers curling around her own. Then she remembered Japheth's face as it had been the other day, so full of pride in his new son. She folded her lips and struggled against the tears prickling at her eyelids.

"I've just talked to Magda," said Coffee quietly, her voice composed, though tears still trickled from the corners of her eyes. "I reminded her that this is a cross we women have to bear, and that there will be other babes, but it never seems to get easier." She squeezed her eyes shut and turned her face against her husband's huge chest. His arms went around her comfortingly and they stood silent, drawing strength from each other.

"Isaiah and Coffee lost their only child to the yellow fever just three months ago," Ryan explained to Kathryn in an undertone. "Sarah was only two years old—a beautiful little girl."

Suddenly, intermingled with Kathryn's grief for little Nathan came a surge of raw fear as she realized that she was now in a time when modern medicine was unknown, where disease and death were part of everyday life. Where any child she bore—perhaps even Ryan's child—might well die before its first birthday. Could anything be worth that? But before panic could overcome her, Ryan was rallying Coffee and Isaiah to action, his words reminding her of her obligation to help these people. Wiping her eyes, she listened closely.

"We can't allow this to delay our plans, I'm afraid," he was saying. "Coffee, the things you will need are in this package. Miss Prescott will assist you while I speak to Japheth and Magda. I'll be back in a few minutes to help you, Isaiah."

He went out and Coffee drew herself up bravely. "Mr. James is right. We have work to do if we are to live to fulfill the Lord's purpose for us." She knelt to untie the parcel Ryan had left. "This is lovely, miss. Are you sure you want me to have it?" She reverently held up the shimmering folds of the black-and-gray gown.

"I got it especially with you in mind, Coffee," answered Kathryn, forcing a watery smile. "Those colors look awful on me, but they should suit you perfectly. Try it on."

Coffee disappeared into a curtained recess at one end of the single room cabin and reappeared a few moments later wearing the dress. "It's the right length, thank heavens," said Kathryn, surveying it critically, "but it hangs a little in the waist. Hold still a second." With practiced fingers, she pinned the offending area and stood back again. "Yes, I think that's all it will need. Take it back off and I'll have it fitted in a moment."

"Oh, miss, there's no need—" Coffee protested, but Kathryn cut her off.

"Nonsense. Why do you think I came along?" She felt a need to keep her hands busy, to keep visions of Nathan—and of little Sarah, whom she hadn't even known—at bay. Coffee seemed to understand, for she returned to the recess without a word and came out after a moment in her old homespun, handing Kathryn the new dress. Kathryn sat down on a low stool, pulling from her pocket the needle and thread she'd brought along, and set to work. By the time Ryan returned, she was nearly finished.

"My, you's quick with a needle, ma'am!" exclaimed Isaiah admiringly, looking to his wife for confirmation.

"You have a gift, miss," agreed Coffee with gentle certainty.

"How are we doing?" asked Ryan with forced briskness as he strode in. His manner was calm and businesslike, but his eyes were red and Kathryn felt another pang. *He'll grow into a man you can be proud of,* he'd said the day Nathan was born. Apparently he wasn't as hardened to such tragedy as she'd assumed.

"Coffee, try this on again," she said quickly, knotting off the last thread. "It should just about do now."

As Coffee retired again with the dress, Ryan brought out a pair of shears and a razor. "Now for you, Isaiah. You've always been known for that bushy mane of yours, so I can think of no better way to disguise you than to shave it off.

Isaiah nodded, resigned, and sat on a low stool so that Ryan could do the deed. Coffee, emerging a few minutes later in the perfectly fitted dress, stifled a gasp at the sight of her husband's hair littering the floor.

"It . . . does make a change, doesn't it?" she managed to say.

"More than I'd have expected," Kathryn agreed. "Let's have a look at you. Yes, I think that will do fine. I'm awfully glad I didn't have to hem it—that would have taken forever by hand." Coffee looked at her curiously, and Kathryn realized that she'd misspoken again. These people would know of no alternative to hand sewing! Coffee's attention was back on her husband, where Ryan was now plying the razor, so Kathryn dared to hope the remark would be quickly forgotten.

"Let's try the wig, Coffee," she said, holding it up. "Sit here and I'll fit it on you." She did so expertly, her theatrical experience standing her in good stead, and in moments Coffee looked like a different woman—a white woman. There was no mirror in the cabin, but Ryan and Isaiah both exclaimed at the change, agreeing that it would do the trick.

A few minutes later, Ryan toweled off Isaiah's shiny dome. "There! Your own mother wouldn't know you now, I daresay!"

Isaiah fingered his head and face in disbelief while Coffee simply stood and stared. Finally, she said, "He's right, Isaiah. I could have passed you in the street myself, I believe."

At that moment, another man burst into the room, panting and sweating. "Masah! Masah! Praise the Lord, Mama Ruth was right. She said as how I'd be like to find ye here!"

"What is it, Jeb?" Ryan asked the young slave.

"Why, they's two of the Warden's men up to the big house, askin' for ye! Mama Ruth said as she thought you was in town, but made a big show o' sendin' me round the fields to look for ye. She done told me quiet like that I'd mos' prob'ly find you here, so I come here fust to ask what I should do."

"Thank you, Jeb, you did right," Ryan assured him. "Can Mama Ruth keep those two in the house for a little while?"

"Yes, suh, Masah! She just took two o' her bodacious chicken pies out de oven, an' she said she was goin' to serve it up to 'em. Ain't no one gone walk away from Mama Ruth's chicken pies!"

"You're right there," agreed Ryan. "All right, Jeb, you take your time riding over the fields, and after a while you mosey on back to the house and say you couldn't find me. Daniel," he turned to the groom, who had come up behind. "Hurry up to the stables, saddle the horses and bring them back here. But be careful to stay out of sight of the house, especially the dining room windows." The groom nodded and followed Jeb out.

"Are all of your things packed up?" Ryan asked Isaiah. "It looks as though we'll have to leave a bit ahead of schedule."

"I packed everything last night," said Coffee. "We can be off at any time."

Everyone sprang into action. Ryan went out to the pump and filled several skins with water, while Kathryn wrapped up the food that Coffee had already set out on the table for their journey. By the time Daniel returned with the horses ten minutes later, all was ready. Coffee brought out the bundles she had packed and Isaiah stowed them in the saddlebags of the larger horse.

"Daniel, I want you to circle around and come to the house from the main road. Tell Mama Ruth that I'm in town conducting business and mean to stay there until suppertime. If the Warden's men want to know exactly where I am, tell them you think I was going to Mr. Haney's office. He's out of town, and I left a message there earlier, so that should ring true. I expect I'll speak to them myself when I return for supper tonight, but it won't hurt to have them chasing around for the next few hours." Daniel nodded and departed again.

Ryan looked at Kathryn. "I was going to have you wait here while I set Isaiah and Coffee on their road, but now you'd better come along in case those two decide to search for themselves. They may want something entirely unconnected with this business, but we cannot be certain."

Kathryn merely nodded, deciding against telling him that she wouldn't have remained behind in any case. She went outside to mount her horse, and the others followed suit.

"We'll take the path through the woods," said Ryan when they were away from the cabins, leading them into the trees that lined these far fields. "I scouted out the land when I first bought this place against just such an eventuality as this." In moments they were all concealed from view, moving carefully along a narrow track that wound between towering pines.

"This path goes on for seven or eight miles and then joins the small south road. That will be the safest route for you to take to Savannah," he said to Isaiah over his shoulder as he guided his horse through the thick undergrowth.

Kathryn was impressed by Ryan's ability to stay on the track. Her eyes could detect no path at all ahead of him, but he unerringly found the way, leading them skillfully and quickly through the dense, almost tropical, growth.

"Mr. James is probably the best backwoodsman in South Carolina," Coffee remarked reassuringly to her at one point. "Don't you worry for a minute that he'll lose his way."

Sure enough, as the sun was reaching its zenith, the path gave onto a much larger dirt track. "You know your way from here, don't you, Isaiah?" asked Ryan. The big man nodded. "You two had best go on, then. If any questions are asked here, you can trust me to lead them a merry chase." The two men clasped hands warmly, there being no words for such a parting, and Isaiah and Coffee turned their horses' heads south.

"I pray they make it," murmured Kathryn, as they disappeared around a bend.

Ryan turned his horse. "They have an excellent chance. But we must hurry if we're not to arouse suspicion." She followed him willingly.

After half an hour, he pulled up in a tiny clearing ringed by azaleas in full bloom with a small stream running through it. "I brought a sandwich along," he said, dismounting. "You are welcome to share it." He helped her down and divided the package evenly. It took them only a few minutes to finish eating, drinking and washing dusty hands at the stream. As they stood to go, having completed their brief meal in silence, Ryan turned abruptly.

"You realize that we are both deeply implicated in this business now, apart from what I may face on our return. Are you regretting your promise yet?" He regarded Kathryn searchingly.

"Of course not. I only wish I could have done more to make up for the damage I've caused." She meant it. Despite the fact that women were often treated like children in this time, Kathryn felt that here, working for something that mattered, she had finally grown up. Ryan seemed to sense her sincerity.

"I misjudged you, Catherine," he said gently. "I'm sorry."

Kathryn was suddenly acutely aware of how alone they were, of how private a place this was. Her heart began to beat faster. Ryan had attracted her from the moment they met and she realized, more strongly than ever, that she wanted him, wanted to feel his warmth pressed against her. No man had ever stirred her senses the way this man did.

Why not now? What if she were snatched back to her own time tomorrow, before she ever saw him again? What if— she swallowed—what if he were arrested, even hanged, for what he did in Charleston? She would regret it for the rest of her life if she let this golden opportunity escape.

"Ryan..." she began huskily. Again he seemed attuned to her thoughts. Before she could say another word, he reached out to her almost questioningly, one hand sliding around the back of her neck, under her thick, dark hair, the other barely touching her fingers, which had risen of their own accord to meet his. Their hands met and clasped, and he drew her gently to him for a deep, searching kiss. She responded hungrily, her hands caressing his back, his shoulders. His embrace tightened and she could sense his mounting passion, a hunger matching her own. Kathryn began to draw him down gently to the thick carpet of pine needles beneath them, still spread with the cloth they had picknicked on, but, frustratingly, he stopped her.

"What are you doing?" he demanded in obvious amazement, though his voice was as husky as hers.

She gazed up at him, her eyes smoky with desire. She *must* have one wonderful experience to remember him by, whatever the risk. "I'm not afraid," she said softly. "Are you?"

He caught his breath and smiled, a serious smile, his eyes probing her very soul. "If this is what you want, Catherine, I won't deny you. But you must be very sure."

Kathryn felt with sudden, searing certainty that she could do no better than to commit herself, her future, to this man's keeping. "I'm sure," she whispered. Determinedly, she began to unbutton his coat, then his shirt. When she had trouble with his cravat, he quickly untied it himself and turned his attention to her clothing.

"We haven't the time I'd prefer to take," he said, deftly undoing the row of tiny buttons down her back and unlacing her corset. "I will try to be gentle."

Kathryn smiled. She was every bit as eager as he. As the last of her garments fell in a heap at her feet, she turned to face him. God, he was magnificent! Kathryn devoured him with her eyes. His hard, muscled frame had only been hinted at before, under the loose shirts and tight breeches he wore, but now he was revealed in all his glory—as she was in hers.

Remembering that time was short, she took a step forward and suddenly found herself in Ryan's arms. This time he did not resist when she drew him down to the forest floor. Urged on by a potent mix of desire and danger, Kathryn caressed him, deliberately rousing him to a fevered pitch. Still, Ryan took the time to pleasure her with his hands, his mouth, until she was moist and ready. She barely noticed the tiny twinge of pain when he finally entered her, so exquisite was the pleasure of it. Together they climbed to the peak, exploding only a few moments later with a release that went beyond anything Kathryn had ever experienced.

Their passion spent, they lay entwined, Kathryn mesmerized by Ryan's heartbeat. Gradually, reluctantly, she again became aware of the passage of time. Now, even more than before, she wanted to be sure of Ryan's safety. Reluctantly, she murmured, "It must be nearly two. Shouldn't we get back?" She knew that she would forever associate the scent of sun-warmed pine needles with Ryan, with love.

Ryan nodded, caressing her as she disengaged herself from his arms. Silently, he helped her into her clothes, fastening the buttons she could not reach. By the time Kathryn had laced up her shoes, he had dressed himself and stood regarding her with an expression she could not read.

Realization slowly penetrated the sensuous languor that still enveloped her. She had not given the slightest thought to playing Catherine's part during their lovemaking. She had been wholly herself—perhaps more so than she'd ever been in her life. For the first time, she really knew who she was. But Ryan didn't know. She could see the doubt, the question in his eyes. Could she tell him? Did she dare? It seemed wrong to hold any part of herself back from him now. But he spoke first.

"Catherine, we have to talk. Now."

CHAPTER THIRTEEN

KATHRYN TRIED TO REPLACE the pins in her hair, but her fingers wouldn't cooperate. Her sense of inner peace had shattered at his words. How much should she tell him? she wondered frantically. Was he ready for the whole truth? Was she? Ryan watched as she fumbled with her hair, retrieving pins when she dropped them and finally pinning up the rich dark mass himself.

"You know we need to talk, Catherine," he repeated. "It may as well be now as later."

She let out her breath, only then aware that she had been holding it. "You're right. I just don't know where to start."

"Then I will. Catherine, I've compromised you—" he stopped, frowning. She knew he was thinking that she hadn't behaved like a virgin at all—nor had she. Thank God the physical proof had been there, at least. He continued more forcefully, "I've compromised you irrevocably now, even if our time alone remains a secret. Please tell me you no longer object to becoming my wife."

Kathryn's eyes widened. He wasn't going to demand an explanation? She wasn't sure whether she should be relieved or insulted. Likely he took credit for her expertise himself—just like a man! But it hardly mattered right now. He was right. She *had* been compromised—or at least Catherine's body had—and she would have to abide by the standards of this culture. Still . . .

"I'll marry you, Ryan," she said, "but only if it's what *you* really want. Is it?" The answer mattered much more than she had expected it to.

"Catherine," he said softly, holding out his hands to her. She came willingly but he held her at arm's length, looking deep into her eyes, this time letting her read his feelings instead of striving to read hers. What she saw there made her gasp. "I love you, Catherine," he said, confirming her wonderful discovery. "I don't know how it happened, or when it happened. It wasn't true when I first proposed, as I think you knew. My reasons were completely different then. But now I love you and I want you to be my wife more than I've ever wanted anything. Will you?" His voice was infinitely tender, and Kathryn thought her heart would burst from the emotions swelling it. There were tears in her eyes when she answered.

"Yes, Ryan, I will. I love you, too, in a way I never knew it was possible to love. I'll marry you." She spoke it as a vow, and he seemed to accept it as such. He drew her to him and kissed her, not passionately but solemnly, to acknowledge the promise.

"And now we'll have to hurry," he said in a different tone, as he released her. "If I'm to divert suspicion from Coffee and Isaiah's flight, I need to get into town immediately to provide myself with an alibi. I'll take you home first, or to the Blake house, if you prefer."

"I told my mother I was spending the day with Priscilla, so I'd better go there, I guess. Besides, I'd like her to be the first to hear our news."

"She mustn't make it public until I've called on your father," he cautioned. "I'll try to do that tomorrow, if I can."

Kathryn nodded, then looked up at him anxiously. "Ryan, are you in any real danger now? I think I deserve to know."

"I'll let you know as soon as I do. But to discover that, I must first return to town. Up with you, then, and let's be off!"

He tossed her into the saddle, and they continued on to where the track joined another. Ryan assured her it would get them to town more quickly than retracing their route.

"We have no wish to be seen coming from the direction of Fair Fields," he added. "This way, I can take you to the Blakes's by a roundabout route and ride into Columbia alone, with no one the wiser about us having been together. I don't want my bride-to-be's reputation tarnished." She laughed at that and he urged the horses faster.

"OH, CATHY, I AM SO happy for you," exclaimed Priscilla in genuine delight at Kathryn's news. "I can scarcely wait to see Leslie Allerby's face when she hears the announcement."

Kathryn glanced nervously at Priscilla's bedroom door. They finally had a brief respite from her younger siblings, but Kathryn wouldn't put it past fourteen-year-old Denise to listen at the keyhole. "You can't tell anyone yet, Priscilla!" she cautioned her friend. "Ryan still has to talk to my father."

"As if he would refuse. Oh, Cathy, you look so happy! You do love him, don't you?" Ever romantic, Priscilla's eyes shone.

Kathryn nodded. "I've never . . . I mean, I never thought I could love anyone this way. And he loves me!"

"Did he say so?" Priscilla settled herself more comfortably among the pillows, ready to hear every detail. Kathryn couldn't oblige her, of course, but finally said enough to satisfy her.

"It's just as well," said Priscilla thoughtfully when she finished. "My Polly told me that you had been seen riding alone with him. She got it from her sister, who spends time with one of your father's stablehands. Now your betrothal will be announced before that little tidbit can become common knowledge. Why *were* you riding out with him alone, Cathy?"

"Shopping," she replied blandly.

Priscilla regarded her doubtfully. "Well, I don't think my Polly will spread it any further. She seems to like your Mr. James, though I can't think why, as he is one of the cruelest slave owners in South Carolina."

Kathryn almost corrected her, but stopped herself in time. She knew now why Ryan had allowed those particular rumors to circulate, and she couldn't risk his safety with the truth. "Never mind that," she said. "I wanted to ask if you will be bridesmaid at my wedding." This turned the conversation back into safer channels until she felt she could reasonably go home.

Kathryn hardly remembered later how she passed the evening. She responded automatically to her parents' conversation while her mind flitted about like a hyperactive butterfly. She thought of her real parents and what they would think of her engagement, of Coffee and Isaiah's escape to New York, of what the future might hold for Ryan and herself—and, of course, of the incredible lovemaking they had shared that afternoon.

The only thing she tried not to think about was the possibility of returning to 1994. That was clearly out of the question now. Catherine was doubtless better off in the future, she reasoned, and as long as she stayed away from that damned clock while it was striking she should have nothing to worry about.

Ryan had told her not to expect him that evening, but she couldn't help worrying about him all the same. What if one of the other slaves talked? What if a reward were offered? As she prepared for bed, she was so preoccupied she barely noticed little Alma's sniffling. The girl refilled the ewer and pitcher on her dresser for her evening wash, her breathing ragged, and as she turned to leave the room another stifled sob escaped, finally catching Kathryn's attention.

"Alma? Are you all right?" she asked, shaken out of her self-absorption. The slave girl stopped to turn huge, over-flowing eyes toward her young mistress, nodding hastily.

"No, you're not. Come over here and tell me what's wrong." She patted the bed invitingly, but the girl hesi-tated, taking only one tentative step toward her, fear and uncertainty replacing the misery in her eyes.

"Please, Alma, you can trust me. I promise." Kathryn coaxed her as she might a very young child or a frightened animal.

Alma took two more steps, then three. Suddenly her re-serve broke and she flung herself into Kathryn's arms, sob-bing as if her heart was breaking. "Oh, miss, oh, miss!" she cried over and over while Kathryn stroked her shoulder, trying to calm her.

"It's all right, Alma. Whatever it is, we can make it all right," she said, awkwardly trying to soothe the distraught girl. Gradually Alma's sobs quieted and she sat up, wiping her eyes.

"Thank ye, miss. Guess I needed a good cry. I does feel better now." She rose to go.

"Wait, Alma! You haven't told me *why* you were cry-ing."

"Wal, miss, it ain't hardly no use. Ain't nothin' you could do, noways."

"Now, how do you know that? Try me."

Alma regarded her doubtfully for a moment, then sat back down. "It's my brother, miss, my Elmo, what belongs to Mr. Allerby. I thought we'd been right blessed to be sold so close together, so's we could see each other once in a whiles, but now I wisht he'd been sold to anybody else! Mr. Allerby, he's goin' t' kill Elmo, I just know it!"

"Why, what has Elmo done?" asked Kathryn, doubtful now herself. What could she possibly do about Allerby's treatment of his own slaves?

"He ain't done nothin' 'cept not be big and strong enough to suit his master. He was bought for a houseboy, when we was brung from North Carliny two, three years ago, but the missus took a dislike to him and sent him out to the fields. He ain't no field worker, Miss!"

"How old is he?"

"Same age as me. We's twins, and allus been real close like. I guess I's about fourteen, from what Nancy says, so Elmo'd be the same. And he ain't no bigger'n me, neither."

"And Mr. Allerby expects him to do the same amount of work as an adult?" Kathryn was aghast.

Alma nodded. "He whips him if he don't finish his task by dark. And now he's adding five lashes every day he don't finish!"

"And, of course, the more he's whipped, the weaker he gets, so he doesn't have a chance," Kathryn finished, feeling ill. A desperate resolve was growing in her.

"That's right, miss. I seen him today, when Cook sent me over that side of town to buy some bacon. He says he's gone cut and run. Oh, miss, Mr. Allerby, he already had two slaves whipped to death for trying to escape! Elmo's got no place to go but the woods, and the dogs'll catch him sure!" She started to cry again.

"Alma, listen to me," said Kathryn with such authority that the girl stopped crying to regard her expectantly. "I'm going to take care of Elmo. You can trust me. I'll tell you how as soon as I can, but you're not to worry anymore. All right?"

Alma nodded, her eyes wide and trusting. Kathryn flinched at the simple faith she saw there, hoping she could justify it. She would. She had to.

"Okay, go on to bed, Alma. Everything's going to be all right." Alma gave her a wavering smile, the first Kathryn had ever seen on her face, and went from the room, leaving Kathryn to figure out a solution to Elmo's problem as she prepared for bed. Should she ask Mr. Prescott to buy him? She'd talk to Ryan tomorrow and get his opinion. He'd know what to do. The thought of Ryan recalled that afternoon and she soon fell asleep, dreaming of their future together.

Kathryn slept late the next morning, and when she came down her mother greeted her with a broad smile. "Cathy, you are a very lucky girl!" she exclaimed the moment she saw her. "Your father will want to speak to you at once, I'm certain." She hurried away to the room that doubled as a small library and Mr. Prescott's study, leaving Kathryn to follow more slowly. She suddenly realized what must have happened and her heart began to beat faster.

As she suspected, Ryan was with her father. At her entrance, Mr. Prescott said cheerfully, "I want a word alone with my daughter now, young man. Suppose you wait for her in the garden. That seems an appropriate place for such matters." Ryan gave her a half wink as he went out, and the warmth that she felt broadened her smile as she turned to face Mr. Prescott.

"Well, my girl, I can see you know all about this business, as I might have expected, and you look happy enough, I'm glad to observe. I believe he'll make you a good husband, as well as a wealthy one, but it's what you think that matters. You'll have him?"

"Yes, Father, I will. And I do believe he'll make me happy. His wealth doesn't matter at all." Kathryn was serious now, touched by his evident concern—more than she'd expected.

"Ah, youth. Think they can live on love and air. You'll be glad of the money, too, by and by, when you've children to feed and clothe. But enough of that! Your young man is waiting to make his formal addresses in the garden. You'd best go to him." He turned away quickly, and Kathryn wondered if she'd imagined the glimmer of a tear in his eye.

In the garden, Kathryn and Ryan embraced quickly and discreetly, aware of the watchful back windows of the house. "Let's make it official now, Catherine," said Ryan as he released her. Going down on one knee, he inquired formally, "Miss Prescott, will you do me the honor of becoming my wife?"

"Thank you, kind sir, I will," she replied in the same tone. Then she grasped his hand and pulled him to his feet. "Sit down and tell me everything that happened yesterday. We should be left alone for a while, so this is a good time to talk about it."

"I'd like to be left even more alone," said Ryan suggestively, with a leer that made her laugh, before he capitulated. "All right. Everything went according to plan, though it's as well I started back when I did. Those two guardsmen were just beginning a tour of the slave quarters when I returned. They started at old Joe's, thank God, and he held them up until I got there."

"Joe? I don't remember him."

"You haven't seen him. He's my overseer."

"I thought you said you didn't have one," said Kathryn in surprise.

"Technically, it is illegal to leave a plantation of slaves without a white overseer—leads to insurrection. So, technically, I have one. Old Joe. Though his eyes are too bleared by whiskey to oversee much of anything twenty-three hours out of the twenty-four," he said with a chuckle. "But he has a very high opinion of his position, and had launched into one of his rambling speeches about how if anything was going on at Fair Fields, he'd be the first to know it. I think those guards were downright grateful to me for rescuing them, to tell you the truth."

Kathryn laughed with him. "So Coffee and Isaiah—and you—are out of danger?"

"For the moment, at least. The Captain of the Guard must not have suspected much, or he'd have come himself. No one on my place would swear to anyone of Isaiah's description, so there's no proof he was ever on my plantation at all, just hearsay. He never went into town, you see. And Allerby heard nothing about Coffee, which means any search will be for one person, not two. They've an excellent chance of making it to New York."

"I'm so glad. But what about you?" This was the question that really mattered to Kathryn. "Did Allerby's questions stir up any suspicion?"

"Apparently not—they asked only about Isaiah. Suspicion alone can't hurt me, anyway. They need proof, and I'm certain now they have none, or I would already have been arrested—or, should I say, they'd have *tried* to arrest me." He gave her a cocky grin.

Kathryn very much wished now that she didn't have to bring up the next subject, but she'd given her word. "Ryan, I have a problem, and you are the only one I can ask about it."

Immediately, he sobered. "What is it, Catherine? Your parents—"

She shook her head. "It's not exactly *my* problem, except that I've promised to help. Little Alma, the chambermaid, is very worried about her brother, who belongs to the Allerbys. He's being horribly mistreated and she's afraid he'll either be whipped to death or try to escape and be killed in the process. Do you think I should ask my father to buy him?"

Ryan was silent for a moment, then said slowly, "I hate to tell you this, Catherine, but your father isn't known for his kindness to his slaves any more than Allerby is. The boy's lot might improve, or it might not, but consider this; your father will want a reason, and if word gets back to Allerby that the boy has been telling tales, even to his sister, he'll likely be in worse straits than he is now."

Kathryn's face fell. "I hadn't thought of that. Then I can't do anything? Poor Alma—I *did* promise her. And we can't just let Allerby kill him—he's only fourteen years old!" Biting her lip, she implored Ryan with her eyes.

His own softened in return. "No, we can't," he said with sudden decision. "He's had two or three killed already, one of whom I tried to buy when I saw what was going on, but Allerby wouldn't sell. He's a vindictive little bastard, and takes the worst of his nature out on his slaves—he and his brute of an overseer. Somehow, we'll contrive the boy's escape. What is his name?"

"Elmo. He's Alma's twin brother."

"Elmo. Hmm. Was he once a house slave?" Kathryn nodded. "I think I remember him. Scrawny lad. Allerby had no business making him a field hand. Can Alma get word to him for us?"

"I think so," said Kathryn. "I can send her there myself if necessary."

"Good," said Ryan, leaning closer, "here's my idea . . ."

FOR THE NEXT FEW DAYS, Ryan played the role of devoted fiancé, staying for dinner, tea and supper. Kathryn loved it. True, they were almost never alone and had to listen to Mrs. S-P's interminable plans for the wedding, announcements and trousseau, but they were together, which was enough— or almost enough. During the few hours Ryan spent away from the Prescott house, Kathryn pored over the fashion plates her mother had brought. Beautiful clothes had always been a passion of hers and there'd been nothing in her time to compare with what she saw here.

Kathryn and Ryan managed to snatch a brief hour alone in the gardens the day after their engagement. They sat on the stone bench near the rose bower, Kathryn's head on Ryan's shoulder, his arm about her waist. It was as though

neither quite believed the marvel of their love yet, and
wanted to slow time while they grew used to it. After a long,
happy silence they began first tentatively, then eagerly, to
discuss their future together. They would live at Fair Fields,
they decided, coming to town only when necessary. No dull
business considerations would be allowed to intrude on the
paradise they would create.

"I hired a new overseer this morning," Ryan told Kathryn in the midst of these rosy plans. "He is just what I'd
hoped for."

"I didn't know you were looking for one. You have old
Joe, after all." She sat up a little straighter in surprise.

"Well, I've been thinking that I might not want to de-
vote *all* of my time to growing cotton—especially over the
next year or so." His slow smile told her what he intended
to spend his energies on, and she snuggled closer to him,
approving thoroughly.

"Such as while we're on our honeymoon?" She walked
her fingers up his arm.

"Such as. At any rate, Peter Morrison is a fine young
man, lately from New England, who shares my views on
how to get the most from one's workers. I feel I can trust
him to manage Fair Fields as I would myself, whether I'm
absent or simply...occupied." He leaned down to gently
nibble Kathryn's ear.

The only thing marring Kathryn's contentment was a little voice that wouldn't quite be silenced. It kept telling her
that she owed Ryan the complete truth about herself. *Later!
Later!* she told it, pushing it to the back of her mind and
willing herself to forget she had ever lived in the future. It
almost worked.

Neither of the Prescotts could lavish enough attention on
their soon-to-be son-in-law, or show enough deference to his
opinions on matters great and small, from the wine best
served with supper to the number of fields Mr. Prescott
should plant next season. If Kathryn hadn't been so happy,

she might have been embarrassed about their attitude. Still, his constant presence made it easy to arrange, through Alma, the plan for Elmo's escape.

KATHRYN AND RYAN waited in the woods near Allerby's plantation, where they'd arranged to meet Elmo one hour after moonrise, their horses occasionally snorting or stamping in the soft pine straw. Kathryn had found it absurdly easy to escape the Prescott mansion undetected. She'd merely waited until everyone was asleep and let herself out of the front door. Ryan had been waiting for her in the stables, her mare already saddled. Surprisingly, he hadn't even tried to talk her out of coming—not that he would have succeeded, of course.

She was just leaning over to ask Ryan how long they should wait when she heard a furtive scrambling in the underbrush. Watching Ryan, she realized he must have noticed it long before she did, for he didn't react at all, but kept stroking his horse's neck to keep it silent. Belatedly, she did the same. The rustling quickly grew louder, and in moments a slight shape stood before them, a darker shadow in the general gloom under the trees.

"Miz Prescott, that you?" came a hoarse whisper.

"Yes, Elmo, it's me," she replied just as quietly.

"Let's get farther away before we say anything else, shall we?" suggested Ryan, reaching down with one hand and swinging the boy into the saddle in front of him. Kathryn heard Elmo gasp, but thankfully he did not cry out, and they walked their horses slowly, almost noiselessly, deeper into the woods for what seemed an eternity. Finally, Ryan pulled to a stop, setting the boy down and dismounting. Kathryn did likewise.

"Now, Elmo, let's have a look at you," said Ryan, still softly but no longer in a whisper. Kathryn was dismayed at what she saw by the light of the three-quarter moon. Elmo was certainly no larger than little Alma, perhaps not as large. But worse than that, the boy could scarcely stand, he was so weak. He leaned against Ryan's horse while his benefactors examined him.

"Ryan, he'll never make it on foot," whispered Kathryn in urgent concern.

"But we daren't take him back. Even now, his absence might have been noticed. The hue and cry could begin any moment. Elmo, can you ride?" asked Ryan abruptly.

"Yes, Masah, I allus used to take the horses down for water when I worked up at the house." He seemed to accept Ryan's presence without need of explanation—or perhaps he was simply too far gone to care.

"Good," said Ryan. "You'll have to take my horse if you're to make it out of South Carolina. That will make it harder to set the dogs on your trail, as well." Ryan tossed the boy up into the saddle as if he were a sack of meal, and continued. "You must make your way to North Carolina, to the town of Goldsboro, and find the Quakers there. They will help you on the next stage of your journey. Here is a letter saying you are returning to your master in Goldsboro, which will allow you to ask directions without arousing suspicion." He handed Elmo a folded paper. "There is food and a little bit of money in the saddlebags, which should sustain you that far. Good luck, lad, and be off!"

Elmo needed no further urging. He dug his bare heels into the huge gelding's flanks and headed north through the trees at a slow trot. As the sound of his retreat faded, Kathryn regarded Ryan accusingly. "You never said you were giving him your horse! It could be recognized."

"That is a chance I'll have to take," he replied. "It was obvious the boy hadn't a prayer on foot." She opened her mouth to protest, but he stopped her with a deep, demanding kiss. "Were you not wondering why I let you come along?" he asked a moment later.

"I should have guessed," she said with a throaty chuckle. As before, the sense of danger and urgency heightened her arousal. When he lifted her skirts instead of undoing her dress, she fumbled with the fastening on his breeches. This time there was even less leisure for exploration but she didn't care. She only wanted to feel him inside her once again, before fate could tear them apart. They were both still partially clothed when he entered her and for a space of time their sighs mingled with the other night sounds.

"HOW LONG HAVE YOU BEEN involved with the Underground Railroad?" asked Kathryn languidly a while later as they walked hand in hand through the woods, Ryan leading her mare.

"The what?" His hand tightened on hers in surprise.

Oops. "The, ah, organization of people that helps slaves escape to the North." Of course it wouldn't be called the Underground Railroad yet—there weren't even any *railroads* yet!

"It's hardly an organization," replied Ryan, still looking at her strangely. "There are a few scattered individuals who are willing to take risks to help fugitives, some on principle and some for the sheer thrill of it." Ryan's tone implied he was one of the latter, but she knew by now that he had the firmest principles of anyone she'd ever met. Kathryn said nothing, still embarrassed by her blunder.

"Of course, some of these people know of others," he continued. "There may well be many more than I'm aware of. But what did you call it?"

"Never mind," said Kathryn quickly, wishing she hadn't brought up the subject.

"Underground Railroad, that's what you said, wasn't it?" She nodded reluctantly. "Strange," he said slowly. "I was going to tell you later on, when I had more facts. Robert Mills has been trying to get me to invest in his canals here in South Carolina, but a man I correspond with in Pennsylvania has advised me to put my money instead into something new they're doing up there—something he called a railroad." His gaze was penetrating. "But there is no way you could have known that, is there?"

"Of course not," said Kathryn, fighting to keep from dropping her eyes. "I . . . I heard the term in England. They're experimenting with railroads there, too, you know." She had no idea whether this was true, and could only hope that Ryan wouldn't know, either.

"Are they doing well?" he asked with interest.

"Much better than canals," she improvised. "I think your money might be better invested in them." As his future wife, surely it was her duty to help and advise him.

Ryan nodded slowly. "You may well be right. I'll look further into it." It apparently did not occur to him to wonder how Kathryn might have found out about something so unladylike as railroads during a London Season.

You're going to have to tell him the truth, you know, said that small, persistent voice in the back of her mind. *Why are you procrastinating?* But she knew that it was fear that held her back—fear of losing his love. *I'll tell him before the wedding,* she promised the nagging little voice. *Definitely before the wedding.*

"Catherine, I've been thinking," began Ryan after a brief silence. As she turned to him, a shot rang out in the near distance, deeper in the woods behind them.

"Elmo!" they both exclaimed, staring at each other in horror.

Before Kathryn could utter another word, Ryan was uncinching her mare's saddle strap.

"What . . . what are you doing?" she asked shakily.

"I'll do better bareback than sidesaddle." His voice was calm, purposeful. "Can you find your way home alone from here?"

She grasped his arm. "What are you going to do?"

"I'll know when I see what has happened. Wait here for fifteen minutes. If I don't return by then, get yourself home.

I'll call on you tomorrow if I can." Pulling away from her, he turned to mount the mare.

"No, wait! I—" He stopped her with a stern glance and she subsided. Reluctantly, Kathryn realized that if she went along, she might very well place him—and Elmo—in even greater danger. "Be careful, Ryan!" she pleaded with sudden foreboding.

"Always," he replied and kicked the mare into a canter.

The next few minutes felt like hours to Kathryn as she waited alone in the forest, straining to hear something, anything, over the nighttime woodland noises. Once she thought she heard distant shouting, but she couldn't be sure. How long had she been waiting? She had no intention of leaving until Ryan returned, even if it took him till dawn. Torn between frustration and boredom, she began walking in the direction Ryan had gone.

Before she had covered more than a few dozen yards, however, she heard hooves approaching. Slipping behind a tree, Kathryn peered fearfully into the darkness. Through the gloom, she could see the outline of two horses, one with a small figure slumped over the back, both being led by a larger figure that she was almost positive was...

"Ryan?" she whispered loudly as they drew near.

"Catherine! Thank God. I was afraid you'd gone back. Here, I need your help!" He reached up and slid Elmo's apparently inert form off of his chestnut gelding.

Kathryn hurried forward, nearly tripping over a tree root in her haste. "What happened? Was he shot?" She was on her knees now, pulling the ragged shirt gently away from the boy's body.

"Yes, in his left arm. One of Allerby's men saw him. Careful, there!" he cautioned her as she moved Elmo slightly to pillow his head on her saddlebag.

"Do you have a knife?" she asked Ryan worriedly. "This sleeve will have to be cut off." Ryan silently proffered his blade and she slit the material over the boy's arm. "Do...do you know anything about getting a bullet out?'' she finally asked, hoping she would not disgrace herself by being sick. She'd never seen so much blood in her life. At least, in the tree-filtered moonlight, it appeared more black than red, which helped a little.

"I thought all women were natural nurses, but I guess I was wrong,'' said Ryan teasingly. Then, catching a glimpse of her strained face, he sobered. "You don't have to watch if you'd rather not, Catherine. I've taken out plenty of bullets in my time, and I can manage alone.''

Kathryn drew a deep breath and squared her shoulders. "I'll help. Tell me what to do.''

Ryan gave her another searching look, then nodded. "All right, then. Hold his arm still.''

She did, but asked, "Shouldn't we do something to stop the bleeding? How about a tourniquet?''

Ryan looked at her in surprise. "Isn't that some French technique? Did you hear of it in England?''

"Yes,'' she said shortly, removing the sash from her dress and winding it around Elmo's arm, just below the shoulder. With a stick, she was able to twist it tightly enough to slow the bleeding.

"Impressive,'' commented Ryan, watching her. Kathryn felt that she'd done the job very clumsily, working only from a general idea of how tourniquets functioned, but it seemed effective enough. She watched as Ryan took out his knife again and approached the blade to the wound just above Elmo's elbow.

"Wait!'' she suddenly exclaimed. "Is that knife clean?''

Ryan regarded the blade with some perplexity. "It looks all right to me,'' he said.

"But it should be sterilized! The wound will get infected if it's not!''

"Steri . . . what?'' Ryan was startled.

Damn! They don't even know about germs yet! She thought furiously. "Could we build a fire? Just a small one?"

Ryan looked at her as though she were crazy. "And let everyone within miles know where we are? The fellow who shot Elmo should sleep for a few hours after the knock on the head I gave him, but I wouldn't want to gamble on it. That shot might have brought others out to look. And why in hell do we need a fire, anyway?"

Kathryn sighed. "Okay, no fire. How about alcohol? Do you have any kind of liquor in your saddlebags?"

"Yes, but—"

"Good. Get it out quickly!"

Ryan did as she asked, doubtfully handing her a small brown bottle. "It's pretty strong stuff. Are you sure this is the time—?"

"It's not for me." She uncorked it and sniffed. Whatever it was, it smelled strong enough to kill germs. "Hand me your knife." Ryan handed it over, looking dazed, and she poured some of the whiskey over the blade. Then, for good measure, she poured some into the wound.

"There," she said. "I don't know how much it'll help, but it's better than nothing. Go on," she prompted as he continued to stare at her. "Get that bullet out before he wakes up!"

Elmo began to groan just as Ryan finished his grisly task and held up the metal ball that had been lodged near the bone. "He'll have a chance now," said Ryan. "Undo that fancy tourniquet of yours so the blood can clean out the wound and we'll bind it."

"How will he ever make it North now?" asked Kathryn as she obeyed. "He won't be able to ride for days." Now that the operation was over she was able to think again, and to recognize the problem they faced.

"I'll have to take him," said Ryan simply. Kathryn drew in her breath sharply, though deep down she had known what he would say. "And no, you can't come," he continued, intercepting her pleading look. "I know the country like the back of my hand, and it will be easier with just one horse. I'll get word to you as soon as I can, I promise. I love you, Catherine!"

Their lips met in a fierce parting kiss, and then she was helping to load the semiconscious Elmo onto Ryan's gelding in front of him, where he could support the boy in case he fainted again. She held up a hand as they rode slowly off, sudden tears stinging her eyes. "God protect you both," she whispered as the trees obscured them from her sight.

CHAPTER FOURTEEN

"I DON'T KNOW," said Annette worriedly the morning after the race. "I'm not sure this is such a great idea."

"Why not?" asked Catherine. "I've already told him the truth. I simply want you to verify what I've said."

"You *told* him? What...what did he say?" Annette sat down abruptly on Catherine's bed.

"At first he thought I was mad—or at least confused. But I think he may be beginning to believe me. I know you can convince him, Annette. He has no cause to doubt your motives."

"And he has cause to doubt yours?"

"Kathryn's, at any rate. He told me last night that she still bears a grudge for his interference in her life two years ago. Though from what he told me, it sounded as though he had every reason to take her to task—drinking alcohol and encouraging the attentions of young men."

"Yeah, Kathy was quite the party animal in school. But that's not so scandalous these days, Catherine, really. And she was an expert at letting a guy know when he'd gone too far—she could cut them down to an inch with two words when she wanted to."

Catherine considered that for a moment, then suddenly chuckled. "I was thinking about Ryan James," she explained in answer to Annette's surprised look. "I was all but engaged to him before we exchanged places, and he rather frightened me. But I somehow suspect that Kathryn may be just the one to put him in his place!"

"She can do that if anyone can," agreed Annette. "The more I think about this switch, the more I think there was some purpose in it."

Catherine abruptly sobered. "I do hope you are right, Annette. But will you speak to Logan with me?"

"Okay. I just hope he doesn't try to have both of us committed!"

They went downstairs to breakfast and discovered that Logan had already left the house.

"He said something about an appointment," Mr. Monroe told them with a shrug. "I don't think it has anything to do with that Lake Murray project, though, since we're not due out there until three. He said he'd be back before noon, so I didn't pry."

Logan had doubtless gone to the doctor, as he had said he would, Catherine realized. She said nothing aloud, however, for she recalled that Logan had not wanted Mr. Monroe to learn of his accident.

Shortly after eleven, Logan returned and Catherine was pleased to see that he appeared completely recovered from his ordeal of the night before. As soon as he saw her, however, he frowned and she knew he was remembering her revelation.

"Please, Logan, come sit down," she said, beckoning him into the living room where Annette waited. Both of the Monroes had gone out a short time earlier but would be back for lunch. This was the perfect time. "Annette has agreed to discuss my, ah, situation with you."

Logan rubbed a hand over his face. "I'd almost managed to convince myself that I dreamed that whole conversation last night. Guess not, huh?" He came in and spread himself across one of the little antique sofas. "Okay, Annette, fire away. Catherine said you were going to tell me about the diary?"

Just as Catherine herself had done last night, Annette recounted what had happened the night of the costume ball.

"I knew the minute she opened her mouth that something was wrong, but it wasn't until I saw Kathy's handwriting—and it definitely *was* her handwriting—in that diary, just as old and faded-looking as Catherine's writing from before, that I believed her," she finished.

Logan looked up sharply. "Her handwriting, you say? Just a minute." He got up and went to the little writing desk in the corner of the room and pulled out a sheet of paper and a pen. "Catherine, write something for me. Anything."

Puzzled, Catherine joined him at the desk and complied, copying a sentence or two from a letter that lay open there. "Like that?" she asked.

For a moment, Logan didn't reply but stared down at what she'd written. "That letter you copied is one from Kathy to her mother."

Catherine blinked and saw that it was true. The handwriting was the same as the one in her diary.

"Your...your writing is completely different. I guess you could have done it on purpose, but..." He swallowed, then met her eyes, glanced over at Annette and then back to her. "You really are from the past, aren't you?"

Catherine nodded, watching his face warily. Would he be pleased or angry?

He let out a long sigh. "This is pretty hard to absorb. I can't believe you managed to fool me and your parents, acting like Kathryn without knowing anything about her, or about this time."

Catherine smiled tremulously, relief flooding through her like a sweet, warm tide. "Annette helped a lot, as I told you. And it is amazing how people tend to see what they expect to see," she said, moving back to the sofa. Annette excused herself with a wink, and Logan, barely seeming to notice, sat beside Catherine to listen raptly as she detailed what the past week had been like, omitting only her attraction to Logan himself.

"So," said Logan as she finished her narrative, "you've enjoyed the 1990s so far?" She nodded. "I'm glad. But the question now is, what do we do about Kathryn? She may be enjoying 1825 as much as you're enjoying the present, but I'd feel better if I knew for sure. Even if she didn't ever appreciate it, I still feel sort of protective of her."

"I understand," said Catherine slowly, remembering her experience last night by the clock. She was being selfish, wanting to stay in this century with Logan, at Kathryn's expense. If her counterpart wished to return, and if it were possible, then she would have to allow the exchange to take place.

"Still, I don't imagine you can just switch back for the wanting to," he mused.

Catherine tensed. She would have to tell him. "I...I don't know. Perhaps—"

But he cut her off. "So I think the thing to do is to take advantage of whatever time you'll have here, however long it is," he said decisively. She looked up hopefully. "How would you like to see 1994 my way?"

He was grinning like a little boy, his hazel eyes twinkling, and Catherine thought he had never looked more handsome. "What do you mean?" asked Catherine breathlessly. Being this close to Logan did odd things to her, making her forget her resolve. "I have seen the mall, and television—"

He held up a hand. "You ain't seen nothing yet, kid. Trust me. I'll have to get a few business details ironed out, and then I plan to take a real vacation. And you're taking it with me!"

Guiltily promising herself she would tell him about the clock later, Catherine agreed.

THE NEXT MORNING, to her parents' evident surprise, Catherine suggested that they all attend church. She was relieved to find that the Episcopal service had not changed out of recognition since her time—nor had Trinity Church, for that matter. It had apparently escaped the Civil War fires that destroyed so many of the buildings she remembered.

During the quiet before the service, she prayed fervently that her exchange with Kathryn was God's will—and that she might be allowed to stay in this time, with Logan. Also that Kathryn, in the past, would find a rich and fulfilling life. Afterward, she felt somewhat calmer, ready to face whatever Logan—and the future—held in store for her.

To her surprise, there was no opposition to his plan from either of the Monroes. "I think it's a marvelous idea," Mrs. Sykes-Monroe gushed when Logan mentioned his plans at dinner Sunday evening. "It will give you and Kathy a wonderful chance to get back on your old, familiar footing." Catherine winced, strongly reminded of her real mother's matchmaking attempts with Ryan James—though she would never have suggested going off alone with him overnight before the wedding!

"I think a little vacation will do you both good," Mr. Monroe agreed. "You have a reputation for working yourself too hard, Logan, and I'm sure Kathy could use a change of scene. Why don't you take her to the country? That should be a relief after two years in D.C."

"We might work that in," said Logan noncommittally. Catherine could see that he was suppressing a smile at her shock at her parents' wholehearted approval of what seemed a scandalously immoral idea to her.

"The timing is great," Annette chimed in. "Dave called just this afternoon to say he's flying home next weekend, and he wants me to come back with him to Kansas for a week or two."

"A week or two is just what we had in mind, too," said Logan, looking at Catherine as if for confirmation.

Though she knew she should feel trapped by their evident collaboration, she could not manage to feel anything but happy and excited. She had been used to having her life ordered by others for as long as she could remember, but never to such good effect as this.

"Yes, that is just what we had discussed," she said firmly, earning a look of surprise from both Logan and Annette. On sudden inspiration, she added, "I have a few things to take care of in Washington, so we will probably spend a day or two there, though certainly not the entire time." She had wanted to see that city ever since discovering that Kathryn had lived there for the past two years. She hoped her desire would not conflict too badly with Logan's plans.

As IT TURNED OUT, Logan had already intended to take Catherine to Washington as part of his "grand tour," she discovered later that evening as she, Logan and Annette met to discuss strategy in Annette's room.

"You were great at dinner, Catherine," exclaimed Annette. "For a minute I thought you and Kathy had switched back! 'I have a few things to take care of,'" she mimicked, her nose in the air.

"Before you announce any other plans to your parents, though, maybe I should share our itinerary with you," said Logan. "I thought we'd start with the beach—Hilton Head Island should be warm enough for swimming by now. And before you ask," he continued, "I plan to book us separate rooms everywhere we go. I don't want to shock you *too* badly...at least not right away." Catherine blushed, predictably, and Logan grinned. She was glad, though, to have that question answered without the embarrassment of asking. "It's nice to find a girl these days with old-fashioned values," he said with a wink.

"And we're talking *old*-fashioned," interjected Annette, plainly relieved to have Logan in on the unsettling secret.

"I see the world has lost its morals since my time," quipped Catherine, entering into the spirit of the conversation. "I'll simply have to put them back."

"Good luck!" exclaimed Logan and Annette together, and the three of them dissolved into laughter.

The next three days passed in a whirl of shopping and packing, with Annette offering plenty of guidance. During one trip to the mall, as they passed one of the larger department stores, Catherine's eye was caught by a display composed of three nearly naked mannequins arranged around brightly colored towels and sand.

"What on earth can they be selling in there?" she asked in a shocked voice.

Annette followed her gaze and began to chuckle. "I'm sorry, Catherine, I'm sure it's not funny to you. You're perfectly right, today's swimsuits *are* indecent—there's no other word for them—but everyone wears them, anyway. Even women who don't have the figures for them. Come to think of it, we should get you one, since you'll need it for Hilton Head."

"Not like those, surely!" Embarrassed, Catherine averted her eyes to avoid staring at the models before them.

"No, I'm sure they'll have some one-pieces, too. Let's go look." Catherine trailed after her doubtfully, wondering again if she would ever really fit in here. So much of the future was beautiful, even luxurious, but as she'd said the other night, morals seemed to have all but evaporated. She had been anything but a prude in her own time, constantly being taken to task by her parents for her disregard of convention, but here...

They reached the racks of swimsuits, and Annette held one of the more modest designs up for Catherine's inspection. It had a very low back, but the front was not too revealing. The stretchy black fabric was covered with bright pink roses. It was quite striking, really, and eminently more suited to its purpose than anything worn for bathing in 1825. Catherine picked up two others of similar style to try on, and then, in a spirit of fun, seized one of the ridiculously skimpy bikinis, as well. Annette gave her an encouraging thumbs-up as she went into the dressing room.

Once alone, she first tried on the outrageous bikini, her spirits still high, and turned to examine herself critically in the mirror. She was startled to see how well it looked, even though she blushed at the very thought of anyone seeing her in it. Every curve of breast and hip was outlined, even those that weren't exposed. She was even more startled to notice that the white, untanned portions of her body conformed very closely to the lines of the indecent garment. Kathryn must have spent a great deal of time outdoors in a similar suit. Logan and Annette had implied that she was rather wild, but really—!

After that first suit, the others seemed positively modest by comparison, and she finally settled on the black-and-rose one Annette had first held up. It still outlined every curve, but at least the curves were covered, for the most part.

"I might as well wear a coat of paint, for all the concealment this offers, but I suppose it is practical," she commented to Annette after paying for the suit.

"Don't worry, you're hardly alone in your opinion of modern swimwear. Even I can't imagine anyone wearing some of these things. Look at this one, for instance!" She held up a metallic gold bikini with star-shaped cutouts on the seat.

Catherine stared for a moment, then gasped with laughter. "Oh, no! That one must be a jest. And look at this!" She picked up a lime-green suit that seemed to be constructed entirely of strings—and very few strings, at that— and both girls dissolved into giggles. She turned to put the green suit back, still grinning, and found Logan standing beside her.

Catherine flushed scarlet to have been caught holding such an obscene garment by anyone, especially Logan. She desperately tried to think of something—anything—to say, but Annette rescued her long before inspiration struck.

"Why, Logan! Fancy meeting you here. Shopping for la-dies' lingerie, are you?" Her eyes also still twinkled with fun.

"No, as a matter of fact I was hoping to find you two be-fore you'd eaten lunch. I've been combing the mall for nearly an hour and was drawn by the sound of familiar laughter. Are you planning to buy that?"

His expression was suggestive, causing Catherine to red-den even further. "I...no. That is, I was just putting it back. I bought this one." She held up the black-and-rose, feeling that even that suit should not properly be seen by male eyes.

"Very nice," he remarked. "And it will undoubtedly suit you better, though few men would agree with me, I'm sure." To her relief, he turned back to Annette and she quickly stuffed the suit back into its bag. "Lunch, ladies?"

CHAPTER FIFTEEN

FINALLY, SUDDENLY, it was time to leave. Catherine had seen little of Logan since their lunch at the mall, as he had been working long hours to tie up his business obligations for the next two weeks. As a result, she now found herself unexpectedly shy of him. She could scarcely believe that she was actually doing this—going off alone with a man for two whole weeks. But nothing would have made her back out now.

The reassuring smiles Logan shot her way as they packed his sports car only made her heart beat faster, and it was with considerable nervousness that she got in the car and waved goodbye to Annette and her parents.

"So tell me, Catherine," said Logan conversationally after the Monroe house was left behind. "How long did it take to travel to, say, Charleston in 1825?" He'd noticed her nervousness and wanted to put her at ease. He also wanted to impress her thoroughly with the wonders of the future, so that she would want to stay, though he hardly admitted it to himself. Guiltily, he pushed thoughts of Kathryn from his mind.

"Charleston?" Catherine appeared to relax somewhat, as Logan had intended. "One full day on horseback, pressing hard, if the roads were dry and one could change horses. By carriage, it generally took two. Of course, if the roads were mud, it could take much longer. How long does it take now?"

"A little less than two hours." She looked at him doubt-fully. "Well, just think how much faster we're going. Once we're out of the city, we'll be able to go sixty-five, which is better than a mile a minute."

She blinked, working it out. "So how long will it take to reach Hilton Head Island?"

"A little longer, about three hours. I've reserved rooms for five nights there, then one in Charleston, and the next few in Washington, D.C."

"Are we going to be able to drive all the way to Washington in one day?" she sounded incredulous.

"We could, but I have other plans."

"What?"

But he only smiled enigmatically and said, "You'll see." He savored the surprise he had in store for her. This was going to be fun.

"I haven't seen any fields planted with cotton," she commented some time later.

She seemed much more comfortable in his presence now, he noticed with relief. For his part, he had a hard time keeping his eyes on the road with her so near. "No, South Carolina is mostly a tobacco state these days," he replied. "I think cotton is mainly grown in the southwest now, in Oklahoma, Arkansas and Texas."

"I remember those states from a map in one of the books Annette got for me, but none of them were part of the Union in 1825. There are fifty states now, correct?"

"I keep forgetting how much you have to learn. Right, there are fifty states. I'd like to show you every one of them someday." Despite his best efforts, he couldn't keep a certain warmth from his voice.

She pinkened slightly, but only asked, "Which is the most recent?"

"Hawaii. It was added in the late fifties, I think. The 1950s, that is. Now that's a state I *do* plan to take you to, if all works out according to plan."

"On this trip, you mean?"

"Uh, no. But hopefully not too far in the future." He mustn't push her too fast, he reminded himself. Catherine was from another time, with different customs. If he frightened her, she just might decide she was better off back there.

They pulled into the resort hotel on Hilton Head Island just after midday. Catherine was astonished at the size of the complex—it was as large as the mall, and much, much, taller! "We're going to stay here?" she gasped.

"That's right," said Logan, plainly enjoying her reaction. "Come on, let's go check in."

Catherine had thought that London society had reached the ultimate in luxury, but she found she was wrong. The lobby of the huge hotel was a marvel in marble and glass. A porter carried their luggage and showed them to their rooms, as he might have done in a grand hotel in the London Catherine remembered. Except for the elevator, of course. This one was not glassed-in, but the feeling of moving rapidly upward still caused a strange sensation in her stomach.

Logan took a few minutes to show her the various amenities of her room, which was the epitome of understated elegance with rich blue carpeting and matching drapes that opened onto a balcony with a view of the Atlantic Ocean.

"The ocean looks so much calmer from up here than from the deck of a ship," she commented when he proudly displayed the vista.

"You've sailed?" he asked in surprise.

"To England and back. I told Annette, but I had forgotten that you wouldn't know. Are ships much faster now, as well?"

"Probably, though I'm not sure. I've never been on one." Her look was disbelieving. "There are other ways to travel now that have made ships almost obsolete, except for pleasure cruises. But that's part of my surprise, so don't ask for details, yet." She grimaced at him and he laughed. "Get into your suit and we'll hit the beach. I'll meet you in the hallway in five minutes." He put one arm around her shoulders and gave her a quick squeeze.

The sensation that flowed through Catherine at his touch was electric and made her aware of his body and her own in a way she had not been before. When the door closed behind him, she took out the swimsuit that had looked comparatively modest in the store, but which now looked scandalously indecent. Her courage nearly failed her. Could she really bring herself to wear it in front of Logan?

Taking a deep breath, she put it on quickly and surveyed herself doubtfully in the large mirror over the vanity. It covered far less than the underthings she had worn in 1825. Snatching up the beach cover-up she had bought to match the suit, she wrapped it around her. That was better. Nervously, she stepped into the hall.

Logan was already waiting for her, wearing nothing but a pair of swim trunks and a towel draped over his shoulders. Catherine tried to avert her eyes from his marvelous body—who would have guessed he would have all that golden curling hair on his chest?

"I, ah, I don't know how to swim," she said lamely as he extended his arm to her. She placed her hand on his arm, acutely conscious of the feel of his bare skin beneath her fingers.

"I'll teach you," he said, a flicker behind his eyes telling her that he guessed her thoughts.

As it turned out, the water was really too cold to do more than splash around in the little breakers on the sand. A beach was a new experience for Catherine, since her only previous contact with the ocean had been on ships leaving from large, crowded ports. Logan alluded to the beautiful beaches of Hawaii, with another half promise to take her there, and her heart soared. Had the world been as beautiful in 1825? Somehow, she didn't think so—not without Logan.

Looking around, she saw that her suit was indeed one of the most modest on the beach. *Why, just look at that blond girl in that tiny little suit!* she thought, appalled. *She's hanging out of it in every conceivable place!* She looked quickly at Logan to see if he was watching the obscene spectacle, but he appeared not to have noticed.

"Why don't you let me put some sunscreen on your back," he suggested, catching her eye and giving her a slow, warm smile that made her tingle all over. The sun picked out highlights in his golden hair, making him look more handsome than ever.

"Sunscreen?"

He held up a small brown bottle. "It screens out the sun so you don't get burned. You're so pale, I think you need it."

"Pale? You should have seen me in 1825." She laughed, turning her shoulders to him so that he could apply the magical lotion. "This sunscreen would certainly have sold well in my time," she said to distract herself from the pleasure of his large, warm hands spreading the cool lotion over her back and arms. "White skin was all the rage then." What would it be like to have those hands massaging the rest of her body? She cut off that line of thought hastily.

"Shall I put some on your back?" she asked boldly when he had finished, hoping he would not see through her feeble ruse to touch his body.

"Yes, thanks" was all he said, handing her the bottle as if there was nothing in the least improper about it. She was sure he could feel her hand trembling as she smoothed the sunscreen across his broad back and shoulders. Every time she touched him she felt the pull of a bond between them, more and more powerful. Could he feel it?

As she finished applying the lotion, Logan wondered what had happened to him. Where was his devil-may-care attitude, the humor he tried to bring to every situation? Something about this girl robbed him of his detachment, drawing him in tightly to an emotional intensity he knew was out of all proportion to the short time he had known her. He had desired other women before, even loved them, lightly and briefly, but this was different. It was as though Catherine were a part of him. The thought of losing her was more than he could bear. In fact, he'd deliberately ignored what might be happening to Kathryn, his childhood friend and surrogate sister, rather than risk that loss.

Striving to project a casual lightness that he didn't feel, he rolled over to face her, asking, "What would you like to do while we're here? The twentieth century and I are at your service."

She put her head to one side, considering. Though her features were Kathryn's, there was an animation, an openness about her expression that made her a completely different person. Looking at her now, Logan couldn't imagine how he'd ever been fooled.

"I'd like you to teach me how to drive a car," she said at last.

"To... Well!" He gave a startled laugh. "Not what one normally thinks of doing for a romantic beach vacation, but your wish is my command. My car is a stick shift, though, which will make things harder. We'll need to find an empty parking lot so you can learn to work the clutch—if you really want to do this."

She nodded firmly, her charming face determined. "If I am going to live in this time, I'll need to learn the skills that go with it. And riding and driving—carriages, that is—were always passions of mine."

With an effort, Logan stopped himself from making a comment about other passions he'd like to teach her. She stirred him so strongly it was all too easy to forget the cultural gap he'd have to overcome before she'd be ready for *that* kind of instruction. ''We'll try to get in a lesson before dinnertime, then,'' he said instead.

To Logan's amazement, Catherine proved an extremely apt pupil. He remembered the one disastrous driving lesson he'd tried to give Kathryn when she was fifteen. She'd been unwilling to listen, afraid of the car, and had stormed off after ten minutes shouting that he had no business telling her what to do. By contrast, Catherine listened and appeared to absorb every word he said.

''So I should start pressing the accelerator *before* I've let the clutch all the way out?'' she asked.

''That's right. Sort of ease off the clutch and ease onto the gas at the same time.''

She followed his directions and the car moved forward almost smoothly, with no bucking this time—and on only her fourth try. Logan recalled that it had taken him dozens of tries, when he'd first learned to operate a clutch. ''That's wonderful!'' he congratulated her warmly, feeling a glow of pride in her accomplishment that he hadn't felt when it had been his own.

''May I drive back to the hotel now?'' she asked eagerly after circling the large lot without incident, even shifting into second gear at his direction.

''Whoa! I don't think you're quite ready for traffic yet,'' Logan cautioned her, though admiration for her spunk swelled within him. ''This was just your first lesson. Maybe tomorrow or the next day you can take it on the road.''

Catherine pulled the car to an almost-smooth halt, with just one jerk at the end, and turned a glowing face to him. ''Oh, Logan, I don't know how I can ever thank you for this! I feel as though all of my dreams are coming true.''

Again, he had to bite his tongue to keep from making a suggestive reply. ''If you're happy, that's thanks enough, Catherine. Let's head back and have some dinner, okay? We'll continue your driving lessons tomorrow.''

They dined in the sumptuous hotel lounge overlooking the water, and afterward went for a barefoot walk on the beach. Catherine had never imagined anything so romantic. Moonlight glittered on the waves and the sand was damp and coarse beneath her feet. Logan walked by her side, almost, but not quite, touching her.

She couldn't help remembering the two novels Annette had given her to read, a far cry from those of Jane Austen or even Walter Scott. Would Logan expect her to behave as the women in those books had? Would he do the things that those heroes had done? A shiver of anticipation and alarm went through her at the thought. But that was fiction, she reminded herself sternly. Annette had warned her not to take those novels literally. Still, she was more than a little bit disappointed when Logan left her with no more than a smile and a touch of his finger on her cheek when they retired to their separate rooms for the night.

She scolded herself for that disappointment, telling herself that she should be relieved. If he had done more—if he had kissed her—she knew she would have wantonly revealed the depth of her feelings to him. She might even have encouraged him to do things that would have compromised her irrevocably. And until she knew for certain that she would be staying in this time, she could not risk that sort of commitment. Strangely dissatisfied, she got ready for bed.

The next morning, she was eager to continue her driving lessons. Somehow, she felt that if she could master the skills of this time she might be allowed to stay, illogical though she knew that was. In addition, she wanted to make Logan proud of her, and in that, at least, she seemed successful. After only an hour of additional practice he allowed her to drive his car out of the lot.

"We'll stick with this residential area for now, where there's hardly any traffic," he said. "I can't believe how fast you've picked this up. You're the best student I've ever had!"

She glowed at his praise, glancing at him with a smile of thanks. Unfortunately, she swerved slightly at the same time.

"Steady, steady," he cautioned. "Keep your eyes on the road."

"I forget how much more responsive this steering wheel is than carriage horses," she said ruefully, feeling a bit foolish. "Of course, a horse can be every bit as tricky when one is riding."

"Really? I wouldn't know," replied Logan.

She dared another quick look at him, this time keeping a firm grip on the wheel. "You don't ride?" To her surprise, he looked slightly uncomfortable.

"Never had a reason to learn, though Kathy tried to get me to, once or twice. She was gung-ho about it in her teens."

"Well, then," said Catherine, smoothly making a right turn onto another quiet street, "as soon as I graduate from this course, it will be your turn for some schooling. I will teach you to ride!" Logan looked less than enthusiastic, but didn't argue.

THAT AFTERNOON, LOGAN pronounced Catherine fit for the open road. He still couldn't believe how quickly she had learned to drive, though she explained to him that she'd had quite a lot of experience with carriages, and that maneuvering in automobile traffic, though at higher speeds, wasn't all that different. "At least the pedestrians stay out of the road here," she'd said.

Now, though, he'd have to live up to the other half of the bargain and learn to ride a horse—something he wasn't really looking forward to. He'd rather spend their remaining time here walking on the beach, gradually breaking down the cultural barriers separating them, though going so slowly was nearly killing him. On second thought, maybe horseback riding lessons were safer.

They found a stable the next day that was willing to rent them two horses by the hour without sending anyone along with them, once Catherine showed that she knew how to handle a horse by saddling and mounting one unassisted. Logan was suitably impressed and knew he made a poor showing by contrast, climbing up the side of his mount as if it were a wall.

"These poor brutes don't have enough spirit to teach you much," Catherine said to him once they were out of earshot of the stable workers, "but at least you can learn the basics. Let go of the saddle and pick up your reins, so. You're not directing that horse, you know, it's just following mine." She was half turned in her saddle, smiling back at him, effortlessly guiding her own beast, Logan saw with appreciation—and a touch of envy. That must be what his driving had looked like to her, he supposed. He picked up the reins.

"Now, we'll just walk a bit before trying a trot," she said as he pulled up almost even with her. "I rather doubt we'll be able to coax them much beyond that."

"A trot will be plenty," he quickly assured her. She laughed, a sound he knew he'd never tire of hearing.

By the time their hour was up, Logan felt almost comfortable on the back of the horse, though he knew he hadn't made a fraction of the progress Catherine had in the same time behind the wheel. If things went as he hoped, he'd make sure she had a horse of her own in the not-too-distant future, since she so obviously loved them. Maybe he'd buy one for himself, too.

CATHERINE HATED to leave Hilton Head two days later, when it was time to check out of their wonderful hotel. She couldn't imagine ever being so happy anywhere else. Still, it was probably just as well. Logan—his face, his voice and, yes, scandalous as it was, his body—seemed to be all she could think about. Perhaps away from the magic of the island she would be able to think rationally again, to consider what she should do about the future, hers and Kathryn's.

They reached Charleston a mere two hours after leaving their hotel and Logan drove directly to the restored section of the city, parking the car at a garage on Meeting Street. "Let's walk a little," he said obscurely, earning a curious look from Catherine.

Once they turned the corner of the parking garage, she understood—it was as though she had been transported back in time again. She had been in Charleston only twice before, on her trips to and from London, but she could swear that this portion of it was just as it had been. In Columbia she had seen two or three restored mansions that she remembered, but here entire blocks had been preserved.

She said little as they walked past the beautiful single and double houses that she had seen before—was it weeks ago, or 170 years ago?—but she trusted that Logan knew her well enough by now to understand how touched she was that he would bring her here. "Thank you," she said when they returned to the car an hour later. "I see now that the past really isn't gone, after all."

Logan smiled down at her. "I hope this is all you'll want of it, Catherine. I can't stand to think that you might be taken away from me now."

Catherine's heart skipped a beat. It was almost a declaration. She'd longed to hear it, but he had to know the truth before she could accept it. "I want to stay more than anything," she said, her heart in her eyes. "But . . . what about Kathryn?"

He frowned. "Kathryn? I'm sure she's doing fine—"

"Logan, there's something I have to tell you," she interrupted, determined to see it through before she lost her nerve. He cared for her, she knew that now, but how much? "I think there may be a way I can change back with Kathryn."

"How?" He was eyeing her warily now, suddenly tense.

"One night—" she couldn't bring herself to say which one "—as I was walking past the grandfather clock, I felt a sort of tug. I...pulled back. I suspect that if she and I were to both stand by the clock long enough, we might manage to switch again." She watched his face anxiously, but it told her nothing.

"Do you want to go back?"

Catherine dropped her eyes. "No," she said in a small voice. "I don't. Is that very selfish of me?"

"If it is," he said tenderly, "then I am every bit as selfish." She looked up hopefully to find a wealth of emotion in his earnest gaze. "Whatever is going on with Kathy—and I've convinced myself that she's all right—I can't stand the thought of losing you, Catherine. Please promise me that you won't try out your theory. It probably wouldn't work, anyway."

"But—"

He stopped her with a kiss, touching her cheek with gentle fingertips. It was the first kiss they had shared since that night they'd seen *Star Wars*. She reveled in it, responding eagerly. They clung together for a few brief seconds before awareness of their surroundings pulled them apart.

"Come on," said Logan when he released her. "It's time we checked into our hotel."

He lifted out their overnight bags, and they walked the short distance to the lovely antebellum-style hotel overlooking Meeting Street where he had reserved their rooms. After that kiss, Catherine found herself wishing, again, that they would be sharing a room, but she dared not say so. She felt she could tell Logan almost anything, but not that.

He installed her in her room, which at first glance might have been that of 1800s Charleston, and told her to be ready for dinner in half an hour. While she dressed, the illusion of the past became so strong that Catherine began to fear she had somehow been pulled back to her own time, even without the clock. It was with profound relief that she found the modern bathroom adjoining her room, which proved to her satisfaction that she was still in 1994.

"For a few moments, I felt that I was going to walk outside and find that I was back...back then," she couldn't help saying to Logan as they stepped out into the early dusk settling over the city. "The past seems so close here. *Too* close."

Logan put an arm around her shoulders and drew her against his side possessively. "We'll be out of here in the morning. Then I can promise you you'll have no doubts at all about what time you're in!" She looked up at him curiously, surprised at the fierceness in his tone. She decided to save any questions for later.

They dined at a restaurant in a restored house in the historic district, which would have been more charming for Catherine, if Logan had not constantly pointed out small anachronistic details, such as the ice floating in their water glasses, that would not have existed when the house was built. He muttered something about McDonald's as they were leaving, but she was unable to coax him into repeating the remark.

Walking slowly back to their hotel they said little, each delighting in the physical presence of the other. Their hands met, as if by chance, and clasped. Outside their rooms, they lingered in the hallway, making inane remarks about the buildings they had seen, as both tried to postpone the inevitable parting for the night. Catherine longed to invite Logan into her room, but could think of no pretext for doing so.

"What time do we leave for Washington in the morning?" she asked, stalling.

"Our fl...that is, we need to leave the hotel by eight-thirty," replied Logan, the twinkle that had been strangely absent during the evening returning to his eyes. "It's time you *really* experienced the modern world."

"Logan, what are you planning?" she demanded, more curious than ever.

"You'll find out in the morning. Good night, Catherine." He bent his head to kiss her in parting, but neither of them were prepared for the shock that went through them as their lips touched. The kiss in the parking garage had been nothing compared to this. Catherine's arms went around his neck of their own volition and he clasped her tightly to him. At the sound of footsteps on the stairs, Logan swore softly under his breath and released her.

"Catherine, I..." he began shakily. She looked up at him expectantly, ready to do whatever he asked. "Never mind. Good night." He backed away quickly and disappeared into his room, leaving her trembling and confused.

Her hand shook as she fitted the key into the lock of her room. Why had he left her like that? Why? She was sure he had wanted her as much as she wanted him. Perhaps he was unwilling to commit himself, knowing that she might not stay, she thought, leaning against the inside of her closed door. *I'll have to convince him the bond between us is strong enough to transcend time. He's the one I've waited for—the reason I came here. I know that now.*

CHAPTER SIXTEEN

"Is WASHINGTON A VERY large city now?" asked Catherine as she and Logan drove away from their hotel the next morning. "I remember Leslie Allerby telling me that her mother visited it once and thought it a grubby, muddy place not fit to house the President. Of course, Mrs. Allerby was from Philadelphia, so she probably had reason to be biased."

"Well," Logan said, laughing, "there are still those who would say it's not fit to house the President, but it's grown enormously since your time. I'm taking you there mainly for its educational value, though. There's a museum there I'm pretty sure you'll enjoy. By the way, how long would you say it took to travel to Washington in your day?" His eyes danced wickedly.

"You love doing this, don't you? I'm not sure, but certainly several days. I never traveled there myself. I suppose it can be done in less than a day now?"

"Well, it's actually a full day's *drive* from here, but I expect we'll make it in under two hours." The sideways glance he gave her was full of fun, and she could not resist rising to his obvious bait.

"Do you mean we're not driving? How *are* we getting there, Logan?" They were on Interstate 26 now, going north at nearly sixty miles an hour, by the speedometer. He was right; even at a mile a minute it would take many hours to reach Washington by car.

"Look up ahead," he said in answer. She looked and saw a large sign that read Charleston International Airport. Logan took the exit indicated and smiled smugly at her. "Didn't I say I had a surprise for you?"

The word *airport* meant nothing to Catherine, so she remained silent for a few minutes until she saw a huge silver object rise above the buildings they were approaching. "Look! Logan, look!" she cried, pointing. "Is that a rocket ship? Is that what the men rode in to the moon?" She had scarcely believed that portion of the history book, but here was the evidence before her eyes.

Logan tried unsuccessfully to turn a guffaw into a cough, which earned him a reproachful glare. "I'm sorry, Catherine, really I am," he said contritely. "But no, that's not a rocket. It's an airplane. That's my surprise."

"An airplane?" The picture of an airplane in the history book had looked nothing like that. In fact, it only held one person. "But it is so big! Annette pointed one out to me in the sky once, and it looked quite tiny. Is it like a rocket?"

"Well, a little bit, I guess, but it doesn't go into space, just up in the air. And it can carry a lot more people. You'll see. I'll let you form your own opinion." He had no intention of so much as hinting that some people were afraid to fly; he wanted her to enjoy the experience. She certainly didn't *look* fearful, he thought, studying her face as they got out of the car a moment later. Catherine was looking around eagerly, apparently hoping to glimpse another airplane.

The airport was not particularly crowded at that hour of the morning, and they were able to check in quickly and proceed directly to the boarding gate. Catherine would not sit down to wait, to Logan's amusement, but stood with her face pressed to the glass of the huge windows, watching the planes land and take off.

"Don't ask me to explain how they fly," Logan cautioned her in an undertone when she turned to him excitedly. "If you're really interested, I'll get you a book on the subject." Just then, an announcement was made for the first-class passengers to begin boarding. "That's us."

Catherine accompanied him eagerly, her head swiveling from side to side in an effort to see everything at once. Just ahead, a small boy of perhaps four or five hung back from the doorway, shaking his head vigorously as his mother tried to coax him forward. Without hesitation, Catherine stepped up to them.

"Hi, I'm Cathy," she said cheerfully to the little boy. "What's your name?" The harassed mother glanced at her in surprise, but did not interfere.

"J-Jimmy," he said with a hiccup.

"Do you know what, Jimmy?" she asked, and he shook his head. "This is going to be my very first time ever on an airplane, and I'd feel ever so much better if a brave fellow like you would hold my hand while I got on. Would you do that for me?"

He considered her solemnly for a moment, then nodded. "I guess so." He held out his hand and she clasped it with a great show of gratitude. "Don't worry, Cathy," he said confidingly as they moved down the passageway to the waiting plane, his mother and Logan trailing wonderingly behind them. "My mommy says flying is the safest way to travel nowadays."

"Thank you, Jimmy, I'm glad you told me that," she said, smiling down at him. "I think you need to go sit with your mother now, but I'm sure I'll see you while we're in the air." Jimmy nodded and allowed his hand to be transferred to his mother's.

"Thank you," the woman whispered as she led him down the aisle ahead of Catherine and Logan, who moved to stand beside her. They could hear Jimmy's clear voice explaining how he had helped "Cathy not be afraid" as they took their seats.

"You handled that very well," commented Logan with a penetrating look. "Do you have little brothers and sisters?"

Catherine gingerly seated herself in the plush window seat. "No, although I've always gotten on well with children. My mother had two more after me, but both died as infants—a boy and a girl."

"I'm sorry," said Logan.

"I was, too, especially the second time, for I was old enough to understand. But it is one of those things that happen in life. I doubt you could find more than one or two families in Columbia that hadn't lost at least one child. When little Amy died, though, I swore I would never have children myself because it was so terrible to have them die." She tried to laugh at her childish foolishness, but couldn't quite.

"That's something else I think you'll like about the present," said Logan softly, deeply touched. "Very few babies die now. And people live much longer."

"So twenty isn't so old, now?"

"You're twenty?" he asked in surprise. Catherine nodded. "That's odd. Kathryn was twenty-three. Which means you are now, I guess—and she's twenty. She should like that."

But Catherine frowned. "I hope people live at least three years longer now."

"It's not too uncommon for people to live to one hundred today," Logan informed her.

"Oh! I should feel sorry for Kathryn then, instead of feeling cheated of three years," she exclaimed. "One hundred!" She shook her head in wonder, but then her attention was drawn to the little window beside her as the plane began moving.

Logan reached across to help her fasten her seat belt and told her to keep watching. After a few turns, their speed increased—as did the noise the airplane was making. It was almost as bad as the speedway had been. Suddenly, the rumbling sound ceased and the ride became noticeably smoother. At the same time, the ground appeared to be farther away.

"We're in the air!" Catherine watched delightedly as objects on the ground grew smaller and smaller. Looking down at the ground, she had no warning before the view suddenly became a white blank. "Oh!" She grasped Logan's arm. "What happened?" Her face showed the closest thing to fear he had yet seen from her.

"Nothing happened," he assured her. "We're just flying through a cloud."

"Aahh! You mean we're *inside* a cloud right now?" She turned back to the window wonderingly.

"In a couple of minutes we'll be above them," Logan said. "I think you'll like that view."

She watched as the airplane continued to climb until it emerged into blue sky floored with fantastic, puffy white shapes. It looked solid enough to walk on. "It's like heaven," Catherine breathed reverently. "Are you sure I haven't died?"

Logan pinched her arm playfully and she jumped. "You seem pretty much alive to me." She wrinkled her nose at him and turned back to contemplate the beautiful scene outside.

The flight was all too short for Catherine. A light breakfast of coffee, French croissants and strawberries was served to them, and she made one foray into the economy class to make sure little Jimmy was enjoying his first flight as much as she was. She also discovered that there was actually a bathroom on board the plane. Well, one couldn't actually bathe in the tiny cubicle, but still . . . ! Then, suddenly, the pilot was directing their attention to the Fasten Seat Belts sign and informing the passengers they would be landing in ten minutes.

Catherine had thoroughly enjoyed the flight, but she found Dulles International Airport more than a little bit intimidating. There were so many people, and they all seemed to be in such a hurry! She drew closer to Logan, and he looked down at her in some concern.

"Are you okay?"

"I . . . I suppose so," she said. "London was just as crowded, but the people there didn't seem to move so quickly."

"From your description of the clothes they wore, they probably couldn't," commented Logan, and she grinned in response. "That's better. We'll claim our bags, rent a car and get away from this madhouse, all right?" She nodded, already recovering from her brief panic. "I'm afraid this is just a taste of what big cities are like these days," he said as they matched their pace to those around them. "Maybe I shouldn't have pushed you into this so soon."

"No, I want this, Logan, truly. Already I am getting used to it. I remember now that London took some adjustment for me, as well. I will be fine, you'll see."

Catherine loved what she saw of Washington, never knowing that Logan carefully kept her from the poorer areas of the city. She was especially intrigued by the Smithsonian Institution's Museum of History and Technology, where she was able to trace the development of every technological advance she had seen (and many that she hadn't) from her time to the present. Logan had to drag her away from the Air and Space Museum, as well.

"I knew you would like this place, but I underestimated you!" he exclaimed. "We can come back before we leave if you want to, but I want you to see as many different things as possible."

She followed him reluctantly, still looking over her shoulder at the Apollo module on display, but soon found that the other sights had charms of their own, as well. She read every word of the Gettysburg Address inscribed in the marble walls of the Lincoln Memorial next to the huge, seated figure of Abraham Lincoln. She marveled at the wisdom of this man who had still been in his teens in 1825. The Jefferson Memorial, though not so grand, touched her more closely as a monument to a President who had served during her lifetime.

Next, Logan took her to the top of the Washington Monument, which made Catherine more nervous than flying had. The elevator went up so quickly, and for such a long time, that her stomach began to turn.

"You don't get airsick on the plane, but you get green around the gills in an elevator?" Logan chided her when she confessed her queasiness to him.

"I was never seasick, either, though we had some rough weather on the way back to America. But this is different!"

Logan put his arm around her shoulders and held her close until the elevator stopped. It helped immeasurably. The view from the top was spectacular, but Catherine couldn't quite believe that the panorama of impossibly high buildings and traffic-choked streets was real. It seemed more like a painting, the edges hazed by an artist's brush.

They changed for the evening in their beautiful hotel on Pennsylvania Avenue overlooking the Ellipse and then took a taxi to the Potomac River, where Logan had arranged for a dinner cruise aboard the *Spirit of Washington*. Though the food was delicious, Catherine scarcely noticed what she ate, so mesmerized was she by Logan's presence across from her and the brilliantly lit city slipping by on either side of the boat. After dinner, there was dancing to a live band.

The only part of the evening Catherine clearly remembered was one very special slow dance, to a tune Logan told her was an oldie by the name of "Color My World." There were no specified steps, but as she swayed to the romantic music in Logan's arms, she couldn't help thinking that the "scandalous" waltz was very tame compared to this sort of dancing.

Logan held her close—very close—one hand pressed firmly to her back. Her face was near his throat and she was overwhelmed by the masculine scent of him. She was reminded of that kiss outside her hotel room in Charleston that had seemed to promise so much more—a promise she wanted more than ever to fulfill. She looked up at Logan questioningly, wondering if their closeness was affecting him similarly, and he smiled into her eyes in answer. Catherine blushed deliciously and looked down at his shirtfront.

It was long past midnight when they returned to their hotel to part outside Catherine's room. Again they kissed passionately, emotions mounting toward some indefinable climax, but again Logan released her abruptly. This time when he turned away from her, Catherine touched his arm, halting him. When he faced her, she gasped at the torment in his eyes.

"Oh, Logan," she whispered. "Are you so unhappy? Or does what's happening between us . . . frighten you?"

He choked on something between a laugh and a sob. "Unhappy? Frightened? Oh, Catherine, if you only knew—!"

"I want to know. Please tell me," she implored.

His eyes searched hers before he answered. "The only thing I'm frightened of is hurting *you*. Of pushing you faster than you're ready to go."

Relief washed through her. "Then you have nothing to fear, Logan," she assured him. "There is nothing you could ask of me that I am not ready to give." She trembled at her own boldness, but it was true. She would give herself to him on the roof of the hotel if he wished it.

"Do you mean that, Catherine?" She nodded shyly and he gathered her into his arms again.

"Won't . . . won't you come in?" she asked when she could speak again. For a few painful heartbeats she thought he might decline, but then he smiled.

"If you promise to tell me to leave if I make you uncomfortable," he said.

"I promise," she replied, knowing that he never could. She opened the door to her room and he followed her inside. The door was barely closed before they were in each other's arms again. "Oh, Logan," she murmured. "I have so wanted you to do this."

To her surprise, he chuckled. "And to think I was denying myself for your sake, you temptress. You knew all along what you were doing to me, didn't you?"

She turned innocent eyes up to him. "I?" But she could not keep her lips from twitching.

"You."

He kissed her thoroughly, his hands roaming up and down her back. When he began to unzip her dress she made no move to stop him, instead unknotting his tie and unbuttoning his shirt. These new zippers impressed her again with their convenience as desires she'd barely guessed at flamed to life within her.

Though she longed to feel his whole length against her, he took his time, caressing every inch of her as he stripped away her clothing. Finally, after an exquisite agony of gentle prelude, he joined her, naked, on the bed.

"Tell me what you want," he whispered, his lips tickling her ear. "I never want to hurt you, Catherine. You're too precious to me."

"I want *you*, Logan," she breathed, trembling with eagerness. "All of you that you can give me. Now."

Still he went slowly, stroking and fondling, kissing and nuzzling, until she was at fever pitch, her body clamoring for release. Finally, lingeringly, he entered her. She gasped with the wonder, the ecstasy of the sensations that rolled over and through her, lifting her up to heavenly regions she'd never dreamed existed. There was no pain, only pleasure and a sense of rightness, of belonging, that went even deeper. Logan clasped her tightly to him after he was spent, and they lay there, silently entwined. Catherine had never been so happy in her life. Blissfully, she drifted off to sleep.

When she awoke the next morning Logan was gone, but as she finished dressing he returned, bearing an armload of red roses. "For the start of a special day," he said warmly.

"Oh, Logan—they're lovely!" Joyfully, she inhaled their heady fragrance before turning to arrange her gift in the two vases already in the room. She should be embarrassed, she supposed, by what had occurred between them last night, but somehow she wasn't.

He smiled and a tingle ran down her spine. Now she knew just how much that smile promised. "I'm glad they make you happy," he said. "I've arranged for breakfast here in your room, since it has such a spectacular view." A moment later a tap came on the door and a uniformed bellboy wheeled a cloth-covered table with covered platters to the spot by the window that Logan indicated.

During the meal Catherine and Logan spoke of such small matters as their sightseeing plans for the day, but there was nothing trivial about the lingering looks they exchanged. A deep current of emotion ran beneath their surface conversation.

"This setting is so romantic," said Catherine with a sigh as they finished their meal. She almost hated to leave this room.

Quietly, his tone full of meaning, Logan replied, "That's why I arranged it." Catherine looked at him questioningly and blushed at what she saw in his eyes. She hoped her own were speaking as fluently.

Logan took her hand, his expression as serious as she'd yet seen it. "Catherine, we've known each other for such a short time, but somehow I feel I've been waiting for you all of my life."

Catherine caught her breath. He had felt it, too! She started to speak, but he stopped her.

"I know we have no guarantees for the future, that there are questions to be settled, but—" He hesitated, searching her face. "I love you, Catherine," he said with sudden urgency. "Will you marry me?"

She smiled, feeling a need to lighten his mood somehow. "Of course I will, Logan—I really haven't much choice now, after all, have I?" She intended her tone to be teasing but was startled to see a flash of pain in his eyes.

"I thought you might see it that way," he said. "In fact, I suspect now that may have been my motive—well, one of my motives—" a ghost of a smile crossed his face "—for, er, compromising you last night."

"Logan, I made that decision of my own free choice," she reminded him. "I knew full well what the consequences must be. You must not feel that you have forced me to anything."

His smile was rueful now. "That's just it. You're not obligated by...what we did. Not in this time, much as I might wish otherwise. Whether you marry me or not is still your choice."

"But—" she hated to ask, but forced herself to "—what of Kathryn?"

Logan closed his eyes. "Damn! I'd almost forgotten Kathy! Of course I'm still worried about her, but..." He looked at her again, a wealth of emotion in his eyes. "You are far, far more important to me. Can't we...just assume that she's all right and go on with our lives? There's really nothing else we *can* do, is there?"

Catherine bit her lip, unwilling to repeat her theory about the clock after the way he had responded before. Nor, in her heart of hearts, did she really want to.

"I'll marry you, Logan," she said finally. "Nothing could make me happier than to be your wife. But...should we take our own happiness at the expense of Kathryn's? If a way opens that we can verify Kathryn's fate, I truly believe we should do so."

"I suppose so," he said reluctantly. "But *only* if it won't risk you in any way. You promised, remember?" At her nod, he smiled broadly. "And for now—" he rose and came toward her, his eyes smoldering "—let's see just how happy I can make you."

CHAPTER SEVENTEEN

"HERE, DEAR, I WANT YOU to look at this peach wool traveling dress," said Mrs. Sykes-Prescott, showing Kathryn a ladies' journal. "I believe it would do nicely as part of your trousseau, don't you?"

Kathryn gave some appropriate reply, as she'd been doing in response to similar comments all of yesterday and today, but her mind was far from such mundane matters as wedding plans. She was in agony to know what had happened after Ryan left her. Had he been recognized? She actually found herself wishing that he'd killed the man who had shot Elmo rather than taking an extra risk. It was a horrible thing to wish for, she knew, but she couldn't help it. She was beginning to think that even bad news would be better than this interminable waiting.

When she heard the front door, it was all she could do to keep her seat. Mr. Prescott was back from town, where he'd gone shortly after breakfast. When he entered the parlor her eyes flew at once to his face, trying to tell from his expression whether he had heard anything about Ryan. He looked grave, she thought, but hoped she might be imagining it.

"I'm so glad you're home, dear," said Mrs. S-P blithely. "We've been discussing the flowers we should have at the reception, and I have been unable to get any sort of a decision from your daughter." She cast an indulgent glance in Kathryn's direction. "I believe she is in the sulks because her beau hasn't been to call for two days, though I told her he must have business to attend to. What news in town, Joseph?''

Mr. Prescott frowned at the question and Kathryn held her breath, but Mrs. S-P continued to chatter about wedding plans.

"I forgot to tell you, Cathy, my love," she said, "but I wrote up the announcement this afternoon. Tomorrow I'll have it sent round to the *Columbia Telescope* and the *Gazette*. Would you care to see it?" She rose to locate it in the small writing desk in the corner.

Mr. Prescott looked up sharply. "Is it not yet in the papers, then?" he asked.

"No, dear, I have been so distracted, it was not till today that I could pull my wits together enough to write it up. It should have gone in yesterday, I know, but—"

" 'Tis just as well," broke in Mr. Prescott decidedly. "It shan't go in tomorrow, either, if you please."

"But, Joseph, they have been betrothed three days already!" protested his wife. "People like to know these things."

"People can wait. There are inquiries I wish to make first."

"Why, Father?" asked Kathryn, her voice sounding stilted even to her own ears. "What sort of inquiries?"

"I heard something today that...well, let us not be hasty. I should know something definite by the end of the week. I shall tell you then. It is possible that our Mr. James is not precisely what he seems."

"You seemed very pleased with him three days ago," Kathryn pointed out. "Does he turn out to be married after all?" The question successfully distracted Mrs. S-P, who fell back on the sofa cushions with a gasp, seizing the smelling salts that she always kept nearby. Mr. Prescott was not so easily sidetracked.

"Not to the best of my knowledge," he conceded coolly. "So calm yourself, my dear," he advised his wife.

"What is it, then?" demanded Kathryn. If she had to wait any longer for the news, she'd become a nervous wreck. "As his promised wife, don't I have a right to know?"

"Yes, dear, do tell us," added Mrs. S-P faintly, recovering somewhat on being assured that Mr. James was not a would-be bigamist.

Mr. Prescott looked from one lady to the other and sighed in resignation. "Very well, as I was so unwise as to say anything at all, I suppose I must tell you what I know thus far or risk sending both of you off with the vapors or some such thing. The news in town is that James stole one of Allerby's field hands the night before last, presumably to help him escape. There is a witness who claims he saw James with the fugitive—he also claims that James knocked him out cold when he fired on the escaping slave. The man is one of Allerby's white servants, who is a less than reliable witness, I must say. Even he admits he was drunk at the time. However, James's disappearance adds color to his tale, I fear."

"Disappearance?" Kathryn managed to echo.

"He is not in town, and he's not at Fair Fields. The Captain of the Guard went himself to question him after Allerby reported the theft. I intend to give Mr. James another day, at the least, to come forth to clear himself, and to disprove some other rumors regarding abolitionist tendencies before condemning him in my own mind. But now that I know his connection with our family is not yet public knowledge, things are easier for us. Even if Allerby's charges prove untrue, I have no wish to ally my name with that of a rabble-rouser."

Kathryn struggled with herself to keep from pointing out that her parents hadn't bothered to find out anything about the man except the size of his bankroll. "This sudden concern comes a little late" was all she said.

"But not too late, thank God," Mr. Prescott declared firmly. "I'll inform you of my findings when I have them, ladies. Good night." He rose and left the room, leaving the two women to stare at each other in consternation.

"Perhaps," said Mrs. Sykes-Prescott after a lengthy pause, "we have been a trifle hasty in agreeing to your engagement with a man we know so little about."

"I believe I'll go up to my room until suppertime, Mother." Kathryn stood quickly, afraid her tongue would betray her if she stayed to hear any more of this hypocrisy. "I see no point in discussing it until we know more." She left Mrs. S-P to rationalize her past behavior by herself.

For three more agonizing days, Kathryn kept up a careful pretense of calm. It was abruptly shattered when Mr. Prescott strode into the house on Friday to declare that the wedding was definitely off.

"You can't mean that, Father!" Kathryn stared at him in disbelief. She had nearly convinced herself, during the long, sleepless nights, that Ryan's fortune, and her affection for him, would outweigh other considerations with Mr. Prescott once his temper had a chance to cool.

"I most certainly do. Do you know what James is? A damned abolitionist! I won't have any such kind marrying into *my* family!"

Mrs. Sykes-Prescott gasped. "Oh, Joseph, are you sure? I'm certain *I* never heard any such thing!"

"No, he's been damnably clever about it. He even went so far as to have his slaves spread rumors of his harshness. But I've talked at length to Allerby and his man, and spent three days going through the records at the State House, and no doubt remains, no doubt at all. The man's been freeing his slaves almost since he came to Columbia, which is his right, of course, but damned strange to my thinking. But when he tries freeing someone else's, he's gone too far. Slave stealing is a hanging offense!"

"What evidence is there against him?" demanded Kathryn angrily, pushing away the surge of terror those last words evoked within her.

"Evidence? Why, the man was seen! Allerby's under-groom positively identified him. I spoke to the man himself. He has the bruises to prove James knocked him down."

"Or that someone did!" retorted Kathryn hotly. "No doubt he concocted this story to cover some guilt of his own. You said yourself he was drunk at the time!"

"Being drunk is no crime. What James did is. And that is not all I got from Allerby. It seems our Mr. James was very thick with the Negroes, both slave and free, when he was in Charleston. Allerby even heard rumors he was acquainted with that blackguard Vesey, who masterminded the uprising there."

"So his crime is in the friends he keeps?" Kathryn fanned her outrage to keep panic at bay.

"The friends a man keeps says a lot about him," replied Mr. Prescott pompously. "Allerby has influence in this town, and aims to see your Mr. James rot in jail. At any rate, we don't want a stain like that on our family name."

"Certainly not," echoed Mrs. Sykes-Prescott from her corner of the parlor. Kathryn shot her an accusing look before turning back to her father.

"You're saying Mr. Allerby has enough influence to have an innocent man arrested?"

"Innocent! Do you still try to deceive yourself? Allerby is a Warden, and a close friend to every powerful man in Columbia, to include Judge de Saussure. He can make life here very unpleasant for James, even if all charges against him are disproved. The Guard has already gone after him, though with his skill in the woods I doubt they'll have much luck. He won't dare return to Columbia, though, so we're well out of it. James may be a knave, but he's no fool, not if I'm any judge of character."

Kathryn bit back the sarcastic comment that leapt to her lips, and wondered how she might be able to warn Ryan, or, if worse came to worst, to flee North by his side.

"I... I believe I'll go visit Priscilla, Father," she said as casually as she could. "She'll want to hear this news, I know." She rose to leave the parlor, but Mr. Prescott's next words thwarted her plans.

"No, you will remain in the house, Catherine. I wouldn't put it past young James to make some attempt to kidnap you, even by proxy—and, like as not, you'd go along with it, such is the foolishness of youth. I want you here where your mother can keep an eye on you for the next few weeks, or until that rascal is apprehended."

Kathryn struggled to find some appropriate retort, tears of rage and frustration building behind her eyes. Rather than allow the Prescotts to see her cry, she flung herself from the room, almost colliding with little Alma in her haste.

"Oh! Excuse me, Alma, I must go upstairs." Her voice broke and she turned quickly away. Alma was the last person she wanted to see right now, since it was through Kathryn's favor to her that Ryan was now in such danger. She felt so helpless!

Alma followed her to the foot of the stairs, however, and put a tentative hand on her arm. "Miss, I... I's got somethin' for you," she whispered. "I know I shouldn't say nothin', but I wanted to thank you all the same." She pressed a small square of paper into Kathryn's palm with a smile and disappeared into the dining room.

As soon as she reached the privacy of her room, Kathryn unfolded the note with shaking hands. As she had hoped, it was from Ryan.

Dearest Catherine,
I pray this finds you in time. E. is safe with the Qs for the present, which I knew you would want to know. It appears that my absence will be necessary for some time to come, but I was loath to leave without asking, just once, if you would come with me. If you will not, I perfectly understand and will not love you the less for

it. If you wish to join me, I will contrive to be beneath your window at midnight. Were I wise, or even prudent, I would know better than to ask, but when was a man in love ever wise? If you are not there, I will understand and try to forget, as must you.

                                                            Ryan

By the time she reached the scrawled signature, Kathryn's tears were falling freely from the fullness of her heart and the relief she felt. She'd always prided herself that she never cried, but all that mattered now was that he'd come back for her. How could he think she might refuse? Cheerfully blowing her nose, she looked around, wondering how much in the way of necessities she could fit into the small suitcase she'd seen in the closet.

Packing would have to wait until after dinner, though, for the clock was already striking noon. With her heart a hundred times lighter than it had been only ten minutes earlier, she thrust the precious note into the top of her corset and left her room to trip happily down the stairs.

On the landing, she paused to look up at the clock, still bonging away. Only twelve more hours, she thought rapturously. Then they'd be safe away from this hateful town forever—together! Maybe in the North she'd be able to help support them by sewing, or by making some novelty that was still unheard of in this age.

Absorbed in her thoughts she noticed nothing out of the ordinary. When she breezed into the dining room, however, she stopped short, frozen in shock. Only one person was there ahead of her, but it wasn't either of the people she had almost come to think of as her mother and father. Instead, it was the last person she had expected to see—someone, in fact, she had thought she'd never see again. It was . . . Annette.

CHAPTER EIGHTEEN

"CATHERINE, WHAT'S the matter?" asked Annette, turning at Kathryn's entrance.

"A-Annette?" whispered Kathryn. "How did you..." She looked around her at the room, then down at the turquoise slacks and flowered blouse she was wearing. "I mean, how did *I*... Oh, *shit!*"

"*Kathy?*" Annette fairly squeaked. "Here, quick! Sit down. You look like you're about to faint." She hastily pulled one of the chairs away from the table, and Kathryn slumped into it. "Is... is it really you? You're back?" Annette looked almost as shaken as Kathryn felt.

Kathryn nodded helplessly, looking around her again. "It sure looks that way." She sat up suddenly. "Annette, I've got to go back! Ryan will think I don't want to go with him tonight!"

"Ryan? Go where? Kathy, you just got here!"

"I know, Annette, and I'm awfully glad I got this chance to see you one last time, but— Wait a minute! You knew about the switch? Do my parents know?"

Annette shook her head. "No, only Logan and me. But first, tell me about Ryan and what's been going on with you. Then I'll tell you all about Catherine—I think you'd like her, by the way. She's not a bit like you." She grinned in sudden delight at her friend. "Oh, Kathy, it's great to talk to you again! But quick—tell me everything, before the others come down."

Kathryn launched into an abbreviated version of her experiences since that fateful night nearly a month ago, but had by no means finished when steps were heard in the hallway. Her mother and Logan Thorne came in and took seats at the table, Logan smiling at her with a warmth that she failed to understand. Had he and Catherine somehow become friends during her absence?

The cucumber-and-cream cheese sandwiches were a far cry from the sumptuous meals she'd been enjoying with the Prescotts, but Kathryn barely noticed, she was so frantic about Ryan. When she responded to a question of Logan's he became suddenly silent, glowering suspiciously across the table at her, but she could not be bothered to wonder why.

"Kathy, have you definitely decided on lavender for your bridesmaids?" asked her mother as she rose from the table. Annette had managed to dominate the conversation with trivia up to that point. Kathryn gaped at her, but before she could respond, her mother continued, "Because I saw the prettiest dresses at Rich's this morning that I think you should see. Let me know if you want to drive over there tomorrow."

Kathryn nodded dazedly, afraid to say a word, since Annette had said her mother didn't know about the switch. Bridesmaids? she thought wildly as her mother left the room. What had been going on here? She turned an accusing glance on Annette for not telling her, and her friend threw up a hand defensively.

"Okay, okay, I'm sorry. I wanted to break it to you gently, but there wasn't time."

"Excuse me," interrupted Logan dangerously, "but would one of you tell me what the hell is going on? When did you get back, Kathy? And where is Catherine?"

"Presumably back in 1825," said Kathryn, more calmly than she felt. "And what is this about a wedding? *Whose* wedding?"

"Ours," replied Logan, his forced smile betraying an anguish that Kathryn understood only too well.

"Okay, you two," said Annette in a rallying tone, "let's all go into the living room and hash out what's happened so far before we do anything else."

It was well over an hour later before both stories had been told to everyone's satisfaction and all questions answered for the moment. "Now, all we have to do," concluded Logan, "is reverse this second switch. No offense, Kathy, but I want my Catherine back!"

"None taken, Logan. She sounds like a wonderful girl. And I agree completely. Not only do we have to switch back, we have to do it before midnight tonight, or I'll probably never see Ryan again!" Her eyes misted again, to Logan's and Annette's obvious amazement.

"All right, then, let's get to work!" said Logan briskly, though Kathryn could tell he was struggling with strong emotions himself. "Catherine told me she thought the clock was involved. But she had agreed—" He pressed his lips together and glanced away.

"Yes," said Kathryn excitedly. "The grandfather clock! Both times it was striking the hour and I was standing right in front of it. I assume Catherine must have been, too."

"Then in order to switch back, you just have to stand in front of that clock exactly on the hour." Logan's relief was obvious. He looked at his watch. "It's twenty minutes to two now, Kathy. Is there anything you want to do here for the next few minutes?"

She nodded. "I'd like to see Mother again, now that I know what's going on. I'd really like to see Dad, too, but he probably won't be home for hours, and I'm *not* willing to wait!" She was as relieved as Logan, now that she knew Catherine's motive to return was as strong as her own. "And believe me, once we switch back, I'm never going near that clock again!"

Mrs. Sykes-Monroe appeared surprised and delighted not only at her daughter's unusual affection, but also at her sudden interest in family history after so many years of indifference about the subject. "I knew one day you'd be glad of all my research," she said smugly. "It's the idea of getting married and starting your own family, I'm sure. That's when I became so obsessed with our 'roots,' so to speak."

She wasn't able to answer Kathryn's question about the fate of the one ancestor she was interested in, but she referred her to the filing cabinet that Kathryn had always jokingly called "the family jungle."

"It's all in there, sweetheart, if you really want to know about her. I'm due at the hairdresser's, but if you still haven't found what you need when I get back, I'll be glad to help."

Kathryn thanked her with a warm hug and waved her out the door. It was only a couple of minutes until two by then, so she could only glance regretfully at the trove of information in the files as she headed out to the landing. She'd just have to find out what happened by living it.

Logan and Annette were already waiting by the clock when she got there. There were quick goodbyes all around and then Logan began a countdown on his watch. "...Three...two...one. It's two o'clock. Is anything happening?" Kathryn shook her head. "Well, we'll wait five minutes or so. Since this clock is broken, we can't be sure that the one in the past is exactly synchronized with my watch."

At two-fifteen, they gave it up. "What we didn't consider," said Kathryn as they all trooped back downstairs, "is that Catherine has to be doing this at the same time. Maybe she couldn't for some reason. I'll just have to try every hour and hope she does the same."

She forced herself to speak brightly, trying to convince herself as well as the others. "At least now I'll have time to go through Mother's papers. Who knows? Maybe I'll find something that can help Ryan when I get back.''

With that goal in mind, she spent the next hour, and then the next, poring over her mother's hoarded diaries, notes and documents, breaking at three o'clock and then at four to stand by the grandfather clock. Logan left to meet a prospective client at three-thirty, optimistically bidding her goodbye.

"Don't think me rude when I say I hope you'll be gone when I get back," he said with a crooked smile. Kathryn met his eyes, which mirrored the frustration of her own.

"You and Catherine have a good life together, Logan," she said sincerely. They clasped hands briefly, and he departed.

After the four o'clock failure, Kathryn reluctantly went back to the family archives, wondering what she hoped to find there. It was no wonder her mother hadn't been able to remember anything about the early 1800s, since almost no records existed for that period. The only thing she found was that in 1825 the price of cotton nearly doubled. That news might be financially helpful to Ryan, but it would hardly get the law off his back.

She couldn't even find a record of that particular Catherine's marriage, something she had wanted very much to see. Most of the diaries and memoirs dated from the 1850s onward, and Kathryn glanced through them almost mechanically, on the off chance that she might find something useful—the recollections of a daughter or granddaughter, perhaps.

Suddenly, the name of Allerby caught her eye on the flyleaf of a small handwritten book dated 1852. Looking closer, she saw it was the memoirs of Caleb Allerby, an escaped slave, detailing his early life and adventures before and after his escape. The writing was hard to decipher and the grammar and spelling were atrocious, but the story it told was clear enough and of more than a little interest to Kathryn.

Caleb, it seemed, was born in 1822, the son of a mulatto slave woman and her master, Jonathan Allerby. His mother was kept on the plantation primarily to serve her master's carnal needs until he tired of her and sold her to a trader headed south when Caleb was ten years old. The book went on to describe Mr. Allerby's cruelty to his slaves and Caleb's subsequent attempts at escape, but Kathryn didn't read much further.

So! she thought in grim satisfaction. *The high and mighty Mr. Allerby had a mulatto mistress.* She wondered what Mrs. Allerby would say to this news—and what price Mr. Allerby would be willing to pay to keep her from finding out.

Kathryn carefully replaced the various papers in their proper folders and boxes in the file cabinet. She was fairly sure she could put this little tidbit to good use for Ryan's sake . . . *if* she ever got back! It was a quarter to five by this time, and she decided to stand by the clock early for good measure. Annette, fresh from her afternoon nap, came out to sit on the steps and talk, attempting to keep Kathryn's mind off another failure—for fail she did.

"Listen, Kathy, I've been thinking," said Annette. "Maybe Catherine wants to see her parents and friends before she switches back, sort of like you have. She's bound to hear about your engagement to Ryan, and know you want to return. Besides, she's supposed to be marrying Logan in a few weeks."

Kathryn tried to take as much comfort as she could from these words, but she couldn't help wondering if whatever capricious fate had switched them in the first place intended leaving them back where they had started. It seemed all too likely.

Mrs. Sykes-Monroe came home shortly after five, followed by Logan and Mr. Monroe, who had met in town.

Dinner was a fairly lively meal, with Kathryn enjoying her family more than she had in years, though she managed to excuse herself from the group at seven, and again at eight, to keep her vigil on the landing. Both times she returned to give Logan and Annette the bad news with a slight shake of her head. She could see that Logan was beginning to despair as much as she was.

At ten o'clock Kathryn's parents went up to bed and she walked up the stairs with them in order to be by the clock on the hour. At eleven-fifteen, when Kathryn still found herself in 1994 after her tenth attempt at exchanging places with Catherine, she sank down on the steps between Logan and Annette with a sob.

"It's not going to work!" she cried dismally. "Either we're not allowed to switch again, or Catherine doesn't want to. Oh, I'm sorry Logan!" she exclaimed, seeing his stricken look. "I forgot that this is as important to you as it is to me."

He attempted a smile. "What I haven't told you, Kathy, is that Catherine may have done this on purpose. She felt guilty about leaving you back in her time, possibly against your will, and talked once or twice about trying to change back, just to check on you. But I talked her out of it, or at least, I thought I had. I was afraid something like this would happen." His expression was bleak now.

"I'm sure she'll try to come back, Logan," said Kathryn in as rallying a tone as she could manage. "And I'll keep trying, even if—" she swallowed "—even if we don't make it by midnight. But if we don't, Ryan will leave without me. He'll think I don't love him..." She put her head in her hands to hide her tears.

Annette patted and soothed her, and Logan mumbled some unintelligible words of encouragement, though he ran distracted fingers through his hair.

"You two go on to bed," Kathryn urged after a moment, composing herself. "If it doesn't work at midnight,

I'd rather be alone, anyway. I . . . I guess I'll see you in the morning.''

Reluctantly, Logan and Annette left her sitting on the top stair of the landing, wishing her good-night and goodbye, though they weren't very convincing in their farewells.

Kathryn sat alone, watching the minutes tick by on her wristwatch, remembering her first meeting with Ryan and every moment they had shared since. She fought back the tears when she recalled the hopes and dreams they had shared—was it only a week ago?—in the garden.

Then, it was time. Time for the final attempt. After this, it really wouldn't matter whether they switched back or not, though she would keep trying, for Catherine's and Logan's sakes. Kathryn stood, her shoulders slumped in anticipated defeat, and stared up at the frozen hands of the grandfather clock.

She closed her eyes. ''Please, please,'' she whispered.

A SUDDEN, LOUD *BONG!* took Catherine by surprise. Startled, she looked up at the clock, and it struck the hour again. Both hands were pointing straight up, when only a moment ago they had still been frozen at twelve-twenty, as they had been since her arrival in this time. Almost reluctantly, she looked down at her clothing. Her turquoise slacks had disappeared, to be replaced by a full-skirted, tight-bodiced pink satin dress.

She was back in 1825.

She really hadn't thought it would work. When she and Logan returned to announce their engagement, her parents had been overjoyed, as had Annette, when she returned from Kansas two days ago. Catherine's only regrets were that her parents, back in 1825, could not share in her happiness and that she still did not know what had happened to Kathryn. The diary had yet to be found.

On a whim, she had decided to stand by the clock for a few moments on her way down to lunch. The chance of

Kathryn being there at the same time was slim, she knew, but at least she would have tried. But now it had worked—and what was she to do about it?

On sudden decision, she turned and went back up to her room to sit down. She knew, in a detached part of her mind, that dinner would be served below almost immediately, and that Kathryn had no doubt been on her way to partake of it, but it was absolutely essential that she take time to adjust her thoughts before confronting her parents—her real parents!—downstairs.

Logan! Suddenly his image was forefront in her mind. He had asked her not to do this, and she had promised him that she would not. And now Logan would not even be born for more than one hundred years!

"Why didn't I listen to him?" she groaned aloud. They would have to trade back, she thought. That's simply all there was to it. But—what if Kathryn didn't want to? She had to find out how matters stood here in 1825. And to do that, she would need to go downstairs. At least she would see her parents again, whatever happened.

"Good day, Mama, Papa," she said warmly as she entered the dining room. She could not understand their surprised looks. Why, her father's expression was positively suspicious!

"I . . . I had feared you might not join us, dear," said her mother, her voice tentative, her eyes anxious for some reason.

"I apologize for my tardiness," replied Catherine, wishing she could ask outright what was going on.

"Oh! That's . . . quite understandable, dear," said her mother with what Catherine could swear was a pitying smile.

"Is it?" she couldn't resist asking.

"Well, you know," said her mother vaguely, "these things often take time to get over. But, Joseph!" She brightly changed the subject. "What were you just telling me about the new stallion Wade Hampton has purchased for his stables?''

Catherine's interest was caught in spite of herself, and she listened to her father's discussion of the horses and how they might increase the value of the Hampton racing stables. She really had missed her father! After a while, though, the conversation reminded her of Logan's promise to buy her a horse after they were married. She *must* determine what had gone on here with Kathryn!

Mr. Prescott left the house immediately after dinner, claiming business in town, and Catherine turned to her mother as soon as they were alone. "What had you planned for me today, ma'am?" she asked, hoping that Kathryn would not have already been told in detail. In fact, her mother looked surprised again.

"Why, I ... that is, I wasn't certain whether ... Though I should very much like to attend the rout Mrs. Nott is giving tonight. If you feel up to it, of course?"

"Do you think I should go?" Catherine asked, watching her closely.

"Well, there is certainly no reason you shouldn't, other than your own inclination," said her mother. "As the announcement never went into the papers, you should not be subjected to impertinent questions. To my thinking, an engagement is not quite official until it is in the papers, if that is any comfort."

Catherine nodded, though she felt nearly as unenlightened as before. Had Kathryn been engaged—or almost engaged? The idea of going out to a party appealed to her. It would give her a chance to see her friends and neighbors here one last time, though of course, she wouldn't be able to tell them goodbye. It was obvious her parents were unaware of the switch, so she doubted that anyone else knew of it. Still, she would like to talk to Priscilla, at least. They had practically grown up together, and she had hardly seen her at all since her return from England.

"Yes, Mama, I should like to go to the Notts's rout," she said decisively. She and Kathryn could switch back tomorrow as well as today. No doubt Kathryn would like the chance to see *her* friends and family, as well. And surely, even if she were reluctant to come back to 1825, Logan would manage to convince her. Still, remembering some of the things she had learned about Kathryn Monroe, she couldn't help feeling somewhat anxious.

By the time the Prescotts left for the rout at five, Catherine had determined, by remarks her mother had let fall, that Kathryn and Ryan James had become engaged and that it had been broken off, apparently *not* by Kathryn. Had Ryan cried off? That would explain her mother's pitying attitude, and it would be just what Catherine would expect of him. And if that were the case, then Kathryn might well wish to be as far away from him as possible. She longed to ask for details. Perhaps she would discover more during the course of the evening.

The Notts were one of the wealthier families in Columbia, known for their entertainments, and this rout was no exception. Fresh flowers were everywhere, and one of the three bands in the area had been engaged to play. Catherine located Priscilla soon after their arrival, and her friend seemed as anxious to talk as she was.

"Cathy!" she exclaimed, drawing her into an alcove behind a potted fern. "Is it true what they are saying in town about Ryan? Is the Guard really after him? Is that why your engagement was never made public? I don't wish to pain you, but I have been positively eaten up by curiosity!"

"Well," began Catherine, desperately casting around in her mind for an appropriate answer, "everything is still very much up in the air."

Priscilla nodded wisely, just as though Catherine's reply had made sense. "I quite understand. You poor dear! When I think how happy you were when you told me the other day, I could just weep for you. But perhaps everything will come

right, after all. I cannot believe Mr. James could really be a
criminal!''

Catherine's overwhelming relief was tempered by aston-
ishment. Ryan had fled town with the law after him? Poor
Kathryn! If what Priscilla said was true, she had fallen in
love with him. She remembered thinking that Kathryn
Monroe might be the very woman to handle Ryan James.
She smiled, startling Priscilla.

"Yes, I am convinced everything will come right," she
said with sudden certainty. If she loved Ryan, Kathryn
would definitely want to switch back, especially if he were
in some sort of danger.

Her spirits considerably lighter, Catherine was able to
enjoy the rest of the evening, though she found herself
missing Logan increasingly as the night wore on. She talked
with her friends, discovering a fondness even for those she
had least liked before, her perceptions colored by the
knowledge that she would probably never see them again.

The clock was striking eleven when the Prescotts returned home. Catherine knew now why her parents had regarded her so strangely earlier. No doubt Kathryn had made
quite a scene when told of Ryan's supposed crime, whatever it was, and on being informed that her engagement was
off. Catherine could easily visualize her father's demeanor
while delivering such an edict, and could well imagine that
Kathryn would not be one to take it tamely. Should she try
standing by the clock tonight? That would mean staying up
till midnight—and she was already so tired. Surely, tomorrow morning would do as well. Wearily, she dragged herself up the stairs to her bedroom.

Nancy was waiting there for her, and she greeted her old
servant with a warmth that surprised the woman. "Just
undo the back for me, Nancy, and go on to bed. I can do the
rest myself." Catherine had become quite accustomed to
doing without a maid during the past month, and now felt
a little embarrassed to have Nancy undress her.

"If you're sure, Missie," said Nancy, stifling a yawn.

"Quite sure. Run along, now." Nancy did not argue further, but left with a smile and a nod, closing the door behind her.

Slowly, Catherine drew off her dress and unfastened her corset, thinking back over the bits of information she had gleaned that evening. What had Ryan James done to Mr. Allerby? she wondered. She had discovered that it was he who had brought charges. She smiled to herself, thinking that perhaps Ryan was not such a bad fellow, after all. She had never cared for any of the Allerbys herself.

As she removed her corset, a scrap of folded paper fluttered to the ground, having apparently been tucked into the top of the garment. Curious, Catherine bent to pick it up. Unfolding it, she read through the note, obviously from Ryan to Kathryn, delivered that very day. Midnight! He was coming for her at midnight! And for aught she knew, Kathryn planned to go with him. At any rate, that was a decision Kathryn must make, not she.

It was half past eleven already. Quickly, she refastened her corset and pulled a dark traveling dress from her wardrobe, one that fastened down the front. Once dressed, she pulled out her small valise and packed the few necessities that Kathryn might need on a journey. There! At least now if she wished to go she would not have to waste time with preparations. Catherine tiptoed out into the hallway and down to the landing to check the time—five minutes. She went back to her room and opened the window, leaning out to see if perchance Ryan might be early. Yes, there was someone down there, with two saddled horses.

"Ryan!" she called in a whisper.

"Catherine?" he called back. "Are you coming?"

Catherine drew her head back in. Was she? What had Kathryn planned to do? Leaning out again, she whispered, "I'll just be a few moments." She pulled the sheets off of the bed so that they would be there to use as a rope if Kathryn needed one, and ran to her desk to scribble a quick note. Tucking it through the handle of the valise just as the clock began to strike, she ran from the room.

THE CLOCK STOPPED striking. Kathryn opened her eyes and looked down at the brown wool dress, tears of joy stinging her eyes. But there was no time to lose! Would Ryan still be waiting? Turning, she hurried up to her room, but paused when she saw the packed valise with the note through the handle. She ran across to the open window, her heart in her throat until she saw the shadowy figure below. "Just a minute, I'm almost ready!" she called down, almost giddy with relief.

"You said that before," Ryan whispered back, but she had already returned to the note.

> Kathryn, I have packed everything you should need if you have decided to go with Ryan. The sheets will make a sturdy rope. I have used them for that purpose many times before when I was younger. I am sorry I waited so long to exchange places—I did not know of your proposed elopement until half an hour ago. I wish you much happiness in life, whatever you decide to do.
>
> Love, Catherine

Kathryn smiled and tucked the note into her pocket. Carrying the valise to the window, she tossed it down to Ryan before knotting a sheet around the center bar of the window frame.

"Catch me if I fall," she whispered, and lowered herself into his waiting arms.

"You truly mean to come with me, Catherine? Are you sure?"

"Absolutely." She clung to him for a moment. "Oh, Ryan, I was so worried! You took a terrible risk coming back for me."

Ryan allowed himself to feast his eyes on her beautiful face, her blue eyes dark with concern for him—for *him!* Could he really deserve the love of such a woman after the life he had led? "I love you, Catherine," he told her from his heart, "and I won't lie to you. There will be danger and considerable hardship until we reach the northern states."

"The greatest hardship I can imagine is living my life without you, Ryan. Let's go. I have something to tell you on the way, something you're going to find hard to believe. . . ."

EPILOGUE

ANNETTE WAS POSITIVE she'd never seen a more beautiful
bride. Looking at Catherine as she stood in the receiving line
next to her new husband, Annette suddenly understood
what the phrase "glowing with happiness" meant. She
waited until some of the confusion around Logan and
Catherine died down, then rustled forward in the full-length
lavender maternity dress she'd worn as matron of honor.

"Congratulations, you two! I haven't been so happy since
I married David. Catherine, I put my traditional wedding
present with the other gifts, but there's something else I
wanted to give you personally. Here." She held out a small
rectangular package wrapped in silver paper.

"Oh, Annette!" Catherine gave her friend a quick hug.
"As if you haven't done enough already. Where is David?"

"He's over there, talking to a couple of college buddies.
But come on! Open it before anyone else comes over to
congratulate you."

Catherine obediently tore off the gift wrap. "My diary!
Oh, Annette, when . . . where did you find it?"

"Mrs. Jefferson, who lives two doors down from us on
post, found my purse wedged way inside her hydrangea
bushes last week. The purse snatcher must have thrown it
there the same night he stole it. It was there all the time! The
only thing missing was my wallet. The purse was pretty
much ruined, from being out in the rain and all, but the
stuff inside was fine. I guess vinyl is better than leather for
some things!" She laughed. "I have to confess, I already

peeked at the end—I didn't want to risk giving you bad news on your wedding day!''

Catherine forgave her with a smile. On this day of all days, she felt she could forgive anything.

"Let's go outside while you read it," suggested Logan, putting an arm around her shoulders. "I don't think anyone else has gone out there yet."

Catherine nodded and he led her out onto the wide terrace of the posh country club where the reception was being held. There was a redwood bench conveniently placed out of sight from the windows, and she sat down to open the little book while Logan kept a possessive arm around her waist. She flipped through her own entries and Kathryn's first passage, which she had already read on her first night in 1994—it seemed so long ago now! The next entry was the last in the diary, dated April 1, 1827.

Ryan and I are back in Columbia, probably for the last time. We are in town for only a few days to wind up our affairs here. Ryan is selling Fair Fields, after holding off for a while on my advice. Whether he believed my story of coming from the future at first I don't know, though he said he did after seeing Catherine's note. But when the price of cotton soared to twenty-seven cents a pound, just as I said it would, he was convinced! He's investing his profits in Pennsylvania railroads, at my suggestion. We've been living in Philadelphia for the past year, and have been so happy there that we plan to make it our permanent home.

Mr. Allerby was persuaded to drop all charges against Ryan after receiving an "anonymous" letter, so we could come back here to live if we wanted to, but we don't. The people of Philadelphia are much more open-minded and we're both more comfortable there. I'm also anxious to get back to little Kathryn, whom I left in the care of her nurse rather than drag her along on this trip. She was one year old the week before we left, and is absolutely gorgeous!

I'm leaving the diary in the cubbyhole of the desk where I first found it, in hopes that you, Catherine, will be able to read it someday. Ryan and I are divinely happy and I pray that you and Logan will be likewise. I have no doubt that we exchanged places for exactly this reason. Ryan and I were obviously intended for each other, and I suspect that you and Logan were, too.

We plan to be active in the Underground Railroad that is developing in Philadelphia—ask Logan what that means, if you don't know. Give everyone in 1994 (or whenever you read this) my love, and tell Logan I said to treat you like the queen you are. Thank you, Catherine, for the gift of your spot in history. I truly belong here.

All wishes for a happy life,
Kathryn Sykes-James

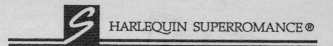

HARLEQUIN SUPERROMANCE®

COMING NEXT MONTH

#594 THE PRINCESS AND THE PAUPER • Tracy Hughes
Jessica Hartman's beloved father was gone, leaving maddening
instructions in his will. In order to inherit her share of the ailing
company that bore her name, she would have to work side by side
with her estranged half-brother. Like it or not, she would have to
confront the forbidden feelings Cade ignited in her.

#595 NOT QUITE AN ANGEL • Bobby Hutchinson
Sometimes private investigator Adam Hawkins thought
Sameh Smith was from another planet. In her endearingly clumsy
way she helped derelicts, street kids and prostitutes. But she was
also a mystery. She had no personal history prior to April 1994,
and Adam was determined to find out why.

#596 DANCING IN THE DARK • Lynn Erickson
Alexandra St. Clair Costidos wanted her son back. His influential
father had spirited him away to an impregnable Greek island to
punish her for leaving him, and the law could do nothing. It was
time for drastic measures. Alex hired mercenary John Smith to
help her, but even if she regained her son, she was in danger of losing her heart.

#597 THE YANQUI PRINCE • Janice Kaiser
Reporter Michaela Emory thought it was time to take some risks.
How else could she have wild adventures and meet the man of her
dreams? Suddenly, she got the chance to do both when she flew to
South America to interview the legendary Yanqui Prince. A mod-
ern-day Robin Hood, Reed Lakesly was renowned for his courage
and charisma. Suddenly Michaela had more adventure and passion
than she'd bargained for....

AVAILABLE NOW:

#590 KEEPING KATIE
Patricia Keelyn

#591 TWILIGHT WHISPERS
Morgan Hayes

#592 BRIDGE OVER TIME
Brenda Hiatt

#593 GHOST TIGER
Janice Carter

Fifty red-blooded, white-hot, true-blue hunks
from every State in the Union!

Look for MEN MADE IN AMERICA! Written by some
of our most popular authors, these stories feature fifty
of the strongest, sexiest men, each from a different state
in the union!

Two titles available every other month at your favorite
retail outlet.

In April, look for:

LOVE BY PROXY by Diana Palmer (Illinois)
POSSIBLES by Lass Small (Indiana)

In May, look for:

KISS YESTERDAY GOODBYE by Leigh Michaels (Iowa)
A TIME TO KEEP by Curtiss Ann Matlock (Kansas)

You won't be able to resist MEN MADE IN AMERICA!

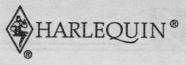

◈ HARLEQUIN ®

AZALEA

Another superb novel from
Brenda Hiatt!

If you enjoyed BRIDGE OVER TIME,
you'll love AZALEA, the story of a
young American woman who takes
the Regency ton by storm.

AZALEA, a book so special, we've
chosen it for our new Regency
promotional series, giving you
more value for your dollar.

Look for AZALEA in
Regency Diamonds, coming
this August to mainstream
bookshelves everywhere.

Harlequin Regency Romance,
a new way of looking
at the past.